Crescendo

Crescendo

Sabrina Strong Book 5

Lorelei Bell

Copyright (C) 2016 Lorelei Bell
Layout design and Copyright (C) 2019 by Next Chapter
Published 2019 by Sanguine – A Next Chapter Imprint
Cover Design by Melody Simmons from eBookindiecovers
This book is a work of fiction. Names, characters, places, and incidents are the product of the author's imagination or are used fictitiously. Any resemblance to actual events, locales, or persons, living or dead, is purely coincidental.
All rights reserved. No part of this book may be reproduced or transmitted in any form or by any means, electronic or mechanical, including photocopying, recording, or by any information storage and retrieval system, without the author's permission.
Visit the author's website at
http://loreleismuse-lorelei.blogspot.com/

Acknowledgments

Thank-yous go out to Steve Kloff, and Jennifer Weydert for information regarding plasma services

Dedication

To my husband, Dennis, who allows me to be me!

Contents

1	én garde	1
2	War	7
3	The Never Ending Dance	11
4	Tunnel at the End of the Light	21
5	Somewhere Over the Rainbow	32
6	Going Down	44
7	You're Fired	55
8	Lights, Please	61
9	Blood is the Life	68
10	Surprise!	75
11	Throwing Sticks	84
12	House of Cards	91
13	Truth or Consequences	106
14	Cold	119
15	White-Out	127

16	Over-night Guests	141
17	Chance	159
18	Deception	178
19	Priory of Sion	183
20	Good Witch	203
21	Bad Witch	213
22	Power	227
23	The Bait	240
24	Ultimatum	249
25	Sacrifice	257
26	Mayhem	268
27	Thunder	280
28	Reprieve	288
29	Awakened	295

Chapter 1

en garde

The man with shoulder-length, dark blond hair and edgy smile sat motionless in in the shadows, in a wooden bar chair, waiting. No one had really noticed him, but then he had made sure that they would not. Wearing a black suit and silk shirt, his white silk tie almost glowed. Leif Sufferden realized he was a tad over dressed for the rough-neck bar in Batavia where several fist fights broke out on a nightly bases, stabbings were not unheard of, and the police had had the place shut down for various violations in the past. Why, only in the past week someone had been stabbed to death, right here. There had been shootings, too, of course. But, tonight, "Side Winders" happened to be open, and its customers couldn't be happier, unless they were high on something other than liquor and weed.

A smile crimped Leif's lips while he watched the blond woman strut in from the street on four-inch heals into the dank bar. They were blue to match her eyes, not that anyone would notice this little detail, but he did. Their eyes met. He slid his eyes in the direction of the pool table closest to him. She gave him a small nod. Her smile broadened to reveal white teeth. Her fangs hadn't come out as yet. She always did have great control. It was one of the things Leif admired about Darla. Her control. That, and her zeal for violence.

All male eyes in the room were zeroed in on Darla like a heat seeking missile. Who could blame them? Wearing a halter top and the shortest possible micro-mini, her heavily made-up eyes darted across the faces of four men who were playing pool. Conversation around the pool table had come to a halt. She had suddenly become the one and only highlight in their uneventful evening. She boldly eyed them right back. They noted she was by herself. A lone woman who walks into a bar—especially one of this ilk—was just asking for trouble. On top of it, she looked like a hooker. No matter what, it looked like their luck had changed quickly as she twitched her way toward them, her movements more pronounced. Looking hungry, her eyes became more cat-like as she licked her lips, like she might take a big hunk out of one of them.

She stepped around their stilled bulks, wiggled her small ass with exaggeration, smiling and making eye contact with each one as she strutted by, sliding the fingers of one hand across the bumper of the table. Pausing next to the biggest one, she looked him up and down. He had the usual biker tats—a lot of skulls and spiders—and a skull logo displayed on his clothing. His hang-over beer gut gave the impression he did more drinking than anything else. An ugly scar down the left cheek that interrupted the two-week old beard sprouting around his chin and jawline told the story of a guy who had seen a bar fight up close and personal.

"Hullo," she purred, then licked her rubied lips. "How's the game?"

"Oh, fine," the large man said. The others pumped their heads, chiming in agreeing noises. "In fact, I think it just got better." He and the others rumbled with knowing chuckles.

"Mind if I join you?" she asked, her hand sliding up his sausage sized fingers.

"Not at all," the large one said, motioning toward the table. "Here, you can use my cue stick." He held it out to her, showing his more gentlemanly side, a wide grin to sell it.

"Thank you." She took the cue stick from him, holding his gaze for a long ten seconds. She fingered the tip with a red lacquered nail and returned his gaze. "I know just what to do with it, too."

The men all chuckled as though they were in on the joke.

She propped her ass onto the bumper portion of the pool table, and settled the larger end of the cue stick between her parted legs. The men leered and chuckled at her act.

"Hey! No sitting on the pool table!" the owner cried from the back of the bar.

"Aw, shut the fuck up, Hank. We're just havin' us a little fun here!" shouted the large man. He looked down at the blonde, almost expectantly.

She wiggled a finger in the universal "come closer" signal. He did.

"What's your name?" she asked.

"Stan," he said. "Stan Baker."

"Hello, Stan Baker," she said. "Let's get to know one another." Putting the cue stick down, she spread her legs further apart.

"Okay, pretty little girl," he said, moving in front of her, but not yet touching her, while the others looked on, making groaning noises, wishing they were in his spot.

"You want me, don't you, Stan?" she asked.

Stan let out a bark of laughter. "Does a bear shit in the woods?" The men laughed. By now those around the other two pool tables, and some men at the bar had turned around to watch the scene.

"Come here, then. Kiss me," she said, leaning forward. She puckered up her red lips.

"Alright." The other men made sounds of encouragement as their large companion placed his hips between her knees. His large hands went around her small waist as he nudged himself between her thighs. Her skirt hiked up so far, he wondered if she had a thong on—or nothing at all. Either way, he was going to score tonight. Her legs wrapped around his large girth while her hands went up his chest. Her fingers twined behind his neck. She didn't flinch from his bad breath, or his over-powering body odor, but allowed him to bring her in for a kiss. His buddies made noises again, nudging one another.

No one noticed the man in the suit, Leif, had risen from his chair in the far corner. Arms folded, he watched with passive interest while the man pressed Darla back onto the pool table. The kiss lasted for more than twenty seconds. He did wonder when Darla would make her move. She liked playing with her food.

Three vampires stepped into the bar, and scanned the room until their eyes met Leif's. He nodded at them, and slid his gaze to where Darla was in a romantic tryst with the large man. The only female in the group cast her light brown eyes to the biker and Darla, then back to Leif. Her name was Kadu Litore, a Jamaican-American. Leif thought she had been one of his better turns. She definitely enjoyed the hunt, now that they were free to hunt humans. She smiled brilliantly, and already her fangs were out. She licked her lush lips in anticipation. Her slightly dusky chocolate skin looked as though it were oiled. Her bare arms and legs didn't agree with the cold weather outside. One would think it was a ninety degree day, but it was only in the twenties with a bitter north wind. That alone should have tipped anyone off what was going on here. But it didn't. Every human was either into the game on the telly, their drink, or looking at the scene at the pool table, unaware that they had been invaded by vampires.

Leif watched Kadu, the only other female vampire, approach the bar. The other two, males, waited for a signal from Leif. Licking their lips as they sized up the rest of the crowd. Their eyes had slid to the bar where the only human women sat drinking.

Four more vampires strode in. They each acknowledged Leif with a slight bow. His hand out, Leif gestured for them to mingle with the crowd in the bar, and choose their warm meals. A crowded bar was something like a smörgåsbord for a vampire. A human's warm blood scent on the air made them lick their lips in anticipation.

Smiling, Leif turned back to check the progress of Darla with the large biker. Suddenly, the biker jerked back from her. Hand going to his face the biker said, "You bit me?" He looked at his hand. There was blood on his face where he'd smeared it.

She chuckled and nodded.

The men around them jeered.

"Oh, so you like it rough, do you?" he said more gruffly.

"Yes. And you had better like it, too," she said with a little playful snarl, her delicate nose crinkling.

"Oh, I do, darlin'. I do," he said. His hand went back as if to strike her. It swung down toward her face. In a lightning move, Darla caught his large fist and held it. His eyes became big with surprise that the petite blond could hold him off so easily. Startled, the other men around them shifted, exchanging looks with one another. No one was laughing now.

In a lightning move, she grabbed his hair and yanked his face toward her, smashing his lips against hers. The biker braced himself against the table with both massive hands, but relaxed into it. His sounds of delight suddenly turned to screams, which he couldn't really get out because their lips were clamped together. Dark blood rivered from their locked lips while Darla held the biker's mouth against hers, both hands behind his head, with a grip like a python's. His hands clawed and grasped her hair and pulled, doing everything to disentangle himself from her. He lifted his and her body off the table, trying to free himself, trying to get the scream past their locked lips. She didn't budge, she didn't give an inch.

Leif felt his smile widen and a chuckle bubble up. "Kitten," he said quietly, but knew she would hear him. "Let the poor bloke go."

The three companions moved in, about to intervene. Seeing this, Leif shot across the room so fast, he seemed to disappear and reappeared in front of the three with a cue stick braced across his hands pushing them back.

"Tut-tut, gentlemen. The lady is busy at the moment. You can wait your turn," Leif said with a British accent and cocky smile creasing his handsome face.

The man with long greasy hair, lunged toward him. Leif threw a punch to his face, knocking him back where he fell to the floor. He didn't move again.

"Like I said, wait your turn," Leif said, with more warning in his voice. He held the other two men in his thrall. They now had no desire to move or do anything. Over his shoulder he said, "C'mon, Darla, luv. We need to party. Let the poor bloke go."

His muzzle freed, the biker's screams filled the room. People turned to see what the commotion was all about. Suddenly the blonde woman, Darla, pushed the man away with a force that sent him blundering back, arms cartwheeling. Blood bubbling out of his mouth, he bounced off the wall, and fell to the floor, sobbing and uttering incoherently as though he had no tongue.

The woman sat up, and spat a large red piece of meat out of her bloody mouth. She licked her lips, then took a finger and wiped around her mouth to swipe at the blood. She stuck her finger into her mouth and sucked the blood from it. Flopping onto her side on the pool table, she looked down at the biker and said, "What's the matter? Vampire got your tongue?"

"Everyone," Leif called out, "feed!"

Kadu turned to the man at the pin ball table, grabbed him by the collar, and yanked him backward. Fangs extended, she sunk them into his neck from behind. His surprised scream became one of submission. His knees buckled, and he sank to the floor where she followed him.

The two male vampires at the bar had already put thralls on the women, and now began to feed.

Leif shoved one of the two men left standing toward Darla. She grabbed him and hauled him down on the pool table, arching his back until his throat was exposed. She buried her fangs in his neck.

Leif growled at the last man nearby, he grabbed his arm and drew it up to his mouth. Fangs sank into warm flesh. Crimson ichor pooled into his open mouth, and only now he realized how hungry he was.

The man's arm was suddenly yanked away from his mouth. Leif jerked back and found himself looking up at a tall Native American wearing jeans and a blue jean shirt with a southwest design embroidered into the yoke.

"I don't think you asked if you could *take* his blood and I'm pretty sure he would have said no," the Indian said.

"You? You're—"

"Dead? Try Undead." Dante grabbed a cue stick from the table and twirled it like a propeller before Leif could make his move.

Chapter 2

War

I landed into the bar a few seconds behind Dante, using the ley line. The dank bar and the heavy smell of old smoke and beer caught me by surprise, but I didn't let it slow me down. In one sweep I saw vampires everywhere drinking from their hosts, knowing full well they had been attacked. They had no way to resist the vampire's thrall. My hand went to the snaps of my dagger sheath at my thigh. With a flick I let the Dagger of Delphi loose. Like a silver arrow it darted to the nearest vampire, and plunged into its chest. With an inward gasp, the dark-skinned female vampire fell to the floor, her heart poisoned with silver.

A mere two seconds later, the air twanged with another's presence. I turned my head to find red-headed Quist standing over the female vampire which the dagger had dropped. He lunged with the laser wand he held, and ran it across her long neck. Deadly accurate, it severed the female vampire's head cleanly. Within a few seconds, the body began to fleck with decay. Must have been a new turn. Older vampires took longer to decompose.

Dagger of Delphi flew off to the next vampire—a woman with long black hair, hovering over a man at another pinball machine. But it couldn't get to her chest and hovered, waiting. *Shit.* I grabbed up a cue ball from a nearby pool table and threw it with keen accuracy, hitting her on the shoulder. She snapped her head my direction and pulled back from her human, letting them sink, and then drop to the floor. Her eyes glowed red, her mouth rimmed with blood.

"Look, honey, that's no way to get a date," I quipped. She turned fully toward me, her grimace terrifying, the bottom half of her face painted in the gore of her feast. She lunged toward me. She didn't get far. The dagger plunged into her chest. Her body buckled instantly.

Once she was down, Quist moved in and lopped off her head with the laser. I couldn't believe it no longer bothered me to see him do this—to watch a head roll away from the shoulders completely detached. Well, as long as they were vampires, it didn't bother me at all.

The Dagger of Delphi went on to the next vampire, and the same sequence was repeated. In the background I heard fighting. I turned to see the flurry of motion. Dante was fighting someone. I knew him. Shoulder-length caramel-colored hair, the handsome cocky look on his face. Leif Sufferden. Exactly who we had been watching, and we'd found him and his cronies in the act of feasting on humans. Not illegal, according to vampire law, but I wasn't about to agree with such behavior. Especially since the two who were now in charge of N.A.V.A.—North American Vampire Association—were my enemies.

I moved forward, but someone grabbed me by the hair and tugged me around. This couldn't be more like being on a roller derby rink.

"OW!" I cried. *Shit!* That hurt enough to bring tears to my eyes. My head had been pulled back with such violent force, I was momentarily stunned. In the next second I found myself staring up into a vampire's face who I feared almost as much as Leif. My throat exposed *oh-so* conveniently to her.

"Ohhh, yum," Darla managed to purr her delight in having caught me in her talons.

"Help!" I cried.

She smiled. "Oh, you can do better than that." Lips rimmed in crimson, she opened her mouth, and moved in closer toward my neck, her eyes had become black marbles in her head, and her fangs like sharpened white fence posts. All this filled my vision while I worked to resist her. But she had a hold on me, and I couldn't pull my mystic-ring hand around to shove her away.

"Sabrina!" Quist shouted. "Sabrina!"

My spine forced against the rim of the pool table, the pain gave me enough awareness to pull my eyes away from hers. It really pissed me off that Darla was able to catch me off guard like this.

"Let go of my hair you bitch!" I finally slid my right hand out from behind myself and thrust the mystic ring into her face. Darla released my hair and threw me a startled look. I returned a scornful one. While she tried to puzzle out what had happened—how I had managed to thrall her, instead of the other way around—I said, "Take a flying leap!" With a flick of my hand, Darla went flying through the air. She landed, crashing into pool cues in a corner. Her shock wore off quickly as she sprang to her feet, growled, and gnashed her teeth at me.

Then the unexpected dart of silver shot across my sight and jammed into her chest. With a sudden intake of air, she stumbled back, hands flaying, feet going out from underneath her. She fell with a sharp grunt. Downed like a bowling pin. She screeched in pain and tried to pull the dagger out. I'd learned that the dagger, once it had found its target, would not relent. No vampire could pull it from their own chest.

Quist darted toward her with the laser.

"No!" I said to him. He looked sharply to me, a hard frown etched on his freckled face. I drew my hand out. "Dagger of Delphi, return to me," I beckoned to my weapon. The dagger obediently pulled itself from Darla's chest. At that same moment Dante's dark form drew up on the other side of me. He threw something that twirled through the air and stuck into Leif. He dropped to the floor only three feet from us, a broken cue stick embedded in his chest. He was still alive, but struggling to pull it free.

"You bitch!" Leif hissed, voice rough.

"I want them to go back to her," I said to Dante and Quist. "In whatever condition. Let Ilona know we're watching them and we're willing to stop them."

Distant sirens wailed. Police and other first responders. They'd be here in two minutes.

"We have to leave," Dante said. I looked around the bar. Humans who were still able to stand, staggered around, bleeding from the vampire bites. Gasps, moans, and expletives as the vampire thrall no longer affected them. They eyed us fearfully. As fearful of us as they were of the vampires. There was no time to alter their memories.

The vampires who were still alive, misted out of existence, one by one, like the cowards they really are.

Leif pulled the make-shift stake out of his chest and threw it to the floor. He looked up at me, murder in his eyes, and a bloody hole in his chest. "I'll get you for this, you bitch!"

I wasn't daunted by his vulgar language, and said, "Give a message to Ilona. If she doesn't rescind the Hunting Human Law, she'll be next." By this time my body was shaking from the adrenaline pouring through me.

"I'll get you for this, *bitch*." Leif hobbled over to Darla, his Life-time mate, clutched her by the middle and vanished.

I grabbed Dante's and Quist's hand. We locked onto the ley line and were gone.

Chapter 3

The Never Ending Dance

I opened the quart jar of stewed tomatoes and poured them into the pot of soup and watched the chunks of tomatoes swim around the heavy cast iron pot while stirring it. The memory of when Constance and I had taken our harvest of tomatoes in our respective gardens and had canned them—forty-eight quarts—interrupted all other pressing thoughts. I was able to step back in time when none of this had been my reality—way before I had begun thinking about getting a job, and *vampire* was not in my vocabulary. We had divided the quarts up equally. I actually didn't think I would use twenty-four jars of tomatoes because my father had died a few months ago, and I was living alone. But tonight I had a house full of men. Not all would be eating my beef soup, but a few of them were humans who were hungry and would greatly appreciate my cooking, such as it was.

Quist and Fritz's voices filtered out to me over Christmas tunes playing on the CD player in the corner. I smiled. It was good to hear human voices joking and carousing in this house again. I'd missed it terribly.

Earlier, we didn't do any hi-fives when we returned to my house, about two hours ago. Some of the people in that bar had been hurt bad by the vampires. I wasn't at all sure how the big biker guy would be, whose tongue was bitten off by Darla. Dante had informed me moments after we'd returned that he'd stayed with them—invisible—to see the aftermath. As our spy, Dante was more than just useful, he was necessary to our survival. He was the eyes needed to find vampire nests, or attacks when they happened, or know what they were cooking up and the enemy had no idea how we did it. Being an Undead was handy in that way, I suppose.

"Sabrina?" Fritz called.

"What?" I called back, returning the heavy lid to the pot of soup.

"Come and see the tree. We're going to light it up."

"Okay." I reduced the flames under my pot of soup and stepped into the living room where they had re-arranged the furniture. Vasyl appeared as if out of nowhere. His hand went around my waist as I joined the others in the living room. Hobart stood next to the wall, hand on the light switch.

Fritz was on his knees with the plug end of the Christmas lights, ready to plug it in to the socket. I stifled a chuckle as some bit of tinsel had clung to his nappy black hair and, filled with static, moved with his motions around the tree. It looked like a metallic worm doing a strange dance on his head.

"Ready?" Quist said, near a lamp, looking at both Fritz and Hobart.

"Ready!" They called out.

"Lights please."

The lights went out, and suddenly the Christmas tree was lit up. He had used an amazing color arrangement of green, red, and purple that gave the tree a dark, haunting look.

We all gasped appreciatively.

"Oh, I forgot," Fritz said and suddenly, a white strand of lights sprinkled in with the mix went on.

"Oh! Beautiful!" I gasped.

"It is tradition, no?" Vasyl said, gesturing toward the tree.

"Yes," I said.

"OMG!" Fritz cried. "He's never seen a Christmas tree before?"

"No. I have not," Vasyl said.

"Where do you live? In a barn?" Fritz asked.

"*Oui.* It is a very comfortable barn," Vasyl defended, his lips making that French quirky thing, which I found sexy.

Quist and Fritz exchanged glances. They had come into my life only a few weeks ago, but I felt as though I'd known them all my life. Quist was part elf, and had a daring side I hadn't known of until tonight. His wanting to come with us to "kill vampires", had unsettled me slightly. His father had invented the laser wand. What Quist used was the older version to behead vampires and demons.

Fritz didn't do any sort of fighting, but he loved to decorate. Both he and Quist had brought a dozen brightly gift wrapped presents to go beneath the tree. Hobart had cut the tree from a local tree farm and brought over to my house this afternoon. A werewolf, he had become my guardian in the past few months after seeking my help in locating one of his own members who wound up shooting himself after stealing the werewolf gang's money.

"Only now he lives here," I said, in answer to Fritz' question, smoothing my hand over my husband's arm. Vasyl leaned toward me, our lips met in a quick kiss, and I got tingles up my spine.

Embarrassed, I turned back into the room and felt that odd sensation that told me someone else had arrived. At the same time, Vasyl's body stiffened, and he moved in front of me as a barrier.

Stepping out of the gloom of the dining room, a dark shadow with long, black hair appeared, and at once, began speaking as though he'd been here the whole time.

"The humans have been taken by ambulance to a nearby hospital," Dante reported, strolling into the living room. He stopped and looked around. "Why are all the lights off?"

I gestured to the Christmas tree.

"Oh," he said, glancing at it. "Nice."

"Someone get the lights, please," I said.

Quist was closest to the lamp, and turned it on. The room became a little brighter. Fritz rose and turned on another lamp.

"What about their memories? Were they wiped?" I asked.

"The elves worked as quickly as they could, then vanished before the paramedics arrived."

I turned to Quist. His blue gaze met mine. "It doesn't take them long to wipe memories, and give them new ones," he informed.

"Good," I said, my glance falling onto the dark TV. I could imagine what the evening news would reveal about what happened to a dozen people in a bar in Batavia. I wasn't sure how they would explain the guy with the bitten-off tongue, though. I shivered as nausea hit me at the memory of all the blood I had seen, and the thought of loosing a tongue by having it bitten off by a vampire—or anyone for that matter. I shivered, making a disgusted sound. Vasyl's arm went around me.

"There's something else I must speak to you about," Dante said, looking directly at me.

I waited. His gray eyes glanced over the others in the room. His hair was arranged in a loose braid, fastened with a leather thong at the end. He had been my lover when he was alive. After dying, and still in love with me, he was able to return as an Undead a few weeks ago to rescue me from the vampires of a planet called The Black Veil. He's been with me ever since—but at a respectable distance.

"What is it?" I prompted.

"It is a private matter," he said, eyes darting from me to Vasyl and back again.

"*Sacreblu*," Vasyl said. "There are no secrets between us." And, as if to reinforce that statement, he kissed the top of my head and readjusted his hold on me. *There, see? I own her.*

Men.

I rolled my eyes. "Okay," I said and pulled away from Vasyl's python grasp. "I'm going to go into the next room," I told Vasyl, stepping away. "I'll see what he wants, and I'll be back."

"Leave the door open," Vasyl said. He would not trust me alone with Dante, for maybe the next fifty years.

Dante followed me. I stopped and turned. "Fritz, could you go ahead and serve up the soup? I know you guys are hungry."

"No problem, Sabrina," Fritz said, and happily he, Hobart, and Quist headed for the kitchen.

Closed off by two French doors, the den had once been what was called a parlor of my circa 1910 farm house. I presumed it was where people sat and visited, back in the day. There was a fireplace in there, too, and on crisp winter nights like these, when the wind was out of the northwest, a fire would help keep the house warmer. I had not thought of getting a fire going, as I'd been a tad busy.

Dante headed into the room before me. I stepped in ten seconds after and found him before the fireplace. A fire ignited like magic. He was a shaman when alive, but also Undeads had a lot of magic at their disposal.

"Wow. I didn't know you could do that," I said, looking at him in surprise.

He turned back to me. "My powers are coming alive in me, more and more. Those powers that I would have had, eventually, had I lived long enough as a shaman."

"So I see," I said, moving toward the now blazing fireplace. I held my hands toward the warm flames. The room's chill made it feel as though the front door was standing wide open. "The fire will warm this room up. *Brrrr.*"

"I no longer feel cold, heat, pain…"

"But isn't that to be expected?" I said. Dante was always able to shield my Knowing. Now that he was an Undead, all the better his tricks to keep me from reading him. I couldn't read any vampire. Humans were easy. I was not only a touch clairvoyant, I was also the sibyl with my own bag of tricks.

Dante's smile tipped his lips. "It takes a little getting used to."

"What's so private you wanted to tell me?"

"It isn't that I wanted to tell you something private as to get you away from the others so that we may speak." He shifted on his feet and faced me. "Vasyl would have made his usual insults and I wouldn't have been able to get a word out," He finished.

"Okay." He was right about that.

His hands landed on my shoulders and he looked into my eyes. "You cannot allow your brother and his wife to remain outside of your loop any longer. It's dangerous for them to not know about the vampires."

Ashamed, my gaze fell. "I don't know how to break it to them." I looked up into his intelligent face, gazed into magnetic gray eyes. "How do I tell them that vampires exist, and that one lives in my house? That I'm married to him. This is beyond their belief system."

"You must find a way to make them believe. Time is working against you. I've told you what Ilona plans. Don't lull yourself into believing she would leave the rest of your family alone. Especially after tonight. You've dropped the gauntlet with what we've just done. There's no way a vampire is not going to answer to a challenge like that."

"I have been thinking about it. But I don't know how to explain things to them."

"You need to tell them about the vampires, even if you can't tell them who, or what you are right now. You need to warn them, educate them about the possibility that they could become targets."

"Tell them to carry around crucifixes and stay indoors at night, lock their doors and don't open it to anyone? I don't see that I have that sort of power to convince them."

"Introduce Vasyl to them. No matter what, you must introduce him to them, anyway."

"Randy will need more than telling. He'll need to be shown."

"Then, have Vasyl do something to convince them. I'm sure he'll think of something."

"What? Have Vasyl bite some animal? That would horrify them!"

"No, there are other things Vasyl can do. He can disappear, or change into something, like an animal or a bird."

"Or show them his wings." My head sagged. Dante brought my chin up with a finger.

"Their lives are at stake. All of them. Ilona will not stop at your brother and his wife. I've heard that she has fed on, and turned children in the past."

My eyes went wide, a loud intake of air filled my lungs until I let it ease out. I thought of Jana and Tera, my little nieces. I couldn't imagine how their minds would cope with the horrible things a vampire could do to them, or their parents.

"You're right, of course. I don't want to scare their girls."

"Have them come over by themselves, your brother and sister-in-law. They can find someone to babysit for a few minutes. Tell them this is a life or death situation and you need to speak with them."

"You should babysit them," I suggested, smiling.

"I'd love to, and not as a dog this time." We both chuckled.

"I'll think of something." There was a pause in our conversation. He seemed morose. "Are you okay? Do you need to—um—feed?"

He smiled, his hands ran slowly up and down my arms. "I've fed, if that's what you're asking."

"Just now?" My face suddenly warmed and I couldn't look back up at him.

"Believe it or not, vampires still have souls. I fed on those we killed."

"Oh!" I grimaced, now embarrassed even more. I didn't like the idea that Dante could feed on souls of anything that died in his presence. He also fed through sex. Somehow. He had to feed in order to become, or remain a physical being. I didn't know which bothered me more. He would have had to find a donor to have sex with, somewhere. He told me one was Cilia Kline, one of the blood dolls for Lonny Pennyweather. He could be there in a blink, although she was all the way in Colorado Springs.

"You have visitors," he said, kissing my hands quickly. "I must go. If you need me, I will be here." He turned away, and disappeared, as if he went through an invisible door. The sudden change in the atmosphere made me blink, and a few strands of my hair was displaced by a small breeze. The aroma of his pine-scent, suddenly gone, made me sad.

"SABRINA!" The shout came from the other room from both Quist and Fritz. "Someone is here!"

Making a disparaging sound, "—Crap—" I turned and headed back into the living room, and closed the French door. It would be a while before the fire would warm that room up enough.

"Who—" I began but was cut across.

"OMG!" Fritz cried, peeking out the window in the door. "Is that a stretch Humvee?"

He and Quist were both looking out the window next to the door. Vasyl was looking out the picture window, pushing aside the drapes.

"Crap. Is that the brother?" Quist asked.

"Whose brother?" I asked, clueless.

"I shall find out," Vasyl said, and vanished.

I bent to look out the nearest window. Vasyl reappeared outside in the snow. The black vehicle in my drive certainly was a huge, stretch Humvee. It looked mean, and capable of conquering the drifting snow outside with those huge snow tires and high clearance. This could only have been sent from Tremayne's garage. No one else I knew had the money for such a vehicle. And my enemies would not announce themselves quite so lavishly.

Quist and Fritz stood back from the door when it opened. Vasyl entered first. Snow covered his bare feet and half-way up his pant legs. I hadn't been around to remove the snow on the steps or in the drive. In fact none of us had been. We were basically snowed in, but for the fact that Quist and I could travel ley lines and take whoever with us worked well enough for the past few days and nights.

Behind Vasyl a vampire strode in whose face resembled his twin brother's, Leif. For the initial two seconds of his entrance it made my heart kick with fear. But, I knew instinctively it was Heath, and calmed myself. He wore a black suit jacket over a black crew-neck sweater. A red button pinned to his lapel with white lettering read, "GOT BLOOD?" I had to give that pause, too. Vampire humor.

"Heath? What brings you out here? Is everything okay?" I asked.

"I'm to give you this," he said, reaching into his coat pocket and producing an envelope. It was exquisite thick parchment, with a red wax seal on it. *Well, well…*

I took the envelope, glancing at him, unsure. Vasyl stood behind me looking over my shoulder.

"Open it, Sabrina. That seal is Tremayne's, you'll notice, and no one has trifled with it," Heath assured.

I stepped into the living room with everyone traveling along with me like they were all on leashes. I turned on another light near the desk, noticing that my name was scribbled on the front of the envelope in shaky handwriting.

Upon opening it, I found a page of matching parchment inside, folded thrice. I opened it and tried to read the scribblings. The lettering was wiggly, and some words collided with those on the next line. Some lines slanted up, some down. It was as if a child on a bumpy carnival ride had written it. I looked up at Heath.

"Is this from Tremayne?" I asked. "'Coz I can't tell."

"Please, won't you read it, first, Sabrina?"

I glanced back at the letter and then had to squint and struggled to read the lines and words. I had to re-read some of it over a few times.

Dear Sabrina,

By the time you have possession of this letter, I will be a few hours further into my eventual death.

Unless you come to me, as I have made plans for you, I will be dead, I am told I may have only twenty-four to forty-eight hours left.

Please, come help me

I beseech you, as a friend,

Tremayne

My eyes were burning with tears and my stomach tightened in a sickening knot as I read and understood his scribblings. His scrawled signature at the end flew off the page. I felt the letter's urgency, and knew I must do something to un-do what had been done to him.

I looked up at Heath. "What should I do?" I said, tears filling my eyes. "How do I get to him?"

"You're to come with me," Heath said. "He really needs you. No one else can save him."

"No!" Vasyl stepped between myself and Heath, him being much larger, and so menacing even I stepped back from him, fearing he might unsheathe his wings. "She does not have to go anywhere! She stays!"

Coming to my senses, I ran around to get between the two vampires. "Vasyl! Stop!" I said, palms out. I hoped that he would not put Heath out on his ear, because it certainly looked like he was ready to. Eyes larger than normal, which looked scary, Vasyl's body shook as though holding himself back like a vicious dog behind a fence. His lips were pulled back in a snarl.

"It's partially my fault that Tremayne is dying," I explained, my voice harsh. Actually, it was because my dagger had poisoned his blood, but Dante was the one who had wielded it and plunged it into his chest. None of us knew that at the time when it happened. As a matter of fact, I hadn't told anyone else about this, so Tremayne didn't know that Dante had been behind it. He simply assumed that the dagger was acting in my defense against a vampire. I felt it was moot at this point. I'd given him my blood right afterwards, which was nearly two weeks ago. Last I'd heard he was doing fine. Apparently things had taken a turn for the worse.

I pushed, but Vasyl wouldn't budge. Heath stepped back and regarded me. His puppy-dog brown eyes looking hopeful.

I turned to Vasyl. "If Tremayne dies Nicolas will take over. Do you want that?" I turned back to Heath. "Where is he? Tremayne?"

"That I'm not privileged to know. What I *do* know is that I'm to take you to the airport and from there you will be taken to Tremayne."

"Should I pack? Change? Do I have time to eat? Will there be food on the flight?" my questions came rapidly out of my mouth. I already had a vision of a small jet. The runway looked like it was out in the boonies, not in the city.

"No. You don't have time to do any of that. You will not be there that long, I don't think, so you don't need to pack."

My stomach growled. I was looking forward to my homemade soup. *Oh, well.*

"Okay," I said. "I'll get my boots on and my coat." I turned. My vampire husband stood like a wall in my path.

"Sabrina, why are you going to him? Every time you do, your life is threatened. If you never went to him to begin with, you would not be in as much trouble as you are," Vasyl said.

"And he'd probably be alive and well, and not at death's doorstep," I argued.

He spun away, sputtering. "I do not understand this relationship you have with Tremayne. Why do you trouble yourself so?"

"I don't know," I said, moving around him to grab my coat off the hook. "It's like he and I are locked into this survival struggle. I can't survive as a sibyl without him, and he won't survive the night if I don't give him my blood, or whatever else he needs right now." I pulled on my snow boots over my blue jean-clad legs and zipped them up.

Vasyl's hands went up in surrender, spouting excited French.

"It's like some strange dance of life and death, and the song just never ends," I went on, more or less ignoring Vasyl as he kept muttering and walking in circles, hands flying up every other step. I'd never been able to put it quite so simply until now. The funny thing was, it was true, and I knew Tremayne needed me right now more than I needed him. I couldn't refuse to help anyone in need of my services. Not even a vampire magnate, who was also my boss, who had a craving for my blood because it gave him a high like no human blood could. Such is my life.

Chapter 4

Tunnel at the End of the Light

The stretch Humvee's growl filled my ears as I stepped up and ducked inside. The warmth circulated the back compartment making it nice and toasty. Lots of room for a party of eight or ten. The lighting was a weird phosphorous purple, the seat covers done in zebra stripes. No vampire mogul should go without such a party bus. All the better it being a large all-terrain vehicle to drive all the way out to the boonies to my house to pick me up in the middle of a snow storm. Peering at the surround zebra striped bench seats, I chose a spot and sank into them and inhaled the new-car smells. Between the seats, in the center was some sort of black console. I realized it was a combination bar and refrigerator.

Heath ducked inside and sat on the opposite side. I could not look at him without thinking of his brother who I'd encountered only a few hours ago. If Tremayne, who was an old-as-dirt vampire, was gradually dying from the silver blade of the Dagger of Delphi, then surely, it would not take long for death to come to a minion like Darla.

"To the airport." Heath spoke to the driver over a phone hand set. He replaced it in a compartment and closed it.

"Which airport? Aurora? Or…" I asked, my Knowing telling me precisely where at the same time he said it.

"DuKane," he said.

Although not surprised, I nodded politely. I'd had the good sense to grab my purse. As always, my purse had my other weapons of choice, like vials of holy water, and my favorite squirt gun loaded with the same—which had saved my ass a half dozen times, now. I was forbidden to bring the dagger, for obvious reasons, but really, he didn't need to tell me like I was a total idiot.

It would be a long, fifteen minute drive to DuKane if I didn't find something to make conversation with Heath. He was the quiet brother. There were times when I wasn't aware of his presence when he was the only vampire around. Unless, of course, Jeanie was with him. But, she wasn't always in his company.

"Where's Jeanie tonight?" I wondered. Jeanie had been my best friend growing up. She had been abducted by Steve Pumphry, and Ilona Tremayne, and nearly drained of blood. I had to act quickly after we saved her from the rogue vampire house. I'd made the decision to have them turn her. A little guilt still welled within me over this decision even now. Would I never get over this?

"She's with her pod tonight. She's having… issues." A "pod" was a small group of newly turned vampires. They stayed together, much like chicks in a nest—bad analogy, but it was the best I could think of.

"Oh, again?" I said. I wasn't going to touch that. Issues for a newly turned vampire could be anything from reverting back to a wild state of vampirism, where they wanted to kill anything with warm blood in it, to feeling depressed over being turned into a vampire and missing their human life. Neither one I would be able to handle or discuss with any authority.

"She's having a celebration of sorts. It's a vampire thing," he went on. "She's officially one month old."

"Oh, I'm sorry. You want to be with her, of course," I said, twisting the fingers of my gloves.

"I will be. When I deliver you, I will return to the party."

Party? Did he know what I did to his brother? I wasn't sure, and I really did not want to ask. He was a twin. Twins had that uncanny way of knowing when the other was in trouble, or hurt, or whatever. It was probably a good thing that neither were each other's maker. They had been turned back in the '60's, separately by females at a party somewhere in England where they were originally from.

The Humvee turned off the gravel onto a paved road. I gazed out the window to see distant lights of DuKane.

I tried to think of some safe subject to talk about. Everything that came to me I had to discard. He wouldn't know about the state of Tremayne Towers, which were in Ilona and Nicolas' control at the moment. Those two were undoubtedly waiting for Tremayne's death in order to take full control of it, and the Eastern half of the North American Vampire Association. If that happened, my world would be turned up-side down. I couldn't fight thousands of vampires. The few

I fought tonight had made me a nervous wreck as it was. I still was not able to do this vampire slaying thing and be comfortable about it. Although the dagger did all the actual dirty work.

"I've never seen the airport here," Heath said. I looked over at him. "I've actually never paid attention. Where is it?"

"Oh, it's up this road we're turning on to." The Humvee made a turn onto the road that arched over I-88, and into the outskirts of DuKane. The road continued north, connecting other major highways.

"We should be there in five or so," I said and was interrupted by a cell phone's ring.

Heath pulled out his phone. I should have been able to "know" who it was, if they were human. But, since I couldn't get a read, I knew it was either a vampire, or some other magical creature.

"Hello? Yes, we should be there in a matter of five minutes," Heath said. "That's right. Which terminal?… Oh, I see. Right, then. See you in a bit." He ended his phone conversation and put away his cell phone. We sat at a light, waiting.

"So, you have no idea where they're taking me?" I asked.

"No. I was told to deliver that letter to you, which I did. And then I was to continue to escort you to this airport."

The light changed and the Humvee moved forward. I clutched my purse. If I didn't trust Heath as much as I did, I'd swear it was a trap. I'd been herded into traps for the past month or more. But the letter was from Tremayne's own hands, albeit trembling ones. He needed my help. Possibly I was to donate the rest of my blood to him so he could live. That morbid idea floated into my head and I pushed it right out.

We were nearly there. I pointed out over Heath's shoulder. "There's the airport." As I said this a helicopter sank onto the tarmac, which we looked down upon from the bridge that crossed over the train tracks nearby. Blue lights ran along both sides of the runway. Hangers were arranged on one side, farm fields on the other.

Heath turned and looked. "Ah, I see it."

In two minutes we were pulling up a drive toward a hangar where the lights of a small jet glowed. A Lier jet, now that I saw it up close.

"Well, this is where I leave you?" I asked.

"Yes," Heath said. "I wish you luck, Sabrina."

I pulled my purse close to myself, thinking I should shake his hand, but humans didn't shake hands with a vampire if they knew better. "Thank you," I said. "Say hi and—uh—happy… uh, whatever to Jeanie for me."

"I will."

The driver came around and opened the door of the Humvee. I stepped out onto a cleared off pavement and I strode toward the awaiting jet.

"Sabrina?"

I turned back to see Heath hanging slightly out of the door of the vehicle. "I want you to know that if—if things don't go well, I won't hold anything against you. Really. I'll always be your friend."

Tightness closed my throat. I couldn't fathom any vampire saying this to me. Heath's friendship was unwavering. Unable to respond because of emotional over-load, I smiled and waved. A twinge in my nose made me rub at it. I wondered as to whether or not I would ever see Heath again, and under what circumstances. Oddly enough, my visions had not come to me, per usual.

I strode the short distance and climbed the steps of the Lier Jet where the pilot stood. I determined he was quite human.

"Good evening, Ms. Strong," the pilot greeted me. I suddenly felt as though I were in a spy movie, and I was about to meet *007*. This was not the normal thing for me to do—jump in a Humvee, and be taken to a small jet to be flown to places unknown in the dark of night.

I smiled at him. "Hi." Bitter wind whipped at us, cutting off any more niceties, and my wild imaginings of spies or thoughts of having a chat with Daniel Craig, or Timothy Dalton—or my favorite James Bond actor, Pierce Brosnan.

The pilot moved away from the door and I stepped inside the warmth of the luxury jet. He shut the door behind himself and I heard it lock with a slight vacuum seal sound. I was standing in a small seating area that looked more like someone's living room done in white, tans and browns with a little pale green leafy patterns thrown in for color. The pilot continued through to the other end and through another door, which he closed.

The fact a vampire was on the plane nearly shocked me and I had to struggle to keep a poker face. A handsome man with a bad-boy's growth of beard and blue-black hair in a business cut occupied one of the sofas. If I continued with my day dream, I'd have to say he was the most handsome Bond I'd ever seen. He stood and smiled. Teeth showing, but no fangs—thank goodness! Oh, yes. He was a vampire.

"Ms. Strong. Nice of you to join us," he greeted me in a nice, deep voice.

He had dangerous blue eyes. Dangerous because they were magnetic, and especially on such a magnificent looking man. I knew a powerful vampire when I met one, and he was definitely powerful.

"My name is Stefan Capella. I'm to escort you to your final destination." His lips moved sensually. The lower lip sort of dipped down to one side, flashing his teeth as he spoke. He made a slight bow with his head. Again I would not shake his hand. That would be dangerous for me in a half dozen ways.

"Thank you." Wonderful. Another Steve. However, aside from his name, he didn't resemble Steve Pumphry at all. Stefan wore a black suit over a black button-down shirt, and he wore it well, believe me. The orchid tie was the only color on him. Suave features, olive complexion, black hair, plus the name, told me he was Italian, and he oozed vampire pheromones. Luckily for me, the gloves I wore had open mesh over the mystic ring. It was the only pair I owned. I'd asked Constance to help me make them, and they turned out so well that she offered to make me more pairs. I may have to check on the status of them when I get back. In the back of my darting mind I figured it would give me the opening I needed to talk to her.

"Have a seat here," Stefan said, motioning to a set of six—three abreast—unoccupied seats facing forward. They looked more like airline seats, but more plush, equipped with seat belts.

"We'll be taking off momentarily." The windows were small and round, tinted dark—a vampire's jet.

I sank into one of the seats, and pulled on the lap belt. Stefan settled into the one next to me. I did not like being this close to him. A distinctive whine of jet engines, and a tone sounded inside, as a light came on above that said FASTEN STEAT BELTS. Stefan smiled down at me. This was going to be a long flight if I had to keep my eyes off of him. I glanced away. He was trying terribly hard to hit me with his vampire thrall, but he was striking out, and I think his ego was a little bruised.

The jet engines wound up higher and it begin to taxi onto a runway. Out the darkened windows muted lights blinked past my vision.

"Have you flown before?" Steve asked.

"Lots of times," I said. "My father flew." Only not a Lier jet.

"I see. Good." He smiled a relaxed sort of smile that creased his cheeks.

"Where are we going?"

"I'm not at liberty to tell you that."

"Ah. I see. This is a top secret place?"

"Actually, yes. It is." Yep. James Bond had nothing on me.

The jet's motion sped up. I waited for that familiar feeling of when we left the ground. My stomach had that lurching, butterfly feeling. I had always thought it was fun to fly.

"I was told I'm going to see Tremayne. I'm to help him."

"Yes. That's correct," Stefan said.

"Must be really secret," I said. "I'm taken to a small airport and whisked off."

"We can't take any chances. This was plan B."

"Plan B? What happened to Plan A?"

"We had to abort it. This was the best scenario so that no one would figure out where we were heading. Each of us only knowing our part in it, and nothing more. In fact, only the pilot knows where we are headed. I haven't a clue." He smiled, steepling his fingers under his chin. I had been watching his mouth again. At first the movement of his mouth seemed weird, but then as I stared at it I found that the way he moved while talking was mesmerizing. Almost to the point of hypnotizing. I realized in a few short moments that using his lips in combination with those deep blue eyes, he was able to capture and hold an intended victim's eyes.

"Wow. I feel like I'm in a double-oh-seven movie," I said, looking around. I couldn't help it. I did feel like I were in the middle of a Bond movie.

He chuckled and leaned slightly as if to impart some secret. "I have been compared to James Bond in my time."

"You do have a certain Pierce Brosnan look to you," I quipped. He liked that and smiled. Okay, ego check here. "How is it I've never met you before this?"

"I'm actually from New York. I've been called up to take care of Mr. Tremayne's needs out this way."

"And I'm on your to-do list?" The jet banked a hard left. My clairvoyant abilities would eventually kick in and I would know where I was heading. *West...*

"You're the only thing on my to-do list for tonight," he said and winked.

"I feel so special," I said as a chill ran up my arms. Shit. I was looking at his lips again.

He chuckled politely as he pulled out his cell phone.

The jet leveled off while Stefan spoke into his cell phone. "I've got the package," he said, and listened. "Very good. We should be there in a few hours." He closed up his phone and placed it on a side table.

"Nice. I'm a package," I said, faking a happy smile. He chuckled at my little antics.

"Take no offense," Stefan said. "I've been instructed to not use your name in any communications. You are either my package, or The Lady."

"Intrigue. I like that."

The seatbelt sign went off. Stefan unbuckled his lap belt, and drew up in one liquid motion. Like most vampires, he seemed jointless with bones made of silly putty.

"Why don't you join me over here where it's more comfortable. He folded his six foot two length on the cushy white couch. I rose, stepped over and chose the couch across from him. He didn't seem to take offense at that. I'd have to try a lot harder to make him not like me so much. What was the chance of that, I wondered. *None.*

"Would you like a refreshment?" He asked motioning to what looked like a small wet bar.

"Water would be fine," I said. I'd had one too many instances where I drank something I shouldn't have where a vampire was serving it to me.

But instead of making drinks, he pressed some button on the arm of the chair. From the same door where the pilot had gone through, a young Oriental man appeared.

"I'd like you to meet Ty Cho," Stefan said, hooking his leg over a knee. "Mr. Cho, would you kindly serve us drinks? Sabrina would like a glass of water."

The new man stepped into the cabin, wearing tan Chinos, and a sleeveless black shirt with a mandarin collar, showing off his muscular arms. They weren't overly muscular, but well defined. My Knowing told me it was a special way in which he worked out, not with weights, like a body builder. He was knowledgeable in the Martial Arts—exceptional, in fact. He was possibly five-eight, or so—a few inches taller than my own five-four. His black hair came down to his collar, with jagged bangs. His movements were lithe, and precise as he walked to the bar and poured the drinks. I found myself fascinated, and alarmed by what I was able to siphon from him.

"Mr. Cho, has been in my employ for several years," Stefan said, smiling, two fingers steepled below his chin. He sounded admiringly about Cho. "He's quite deadly."

"I know he is," I said with confidence, watching Cho lean over a small counter. His nearly black eyes flicked up to me, and a brief smile stretching his lips before he bent and took a couple of bottles out of a mini fridge. One was a Dasani water, the other was a black bottle of Real Red. He worked on filling a tumbler with ice and poured the water over the ice carefully, and without hurry. The Real Red—100% human blood—was placed in a wine glass. He brought the drinks over to us, and placed the glasses on little napkins. Then he stood off to the side, holding the tray downwards, in front of himself and made a little bow to Stefan, remaining silent.

Cho was human, that was easy to assess. I got a read from him the moment I boarded the plane, but more clearly when he'd entered the room. And yes, he was "deadly" as Stefan had said. The images that came to me were quick flashes, but I got the gist of it. He had caused at least one opponent's death in a tournament in Tokyo—he was much younger then. My guess was he was now in his late twenties. I wasn't sure how many deaths he had dealt under the vampire who now thralled him and was taking me to who-knew-where. Tanned, the strong hands had pulled my attention while he served me my drink. I've seen working men's hands, hands of construction workers, or men who labored. These were not the hands of a man who "worked" with his hands in the way, say, a brick-layer, or a farmer, or a carpenter does. These were clean hands, no trace of roughness, and his nails were manicured, knuckles large. Yet, he could do amazing things with them. I knew precisely what his hands were capable of. And the fingers. I've seen pictures of a tree with odd finger-sized holes drilled into the trunk, while looking through an old text my father had on Chinese physical culture, history, and Zen Buddhism. Those holes were not drilled into the tree with a drill, but punched with the fingers by members of the order of Shaolin priests. If Cho practiced kung fu, he could possibly do such things, like break boards, or bricks with his hands. The veins tracing over the backs were pronounced over the bones, and he had done nothing more than pour a few drinks.

"His hands and feet are deadly weapons, that is," Stefan corrected himself.

I made a noncommittal sound and nodded—all the while smiling to myself—and looked up at Cho. Our eyes met briefly once more. There was a certain shyness about him. Or was it some sort of humility, an Oriental poise, I suppose. I couldn't keep the smile from my lips. And he seemed almost too happy to be part of this whole deal. Excitement oozed from him, much like the vampires pheromones did. Yet, he held himself poised.

"Ty, this is Sabrina. The one we spoke of earlier?" Stefan said as if to remind him. Cho remained one cool dude as his dark eyes slid to rest on my face. He smiled and gave me more of a bow than he had to Stefan. Interesting.

"He will be escorting you throughout the rest of your trip, once we land, that is," Stefan informed me.

"Oh," I said, a little surprised by this. I was going somewhere where I needed to be escorted? "So, where am I going where I need someone who is a black belt in the martial arts?"

Stefan's eyes darted to me startled by how I knew something which we hadn't discussed as yet. Oddly, Cho did not register any surprise whatsoever. "Oh. Of course, you're clairvoyant," Stefan said, finally getting it. He cleared his throat and went on. "It was my mission to find someone who could stay near you night or day, and not be affected by sunlight, yet can—how shall I put it?" Stefan said, fingers steepled once again as he gazed up to find that word. "Kick ass?"

I darted a look to Cho. "I think he qualifies," I said. Cho seemed to like my comment, and his almond eyes thinned to twin black crescents while his lips stretching into an almost full smile, but I could tell he was holding back. He bowed a little deeper to me, his hair shifting like silky strands with the movement.

No one knew that Dante was always with me—an invisible spirit—since he was an Undead. As long as there was a mirror available, I could summon him. I kept a compact in my purse for such occasions. Sometimes he merely showed up—the mirror worked as a bridge between my world and his. At the moment, though, rather than state that I didn't need anyone to help protect me, I kept still. Dante, who was now an Astral Vampire, couldn't always stay by my side in the flesh, as it took quite a bit of energy. My gut told me to keep Dante as the ace up my sleeve. If Dante wasn't needed, then Cho would do just fine. Why let them know I had a secret weapon? It would be unwise to let anyone know I had such a valuable ally.

"May I ask why would I need someone experienced in the Martial Arts in order to get me wherever Tremayne is?" I could not imagine what lie ahead of this journey.

Stefan laced long fingers at chest level and cocked his head, dark blue eyes gleaming. "Oh, I suppose it would be because Nicolas is overly fanatic with protection. We heard he ordered up hard muscle from New York—my area, in fact—to guard the compound. You, a woman alone, well, let's just say werewolves can get downright nasty." Stefan's smile became a sneer. His words made me shudder inside. *Werewolves?*

He lifted his drink to me in a silent toast. I mimicked him, then sipped my drink, faking that I was all hunky dory with that.

Flopping an arm across the back of the couch, he looked at me and said, "I've heard many things about you. One is that you're the sibyl and that you can control demons and vampires. Is this true?"

Smiling I said, "Do you want a demonstration?"

"Yes. Let us put it to the test, shall we?" He set his drink down and stood. "Now, mind, let's keep this on a friendly level. I promise not to do anything to ruffle your feathers, and you'll not throw me across the room. Agreed?"

"Agreed." *Unless you piss me off.*

He came over and sat next to me. "Oh, I do like this side much better." He leaned a little toward me, and breathed in my scent. "You know, if Tremayne doesn't make it, I would gladly hire you on."

As if, loser. I dared to stare into his handsome face and blue eyes, which were now aquamarine blue. It was like he could change their color at will.

"I think you want to go and sit across from me now," I said, pointing to the couch, as though he were my pet bull dog. Stefan stood, stepped across to where he originally started, and sat down. His suit moved in a liquid-y fashion. He settled across from me, looking slightly amazed and also a bit unsettled as he pulled at his neck tie.

"How did you do that?" he gasped, with a shake of his head.

"My little secret." There was no need to reveal my secrets to this one.

He chuckled, having regained his composure. "I'm impressed and intrigued." Right. He smells my blood. That was the one thing that intrigued him the most about me. "If there's anything I can do for you during the flight?"

"Food?" I said hopefully. "And maybe a movie?" This was going to be a long ass flight and I wasn't looking forward to jawing with this handsome Italian vampire from New York who would constantly try and thrall me.

"Food? Oh, yes, of course." Stefan turned to Cho. "Mr. Cho, how is the food for our guest coming along?"

Cho held up a finger. He moved quickly back through the little door.

"In the meantime, I've got something you might find enjoyable." Stefan picked up a remote. Lights dimmed and a screen lowered. The music was from a familiar show. I had seen it when it was on reruns. I figured I might enjoy watching a show about vampires and demons and see how someone else handled staking them for a change.

Chapter 5

Somewhere Over the Rainbow

Snow covered the ground when I looked out of the jet's open door, after we'd landed. The surrounding air field looked flat and barren under the lights. Beyond that, there were almost no lights in the distance. For all I knew we were somewhere in Siberia. *Just how many "Buffy the Vampire Slayer" shows had I watched on that jet?* Aside from the few plane hangars, there wasn't another building anywhere. Trees, in fact, were much less abundant. But then, it was black as pitch out. Icy wind bit my face, and I pulled up my collar, zipped my coat further up to my neck, and wondered why I'd left my knit hat at home. Well, I had no idea where I was going tonight. But once we were down on the ground, I did.

"Is this Kansas?" I asked Stefan who stood behind me on the steps.

"You're good," Stefan said, admiration in his voice as he stood inside the jet's doorway to see us out.

"Where in Kansas?" I asked.

"I'm not allowed to tell you," he said.

Great. I couldn't get a read from him, of course, but I got a general read from someone who knew where we were. I figured the pilot knew.

Cho emerged from the warmer interior and looked around. He had a lightweight leather jacket on. *He'll freeze.* And carried a small duffel bag. Cho had been Mr. Silent the whole trip. It was a good thing that there had been something to watch, because he either shrugged or smiled, or bowed. If I didn't know any better, I'd think he were a mute. But I was quite certain he could speak, he didn't have anything to say or add to whatever the conversation at the moment was, but it was a little off-putting, really.

Another car, this time a plain-old stretch limo awaited us on the tarmac below. I shouldered my purse and descended the steps. Cho's footfalls were quiet behind me. Either his shoes had soft soles, or he was barefoot. We reached the car and the driver held the door for us. I gave one last look at the jet. The door was already closed, and the engines still whining, but it remained stationary. I hoped that we would be returning the same way, and not be abandoned here in Kansas, which was nearly the same thing as Siberia to my thinking.

"Good evening, Ms. Strong. My name's Charley, and I'll be driving you to your destination tonight," the driver said. He smiled at Cho. Obviously, he hadn't expected a second passenger.

Cho bowed to him.

I thanked the white-haired gentleman, who wore the usual limo garb of dark suit, tie and a little chauffeur's hat.

Cho let me duck in first. I chose the closest seat near the door. He slid in and sat across from me. The door closed, and then Charley got in behind the wheel. In another moment, we smoothly pulled away. The interior was lit minimally, like a theater before the show. Enough to see one another, at least.

I bit my lip. I wasn't entirely sure that Cho could speak English. I wasn't exactly a shy person, but normally I'm quiet. Figuring him out was going to be somewhat of a challenge. Although I got reads from him, he was not an easy read by any means. I would have to touch him in order to find out more, and I really didn't want to do that. Instead I'd have to strike up a conversation.

I smiled at him.

He smiled back.

I twisted my lips. Time for twenty questions.

"So, where are you from?" I asked, saying each word carefully, and slowly.

"Al-bu-quer-que," he said just as slow, to tease me. Then he laughed. "I'm American." I don't know why it surprised me, but it did.

I laughed too, hand to my open-mouth, both surprised and embarrassed. "Oh, I'm sorry," I said. "You didn't speak on the jet, so I wasn't sure."

"Yes. Sorry about that." He still looked bemused about it. He twisted his lips and went on. "I've been doing a little play-acting with Stefan. I pretended I was Asian." He shrugged. "I don't know why. Call it my version of fun when I'm bored. But when I met you, I didn't want to do the accent and then have to explain to you why I really don't have one." And yet, here he was explaining.

"Love it! That's funny!" I chuckled again. "Are your parents American?"

His eyes made a roll, and a lot of whites showed when he did. "Yes, unfortunately. As it so happens, my mother is from San Francisco, and my father is from L.A."

"How did you get into the Martial Arts?"

"My father studied the Martial Arts. He had a dojo and taught me. He is my trainer. He is actually at the fourth dan stage."

"I'm sorry? Fourth dan?" I said.

He made a little head movement. "It is someone who is trained in kung fu to an extremely high level," he said.

"What level are you?" I asked. "Because I was told your hands and feet are deadly."

He smiled. "I have trained at the *dim-mak* level."

"Okay, now you're giving me more new words to learn," I said with a chuckle. He chuckled too.

"It has to do with what is called the death touch, but it's more to do with healing, than killing." He shook his head. "I know. I'm confusing you, but it's the Yin and Yang, thing. It's based on the idea that striking certain acupoints or pressure points on the body can either help to heal, or cause instant or delayed death, depending upon how hard you strike."

"Wow," I said. "That's pretty wild." I was at a loss for words at this point. "Have you actually caused a death using this *dim-mak*?" Well, I already knew, but wanted to see if he'd admit it.

His lips went into a purse. "Once. But only once. And I was absolved of it entirely, because my opponent was also using the death touch, and it is illegal in competition. I had no choice. It was him or me."

"I see. So, you were fighting professionally?"

"No. Actually it was after the match. He attacked me. We had already competed, and I won. He was angry, and well, anger isn't such a good thing when you are trained in such things. I had no choice. He came at me, and I struck in order to protect myself." He shrugged.

"And you hit him somewhere—"

"There are many pressure points on the body. One around the left side of the ribs, here—" he put his hand to his own ribs "—a hard strike to this area can rupture the spleen. A strike to stomach point nine on the carotid artery can either instantly kill, or may take years before the person may die. On an older individual with plaque buildup, it would cause a heart attack or stroke probably instantly."

"Wow."

"And Tiger Leopard Fist can burst the eardrums." He had curled his fingers in on his hand, and made a motion toward his head. "Many of the *dim-mak* strikes can cause death hours or days later."

"So, this dude was trying to kill you with *dim-mak*? How did you know?"

He made a small chuckle. "I knew. You know when your opponent is trying to seriously to hurt you permanently.

"I see. What about your mother? She's not into kung fu, is she?"

"My mother? Oh, no. She was a three-time gold medal gymnast for the Olympics."

"Oh, wow! How impressive. And your father is a Martial Arts trainer?"

"He didn't become one until later. Actually he is a lawyer. But, once I got into training and competition, he began to train me full time."

"I don't understand why Stefan wanted to give me a bodyguard with such a high skill in kung fu," I said. Usually vampires were not interested in a human's welfare, especially when we were in their company. I had to presume this was all Tremayne's doing, and not Stefan's, as he would have me believe.

Cho made a little noise in his throat. "He owes Tremayne fealty," he said. "Not only that, I am very honored, since I divined that I was to become your champion. I'm excited at the prospect."

"Divined? My champion?" This wasn't sixteenth century England, I was pretty sure.

"Let me explain," he said. "I use the divination of I Ching. You were in one of my reads."

"*I* was? How could you have found me?" I actually wasn't quite sure what I Ching was, but presuming it was a form of reading the future, I faked it.

"It's difficult for me to explain in great detail to someone who has never heard of it. You see, through several dozen throws of yarrow sticks, and consulting the Book of Changes, plus an astrologer, as well as three mediums, I learned that there would be a woman with great powers of second sight, a seer the likes of which the world had not seen in at least a century, maybe more. And, our paths would cross."

"I'm the sibyl," I said. It seemed that a number of people were able to find me through some method of divination. If it were not by supernatural ways, it was through divination and a good medium, or word of mouth.

He made a small bow. "Yes."

"So, you threw some sticks and found me?"

He chuckled. "Yarrow sticks. There are fifty. Some people use coins, but they are not as accurate." He chuckled, as if that were a private joke. "The closest comparison to the I Ching is the Tarot cards."

"Ah," I said. "Tarot cards. Those I know."

"Six throws will give you a hexagram, and you consult the Book of Changes to know what it means. Of course, I've become pretty good and no longer need to consult the book."

I nodded. "And each hexagram gives you the reading?"

"Correct. Sometimes, though, it is an action, or an inaction. I found out you lived in the mid-west. I began working for the New York vampire headquarters, which Stefan is the head of. My read said that no matter what, our paths would cross. I was patient."

"How did you wind up working for vampires?" I asked, dumbfounded.

He chuckled. "Believe it or not, they offered me great money!" He laughed. "Vampires who are rich throw money around like it was useless paper."

"I know! I work for Tremayne. I needed the money, and couldn't turn him down. I'm his clairvoyant," I said, feeling our camaraderie growing out of our similar jobs.

"Also, I Ching says that there is a possible *gé*."

"How's that?"

"A revolution. A revolt."

"Already happening," I said. "But you should know about it, since you've been working for Stefan."

"I'm kept in the dark. He has told me nothing about anything dealing with their politics. What have you heard?"

"Heard? I'm living it!" I complained mildly. "When I was hired to find out who was killing vampires and drinking their blood, no one knew that Ilona—she was Tremayne's brother's wife—was going to kill Erik. Plus she made an attempt on Bjorn, and a few others—me included—along with them. I was getting close to discovering who was behind it all, and they kept me busy by attacking me in order so as to get things ready for them to take over all of America. Uh, the whole North American Vampire Association, that is."

He nodded, readjusting his ankle over a knee, and holding it with a hand while leaning forward slightly. "Sounds like you've had a thrilling time."

"Thrilling isn't even touching it. Anyway, Ilona has been trying to get rid of me the whole time, along with Bjorn's wife and his brother. Meanwhile, she's also managed to bring back hunting humans."

"Yes. So I've heard. But Stefan is siding with Tremayne, and keeping his minions in check. They use only donors and the bottled blood."

I nodded. "Well, anyway, in the meantime, because Tremayne wouldn't go along with it, he has been declared a rogue. They are trying everything they can to keep him out of power. Or kill him."

"I see. And this is why you are going to Tremayne?"

"Not exactly. Tremayne needs my help. He—well—he may be dying from—" I broke off, my face became warm, and my eyes teared up. Although I was not the one who unleashed the dagger on him, I felt as though it was my fault all this had happened. A multitude of thoughts and worries as to what would happen once I got to my destination brought on a wave of nausea. I looked out the window to see mostly darkness, and only a few distant lights on the dark horizon.

Cho's voice invaded. "Hex two and three is *kūn*. We will not force matters and go with the flow for now."

I turned. "Yes. That's probably a good idea." We spoke nothing more about vampires. Instead, we discovered a small screen behind the front seat, and figured out how to run a DVD on it and watched something inane. I wasn't sure what to expect, once we got to our destination, and feared the more I spoke about it, the more nervous I would become. It was better to be oblivious. For the time being. I couldn't figure out why my Knowing wasn't able to reveal anything to me at this point.

An hour later, our driver announced that we had arrived.

I looked out of the tinted windows. Pole lights glowed eerily inside a compound that looked to me more like a military base, complete with chain-link fence, and a warning sign that gave me shivers. The building inside looked like a small cabin. It stumped me. And then my Knowing kicked in.

A cabin… built recently… everything is below ground. I was getting the word "bunker" from somewhere. Also, werewolves were involved. The muscle Stefan had mentioned, of course.

The limo paused at the gate. Someone came out of a small gate house. Charley powered down his window to speak with him.

"I have Ms. Strong in back," Charley's voice came muffled through the privacy glass. From my spot it was easy to see the shadow of a man lean in toward the driver's window, using an LED flashlight to look in at him. Finally he nodded and went back into his little gatehouse. The gate glided slowly back electronically.

Charley drove us through into the compound. Looking around, and now that we were here, my Knowing fed me more information. This had once been something to do with the military. The revelation was a little scary. Now that the missile—or missiles—were gone, it was benign, of course, and no longer run by the military. But I became confused about why Tremayne was here—and *where* he might be. The lone cabin stood approximately at the center of the compound. I was not getting any readings on where Tremayne might be kept safe and under a doctor's care. My gut began to twist. My Were-senses said this wasn't a good thing.

The limo pulled up to the cabin, next to which was parked a dark, humongous Humvee which still had a military look to it, painted in the drab military camo greens with no "extras". Three large men stepped out the front door of the cabin onto an open porch and down three steps. Charley powered down his window again. The same words were briefly exchanged again. Charley got out and opened our door ushering cold a cold breeze through the back compartment. Cho allowed me to exit first. I paused.

"Ladies first," he said.

"Gee, thanks," I said and moved to get out but stopped. One of the men had stepped up to the car.

"Ms. Strong?" he said, bending down to peer in at me through the open door.

"That's me," I said. He backed up as I stepped onto the gravel. The wind whipped at us, flapping my coat and the guy's camo jacket. The other two remained on the open porch, at military rest. They all dressed the same, in full camouflage, and black knit hats. I saw no hair beneath the caps. No weapons hung on them, which was a relief, but from the looks of them, they could do me a lot of harm physically. Especially since they were not vampires, and I couldn't control them. They were werewolves, like Stefan had said. I detected their scent just as easily as they would mine.

"Come in, please?" He paused, eyes darting to the area behind me. I looked back and found that Cho had stepped out of the limo. In comparison he was slight, looked as threatening as a toothpick. The wind whipped his straight hair across his face and he made no move to shake it away.

"Who's he?" the leader asked, flicking his head in gesture.

"My entourage," I said, tongue-in-cheek, as I smiled back at Cho. It had been our little joke as we'd driven across the open land that if someone asked about him, that's what I would say. They couldn't deny me an "entourage".

"We need to do a search before you are allowed past this point," he said. "Come inside."

"Search?" I looked back at Cho.

"No worries, Sabrina," Cho said quietly moving to join me. But I'm pretty sure the Weres had heard him.

"Who's this?" a second guy asked as we stepped up to the porch, coming between me and Cho.

"This is Cho," I said, anger swelling up. "My bodyguard."

"Bodyguard?" The first one said, an amused smile on his lips as he checked Cho out. From his slim and shorter frame, one would presume Cho was not at all a threat. The three Weres chuckled as though I'd told a pretty good joke. I hoped Cho's easy confidence was not male bravado. But, I had a feeling I was going to see him in action sooner rather than later.

One of the men opened the door to the cabin. I reluctantly went inside. Stepping onto a colorful throw rug, the warmth inside bathed me. A fireplace snapped cheerily at one end where floor to ceiling windows gaped out at the night. A vampire would never live here. My nerves on edge, I glanced around. The cabin's living room adjoined the kitchen/dining area. Off the kitchen, a hall led back to a few rooms. My Knowing told me down the hallway there were two bedrooms and one small, basic bath with only a shower. But more importantly, there was another door around the corner of the kitchen. This led *down. Way down.*

"We need to conduct a search," the leader announced.

"What for?" I asked.

"To see if you're carrying," the second, smaller Were said. He was still taller than either of us and broad of shoulder. Shaped something like what my brother would call a "fireplug".

"Carrying? Carrying what?" I asked, doing my best innocent act.

"Holy water, crucifixes, and that vampire-killer knife of yours," he said in a gruff, but bemused voice.

"Dagger of Delphi," I corrected. "I don't have it on me." But I did have other stuff on me. Damn!

"Empty the purse, miss," the leader said, pointing to the kitchen counter.

With a small gasp of protest, I turned and stepped toward the counter.

"You, too, hot shot," he said to Cho who put his duffel bag up on the counter.

One of the other men pulled on blue urethane gloves, the kind they use at the airports in order to search passengers. *Brother.* My stomach did a slow cartwheel as my precognition fed me a few blipping scenes of what they were going to do. They were actually going to *touch* me?

"Okay, let's see what you have in that bag, sweetheart," the leader said with less mirth this time.

"Fine." I up-ended my purse. All my crap fell out. My wallet was snatched up by a large hand.

"Hey!" I tried to snag it but the brute laughed, stepped away from me and looked through it. He must have found my driver's license because he looked up at me and then at the picture. He looked down and up again. Yeah. It was your normal bad picture from the DMV. At least my hair was combed out this time. Finding nothing further of interest, he tossed it back onto the pile. The other Weres were going through some of it. One found the glass vial and held it up with an expletive, like it were a deadly snake. The other had my water pistol.

"Holy water?" the leader held up the green plastic water gun, shaking it, and then squinted at it. I noticed he had fingerless gloves on. I suppose he wasn't worried about getting any of my cooties on him, but the other two had the blue gloves on.

I shrugged.

"What other goodies have we?"

"Nothing else."

"Where's the knife?"

"It's a dagger," I corrected again. "And I left it at home."

"Better have," he said in a warning voice.

"Wish she brought it," the other said. "I'd like to see what it looks like."

Six pairs of eyes looked at me.

"Well, let's do the search to make sure."

"Off with the coats," came the command.

I rolled my eyes, but complied. Cho removed his coat, and held up his hands in a casual complacent way. On the outside he was cool as ice in January. But I knew he was like a rocket about to launch if something lit his fuse.

"I've got the lady," Fireplug claimed and moved toward me, looking like this was going to be a pleasant experience for him. I wondered if they'd drawn straws or something. *Probably.*

Both men moved toward us. Mine smiled at me and drew his blue-gloved hands over my shoulders, first, and then went down my sides as I held my arms out to my sides. He squatted and ran his hands down my right thigh, all the way down to my ankle. Then he moved to my left leg. His hand touched me in the groin area. I jerked away.

"Hey!" I said, anger boiling up.

"Sorry," he said—not sounding at all sorry—and drew his hands down my leg.

I squinted down at him threateningly. "I'd be careful, if I were you."

Standing, he smiled. "Why?"

"I might have to kick you in the knee."

Amusement played at the corners of his mouth. Chuckling, his hands moved toward my breasts. I jerked back. Playfully he held up his hands as if he were joking around about touching me there.

"You're done searching me," I said, noticing that Cho's body search was finished too. He glanced at all three men who stood around us. I felt like he was measuring them up. He gave me a vague nod. It was a nod, not a bow. I had a feeling he knew what I was about to do. Was he telepathic? I wondered.

I turned my head away, then shifted my body's weight to one foot. Without hesitation I swung my right leg, and my foot connected with the guy's crotch. I watch him go down, holding himself, curled up like a fetus, groaning in pain. God, did that feel good!

"Like I said, I might kick you in the knee."

"You missed the knee," one of them pointed out.

I looked down at the guy. "No. I'm pretty sure I got the middle one."

Cho smiled and said, "*Xùn.* Wind." I didn't know what he meant by that until I saw the larger guy move out from behind him as if to surge toward me. I backed into the counter to keep clear. Cho's body twirled, both his feet came off the ground—all of it so fast I didn't see what exactly happened, but the man's head snapped back. In the next second, the guy was down on the polished wood floor, groaning, holding his face, and Cho stood in a kung fu pose, legs in a wide stance like I've seen in Bruce Lee movies.

"*Xùn*. Wind," Cho said, smiling, hands in a kung fu pose in front of him in case the third guy had some ideas to attack.

I smiled and nodded. "Wind."

Looking nonplussed, the leader assessed the two men on the ground. He shook his head and said, "I was told you'd have some surprises, but I didn't expect this."

"Me either," I said and shrugged, crossing my arms.

Cho relaxed, seeing there was no more threats.

"C'mon. You can pick up your purse, coats, and everything when you leave," he said and moved us through that little hall toward the door which led down, pretty much forgetting his pals.

He opened the door. Cho and I peered down the stairway, which went much further down than a normal basement. In fact there was a landing, and the steps continued down at least another level. At the bottom was a turn. Lighting, I noticed, was anchored low to the walls, pointing downward, and lit the steps well enough to see our way.

"Take the steps all the way down. Someone'll be there to let you inside," the leader said.

"How many floors?" I wondered.

"There's *fifteen*," he said, large front teeth showing, as though he were snarling. "You only go down one level."

"What was this place at one time?" I asked, getting the words *military, cold war, secrecy* and *bombs. Holy crap!*

"It was an Atlas F missile site. It's vertical, which means there's a lot of stairs. You'll be going into the old control room, and there are other complexes that run off the first level. The builder did a damned good job," he explained. "Very cozy down there, now. It's really a nice condo." He laughed and added. "If I could afford it I'd live here."

"I suppose you don't have to worry about tornadoes, here," I quipped.

"Or WMD's," he said with a wry smile.

Cho and I moved through the opening. Our footfalls made light tapping on the well-lit steps as we descended.

I hesitated and looked back up.

"Are you gonna lock us in?" I asked the guy.

"No need," he said confidently and moved away from the door and shut it.

"Sabrina. Come," Cho said from below. I looked down to see him motioning to me.

I relented and went down the stairs. Visions wafted to me. I didn't like what I was seeing.

Since they had stripped me of my purse and coat, I was now weaponless. I couldn't bring Dante in to help without a mirror. But after Cho's little demonstration, I was certain that I didn't need him for this, after all. At least I still had my mystical ring that both controlled vampires and kept me from falling under their vampire thrall.

Chapter 6

Going Down

At the end of the two flights of stairs, we stepped into an extremely short hall, no larger than a closet. Another large werewolf, wearing a dark suit instead of military garb, stood at a door at military rest. His head was completely shaven like his clones up top. He stared straight at me and Cho. His eyes stopped me. They were silver ringed with Halogen-blue. They were so unusually chilling I had to avert my eyes. The strong musky werewolf scent wafted from him. But the underlying scents of new paint, and flooring adhesive was overpowering, and I tried to glide on those smells, instead.

Although Cho didn't look deadly, I knew he was, and would have no trouble with this guy. Yet, I was still fearful. The Were could probably scent the fear in me.

"Hi," I said. Not sure what to say to him.

"Ms. Strong. You're expected."

He turned to a weird looking steel door. It was unusually complex, made of six thick bars and the inner portion of the door was concave—and several inches thick, possibly a foot, maybe more, my second sight told me.

"Blast doors," Cho supplied. "Designed to keep occupants safe during a nuclear attack."

"You seem well-informed," I said.

"Studied about the cold war at the university," Cho said.

Meanwhile, the Were used a small radio to make contact with someone on the inside.

"Yes?" said someone, the radio static thick.

"Ms. Strong is here, master." *Master?* Okay, I was about to go into a vampire nest. It shouldn't have surprised me since they searched me and made me give up my holy water vials and water gun.

"Allow Ms. Strong to enter," the voice said. The voice gave me chills. That was Nicolas' voice. Why was he here? My heartbeat deepened with dread and fear. The wrong subliminal message to send out to any vampire.

The guard turned a leaver, and the door opened out. On the inside it did, indeed, curve inward. The large Were moved aside. I peered through the door. A few steps beyond the threshold, a well-lit hall with creamy walls were awash in amber from lamps met my eyes. It made a turn about half-way in. Another door exactly like this one guarded another entrance, or exit.

"Go on in. You're expected."

Cho moved with me and the big Were stepped in between us, cutting Cho off.

"*He* stays." the silver-eyed Were said, defiant

Cho said nothing and didn't make any moves. We exchanged glances. He shrugged.

"Why can't he come with me?" I challenged, now daring to look straight into those strange eyes. The pupils had gone large, as though he could become his beast at a moment's notice. Maybe he wasn't merely a Were. I could not get any read from him. Weres were difficult to read, not impossible. This was not good.

"The master wants to see you. Alone," Silver-eyes said.

"Go ahead, Sabrina. I'll wait out here," Cho said, smiling, and leaned against the wall, folding his arms. I knew this was all for show, to give the werewolf a false sense of security, and he wouldn't need to worry about him. I chuckled inwardly. Cho had something literally up his sleeve. My Knowing told me he would not wait out in the hall for long.

Knowing who I was about to face, my stomach clenched. I stepped through the threshold and in two steps I turned, and came face to face with Nicolas. I found myself grappling with mixed emotions. Fear and shock took a strangle hold on me at once, and I wasn't sure that this had not been a big hoax to lure me into another trap. *Well, damn it to hell and back!* I hate when I second guess myself.

"Nicolas," I said, working to keep my expression neutral.

"Ms. Strong. Won't you come in?" he said, acting his charming self.

"Why are you here? Where's Tremayne? If this is a trap—"

A calming hand came up. "I assure you it is not a trap," he said in that dark and deadly voice of his. I used to think it sexy. Now it drew heavily on my inner red flag zones. It made my blood run cold, and my knees became like jelly. At the same time, my desires went wacko on me. *Damn!* "You were summoned this way because none of us here can summon you in a vampire way." Yes. Although Nicolas had bitten me, his powers could not override Vasyl's, and I was pretty sure that pissed him off. *Ha-ha, na-na.*

"Yeah. Thank God," I said, just to rub it in.

For a full human heartbeat, he grappled with that. I watched his lips twitch ever so slightly. Then, with a slight movement of his head, chin drawn forward, he took a deep breath and brought his head down to engage my eyes. I stared back defiantly.

"Would you like to step in? I assure you no one is going to harm you in any way." *Yeah, right.*

I looked back out at where Cho remained with Silver-eyes. "Why can't he come in?"

"He was not invited."

"Stefan gave him to me for my protection," I argued.

"Really? Stefan Capella?"

"Yes. He told me that I was to have Cho as my bodyguard."

"We made no such request—"

"You've taken everything from me that protects me," I said, in a challenging voice. "As the sibyl I can have my own elite guard." I crossed my arms over my chest. I knew my rights, damn it.

Nicolas looked out at Cho again. A bemused smile crept across his face. "This is your elite guard?"

Silver-eyes chuckled too, apparently his Were hearing in excellent condition.

"Mr. Cho. A demonstration, if you don't mind?" I said, hand out to him in invitation.

"As you wish, Ms. Strong," Cho said, pulling away from the wall. He bowed nicely to the Were, hands together as though in prayer. Then his hands became a blur. Contact began at the head, then his fists traveled down the chest, which had the big man flopping against the huge steel door. Then Cho flew up and one kick put Silver Eyes on the floor. Unconscious. The end.

I bit my lip. The guy was out like a blown light bulb. *Holy Crap!*

"That is fine, Ms. Strong. Bring your little assassin along," Nicolas said nastily, and turned away sharply.

Cho bowed, again with palms together, to the man on the floor, and stepped into the condominium with me.

I took the condo in with amazed silence. A massive brownish-yellow column in the center flared out, mushrooming up into the ceiling of a living space in-the-round. The colors were a muted sand with amber and a greenish-gray mixed in. The floors were polished wood. From where we stood I spotted an entertainment center located on a shelf up against the column. Beyond this, nudged into the wall was a kitchen with black counter tops and track lighting. A partition wall positioned three feet away from it circled the column. To the left of it were high-backed black lacquered chairs clustered around a long oval table. The chairs had an unusual Victorian styling with black velvet backing. Almost hidden off to the side, I spied carpeted steps that spiraled up around another much smaller cement pillar. It was painted in a way to suggest it was made of marble, but I knew it was not.

"So, here I am. How am I supposed to help Bjorn?" I thought I might as well get down to business.

Someone drifted into the room from those aforementioned spiral stairs. The new arrival was Nathanial, Nicolas' latest scion. His lithe body seemed more anorexic than the last time I'd seen him.

"Nathanial, see if our guests would like something to drink," Nicolas said.

Obediently, Nathanial stepped forward.

"We're fine," I said, giving Nathanial the briefest look. The last time he had confronted me, my werewolf friend, Hobart, put the scare into him. Nathanial eyed Cho as if that particular memory had surfaced. Cho looked as mild-tempered and nonthreatening as Nathanial, with his soft, boyish features. You can't always judge a book by its cover, I always say.

Nathanial paused next to Nicolas looking relaxed and perhaps a wee bit too comfortable with things. We'd have to change that.

"Your weapon. The dagger," Nicolas said. "It must be made of pure silver."

"It is."

"It is highly poisonous to a vampire."

"Yeah. Duh. The Dagger of Delphi is meant to maim vampires and kill demons," I said, chin up. "It was given to me because I'm the sibyl." He hadn't believed I could be the sibyl when we first breached this subject a little over a month ago when I first started working for Tremayne.

Nicolas sighed. "Be that as it may, the poisonous silver has entered his system deeply and at this moment is slowly killing Bjorn."

My chest became tight. "But I'm here," I said, hardly knowing what more to say. Nicolas didn't look upset about it at all.

"You have been hard to reach as of late," he said.

I squinted at him. *Well, excuse me!* "If you want my blood for him—"

"What we need from you is your plasma," Nicolas interrupted my almost tirade. "You happen to be a perfect match for Bjorn."

"Plasma? Really? But I thought my blood—"

"No. Even if we were to drain you completely, your blood wouldn't be enough for him to heal from all the damage that's been done," he explained patently. "The white blood cells, on the other hand, may be his only hope. It's highly experimental, as it has never been tried on a vampire—but we are hopeful that it may help stop the spread of the poison throughout his system."

"I see," I said, feeling suddenly numb. "You say my plasma?"

"Yes. It is all we require from you. It can be done in this facility."

"Really?" I found that my legs had become weak thinking about being probed with needles. Searching for a handy chair, I found none close by, and nearly leaned into Cho. He seemed to sense my weakened state and braced me with strong hands. The contact was brief, but enough to give me more reads of him, which I wasn't at liberty to mull over at this juncture.

"But I gave him blood right after," I said, glancing up at Nicolas.

"I'm afraid that he took a downward plunge soon after. When he received no more of your blood, the silver, still in his system, had begun to poison him."

"I didn't know. I had no idea." I sagged. Cho grabbed me, his arm around my waist, as I fell against him. He was stronger and more solid than he looked.

"Would you like to see him?" Nicolas suggested.

"What?" I looked up. "Can I?"

"Of course," Nicolas said and moved to gesture toward the open stairs. I pulled away from Cho, and followed him toward the steps which led up. I came up behind Nicolas who was half way up the winding stairs, my eyes focusing on his expensive, shiny black shoes (instead of his ass). I noticed the heels were not worn down much. With Cho behind me, I felt safe, at least from attack from behind. Nicolas was still under Tremayne's beck and call, apparently. But I somehow didn't trust his act.

We all gathered before the only door, apparently, on this floor at the end of a short hallway that bent in the concave fashion as the rest of the place had.

He turned to me. "I warn you, it will be difficult to take—how he looks. And the smell is nearly intolerable. You need not stay any longer than a moment, but he will be glad that you came."

I nodded, not quite knowing what to expect. My stomach churned as my werewolf sense of smell heightened my olfactory. I didn't need anything to enhance the smell of rotting flesh mixed with chemical and medicinal odors coming from this room. It was so horrible I had to put a hand to my nose and mouth.

"Here," Nicolas said, turning to Nathanial who handed him something white.

He held out a doctor's mask to me. "It won't help the smell by much, but it is required to be worn when you step into the room."

I slipped it on, fumbling with the strings, but Nicolas tied it in the back for me.

He then turned and knocked softly, holding the doorknob ready to open it. When someone answered quietly—so quiet that even with my Were hearing it was soft as a whisper—he opened the door.

I was hit right away by the stench of rotting flesh. I retched. I couldn't walk into the room until I had hold of my gag reflexes. Cho's hand on me, I glanced back at him.

"Should I come with you?" he asked.

"No. I'm sure it isn't necessary," I said through the mask and held my hand over it, pinching my nose and trying to breathe only through my mouth. I needed some menthol rub to block the nasty smells.

"Sabrina is here, sire," Nicolas said, holding the door open. Tremayne was Nicolas' sire, and although Tremayne was weak, Nicolas must still feel some thread of obligation and duty to him, in his last hours. I still did not trust this fully, and my insides were shuddering.

"Sabrina?" a feeble voice sounding like that of an old man spoke. It was not the rich baritone that I associated with Tremayne. I looked into the room, past the massive white column, which in this case was protected by a white steel railing, to keep a person, I suppose, from tripping on the base that extended a foot away from it on the floor. Lining one wall were brown dressers, cluttered with pictures and vases of flowers. A white afghan was folded over the back of a cranberry-red arm chair at the end of the room. Next to it a small end table with a lamp. The clean aesthetic furnishings and white walls exemplified a feng-shui style that was strikingly different from the rest of the condo.

I could not see past the corner, but I knew someone else was in the room besides the one who occupied the large bed.

The man was sitting up, the bed was the kind that could let the person sit up. At the end was a large, intricately carved wooden chest. It looked old, and yet well cared for. Various monitors were set up to one side of the bed. The heart monitor blipped once while I stood there. Contrary to popular myth vampires were not dead—or "undead". They had a heartbeat, but was very slow. This explained their longevity. Their metabolism was so slow that they could live forever.

My eyes ventured to the person reclined in the bed. His face was ashen in color, with a webbing of wrinkles all over the skin as though it were made of crinkled rice paper. Snow-white hair sparsely covered his head. His hands were wrapped in gauze. My Knowing informed me that the stench was coming from his hands—and other extremities, where the flesh rotted, including the nose, which I found hard to stare at him for more than a few seconds.

I heard a sound, like the crash of a wave, and call of a gull. My eyes were pulled to the wall in front of the bed. There appeared to be a large window, but I knew it wasn't. It was a large-screen TV, showing a sandy beach over aqua waters. Possibly something that made Tremayne happy—the sea, seeing that he was a Viking at one time. I figured it must be a DVD put into a player so as to interrupt all the whiteness and trick the mind into believing they were not down below the earth's surface.

"Sabrina, you came," the man in the bed said in a wispy voice. His lips were thin, and the cheek bones sharp beneath the paper-thin skin. His once aqua eyes were now a dull gray. His lips drew back, revealing dingy, yellow teeth of what may in time become a cadaver. My heart sank further than it had already been. A few strands of his remaining hair fell off his head and landed on his shoulder like gossamer. This could not be the strong, handsome Viking I knew. How could he have gone from that huge, strong, handsome vampire guy, to this, in such a short time? My heart squeezed with pain to see him this way.

"Yes," I said, wavering on the need to exit the room as quickly as possible, and wanting to cry and vomit at the same time. My hand went down and clutched a railing along the wall. "I'm here. I'll help you, if I can."

"Good. Good." The heart monitor blipped again, the sound oddly loud.

A thin woman moved into view—the person I knew to be in the room with him. She floated out from around the wall wearing mint green scrubs, like a nurse. I had only to look at her ears to know she was an elf. His elves took care of him, best they could. But all this made my heart shatter into pieces, while a sharp emotion of desperation filled me. I didn't know who it came from, since I couldn't read vampires, nor elves. *Me?*

"We need to keep him quiet," she said gently, and gestured to us to leave the room. I was relieved to not have to stay in that room another second.

A hand clutched my shoulder and ushered me out. Devastated, I turned into the only available arms as the door shut behind me. I cried against the strong, broad chest. Then pulled off the mask in order to suck in some fresh air that wasn't tainted by death or chemicals.

"Sabrina," Nicolas' voice rumbled above my head, and in the chest I wept against. "Sabrina, you must get hold of yourself."

I looked up, my face wet with tears, and my nose oozing snot—I was a mess. I needed to get away from him, too. I knew my touching Nicolas was a big mistake.

Looking put out, Nicolas produced the usual silk hanky.

I blubbered my thank you, half-way wanting to chuckle because it seemed there had been numerous times when he had helped me dry my tears this same way. I turned away and honked into his hanky. "I'm sorry."

"It is understandable. You couldn't have known that what you had done would eventually kill him."

"I *didn't* do it," I said, my voice a little more angry and edgy than I intended.

"But it is your weapon, is it not?"

Cho moved in a little closer, protectively. Nicolas' eyes darted warily to him. I put my hand out to Cho to keep him at bay. Nicolas could kill him in a blink, if he wanted. I didn't want someone else's life on my conscience because of something I did.

Keeping my eyes on Nicolas, I said, "Yes. But it was put away in a drawer at the time, in another room. I won't go into details as to what we were doing at the time, but I did not have any way of getting to it."

"But, from Bjorn's account there were only the three of you in that room at the time," he argued. *Oh, jeez!*

"Yes, and as we were all... *busy*, it's not likely either me, or the other lady could have gotten up and gone and got the dagger!"

"Who then?"

I realized we were having this discussion right outside the door to Tremayne's room. I stepped away, and Nicolas followed me as I continued down the steps. I didn't stop until I got to the lower floor. Wiping my tears on the black silk hanky, I turned to watch Nicolas and Cho step down into the lower level with me.

"The dagger is able to go after vampires and demons all on its own," I said. "I don't need to touch it." I had decided to not tell the *whole* truth. Dante was the one who took the dagger out of the drawer, came to the room—invisible—and stabbed Tremayne after the whole thing was finished. Dante had meant to stop Tremayne from "hurting" me—at least that was his story. But I felt it was a jealousy thing. Tremayne had finally had his way with me, after tricking me. Somehow I'd been tricked into thinking I'd removed my right-hand glove where I wore the mystic ring, which thwarted all vampire thralls, but had really removed the left hand glove.

Nicolas stepped away from me. "You should never have told me this," he said, irritably.

"Why?"

He turned back to eye me. "Because you have made an enemy out of the vampire world."

"Oh, well, jeez, like this is something new?"

His frown hardened, and one brow arched. "Indeed. You should be thankful you are still alive."

"Is that a threat?" I put my left fist on my waist and held my right hand at the ready.

He smiled, it didn't reach his eyes. "Ilona is not likely to take what you have been doing sitting down."

"You mean my stopping the vampires from attacking humans? Sorry. I'm not going to let them take over my corner of the world," I said.

"Your little forays to kill a few of us is futile." He gloated as though he knew something I didn't.

"So," I said, folding my arms across my chest and stepping a little closer to him, "you're all for the Hunting Humans Act, are you?"

His dark eyes squeezed at me. "In my capacity I must uphold Vampire Law."

"What capacity?"

"I am acting magnate of the eastern half of the United States."

"But Tremayne's against it," I argued.

"He's hardly in a place to uphold or shoot down any ruling no matter what it is."

I stared back at him, realization making my stomach hurt. If Tremayne died Nicolas would be in charge. He wasn't against hunting humans at all, I could see it in his eyes, and he was a pompous Romanian-vampire with plenty of attitude. Not only that, I was certain he knew about Ilona's plans to murder her husband, me, Dante and Bjorn two months back. His previous scion, Toby Hunt, had been the murderer who drank the blood of his victims—vampires—and then became a vampire himself after three consecutive nights of such activities. Bjorn had killed Toby before he could kill me—exacting his revenge on him for killing his wife.

I paused, adrenaline making me jumpy. "I just have one question."

"What is it?"

"If Tremayne dies who would you answer to?"

His chin jutted out. "No one. There is no one else older than I in the whole world of vampires."

"You're mistaken," I said low, holding his gaze. "There's one."

"Who?"

"Vasyl."

He laughed. "He is a rogue."

"Ah, yes, but so is Tremayne even now," I argued. "But he's your sire, and you have to do his bidding. Once he's out of the way, you'll take over the American Vampire Association. I can see how that would work nicely for you and Ilona." I paused and delivered the zinger. "When's the wedding?"

I didn't think I'd be able to surprise Nicolas with my little jab, but I had. Looking away, he adjusted his tie and said nothing.

I smirked. "Bringing me here wasn't your doing at all, but Tremayne's. Yeah, I get that."

He squinted at me, then a smile crept across his handsome face. I wasn't stupid. He was simply going through with the motions, bringing me here, showing Tremayne I had shown up, only to give him false hope. The bastard. I'd had visions of things going way wrong at some point while I was here.

"In fact, I'm guessing, if you had it your way you'd let him die," I added.

"There is only so much I can do," he said, doing a one-shoulder shrug, smiling smugly.

I turned to Cho and said, "You understand that if I never make it to wherever it is I have to go to give my plasma, Tremayne will die." It was cleaver of him to have me show my face to Tremayne, and then, kill me. Or try to.

"You will make it, Ms. Strong," Cho said confidently. "And Mr. Tremayne will live. I have great faith in you, and my throwing sticks." He made a bow.

I bowed back, then turned to Nicolas. "Which way?"

He turned and gave Nathan a nod. I had forgotten all about Nathan.

The little shit pulled out a gun and pointed it at us.

Chapter 7

You're Fired

I wasn't worried about the gun. The gun was a no-brainer. It was Nicolas who I was worried about.

Cho made his lightning move with a swish of his foot. The gun flew out of Nathan's hand, hit the ceiling, fell and discharged with an odd *pop*. The slug must have hit a concrete wall, because it pinged and hit something that stopped it. None of us were hit.

"RI-I-I-ICK!" I yelled, moving behind the large pillar in the center of the room. Nicolas lunged for the gun, pushing his puny scion out of the way. Nathan fell with a thud and slid about a foot on the highly polished floorboards.

A displacement of molecules filled the space around me. Rick, the leprechaun, appeared in front of me.

"Hi, toots." Rick said, his eyes swimming around to take things in. "Whoa, shit!" Upon seeing the gun aimed at us, he snapped his fingers. The gun became a can of tuna fish. Nicolas held it out and then realized he was holding a deadly can of sorry Charley. The look on his face was priceless. He dropped the can to the floor and it rolled along and disappeared behind the massive column, and wound up underneath the elegant dining table.

Nicolas swore in his native tongue. It sounded pretty nasty. Then he pointed at me with his finger—not the nasty one.

"By the way, Ms. Strong. You're fired."

"I beg your pardon?" I said, slightly surprised, and couldn't help a small chuckle. *Oh, ow.*

"You. Are. Fired. Your services are no longer needed."

"Who died and made you in charge?"

"Bjorn. He's given me power of attorney. I am letting you go."

"Oh, well, thank God, because this job really sucks!" Face burning, I turned to leave. The door was still open to the short hall. Both Rick and Cho's footsteps thumping right behind me. Instinct told me not to go out the way we came in. The way I had to go was through the second door to our right. I took three steps and we all stopped. The six thousand pound door was closed.

"Girlfriend, why is it you're always neck deep in vampires whenever you call me?"

"So you feel wanted." I smiled. Meanwhile my heart beat like a bongo drum in the jungle.

"Not in the way I want to feel wanted," Rick said, a sour look on his face. "What's the deal? Where the hell are we?" The usual armless shirt and coat covered him, and he wore a White Sox hat, backwards.

"Down in a subterranean condominium made from an old missile silo."

"Cool!"

"And we need to get to wherever the sanguine team is to take my plasma so that Tremayne will get it and be healed."

"Nice." Rick stepped up beside me.

"Do you know where?" I asked.

"Beats me." The armless leprechaun shrugged. Hands, which were attached to the shoulders by a few inches of wrist went palms up.

"Eh, who's your friend?" Rick looked up at Cho. Cho towered over Rick who came almost to my shoulders.

"Cho, this is Rick. Rick this is Cho. Cho is a black belt. Rick's a leprechaun," I introduced.

"Nice to meetcha," Rick said, and Cho bowed.

"So, where are we headed? This is a dead end. Isn't it?"

"No. It's a door. We need to get on the other side of this door."

"Well, why didn't you say so, toots?"

I had Rick with me. Who needs doors? He snapped his fingers and the door opened. We now looked out into an odd-looking hallway. Odd because the hallway was basically a huge tube with an open metal platform to walk along. I now knew what a hamster felt like.

Cho looked around himself, trying to figure out how the door had opened in an unusual way. He smoothly took it all in with all the aplomb of a Ninja who had just jumped over a two story building.

"Now what?" Rick asked.

I pointed as I walked. "This way."

The tunnel ahead of us narrowed as if into infinity. If I wasn't a clairvoyant, I'd have no idea where I was going. But I knew that I had to get to the end of this tunnel. Our footsteps clanged along over the steel mesh ramp. Cho stayed behind to watch our backs.

"Since you called me, does this mean you're not mad at me anymore?" Rick asked.

I rolled my eyes upward. "Yes. I'm not mad at you, Rick. I can't stay mad at you. You didn't do anything. Or, at least you weren't really aware what Tremayne was up to."

"No. He made it sound like you were into him and he wanted to be with you, and the only way he could do it is—"

I cleared my throat to interrupt him. I did not want him to blabber what Tremayne had wanted to do with me, especially in front of Cho, who was basically a stranger. "I know. But here I am and I'm going to help him."

"That's great. He needs your help," Rick said.

"Tell me about it! I just saw him! Plus you saw how pleasant Nicolas was about all of it."

"You saw Bjorn?" Rick asked, sounding unnerved.

"Yes."

"When?"

"Just now."

"You mean he's here?"

"Yes," I said looking down at him as we strode along.

"How is he? How's he look?"

"Bad. Really, really bad. He's slowly dying."

"Oh, wow. Crap on fairies." He looked up at me. "Excuse my language."

"You're excused. I'm going to give them my plasma. You think it'll work?"

"I don't see why not," he said. "Your blood made him stronger that one time."

"Yeah. That one time. It's been weeks since. Now—God—his face was all old, and his nose and fingers were rotting off him."

"Eww! TMI!" Rick shivered.

We were nearly to the end of the tube-like hall.

"And here we have another huge steel door," I said looking at it.

"What sort of door is this anyway?" Rick asked, puzzled.

"This is a bomb blast door," I said, and screwed up my face. My Knowing was awesome.

"What in Fairy Land is that?" Rick asked.

"They would close it to keep themselves from being knocked out from the blast, or the debris," Cho explained.

"It must weigh a ton!" Rick said. "You want that I get us over to the other side?"

Cho moved in front of us and, hands on one of the steel bars, pushed. The door swung inward. "Three tons to be exact."

I gasped. "How did you do that?"

"It isn't that hard to push. They were made for one man to push open, or close," Cho explained.

"Wow," I said.

"Cool." Rick strode through.

"It's actually amazing that these are intact. Many of them buckled under their own weight," Cho said, examining the door. "There are those who question whether they would have stood a blast at all."

"Yeah, be happy they didn't have to find out," Rick said looking around.

"Yeah. Right?"

"This place is awesome!" Rick's voice went high with excitement.

I stepped into a dim hall lit in calming green lights. Sounds of voices preceded someone surging through the next door. The man appeared and I was never so happy to see Morkel as I did now. I went up and hugged him.

"Ms. Strong?" Morkel said, surprised, not quite understanding my sudden affections.

"We had some trouble back there," Rick said, by way of explanation.

"Trouble? What trouble?" Morkel wondered.

I stepped away from him, letting my arms flop to my sides. "Nicolas isn't a team player."

"How's that?"

"He had a gun," Rick explained.

"Really?" The six foot elf took me in. "Are you alright?"

I nodded. "Yes. Then he fired me." I had to chuckle. Rick chuckled too.

"That's rich," Rick said.

"Fired you!" Morkel said, looking surprised.

"Well, you know that he and Ilona are plotting the overthrow of the NAVA. Sucking humans dry is on their agenda. Then go on to rule the world, eventually."

"No. I didn't—I mean, I knew they were up to no good, of course." Morkel said, still giving me a questioning look. "Didn't you use your ring to control him?"

"Oh," I said, brow rumpling. "I didn't think of it. Everything happened so fast!"

Hand up he said, "Not to worry. Everyone is alright, and you are here, and that's what counts." He turned to Rick and Cho. "Gentlemen, if you don't mind waiting in the waiting room?" He gestured to a small opening. "Sabrina, come with me."

"No problem," Rick said. He and Cho went into a waiting room off the main room.

Morkel led me through a partition. The walls were still circular, and there was the large pillar that held the whole thing together.

"At any rate, as you can see we've been expecting you." Morkel gestured toward three women elves who were waiting for me next to one of those movable partitions. A chair that reminded me a little of a dentist's resided next to a strange apparatus with tubes running all around it and down to what looked like a clear container. It all made me pause. A much cruder form of this had existed on Black Veil. But this was super clean and looked highly mechanical.

"Well, if Nicolas had his way, you'd be waiting forever," I quipped, trying to hide my discomfort over a machine that would somehow separate the plasma from my blood. "Get me hooked up. I just left Tremayne's side. He won't make it through the night."

"We need to do a little prep first," Morkel said. "We already know that you are a donor match for him."

"I had no idea," I said.

"That was why we sent for you. It was imperative that you should give as soon as possible. We'll require you to give again in 48 hours."

"You mean I have to stay here?" I said, not prepared to do that.

"No. There is a donation site much closer to you. The plasma can be sent from there. But tonight we needed you to give the first donation."

"Oh." My relief spilled from me. "Yeah. You'll be able to give him my plasma as soon as I give it, right?"

"Right," Morkel said. "You might as well have a seat." He motioned to the reclining chair. I slid onto the chair, my body quaking. I never liked giving blood, and thought I'd never get used to it.

"We need to take a finger stick test, first," the nurse nearest me said. "It's required to see where the hematocrit and protein levels are at."

I had to take off my left glove—the one closest to the machine. She took my hand with her own disposable Latex-gloved hands and chose the middle finger. She stuck me.

"Ow," I said when I felt the prick at my finger.

"Sorry." She took her sample and swept through the room, and disappeared around the partition.

Morkel seated himself in a chair and leaned forward. "We will make an appointment for you from here at the BioPlasma center near you."

"Okay," I said. "How long will this take?"

"Since we have you already tested for everything, you shouldn't be longer than an hour to an hour and a half." He stood. "I'll leave you to our capable nurses. However, afterwards I must speak to you about what is happening, and what might happen, if Tremayne doesn't make it."

I winced. "I'm hoping like hell that he does make it. If Nicolas and Ilona take over, humans will be attacked everywhere—not *just* in my neck of the woods. And I really can't cover all of the world, let alone the whole dang United States."

He smiled and patted my hand. "We'll take care of you, and Mr. Tremayne. Never fear."

"I'm having Rick take me home, by the way. You probably should have had him bring me here to begin with," I suggested.

"Stefan wasn't overly aggressive toward you, I hope?" he said with concern.

"Oh, no, he was fine."

"Besides, we arranged that Mr. Cho be your guardian, should something happen," he said.

"And it sure did."

Chapter 8

Lights, Please

Exhaustion had caught up with me while they took my plasma. I wasn't comfortable enough to nod off, but my eye lids drooped, and I did shut them a few times. My breathing leveled off. Checking my watch again, midnight had come and gone. I'd been hooked up to the machine for ten minutes. I couldn't take a nap because I had to clench and unclench my fist during this whole process. I glanced over to the machine to see my blood travel through the lengths of tubes and through the odd enclosed round things (I was told it was a centrifuge), on the machine and here the plasma is separated. A murky liquid (my plasma), flowed back into the same tube and was collected in a bag down near the floor. After watching that for a moment I felt light headed again. I quit watching it and looked up at the ceiling.

"Hi, how are you doing?" the elf nurse who stepped into view asked.

"Okay. A little cold," I said, noticing she'd brought me a blanket.

"Here," she said, opening up the blanket and settled it over me. "This should help."

"Thanks." I became cold when the saline solution was pumped in—a weird sensation, like someone pumped me with ice water. Plus, it gave me the oddest metallic taste, like I held a penny in my mouth. I tried to not look or think about my blood being drawn out of me. But it was difficult, as I was totally aware of it all. Like being in a dentist's chair, only not quite as bad.

The nurse dipped and checked the plasma bag. "Everything is going along fine. You should be done shortly." She stood and left me.

Twenty-five minutes later I was done—happy it had not taken a full hour.

"Thank you," I said to the nurse who unhooked me.

The other elf-nurse unhooked the bag of plasma. "Looks like a little over a quart. Nice donation. We'll get this to Mr. Tremayne at once."

"Thank you," I said again for possibly the fourth time.

I was given last minute instructions, telling me to drink plenty of fluids, and one of them handed me a bottle of cold water, and she led me back out to the sitting area. Feeling a little light headed I dropped into the soft leather sofa.

Rick and Cho bounded down the stairs to my right.

"Hey, girlfriend! How'd it go?" Rick asked, enthusiastically.

"Okay." I absently rubbed my arm where the needle had been.

"Cho here is an excellent Wii player," Rick said, stepping further into the room.

"Where were you guys?" I asked.

"Upstairs. They've got a whole game and entertainment room up there."

"Leather lounge chairs," Cho added, smiling over at Rick.

"I could live here!" Rick said with a dreamy look on his face.

Cho sat down in a chair next to me. "All is well?"

I looked into his dark eyes and nodded. "They have the plasma, and took it to Bjorn." I paused. "I need a bathroom."

"They have one through there," Rick pointed. He would know, as he must have used it.

I stood, and felt only slightly woozy, but gathered myself and padded off through the portal that curved around, my hands using the walls for support. I found the bathroom to be more luxurious than I'd expected. Completely tiled in some sort of brown stone, there was a jacuzzi and a large shower with three heads. Nice. I got the feeling that this was the same basic pattern as the condo we had left moments ago, where Tremayne was.

After doing my business I washed my hands with a foaming soap. I looked at myself in the mirror, thinking I could sure use my brush. The sight of the man over my shoulder in the mirror shocked me and I made a start, then felt ridiculous two seconds later. I knew who it was.

Dante came out of the mirror and appeared in physical form behind me. "I've got you." His arms curled around my body to steady me.

"Oh, goddess," I said as I fell into his embrace both elated, and slightly annoyed.

"Will you never get used to finding me in mirrors?" he asked, a little chuckle in his voice.

"No," I said against his chest, and play-slapped him on the shoulder.

"I'm sorry that I couldn't help you, earlier," he said, readjusting his hold on me. "No mirrors. They may have taken them out as a precaution."

"I don't think they could have known about how you get around," I argued.

"Believe me, they know. After seeing me as an Undead, they would know. Besides, I've been watching and listening whenever I can."

"Rats!" I made a dull snap of my fingers. "If Cho and Rick, hadn't been here, things would have gone really bad."

He pulled away from me. I frowned with a thought. "You don't watch me when I…" I trailed off.

He laughed. "I turn away when you are in your private moments. Always." It was weird and disconcerting to know that someone was always able to see me from the other side. He was like a ghost who could appear in the room with me if there was a mirror handy.

"Good." I tried to move away, but he held me still. I looked questioningly up at him. His fingers found and lifted my chin. He looked deeply into my eyes.

"You are sure you feel alright?"

I paused. "Actually, I feel a little light-headed, like someone took a lot of something out of me."

"They did. Let's try something," he said. He leaned in and I let him kiss me. His kisses always made my stomach flutter. This one gave me a fluttering, but also a little thrill went through my body. The thrill left me feeling invigorated.

"Oh, wow…" I trailed off and drew my head down to rest on his broad chest. He held me. I had no idea he could do the same for me that I did for him. He made a low chuckle.

"Better?" he asked.

"Better," I said. His arms left me and I stepped away from him. "Thanks."

"No problem, my Lady." He bowed to me slightly.

I turned and opened the door. We stepped out together. "The others are going to wonder how you got in."

"Let them wonder," he said, smirking.

I laughed and we strolled back into the front room where not only Rick and Cho waited, but also Morkel.

"Dante! When did you get here?" Rick said, looking happily surprised

"Just now," Dante said.

"Wonderful," Morkel said. "Now that we have everyone here, we need to go over a few things."

"When do we go after Nicolas?" I asked.

"We do not," he said, blinking as though I'd interrupted him.

"What? After what he almost did?" Rick protested. "He held a gun on us! He was going to shoot—"

Morkel held up a hand to quiet Rick. "Yes. Especially after what he *almost* did."

"Well, that sucks!" Rick whined.

"As a matter of fact, you are going to take a break in going after the vampires."

"What?" Both Rick and I squeaked. Morkel's steady sky-blue gaze withered my boldness.

"I know that I have been encouraging you in your endeavors, but for right now, we are going to have to have you hold off on this activity."

Rick and I made small noises of protest.

"The reason being is that we've stirred the hornet's nest enough for now. And," he went on, hands clasped together forefingers pointed at me, "Sabrina I needn't remind you that you are the one and *only* reigning sibyl. As such, your life is now way too important for you to be taunting vampires."

I hung my head. Apparently, I was not to become the kick-ass vampire slayer. Damn.

"Also, in light of recent developments, you need to speak to your family members about the vampires. They need to know about them."

My gaze lifted to Dante, who had expressed the same thing to me earlier. He gave me a knowing look, but he didn't gloat. He wasn't like that.

I sat back feeling as though the walls were caving in on me. How would I tell my brother (who would either laugh, or call the men in white coats—or both), vampires existed? And, do it without scaring the living daylights out of his wife (who would also question my sanity).

"But I thought there was a ward on their house," I argued.

"There is," he agreed.

"I put a good one on it," Rick chimed in.

"I know you did, Rick. However, like with Sabrina's house, it is only good while they are in it, or on the property. Once away from it, they are vulnerable."

What was left of my good mood deflated with the crush of this new challenge.

"Now, Dante." Morkel turned to him. "Since you are able to keep watch over everyone wherever they may be, I need your services, if I may?"

"Of course," Dante said.

"I need you to spy on what Ilona is doing at all times. If we do not know what the enemy is doing, she may find some new way of attacking us."

"I can do that, but I need the portal avenue of a mirror. They now know what I am and may have removed all mirrors from wherever they gather."

"That's problematic," Morkel said.

"What about bathrooms?" I said.

Rick groaned.

Morkel darted a look my way. "These could have been removed too, but there must be ways to get around this, surely?"

"Any bathroom will do," Dante said with a smirk.

"If you have no other alternative, try the hotel rooms," Morkel suggested with a smirk. "They can't have removed every mirror in both hotels."

"My suite," I put in.

"That will work," Dante said with a crooked smile. "Then I can move about without being seen, go to wherever they might be."

"Good," Morkel said.

"I wasn't allowed to bring my purse inside. I have my compact in there." I paused, eyes pinched. "Plus other things. I need to get it back."

"And our coats," Cho reminded. "And my things as well."

"Oh, right. The coats and my purse, my wallet, and Cho's things, are all up in the cabin, where we started." I slid my glance to Cho. "Guarded by Werewolves." We exchanged knowing grins.

"Wind," he reminded.

"Lots of wind damage," I agreed and we both chuckled at our private joke.

"Oh-h, I get it," Rick said, as if understanding something more lewd.

"So, you'll work on informing your brother and his wife about the vampires?" Morkel said.

"Yeah." I rose to my feet. *Somehow.*

"I will call you with the appointment for your next donation of plasma," Morkel said. "We will need it day after tomorrow."

"I'll be ready."

"Rick," Morkel turned to the leprechaun.

"Right here."

"You can get everyone up top?"

"No problem, as long as the guys don't mind holding hands." He snickered.

"I'm capable of leaving on my own," Dante said and turned to me. "If you need me, open up your compact and call me. I'll pop in." *Like some sort of weird transmitting device.*

"Right." I looked at Rick and then to Cho. "I think Cho roughed them up plenty, but if they need a repeat lesson in manners, I don't think he'll mind giving them one."

Cho bowed with a smile.

I took Rick's hand and Cho took the other. Rick magically took us back up top, inside the cabin. Whenever he popped me through ley lines it was different than when I do it myself. It's very uncomfortable. I feel squeezed, at first, then as though my whole body was pulled through a keyhole. But not quite as unpleasant as it sounds.

Feet back on the ground—or in this case, polished wood—I looked around myself. Feet rocking as I landed unbalanced and nearly fell, my hand jerked from Rick's grasp.

"You okay, Brie?" Rick's voice rose with concern.

"Yeah, yeah. Crap, it's dark in here," I said, waiting for my eyes to adjust. The only light came from the dying embers of the fire. No lights were on.

"Where's my purse?" I asked, looking around to find the counter where our things had been.

"Your purse is here," Cho said. I turned to his shadow against the glowing embers, looked down to find he had my purse in his hand.

"Thanks." I took it and peered inside to find everything was there. "Where's our coats?"

"I wonder if they hung them up," Cho said, looking around at the walls.

"Wait, what's this on the floor?" Rick said.

"That's them," Cho said.

Hand in my purse, I riffled around. "Hey! Where's my squirt gun!" My hand hit everything, including my brush and one of the bore-hair bristles stabbed underneath my fingernails. "Ow! Damn it!"

"Shhh!"

"What—"

A loud noise shattered the quiet of the cabin, and the flash burned my retinas. The smell of gun powder and my brain panicked.

"Holy shit! Grab my hand! NOW!"

A hand grasped mine.

Something thudded nearby. A crash of glass echoed in my ears as my being was swept away into the cosmos. Cold rippled across my face, then heat, then cold again. I was aware of pain over my shoulder. It was like something was burning me.

Everything stopped, except for the ringing in my ears.

"Oh-oh," Rick said. "Sabrina? You okay?"

Eyes closed, I opened them and saw Rick's face upside down in my field of vision. At the same time, I found myself flat on the floor.

I lifted my head. It felt like a giant water balloon ready to explode.

Cho and Rick were both there at my side helping me sit up.

"Where are we?"

"Your place." *Snap!* Lights went on.

"She's bleeding," Cho said.

"What?" I said. "Where?"

"Shoulder." Rick pointed at my shoulder

I looked down, my eyes straining to see my shoulder. Red stuff—my blood—soaked the front of my shirt. Little pinpricks of stars danced across my vision.

"Vasyl," was all I could manage to say before my lights went out.

Chapter 9

Blood is the Life

Heat enveloped me as I looked around. The land looked like a moonscape.

"Hihanni-waste," Dante said. "Welcome. My Lady."

"Where am I?" I asked, my voice sounding strange to my ears.

"This area is Death Valley, and this spot is called Dante's View."

I looked out at the stretch of parched land. The panorama was that of a mountainside, the colors in the lightest peach, mauve, and ocher.

"I can see why you'd choose to be here," I said. "Your namesake's on it. It's quiet." I looked around. "No one here."

"Very quiet," he said. We looked at one another. His long black hair fluttered in a slight breeze. "You can't come over. Not yet."

"Why not?" I argued mildly. "I'm tired of fighting vampires and the bad guys shooting at me. Maybe finally they got me."

"No. They didn't. I'm sending you back and I'll be there to tend your wound. So... shoo."

* * *

"She's coming around."

"About time."

"Mon amour."

My eyelids felt heavy when I tried to open them. A mauve colored ceiling met my vision as I slitted my eyes. I frowned. "Where am I?"

"Home," Vasyl's voice at my right ear, his breath tickled and I shook my head.

His hand, I realized, held mine. Finally, I peeped up at him. Regally handsome face, I stared into black pupils ringed with light violet. Relief wash over me as I recognized my bedroom, and Vasyl being with me only reinforced my feeling of security. Weakly, I reached up, caught his black coiled hair in my fingers. Silky and thick. A smile stretched my lips. Why had I been dreaming of Dante? The aroma of a barn filled me—Vasyl's individual scent. I then realized my glove was missing. I didn't know where it was, or how it was not on my hand. I allowed the feel of his satiny curls against my fingers sooth me. It was something elementally close to petting a cat.

"You were shot, but the bullet did not enter your body," Vasyl said. "It was only a—how you say—flesh wound?"

"No way!" I pushed up on my elbows. The pain in my shoulder seared through me and I fell back. "Shit!" I looked over at the group clustered in the wide door of the bedroom. I found three pairs of eyes taking me in. "What happened? Do you remember?" I looked to Rick.

"Someone in that cabin shot at us," Rick said. "I got you out of there as fast as I could, but you went down."

Pain in my shoulder twinged like a hot branding iron was put to it. Gasping as I touched it. I examined it out of the corner of my eyes, lifting my shirt away. A large bandage covered it. "Who patched me up?"

"Dante," Rick said.

"Dante and I," Vasyl said with barely veiled contempt. His eyes lifted as he gave Dante a heated glare. He may have been pacing outside, waiting for me to return and realized we were home. I'd missed out on the two men fighting over who would fix my owie. Darn.

"Okay," I said, impatiently. "Someone in that building—not naming names—wanted to shoot me."

"They did!" Rick said, hands out.

"And if it weren't for you, they might have plugged me good," I said.

"Damn straight!"

"How did you get us out of there? Don't you have to grab our hands?" I asked, trying to remember our exit.

"Cho grabbed you and I grabbed his arm."

No wonder I'd had an odd lifting sensation that ended in one of falling.

"Boy, Sabrina, they want you to disappear like Jimmy Hoffa," Rick said.

"You think?" I said. Vasyl plumped up some pillows, arranging them against the head board so I could sit up. I leaned back into them with his help.

"Thank you," I said looking up at him. He smiled in that monastic way of his.

"I called Andrew," Rick said. He only called Morkel by his first name. "Told him what happened."

"Good." I turned back to Vasyl. "What time is it?"

"Three in the morning," Cho said after glancing at his watch.

"Yeah? Wow. I haven't been up this late in a long while," Rick said, then yawned. "Hey, Brie, if you don't need me any more…"

"Yeah, sure," I said. "Go home. And thanks."

"Sweetheart, I had more fun with you on a Sunday night than I would have at Tom's Hideaway," he said and snapped his fingers and vanished.

"Actually, everyone is excused. Dante, thank you," I said and caught his eyes. He made a deep bow to me with a fist over his heart.

"Blessings to you and yours, my Lady," Dante said and straightened. "It has been a long night. And it looks like you're in capable hands." On that note, he vanished also. That left Cho.

"Oh! I forgot." I looked up at Vasyl. "It would seem I've picked up a human protector. Have you met Ty Cho?"

"Yes. He explained everything," Vasyl said, looking okay about it.

"Good," I said, feeling suddenly sleepy, and yawned. "Could you show Ty the guest bedroom upstairs?"

"Of course. Which one?"

"My father's old room should work," I said.

Vasyl kissed the back of my hand and rose. "I will be back shortly."

I smiled at Vasyl, then looked at Cho. "Did you manage to snag your duffel bag?"

"I did," Cho said and bowed. "It has been a pleasure serving you, Sabrina."

My face warmed. "Uh, yeah. Thanks," I said feeling dorkish. It wasn't nearly enough to just thank him. I owed him quite a bit. Room and board would work, I figured. At least for now. Then, as if my brain didn't have enough to ponder, I wondered how long he was staying with me. Tonight? A week? Forever? Was he supposed to go back to Stefan, eventually? I didn't get those details ironed out before shit hit the proverbial fan. I had thought I was to return on the jet I'd come out on. But that all got pushed under the rug. I couldn't worry about such details. I had to assume that Cho would have called Stefan and told him all about our night. I would get an update later on.

I moved to adjust myself in bed. Shooting pain in my right shoulder caught me by surprise and I pulled in a sharp intake of air.

"Ow. Damn it!" I swore. This was the same shoulder as the last time when I was shot, only last time it was my back, this was in my front. Thank goodness whoever shot at me couldn't shoot straight. Of course, it had been dark. But I had a feeling that whoever had shot at me had excellent night vision. That could be either a vampire or a werewolf.

I never did asked if anyone had seen who it was. It was so dark, if anyone would have seen who, it would have been me, with my better night vision. But everything had happened too quickly.

Vasyl's foot falls coming down the steps alerted me. That was a quick tour. I hope Vasyl had shown Cho the bathroom, beforehand. Hopefully he turned on some lights for him, too.

Crap. What was I going to do with another guy in the house? I felt guilty, like the kid who brought home another puppy to feed and take care of. Well, at least Hobart had his own place. He'd been scarce as of late. Today, when he brought the Christmas tree, it was the first time I had seen him in two weeks. I wondered if since Vasyl and I had become husband and wife he hadn't told Hobart to keep away, what with him being a werewolf and our doing it while in our other skins. Yup, I'm pretty sure that was why.

Vasyl swept into the room and pulled the hundred-plus oak pocket door closed. It was called a pocket door because it slid open and closed on casters, and disappeared inside the wall. The racket startled me out of my thoughts. The noise probably had Cho wondering what the hell it was, too. Vasyl's nimble fingers engaged the lock. We were now alone and no one could get to us, unless they could kick an oak door down. Cho probably could do that, but I was certain he was too tired.

"How do you feel?" he asked.

I moved my hand to my opposite shoulder. "Feels achy, and still hurts when I move it."

"You need to rest." He settled on his side beside me. Picking up my hand, he kissed the back of it.

"I have missed you. I wanted to go to you."

"I was fine. I had everyone with me."

Crescendo

"You called Rick, instead of me?"

I twisted my fingers guiltily. "I thought that Rick, with his magic, could do something fast. Like get us the hell out of there. Nicolas held a gun on us. Rick turned it into—" I chuckled suddenly remembering it and now how funny it actually was.

"What?" His lips fought a grin.

"He turned the gun into a can of tuna fish."

"That is good, no?" Vasyl nodded. "I wish you to not go on any more forays again."

"I won't." I was too tired to tell him why.

"Good." He kissed the back of my hand again and then went to kiss my shoulder.

"I need someone to help me out of my clothes," I said with a little pout.

"I would be delighted," he said with a smirk. "Where shall we begin?" He would make a game of it. He moved to my feet. Of course. My shoes. He gently pulled each boot off and set them down on the side of the bed.

"I'm not sure what to do about Ty," I said.

"Ty will take care of Ty," he said and pulled my right sock off.

"You don't mind that I brought him with me?"

"No. You are gathering your forces. There is going to be a war, and you need all the troops you can get." He lowered his face to my right foot. A brush of his lips brought me to hysterical giggles.

He removed the other sock, and reduced me to giggles in the same way. I wasn't sure why I was ticklish on the tops of my feet.

"There is war in this bed," he said, crawling up toward me. My giggles dying while looking into his dark violet eyes and feeling somewhat overwhelmed by his sexual aura, which slowly enveloped me like a warm cocoon.

Fingers easily unfastened my jeans, then hooked into the band. "Lift, *cherie*," he said. I bent my knees and pushed to raise my butt from the bed. He peeled my jeans off revealing lacy black panties.

"Oh, la-la!" His eyes became round and then looked up at me. "These are new, *oui*?"

"*Oui*," I said on a small giggle.

"Does it match with…" his eyes went to my chest.

"Why don't you find out for yourself," I smirked, and with my left hand, flipped my hair out from behind my head to fan it out on the pillow. Like I was such a floozy.

Vasyl was not one to rush things. In fact, that was the one thing I liked about his love making. But, he wasted no time to unwrap me, as it were. A string of words that sounded extremely sexy in French escaped his lips when he unveiled the matching bra. Then he landed gentle kisses over my breasts, stomach and neck while he kept repeating in between kisses, "*Manifique... manifique... manifique...*" as though he'd never touched me before this moment. He'd touched me plenty of times, since we consummated our marriage in Colorado while staying at Lonny's cabin, several days ago.

Right when I thought he would disrobe me completely, he rose over me and his lips landed over mine. That skillful tongue of his able to make my mind numb with anticipation at what he could do with it... elsewhere. My one hand (because of the wound, I couldn't move my other arm much), traced up his arm, which were corded with muscles that I found had contours over contours. Funny that a former man of the cloth would have muscles. But then, those were different times. His black hair slithered around me, almost as though it were a separate entity or another being entirely, and silkily abused my naked flesh. It wasn't unlike the feel of Dante's generous mane, but there were times when I thought Vasyl's hair actually moved of its own will, erotically teasing my hips, thighs and breasts. I questioned my own sanity at times when I was with Vasyl this way. He could do to me things no man had ever done before. I would not have thought it possible, but he was better than Dante in bed. Of course, he had the vampire pheromones going for him, but he never bit me. Not once. How he was able to resist, I hadn't a clue. But I knew he had become a "vegan" in vampire terms, and drank horse blood primarily.

Clever fingers slid my panties down slowly, kissing every inch of both thighs as he went. I giggled as he made a return trip, kissing up and up; my skin tingling with delight as he moved closer to the V of my legs. Stirred beyond comprehension, I moaned when he wound his arms beneath my legs and drew them apart, placing me at his disposal. My senses on fire, it was all I could do to stay sane as he ravaged me with his tongue. I may have shrieked a few times, but I was out of my mind, the erotic pleasure he treated me to, putting me elsewhere completely. In fact, I closed my eyes and saw sparkles as I twisted, clenched and finally that bright light blasted me, and then blamo... orgasm!

Panting, I looked through cracked eyelids. His body settled over me, but only halfway.

"You are bleeding again," he said, gaze on my shoulder.

"Huh?" I looked to see that the bandage was soaked in red. "Crap," I gasped, letting my head drop back into the pillows.

"I did not mean to, but you are so wild," he said.

"I am? You make me that way!" I accused.

He drew his wrist up to his mouth and bit.

"What are you—"

"Drink, *cheri*," he said, placing his bloody wrist to my mouth. I wasn't allowed to resist. The flavor was sweet. I remembered from the first time I had been shot, and he gave me his blood.

I watched his reaction when I placed my mouth over the wound and sucked. He closed his eyes, bit his lower lip and let out a low moan.

I stopped sucking on the wound. "What?"

"It is very erotic for me," he said.

"Really?"

"Yes."

"How so?"

"I cannot explain. It is extremely pleasurable. Almost better than sex."

"Oh. Wow." I drew more blood from him. He moaned again. In my head, I saw short little episodes of Vasyl before we met, whenever I took his blood into me. I stopped drinking, not liking what I saw because he had been with other women. Of course, I knew he had been, but the sight of it made me jealous. The blood never flowed too long and the wound healed over quickly. "You did this to other women. You made them vampires?"

"*Oui*," he said. "It was my—eh—distraction. But I was a new vampire at the time. I have not made another vampire in a century."

He lifted the gauze on my shoulder to check on the wound. He pulled it off. "It has healed over." He dropped the gauze into a small trash bin. Then he licked the residue around the wound.

"I think you will live," he smiled.

I chuckled and drew my arms around him. "Ah, yes, but you might not!" I wrapped my legs around his hips.

"It would be a wonderful way to expire, madam," he growled.

Chapter 10

Surprise!

The weather broke, and the sun came out. I was famished and left Vasyl's side, slipped into the adjoining bathroom. I got dressed, ready for the world, and went out through the other bathroom door that opened out into the dining room.

I've always enjoyed the view outside my house. I liked watching the change of seasons, and today the snow was mounded up, pristine and glistening in the sun, sparkling red, gold and blue as though the white blanket was encrusted with multi-faceted diamonds.

I had checked my shoulder while dressing, and found that it had healed almost completely. Only a thick bit of red scar tissue was my only clue as to how deep it was. It had missed my collar bone, probably by centimeters, and had left a slight groove on the flesh. *Flesh wound.* If it had not been for Vasyl's blood, I would still be in pain, and would probably need stitches, and face weeks of healing.

Not wanting to dwell on who, why, or all of the reasons the nasties wanted me dead, I pulled out a frying pan. I didn't know what Ty would eat. For all I knew he might be a vegan. But, I didn't care. I was having eggs and bacon. Vasyl had told me to eat plenty of protein. I would do as the "doctor" had ordered.

I thought my banging around in the kitchen would wake up my guest, but I was sitting down eating and still no Mr. Cho. It was noon when I cleaned up the dishes. And then I heard some thudding sounds.

I stepped out of the kitchen and listened carefully. The thudding stopped. I stood for the longest time, and did not hear it again. Vasyl, although a vampire, would, on occasions get up, but not on a sunny day like today. I had put very thick blinds and drapes in my north-facing bedroom so that he could get his Z's in a dark room. I knew whatever noise I'd heard was not coming from our bedroom.

Shrugging, I went back into the kitchen and gazed out at the brilliant white landscape, finding drifts had mummified everything, including my Jeep. I didn't need to leave the house for any reason, thank goodness. I had learned to be well-stocked in the winter time. In past winters, my father had hired a man who would plow out our drive during the winter months. Now, I would find, to my great pleasure, that Mr. White would, indeed, still come plow my drive for me. I would offer him money for gas, at least, and he'd wave me off, chuckling. "That's what neighbors are for, missy," the grizzled old man would say to me and climb back into the cab of his small dump truck with the blade. I hadn't seen him since this last snow storm. Possibly he couldn't get out himself.

Across the street my neighbor, Mrs. Bench, had company. The vehicle was not familiar to me. The black SUV was parked far enough into her dive without plowing into the six-foot drift that always formed between Mrs. Bench's house and her small garage. I squinted at it. It was a Jeep Compass, I was pretty sure.

I turned and nearly ran into someone standing quite still right behind me.

"Oh! Shit!" I cried, hand to my chest to keep my heart from jumping out.

Cho was standing two feet from me, and squinted with what amounted to an amused smile.

"You and Dante are going to give me a heart attack between the both of you!"

He backed off, palms together he bowed, his straight hair falling like silky fringe. He had to shake his head when he straightened to get it all out of his eyes.

"Sorry," he said. "I noticed you have much snow."

"Yeah." I leaned against a chair, waiting for my heart to climb back into my chest. "I just ate, but I've got almost anything for breakfast. Even some healthy cereal." I did a mental check of things in my cupboard. I had three boxes of cereal, oatmeal, peanut butter, half a loaf of bread. I also had left over soup. I was happy to find that either Quist, or Fritz had done the dishes and put a container of left-over soup into my fridge last night. God, was that just last night? Seemed like a week ago.

"I am not hungry," Cho said, eyes slitted with his smile.

"What?" I looked at him. "How could you not be hungry?"

"I am fasting." He held a bottle of water, put it to his lips and chugged down about half of it.

"Oh. Okay." I would not have to feed him? How good was that?

On a normal non-work day, I would luxuriate in doing nothing but watching TV, or a movie from my dad's stock of videos, or if there was desperation, clean my house. Then, I remembered Nicolas had fired me last night, and a burning sense of outrage seared through me. My mind replayed that whole scene in that bunker-turned-condo while I did dishes.

Who does he think he is, firing me! What an asshole!

I wondered how things were with Tremayne, this morning after he'd gotten my plasma. I went to check my phone. No messages. My heart dropped at first. But then again, maybe no news was good news. I stood with indecision running through me. Who could I call? I realized I couldn't call Tremayne. I didn't have Morkel's phone number in my cell phone's list. That really sucked. In all the time I had known him I had not once asked for his phone number. *I really suck.*

Shoulders sagging, I located my purse, remembering that my favorite water pistol was missing. *Those bastards stole it!*

My emotions climbing once again, I riffled through my bag. I wasn't sure what I was looking for. Maybe to make sure they hadn't kept my wallet. No. It was there. Momentary fear washed through me and relief replaced it as I opened it up to find all the money and my cards were still there.

They could have found my address by looking at my license. I grimaced thinking about the Were I had kicked in the balls. Great. I was dead meat. I would have to tell Hobart. Maybe he could keep a watch out for them. This was his territory, after all. Any new Were would have to get permission to come into another's territory.

That's when I turned expectantly and my phone rang. I pulled in a breath and let it out. Whoever was on the other end had to be magical, because I couldn't get a read from it. I moved to answer it.

"Hello?"

"Sabrina, dear?" It was Mrs. Bench, across the street. She was a witch, so naturally, I couldn't get a read from her at all.

"Good morning," I greeted her, wondering why she'd called me.

"Bill's sister, Ophelia, and her husband are here, visiting."

After about a second of thought I said, "Oh." My heart was having a hell of a time staying in my chest today. Bill had died in a cave-in in Colorado a week ago. I couldn't fathom why they were here just to see Mrs. Bench. Although I wasn't one hundred percent sure that Bill was actually her grandson, he had lived with her for a few months. I knew that she had grown to love him, either way.

"Someone comes," Cho said, still watching out the kitchen window.

I looked out the window. The black Compass, which had been in Mrs. Bench's drive, was now in mine. I saw a woman in what looked to be a real mink coat and sleek looking boots standing outside at the end of the driveway. A man was with her. They were both heavily dressed, but I could see their faces. They were both very handsome people.

"Sabrina?" Mrs. Bench said in my ear over the phone.

"Yes?" I said.

"You'll have to bring that ward down around your house, in order to let them inside," Mrs. Bench said.

"Uh," I said. Did I want Bill's sister, who was a Nephilistic off-spring, in my house? I debated with myself. What could they possibly do to me? Cho was here and in a pinch I also had Vasyl to protect me.

"Sabrina?"

"Yes, Mrs. Bench. How do I take the ward off?"

"Simply say 'I allow Ophelia and Declan Widdicombe to enter my premises', and that should do it. Then, when they leave, you say you rescind it."

"Okay. Thanks," I said, and we hung up. "Okay, ward, I allow Ophelia and Declan Widdicombe to enter my premises."

I looked down at myself. I was dressed in sweats.

"Holy crap! I have to change." I looked at Cho who had turned around to me. "Could you let them in?"

"Of course," he said, smiling.

I darted through the house and went through the bathroom—because the door to my bedroom was locked from the inside. I didn't want to wake Vasyl unnecessarily. I opened the door to our bedroom and snuck in. As if you could sneak up on a vampire!

I located my jeans, but my shirt was ruined and had been thrown in the trash last night. I spied my black bra on the floor near the bed. I bent to pick it up. A large hand grabbed my wrist. I looked up at Vasyl with a start.

"What is happening?" he asked.

"Someone is here," I said.

"Who?"

"Bill's sister and her husband. They were over at Mrs. Bench's." At that moment, I heard Cho greet them out in the other room. I heard the woman's voice ask for me by name. A tingle in me began low in my spine as I watched Vasyl's alertness blossom.

I didn't expect to get a read from Bill's sister and husband, and didn't. But it sure would have been nice to know what they wanted.

I opened my mouth to speak, and Vasyl stopped me with a finger to my lips.

"Who wishes to see her?" Cho's voice came clear.

"Ophelia, I am Bill Gannon's sister?"

I pulled up, Vasyl's hand still held onto my wrist, stopping me.

I frowned. "I've gotta go and meet her. Her brother died helping me!" I whispered.

His hand released me. I fitted myself into the bra, snugged on my jeans and riffled through my closet, trying to find something that would look nice.

A rap at our bedroom door made me grab the first shirt, ripped it off a hanger, and struggled to get my head through the right hole.

"Yes?" My voice muffled as I struggled to pull my arms through the shirt.

"Ms. Strong. Ophelia Widdicombe, and her husband Declan here to see you." Cho was being very formal in this instance.

Now fully dressed, I unlocked the sliding oak door and peered out at him. "Did you let them in?"

"Yes. There are waiting in the dining room."

"Would you mind taking them into the parlor?" I asked.

"Parlor?" he said.

"It's just off the living room." I pointed. "Through the French doors."

"Very good, madam," Cho said. I had forgotten that he had been Stefan's "boy".

I closed the door and turned. Vasyl was sitting up and pulling on his jeans. I darted him a look.

"What are you doing?" my whisper strained, trying to not let the sound travel as I heard Cho lead the couple past the door.

"I'm coming out," Vasyl said.

"No!" My hands went out to stop him.

He stood, and that hooded look made me back off, momentarily. I knew well his feelings toward Nephilim. This woman wasn't here to harm either of us. How could I convince him?

I stepped up to him, ran my hands over his creamy chest. "At least give me ten minutes with her. I think I know why she's here."

"Very well, *cherie*," he said. "Ten minutes. If they are not leaving in ten I shall come out." That wasn't a lot of time.

"Fifteen," I said.

He squinted at me. "Fifteen, but no more than fifteen."

Turning, I rolled my eyes. I dug out a sweater from one of my drawers and pulled it on over the T-shirt. I slipped my feet into my warm house slippers—not the fluffy ones, but something more dignified—and unlocked the pocket door. As quietly as I could, I drew the door back, slipped out, and closed it again. It banged and I hunched my shoulders at the noise. It would not stay closed unless you locked it, but I was not going to lock Vasyl into the room, although the thought did enter my mind. But, no locked door would keep him out.

I tugged at my sweater, shifting it down in the front. I hadn't hazard a look in the mirror, and there were none out here. Cho must have turned on lights in the parlor because the glow shown through the sheers. I usually left the drapes drawn, as I didn't go into the room very often. Being that it was on the northwest side of the house and cold in the winter. It was usually a dark room. Once in a while, Vasyl liked to sit in there during the day and read. I hadn't thought about how cold it might be in there without the fireplace going. I clicked up the temperature on the furnace and heard the thing flick on.

Cho stood at the entrance on the living room side, and made a little bow to me.

"Thank you, Ty." I moved passed him and found my guests seated on the couch. I stepped in and said. "Hello. Welcome."

A woman with very pale blond hair and sapphire eyes looked up at me and smiled. Her mink coat draped her shoulders, beneath she wore a pale blue dress. The man with dark brown hair and startling blue eyes sat next to her, looking expectantly up at me as I entered. Both of them looked pale, but not as pale as vampires. But, rather, they had flawless skin—hers was a to-die-for peaches-and-cream complexion. Both were uncommonly beautiful. In fact, I was momentarily stunned by their good-looks. And their pheromones took me by surprise, soothing me into a state of complete serenity.

"Sabrina?" the woman said in a rich flute-like voice that nearly stunned me as much as her beauty.

"That's me," I said, feeling like an oaf and so below them it wasn't funny.

"I'm Ophelia Widdicombe, William Gannon's sister?" She had a French accent.

"Bill's sister?" She nodded. I reached over to shake her hand, and then she introduced her husband, Declan. I shook his hand and we made appropriate noises of greeting. I'd taken off my glove, for this one thing. I got no reads, but that didn't surprise me.

"Very happy to meet you, my dear," he said. He had a British accent.

"We are here, eh—" She lapsed into French looking at her husband. She seemed to wrestle with saying what was on her mind, and I was pretty sure it was not because of a language barrier. Her English was impeccable. She spoke in French to her husband, a hand protectively at her nearly flat belly.

"What my wife is trying to say is, well—"

"Thank you," she said, smiling wide with bright white teeth. "We've been trying to conceive and, well—"

My face began to burn with slow realization.

"We are very grateful that you donated," he added, looking at his wife. His hand clutching hers, he drew it up and kissed the back of it. They couldn't be happier. They were expecting a baby. *Oh, hell.*

My mouth dropped open and my hands covered the gasp that came from it.

"Oh, my... I mean Congratulations!" I finally blurted.

"We couldn't have done this without you and my brother's—um—"

"Yes! Of course!" Realization hitting me over and over on the head. I was totally broadsided by this. Bill's father had not said that Ophelia would be one of the women who would be implanted with the fertilized eggs—my fertilized eggs. Or were there more than one? I didn't know, what with the fact that the Nephilim had been having trouble conceiving.

We all laughed at the awkward moment. Although I wasn't quite sure why I laughed. This was the oddest conversation I had ever had. The woman before me was carrying mine and Bill's child. I had learned, through Bill, that the Nephilim could not conceive naturally, and their race were dying out. Bill's sperm was their only hope. His intention was to get *me* pregnant by marrying me. That was not going to happen. Of course, when Bill lay dying in his own blood in a cave-in, asking me to please do this one thing so that his life would not go to waste, I went ahead and donated some of my eggs. I had questioned myself afterwards. Did I do the right thing, as a sibyl, who was a sworn enemy of the Nephilim? I'd convinced myself by asking who was I to make decisions against a people, merely because of the past? They were not the fallen ones. Their distant ancestors were.

"We were choosing names," Ophelia said, "and wondered if you care to hear what we've chosen?"

This surprised me. I was told that I would not be involved with the child's up-bringing at all. Not in any way, shape or form. Why would they care if I liked a name they chose, or not?

"Sure," I said, settling into a reading chair off to one side of the room.

"We like Draven, if it's a boy. But we're stuck on the girl's name. I thought Helena."

"You know I love the name Lucretia," Declan said softly. She patted his hand and smiled.

A numbness came over me and my lips moved without my intending them to. "It'll be a boy," I announced.

They both looked at me sharply, then blinked with confusion.

"Sorry," I said, hand to my mouth, face burning. "That sort of happens." I paused, crinkled my brow. "You know I'm clairvoyant, right?"

This wasn't news to them and they relaxed again.

I wondered suddenly how I knew. But then the next second I realized that the baby had *my* human genes in them. *Oh my God!* The child inside Ophelia was mine. My face became warm again and I fanned myself.

"My dear, a-are you alright? You're all red in the face," Declan said.

I was about to voice my thoughts, thinking again, that maybe I should stay quiet about those crazy inner thoughts of mine, when a noise from the next room caught me. The banging as the pocket door of my bedroom slid opened.

I stiffened in my chair, looked around through the beveled glass of the door, and Vasyl's form stepped in.

I stood as he entered the room. He gave both Declan and Ophelia deadly looks and said, "They must leave this house at once!"

"But—"

"I said *now!*"

"They were just visiting me, telling me—"

"They are Nephilim. They are my enemies!" Vasyl said. His fists were clenched down at his sides, and his eyes had become deadly black—all of his eyes, including the whites. *Holy shit!*

Ophelia and Declan were on their feet, pulling on their coats.

"How rude!" Declan spat. "Who are you?"

"I am her husband," Vasyl said and then went into a long tirade in French that had the two making incoherent sounds and moving quickly out of the house.

Growling, Vasyl moved as if to shove them out the door if they didn't move fast enough. Vasyl's face had become animalish, fangs out, and then his wings came out. *Oh shit!*

Alarmed, I jumped between him and Ophelia.

"Stop!" I cried, hands outstretched protectively. "She's carrying my baby!"

Chapter 11

Throwing Sticks

Vasyl stopped, and looked down at me like I'd dumped ice water on his head. Everyone stopped and stared at me. Cho, who was standing near the door, doing his imitation of Kwai Chang Caine from *Kung Fu*, stopped as if uncertain which way to jump.

"What do you mean?" Vasyl said, eyeing me, absolutely clueless, but brows were drawn, and a crease in his forehead told me the degree of anger he was about to display.

I bit down on my lower lip. Oh, crap. I never told Vasyl that I had donated my eggs to be used for—well, this.

Ophelia chose that moment to say something. In French. Terrific.

Vasyl hissed, showing fang. Lots of it. Spitting angry French, so that spittle flew from his mouth. At the same time, he displayed his horrific wings. I pushed at him, trying to keep him off the Witticombes. I may as well be pushing at an avalanche.

"Stop!" I said, holding my ring up, as if in warning. For good measure I faced both the Witticombes and Vasyl. That worked. For now.

But angry French insults volleyed back and forth between them once more.

I brought up my right hand with the ring and flashed it in front of Vasyl in a warning. I didn't want to hurt anyone here, but if push came to shove, I would.

He stepped back, looking at me like a mad dog. In fact he growled.

"Let these people leave. Okay?" I said sternly. "Then we'll talk." He crossed his arms and glared. "Put the wings away." It was like I was telling a two year old to stop his tantrum and put his toys away.

His eyes fluttered in a strength-gathering moment and the wings vanished.

"Thank you."

He spun away, muttering something in French. I turned back to my visitors, apologetic, but they swiftly left the house. I felt badly.

Once they were out the door, I turned to Vasyl who was in the living room, angry that he'd treated them so harshly.

"They never did anything to you!"

"First of all, what have you done? Explain." His arms still crossed, looking vexed.

I bit my lip before I could answer, because I had to think about it. I began, and then stuttered and stopped. He waited, impatiently drumming his fingers on a bicep.

"Okay, here's the thing. I donated some of my eggs, and they had some of Bill's sperm and they—I don't know how it's done exactly—they made a baby in a test tube—I guess—and they put it inside Ophelia's womb. She's a surrogate mother. The baby she carries is mine and Bill's."

After he digested this, which took a moment or two, he said, "You realize that you have aided your enemies by helping their kind reproduce?"

Dropping my gaze I said, "I hadn't even thought of it that way."

"Now they will have in their possession a being that is stronger than a vampire, Nephilim, and *you*."

Yipes.

"What were you thinking?" His nostrils flared.

"I couldn't refuse him. He was dying!"

"And good riddance!" Vasyl fumed, doing a one-hand flick.

"That's just mean!" I retaliated. "He wasn't a bad person. He could have kidnapped me and done it that way, but he didn't."

"You are too trusting. Too gullible."

"I am not!" I spat back. Maybe I was, but I wasn't in the mood to admit my shortcomings.

He let go a heavy sigh, as if to steady his nerves. He spoke slow and in a low tone as though I were as dense as a boiled egg. "It is very likely that this child, when it grows up, will become your worst enemy."

I thought about it a few heartbeats, doing the math in my head. "I'll be too old to fight him, I'm sure."

"Sabrina," he said with a sigh. "I am your protector, but if you keep on trusting your enemies, you may wind up dead, and I will be unable to do anything!"

"But he told me he wasn't my enemy."

"He lied!" he roared. "Nephilim are very adept at lying and sounding sincere."

I couldn't look at him anymore. I thought I had done a good deed, but turns out I hadn't. If anything, I'd probably made my job harder, and about twenty years in the future will be kicking myself repeatedly, while trying to fight the being I'd created.

"You have been making bad decisions, Sabrina. You must realize the future of all humans depends upon you killing *all* Nephilim."

"All?" I gaped at him.

"Why do you think you are here?" he said.

"I was told I'm supposed to kill nephilim, demons *and* vampires. What about that, Mr. Vampire?" Cocking my head, I shoved my fists on my hips and glared at him.

"I am your protector. That is what I was doing when the Nephilim came after me while I was human, and hunted me down like a cur!" Vasyl growled. "That is the reason I became a vampire!" His hands went out. "If I had died, then the Dagger of Delphi would have never been found. Only *I* knew where it was."

"No. You said the elves knew, and they were the ones who got it for you, from wherever you'd buried it." So there. Nah-hah.

An odd noise of what sounded like pencils falling and scattering onto a floor somewhere halfway caught our attention briefly. Vasyl made a guttural sound and broke into nearly hysterical French, arms flapping, mouth going. I had no idea what he was saying. But I wanted to get as far away from that as I could, and turned away, even as he protested vehemently for me to not go away. Yeah. I don't like people yelling at me. Ex*cuse me!*

The strange clicking and clattering sound came again from the kitchen. What the hell? Tired of listening to Vasyl rake me over the coals in his native language, I stepped away from him toward the doorway of the kitchen. Cho sat cross-legged on the floor, throwing small flat sticks onto the linoleum. They were short and maybe an inch wide with lines and dashes on the ends. I couldn't figure out what the hell they were, or why he was tossing them onto the floor.

"*Sóng*," he said eloquently in Chinese.

I squinted at him. "How's that?"

He didn't look up from his reading. "Conflict. You will settle the argument eventually." He threw again. Then he picked the little sticks up and threw them a few more times, like before. "I still see a revolution, *gé*. And *zhén*—thunder.

There will be a shake up... hmm. Interesting. Also means first son." He looked over his shoulder at me and smiled. "I think you will somehow meet him."

I squinted at him again. "I probably won't ever see him. They were pretty adamant about my not having anything to do with his up-bringing." I was floored that Ophelia had actually come to tell me about her being a surrogate. Maybe she wanted to gloat? Now that they were gone, I wasn't sure.

"No. You will. And..." He threw again. The sticks fell. I didn't know how he was able to read the things. I noticed that the dashes and lines on the ends were different on each one. "In the future, yet, in the now." I scrunched up my nose at him. He shrugged.

"It is all in the reading. I don't make it up."

"We were fighting. Why did you leave?" Vasyl said over my shoulder and I jumped.

"Oh!" I twirled on him. "You can't come in here! It's sunny!"

Angered, he turned and stalked away, hand flying as he went. "I am going back to bed!"

"Good!" I yelled back, watching him go. He slammed the door shut a few times. It was hard to slam a sliding oak door, it would only bounce away from its threshold. With the sound of the metal lock engaging, I knew we were now free of the angry vampire.

Crap. Our fights tended to be over other men in my life. Fortunately, I remembered I needed to take care of something more important than hashing over something I could not change.

"I need to call Constance," I said, and stepped around Cho. The land phone hung on the wall. I worked on how to get them to come over, but leave the children behind in my head before I dialed. Could that be done? Or would it be necessary?

Cho threw his yarrow sticks again, they scattered like little twigs across the floor in front of him. I watched, fascinated while I dialed.

"Moonlight's Antiques and Collectibles," Constance's voice was in my ear. I called her at the shop, knowing she would be there.

"Oh! Hi, it's me, Brie," I said.

"Hi, hon. How are you?"

"I'm fine. Um, are you busy?" I still had no plan.

"Just a few people browsing around. Why?"

"Um, I'd like for you and Randy to come over for… dinner tonight?" I bit my lower lip. I couldn't think of anything else.

"Really? Sure!"

"Well, not if you have plans," I said, hedging.

"No, just leftovers."

I grimaced. I had left-over soup.

"I need to see the both of you, um…" I glanced at Cho and began making a quick decision. "I've got an important announcement to make." I closed my eyes tightly, wondering how I would tell them everything. Especially about Vasyl. This was going to be really difficult.

"Wow. Really?" she sounded intrigued. "Should I bring anything?"

"I'm out of bread. Could you bring me a loaf? I hate to go to the store just for bread." I really didn't want to drive all the way to town for a loaf of bread, and she was right there.

"Sure no problem. What else? Cake?" I looked at the phone. Why would she want to bring cake?

"No, nothing else. Be here around six?" I held the handset with my shoulder as I spoke because my hand was shaking. She'd bring something, I *knew* this.

"Okay. You sure are being mysterious, Brie," she said and chuckled. "I'm dying to find out what your announcement is."

"I know. I've got something very important to tell the both of you," I said, twisting my fingers, since I wasn't wearing gloves.

"Are wedding bells in the offing?" she asked.

I was stunned at Constance's intuition hitting it right on the head. I totally forgot. I *was* married. That would have to be my prelude to the other stuff I had to tell them about. I chuckled. "Not saying," I teased.

"Okay, I guess we'll see you at six," Constance said. "I'm so excited!"

We said goodbye and I hung up. My underarms were sweaty. Wonderful. She thought I was going to announce an engagement. I was already married to a man she and Randy had never met before. And Bill's death might be another announcement, but I really didn't want to talk about that on top of everything else. Especially in front of Vasyl.

"Ty?" I said.

"Yes?"

"How are you with kids?"

"Kids?" he blinked at me. "I've got six siblings. Two are younger than myself."

"How about two girls around six and eight?"

"I love children. Why?"

"You're going to take them into another room—maybe the parlor—and keep them occupied and out of ear-shot. Meanwhile, I'm going to introduce Vasyl to them, and then eventually tell them about vampires. After dinner, of course."

"Vasyl *is* a vampire," he said in a reminding tone as if I were dumb as cheese.

"I know. I haven't figured this all out yet." I bit on my lower lip. My underarms became itchy I was sweating so much thinking about this. "Crap. This won't be easy."

"Start small. Introduce Vasyl to them. Let them get to know him, first."

"Yeah… yeah," I said, my eyes unfocused as I tried to visualize us all sitting down to the table. "Vasyl doesn't eat."

"Can he pretend?"

"I don't know," I said. "He doesn't know I'm going to do this tonight. I want to do it and get it all over with."

The phone rang making me jump like a startled cat.

"Crap!" How was it that I didn't know it was going to ring? This could only be a phone call from a supernatural, and not many of them had my home phone number.

I picked it up and answered tentatively. "Hello?"

"Sabrina? This is Andrew Morkel. How are you?"

My heartbeat doubled. "Oh! Hi. I'm fine. How is Bjorn?" My hand went to my throat—I don't know why.

"There was great improvement. But he isn't out of the woods as yet."

"Okay. In what way was there great improvement?" I asked, doubt running neck and neck with hope.

"The deterioration has stopped. In fact some of the decay has retreated."

"Really? That's great news, right?"

"Yes. However, we need you to go and give your plasma again. I've called the facility and have gotten you your appointment. It's for 2:00 tomorrow afternoon. Can you do that?"

"Yes, of course!" I said. "But how will you get the plasma to him? Won't that take a little while?"

"Sabrina, for as long as you've been in our realm, I would think you'd know we would have a very quick way of getting the plasma here, don't you think?" he chided.

"Oh. Yeah. Duh. Didn't think of ley lines," I said, a chuckle followed from both of us.

"We will have someone there to take the delivery, and as soon as they have it and are out of sight, they'll pop back here with it."

"Sounds good. It seems to be working, then?"

"Yes. So far it does."

I breathed a sigh of relief. "Thank you, Andrew."

"No, Sabrina. Thank you."

We said goodbye and I hung up.

"Well, the good news is that my plasma is helping Bjorn."

Cho smiled. "I am not at all surprised."

I went to my refrigerator. I thought about how much food I would need. Not for us, but for my brother. He ate like a starved caveman. I looked at the left-over soup in the container. I knew that this wasn't nearly enough, even considering Cho was fasting and Vasyl wasn't going to eat. There were still three adults to feed. Somehow soup didn't get me excited either. I opened up the freezer and saw frozen veggies, and some white paper-wrapped meat. In black pen it said *ROAST* on it. This was deer meat that Hobart had brought to me. I wasn't home when he'd left it in my large freezer, in the shop. There were venison roasts and some sausages. More was out in the deep freeze. I took out the large roast and put it on the counter. I'd never cooked a venison roast before. Was it like beef? Who could I ask?

Only one person came to mind. I strode into the dining room and faced the mirror, looking around in it. All I saw was me standing in the dining room. "Dante?"

He appeared in the mirror first, at the edge, and walked out of it. There was a definite shifting of the molecules around me. I turned to find him next to me in the flesh.

"I am here, at your service, my Lady," Dante said, and gave me that fist-to-his-chest bow.

"I need to know how to cook venison. I've got my brother and his wife coming over tonight."

He smiled. "Not a problem."

Chapter 12

House of Cards

The aroma of roast venison and accompanying vegetables filled the house. I thanked Dante for getting it into the oven for me, and he kindly bowed out shortly after, knowing that I was about to take the hardest step ever in my new life as a sibyl. He promised he would be nearby if I should need him.

Earlier, I got a toasty fire going in the den, and put out games, crayons and coloring books for the girls to play with after dinner. Cho would be with them and would make sure that they were occupied while I brought up the subject of vampires to my brother and his wife.

"I will serve dinner," he said, and I gaped at him.

"No. You don't need to do that," I said.

"I used to be a waiter," he said. "Waiting on you and your family would be my honor." He bowed. Well, how could I argue with that?

The sun set well before dinner at around four thirty, and I lit some candles in the dining room. Cho plugged in the Christmas tree, adding to the lights. It looked like a typical old farm house during Christmas time. Charming, in a weird way.

The dining room table was set. Don't ask me why I set it with the good china, and an heirloom linen table cloth but I did. I mean, Randy would never notice, but Constance would and see the trouble I went to. She would know something was up right away. Women know things like that. We're more intuitive than men. Naturally, she thought she'd figured out what my announcement would be. I was gonna shock the hell out of both of them tonight. More ways than one. They would meet my new husband for the very first time. *Glup*.

My roast was nearly done, and it was almost six o'clock. Dante had done a superb job in getting it prepared and put into the oven with the timer set. I only had to baste it once. I figured if anyone knew how to cook venison, Dante would.

When the vampire in the house came out of slumber and opened the pocket door with that distinctive sliding rumble, I knew we had more than one thing to discuss.

Cho and I exchanged glances. Cho smiled.

"I must change." He ducked out of the kitchen and left me.

Chicken shit.

"*Cherie?*" Vasyl's voice sounded calm. That was a good sign. But he was always mellow when he first woke. He would go out and feed soon.

"In here," I said. He knew where I was, but it would have been bad if I didn't answer him. He would presume I was still angry from our earlier fight. I wasn't. My nerves were twitching about this other thing I had to do.

Vasyl's hair was rumpled more than usual as he stepped into the kitchen. And he was shirtless. The shirtless part had my attention. He had that sleepy puppy look. But this was always deceiving, since he was a vampire who had just awaken. He needed two things upon awakening. I could provide only one of those things.

"I've never seen you in that dress before," he said, eyeing me.

"It's new."

"Why are you wearing it? What is that cooking?" He sniffed the air.

"Dinner. My brother and his wife are coming to meet you, and—"

Our eyes met and something inexplicable came over me. I strode wordlessly up to him and grasped his face between both my hands and kissed him soundly on the lips.

"I'm sorry," I whispered.

His lips were on mine while his hands went to my waist. Pressing me to himself, he molded me against him like I was made of clay. Then his hands dropped to cup my behind, pressing me against him where my pelvic bone hit something solid on him. Wordless message received, I drew my arms around his neck, my body melting, submitting to him. His hands went under the dress to caress me more intimately. He then hauled me up against himself and the passion rose. Our tongues mated and my lust blossomed. I moaned into his mouth, trying to make it known how much I wanted to do something about this.

Being that he was vampire and had had my blood, he certainly did understand my needs. Hands bracing my butt, he picked me up, and I entwined my legs around his narrow waist, hooking my ankles. We traveled through the house, my shoes dropping like little bombs along the way. My eyes were closed and my lips were locked on his, but I knew our destination. At least I hoped so. I pried one eye open to make sure. He stumbled when he got to the threshold of the bedroom, and the door rattled against its opening. A muffled chuckle slipped from me. Vasyl growled low and suddenly we fell and landed on the bed. My panties flew off me and then my skirt was unceremoniously lifted and he entered me roughly. Sex at this hour was anything but slow. It was sudden and quick, but after last night, it was enough to satisfy me for the time being. Although it lasted perhaps all of five minutes, it left me panting.

"You've messed up my hair, and my dress," I complained.

"I enjoy messing you up," he said, a fiendish smile in his voice. "You've heighten my hunger, *mon amour*." I looked up to see that his fangs were fully drawn. He moved off me, zipped himself up and rushed from the room before I could sit up. Our vampire quickies had taken me a while to get used to. A vampires' needs were two-fold: sex and blood. They barely differentiated between them, as far as the need. If Vasyl fed from me, he would have stayed and took blood from me. But since he didn't drink my blood—didn't dare—he had to go and feed elsewhere. He had told me that soon after he had been turned, he'd had to learn to drink from animals, instead of humans, because it was known that a sibyl's blood was an elixir that a vampire couldn't resist. The fact that he went to so much trouble to not be tempted by my blood, I guess I didn't mind.

"We're having guests tonight," I called out, not certain if he'd heard me. "My brother and his wife. You're going to meet them!" I groped around for my underwear, and found them on the floor. They always wound up on the floor. "Vasyl?"

No answer. He must have left to feed. I wasn't all that sure where he went to do his feeding. Possibly his barn, but I had no idea where that was. But he could get there in no time.

I skittered into the bathroom, washed myself—*gak*—and straightened my dress and hair. That took all of ten minutes. Afterwards I found my shoes and put them on, then returned to the bedroom where I had to straighten the bed. I turned to the drawers and found the new pair of jeans and a trendy tee shirt I had bought for Vasyl to wear. The jeans were somewhat distressed. I could imagine him in them (too yummy for words). It would be hard enough for me to keep my hands to myself tonight. Any other woman would not be able to keep their eyes off him, no matter what he wore. And he would wear the slip-ons I'd bought or I'd withhold sex for... one, or two hours—tops.

Back in the kitchen I bent to check on the roast. The timer was still clicking down to zero.

Cho was silent on his feet and I didn't know he was there until he said, "Is everything alright? Can I come in?"

I jumped with a start and turned with my hand on my heart, which was now jackhammering in my chest.

"Ty! Don't sneak up on me, please," I said. Then I made a face. Why hadn't I known he was right there? He wasn't magical—I didn't think so, anyway—so I should *know* he was there somewhere nearby.

"Sorry," he said. "I didn't want to disturb you and your husband in your private moments."

I bit my lower lip, a small sound of helplessness escaped as embarrassment filled me. Although he was upstairs he'd heard us. I blinked my eyes closed. That's right. He was in the bedroom above us. *Damn!*

He wore a crisp white shirt, black bow tie (yeah, didn't expect he would have packed that), and black pants and shoes. A basic waiter's uniform. He stepped out of the kitchen. I stared at the spot where he had stood and wondered about him. Unable to make any judgments as to whether or not Cho was merely one of those people who I could not read, I checked the wall clock. Holy crud, it was quarter till six. Where was Vasyl? He needed to get dressed, damn it. Nothing had better ruin this dinner party. Or was it a "dinner party" with only a few people? Two couples, I added up. Four people. Small family get-together? Now I was babbling to myself in my head. *Sheesh!*

A car door slammed. Then another one, and a third one.

I rushed to the window in the door. My brother and his family were here. Panic rose.

"They're here! They're here!" I scrambled around the house. You'd think the King of Siam were about to enter my domain and it was only my brother. But then, this was the first time I had invited them over after my dad had died.

"What do I do?" I asked Cho.

"Answer the door," he said. "Or do you want me to?"

"Oh. No. I'll get it." I didn't want Randy to ask any questions about why an Oriental dude had answered my door.

My brother's loud voice came through the door. "What do you mean 'don't just walk in'," he said as if in answer to something Constance had said. "I used to live here!"

"Yes, but you don't any more, and Sabrina lives here by herself," Constance's lighter voice filtered in.

I grabbed the door knob and pulled the door open to stop the argument and met my brother's gaze.

"Hello!" he said. "Where's the chow?" Then he laughed that characteristic wild laugh of his and stamped his feet of snow on the outside rug.

"Come on in," I said, nearly hyperventilating because Vasyl was nowhere to be seen.

"Oh, who's this?" my brother said, spying someone a little further into the dining room.

I turned, expecting to see Cho. It was not Cho. It was Vasyl. And he was wearing exactly what I had put out for him, sans the shoes. Damn it. I knew he hated shoes, but didn't know why. I'd have to ask him someday. But he had put on the socks. *Thank God for miracles!*

"Oh, um—" I gathered my wits to make the introductions. "I'd like for you to meet Vasyl." And then I realized he didn't have a last name. Or did he? I tried to remember if he had written one down on our wedding license. I really couldn't recall.

My brother thrust out his hand before I could stop him. But Vasyl shook his hand, and nothing untoward happened.

"A pleasure, *monsieur*," Vasyl said and let go of his hand.

"And this is Constance, his wife," I introduced, as she and the children moved into the dining room, the fresh outdoors wafting around them.

"Madam Strong." Vasyl, a true Frenchman took her hand and brushed the back of it with his lips, earning an arched brow of suspicion from my brother and a titter from Constance and the girls. I had to stifle a snicker myself.

"Oh. Here." Constance handed me a foil-covered pie—still warm from the oven—and a paper grocery bag with "Moonlight's Market" printed on it. My bread sat on top. I'd forgotten all about the bread.

"Thanks," I said, taking the items from her. "You didn't have to bake a pie."

"Nonsense," she said, a crooked smile on her lips as she eyed Vasyl. Yep. I knew it. She couldn't help herself.

"And who do have we here?" Vasyl asked, bending slightly at the waist, hands on his thighs, to look down at my nieces.

Jena and Tara stood close to their mother. Jena clung to her mother because she was shy.

"This is Tara and Jena," I said while they both shyly peered at him from their mother's skirts.

Vasyl went into French right away in a nice, mellow voice, calling them *Mademoiselle Jena* and *Mademoiselle Tara*. There had to have been some pheromones hitting them, because they didn't seem quite as shy then, and gaped at him in awe.

"You speak French," Tara claimed.

We all chuckled.

"You know this, how?" Vasyl asked.

"We had a woman visit us in our class who spoke French to us. She taught us some words," Tara said.

"*Oui?*" Vasyl gasped a little, showing interest.

"That means *yes*." she said, hands clutched behind her back while twisting her body back and forth.

We all chuckled and Vasyl patted her on the head. *"C'est chouchou correct et petit."*

Everyone chuckled. Especially when she gave him a questioning expression.

"Um," I said. "Vasyl why don't you take their coats? Put them in the bedroom."

Vasyl took the coats and did as I asked. He was being very accommodating.

Fanning a hand in front of her face, and with a wide-eyed expression, Constance said, "Where on earth did you find *him*?"

I smiled, twisting the fingers of my gloves. "I'll tell you when he comes back. It's actually my announcement."

"What did you do, fly to France and bring him back?" Randy laughed at his own joke.

"No. Not exactly," I said.

"Is he a rock star?" Constance asked, leaning toward me conspiratorially. "You know he looks a little like Johnny Depp."

"No." I chuckled nervously because that's what I'd compared him to.

"Johnny Depp is shorter. Plus, he's married," my brother said pointedly.

When Vasyl returned, I went over and put my arm around his waist, and his arm went around my shoulders.

I cleared my voice. "Uh, Constance, Randy, girls… we're married."

The dropped chins and opened mouths lasted about as long as I had expected—approximately ten seconds—before a rousing "Congratulations!" spurted from them both. Randy had to shake Vasyl's hand again. I hoped this constant contact wasn't going to get him into trouble. But my guess was that since Vasyl was not a feeder on human blood, Randy wasn't going to be missing a pint of blood tonight.

"When did this all happen?" Randy asked, hands to his slim waist, still his jaw was dropped slightly.

"A few weeks ago," I said, ready for the next question.

"What? Why didn't you invite us!" Randy said. Constance childed him.

"Randy, maybe they wanted a private ceremony." She turned to me. "Justice of the peace, right? I'm so happy for you!" Constance pulled me into a warm hug.

"Yeah," I said, feeling bad. "We wanted a private ceremony."

"Well, come on, let's hear how you two met," my brother said, fingers making the universal come-on gesture.

"At work?" Constance guessed.

"Through an acquaintance," I said. It was almost true. My mother introduced us when I was ten, but that would not be in the conversation tonight. It was going to be hard for me to tell them the truth about Vasyl.

At that precise moment, the timer of the oven went off. I moved for it, and suddenly Cho sailed through the house. The pie and bread in my hand was suddenly no longer on the table, but in his hands.

"I've got it," he said as he zig-zagged between everyone with the ease of a snake through the grass.

I got stares.

"Um, our help," I said, shoulders up in a shrug.

"Yes," Vasyl said. "*Chambre aider.*" He looked at me and shrugged too. It was as if that was the only thing we could drum up that explained Cho's being there.

"Ty's sort of our all-around-the-house guy," I explained.

"Really?" Constance said looking as though she might die if I told her any more surprising news about my life. "That's wonderful. I could sure use someone to help around our house." She nudged Randy.

"What? Oh, we do alright the way we are," Randy said in a bah-humbug voice.

"Why don't you go ahead and sit," I said, motioning to the table.

"Oh, look, Randy," Constance said, eyes taking it all in. "She's put out the China and silver." I knew she would notice and then gushed about how much trouble I went through. Well, eventually they'll find out that it was worth it to me to make them comfortable.

We all sat and the conversation went back to where we met. Since I was a terrible liar, I allowed Vasyl to jump right in.

"I saw her from afar," Vasyl said, looking straight at me. His eyes glittered in the candlelight. "I knew from the moment my eyes fell on her that I would have to know her. I would have to meet her, and know her."

"I dreamt of him," I said, nearly tearing up. That part was true. Constance's little whine, pushed me over the line, and tears formed. I knew what Vasyl was talking about. He saw me as a little girl, and then I grew up into a woman and he was always there, watching me from afar. Wanting me.

"So, you met at work?" Randy said.

"No," I said. "It was—"

"I saw her in a restaurant with another," Vasyl interrupted. "I had to find a way to introduce myself to her."

Chin on folded hands, elbows on the table, I listened without interruption. Hearing it from his point of view, and with his accent, even *I* could believe it. Constance would have been entranced even if the pheromones weren't dancing around.

"I had the waiter bring her a drink, telling her it was from me." He shrugged. "It was the ice breaker—as you say." He shrugged again.

"After that we've hardly been apart," I said. Wow. I *could* lie like a rug.

Constance sighed, looking somewhat dreamy-eyed. "How romantic."

Randy, being immune to Frenchmen and apparently to romantic stories, gave her a slitted look.

Cho entered the room then. He poured ice water into everyone's glass. I have no idea where he found the pitcher, but he was surprising the hell out of me tonight. He exited and returned with a bottle of wine. He stopped next to Vasyl, and showed it to him for approval.

Vasyl made one of those Frenchmen scoffs. "Domestic. Bah."

"That's from California. Napa Valley," I said, frowning. "As good as any wine from France." I'd had more than enough arguments about wine with him in this house. Besides he didn't drink wine, so he couldn't talk.

He made a slight motion with his hand. Cho opened the bottle expertly and poured the wine into our two glasses—at that half-way level, like they do in posh restaurants. He moved to pour some into Randy's glass, but Randy put a hand over the glass.

"No thanks." Randy chuckled and looked first at me then up at Cho. "I prefer beer."

"Oh, good heavens," Constance said, "one night without it won't hurt you."

"We do have beer," Cho said, pausing next to him. Eyes glancing to Vasyl he added. "Domestic." His mouth dipped into a boyish smirk. He poured wine into Constance's glass.

"Thank you," Constance said and took a sip. "Oh, that's wonderful!"

I always kept beer in the refrigerator. "If you'd rather," I said to Randy. "Go for it."

"Well, yeah I would rather, if you don't mind." He gave Constance a don't-even-go-there look.

Cho bowed. He took my brother's empty wine glass and darted back into the kitchen. I heard the can being opened and poured. I began to really appreciate Cho's experience in handling everyone's whims and wants around the dinner table. He brought Randy his beer, in a tall, tapered glass, set it beside his table setting, and made a little bow.

"I will serve you all momentarily," he said and withdrew.

"Wow," Constance said low to me. "Could I borrow him sometime?"

"I might be able to let him go some night. If he agrees," I said. I actually didn't know how long I had him for.

"He'd be great for the annual antiques dealers meeting in our region. I'm in charge of it this year."

"So, Vasyl," Randy said, interrupting his wife, "what do you do for a living?"

"He raises horses," I blurted suddenly.

Vasyl's eyes darted back to me. He smiled patently. "I do not have to work. I have a large—eh—inheritance. But I do, as your sister says, raise horses."

"You mean, like racing horses?"

"No. They are merely a past time. A love." He smiled tenderly.

"You don't have them here, do you?" Constance asked.

"No. They are elsewhere."

Cho entered the room with plates balanced along both arms and in his hands. How he did this was amazing to me and he earned some appreciative gasps as he settled each plate loaded down with our food in an eye-pleasing way. I had no idea we had fresh parsley leaf.

When he set the plates before the two girls, he bent, hands on thighs and asked them what they would like to drink. They both said "milk". Cho dutifully brought them out two glasses of milk.

"What is this?" Randy asked. "Tastes like venison."

"It is." I cut off a piece and tried it. Dante had done a superb job. It actually melted in my mouth and was flavorful. I nodded and said through a mouthful, "Very good."

"How fancy! Pearl onions, finger potatoes and small carrots," Constance gasped. "Can I get your recipe?"

I chuckled. "If I can dig it up for you. Sure," I said.

"Randy always brings home a deer every year—"

"Well, not every year," Randy corrected, smirking.

"Anyway, he has the butcher make roasts. Mine always dries out." A gush of frustration came from her.

"It would be fine if you'd just cook it in the crock pot," Randy said to her.

"I do!" she said, looking pointedly at him. "Is that how you did yours, Sabrina?"

"No. This was in the oven."

"How many times did you baste?"

"Only once," I said, smiling, and feeling horrible to not be able to tell her exactly what was done to the roast.

"What temperature?"

Crap. "I think it was low, but I don't remember."

"Two hundred and thirty-five degrees," Cho's voice came from the kitchen. "For two hours."

I smiled at Constance.

The meal was delicious and conversation revolved for a time around my roast, and then back to Vasyl and where he came from. I knew that Vasyl had been in America for a while, but I didn't know exactly when he came here to find me. But he knew all of Europe, and spoke about it as though he flew back

Lorelei Bell

and forth from Paris to America all the time. You wouldn't know he'd been around for over a thousand years.

When conversation died, Constance said, "Oh, Aunt Shirley called the other day. She's wondering when Lindee will be coming home. You know there hasn't been any contact at all from her?"

"I know," I said, and took a sip of wine to bolster my lie. "That was one of the conditions that were made by this rehab place that she had been sent to." I felt a twinge of guilt in my gut. If I had to make up one more lie about where Lindee was tonight, I was going to explode.

"Wow. You think she's changed?"

"Oh, yes. Quite a bit the last time I saw her. She'll surprise everyone," I said. This also reminded me that I would have to go and retrieve Lindee from Black Veil. When the hell would I have time to do that? Especially since Vasyl had made me swear I would never go back to that place again. I could not send Rick because he could lose his powers. Vampires couldn't go, because they had no way back. And I couldn't go against Vasyl's wishes. I had no solution to this dilemma at all. It made me more sad, now that someone mentioned how Lindee's family was looking forward to her coming home for Christmas, which was only three weeks away.

When we were all done with our dinner, Cho removed our plates and returned to place a wedge of pie on smaller pie plates.

"Oh, blueberry?" I said, surprised. "God, I haven't had blueberry pie in ages!"

"It's from a can," she said with a wrinkled nose.

"Well, everyone knows it's the crust that makes it great," Randy said, fork loaded down with a hunk of pie, held to his mouth. I watched the hunk of pie disappear into his mouth. He caught a dribble with a thumb and stuck that into his mouth as well and sucked loudly.

"That's… true," I said, slightly distracted as Vasyl held his fork loaded with pie in front of my face. My eyes crossed to look at it. Constance made an *aww* noise as I opened my mouth. Vasyl held his hand under the piece of pie as he guided it carefully into my mouth.

"Aw, look at the newlyweds," Constance said. "Reminds me of when we—" Constance shut up. Her face turned beet red. Randy eyed her.

"Huh?" Randy said.

"Oh… never mind," Constance said, batting the air with her napkin.

Slightly embarrassed, I couldn't help but snicker at the act of Vasyl feeding me. This reminded me of his prelude to sex. He sometimes enjoyed feeding me. I became really warm at those particular memories.

My nervous stomach prevented me from eating much of the pie. I was about to have to tell them what Vasyl really was. And that vampires were all around us. Plus, that I'd pissed a number of them off and they may be waiting to do something to us all. I couldn't tell them *everything*. No way was I going to tell them that the thing they thought was Grandma Rose at Thanksgiving was really a demon. I don't think I'd be able to convince them. But then I recalled that Rick had rearranged their memories to not include her that night. For all I know, he may have also had them forget his and Tremayne's visit as well.

The last bite of pie was eaten. The girl's plates were cleaned, milk drank. Somehow no one noticed that Vasyl hadn't taken a bite of food. Probably he had thralled them into believing he had been eating along with them. Vampires could do amazing tricks to the human mind.

That was when Cho entered the room juggling fruit. An orange, apple, and one lemon looped in the air, his hands busy catching and tossing them.

"Oh, I definitely need to borrow him," Constance said, chuckling.

We all watched his juggling act. He ended by snagging the apple in his teeth, and took a bow after catching the rest in his large hands. We all clapped.

I knew this was a signal to me that it was time to get the girls into the den so that I could talk to Randy and Constance alone.

"Girls, I've put a few of your toys in the den. And Ty may have a few more tricks to show you as well."

"Yay!" They both jumped off their chairs and darted through the house.

"Walk, girls," Constance said.

They didn't hear her, as they giggled and screamed the whole way, charging ahead of Cho to the den.

We all released a collective sigh when the room became quiet.

"That was a very good meal, Sabrina," Constance commented. "Write the recipe down before I go."

"Okay, but I'll have to get it from the person who made it. I actually didn't make it," I admitted. She should have known, though. I was not that good at cooking anything so complicated.

"Oh, don't tell me you've found a man who cooks?" Constance said looking pointedly and admiringly at Vasyl.

"*Moi? Non!*" Vasyl said. "I do not cook at all." He looked to me.

"Cho?" she guessed looking at us.

"No. It was actually Dante who prepared it. Then he left," I said.

"Oh, Dante," she said and then had that odd look on her face while she glance at both of us. She most likely remembered him being with me, and wondered what had happened, and how I had not wound up with Vasyl, instead. But I could see that she found my choice of husband wasn't at all disappointing.

"Dante knows how to cook venison. I don't," I said with another shrug. They didn't know that Dante had died, of course. I never told them. I had no reason to. "Since he's three-quarters Lakota," I added.

"I'll bet he brought it to you," Randy said.

"Actually—" *oh, what the hell. My life was now a huge lie, anyway.* "Yes, he did." When the lie was easier than the truth, I decided it was easier going with the lie.

But the dinner was not high on my mind, or Dante for that matter. I didn't know how to bring up the subject of vampires. Bluntly? *Hey, guys. Guess what? Vasyl's a vampire!* Or should I go with the coy approach. *"Randy, remember when Mom disappeared—?"*

No. That would have a real contradictory affect. Randy would hate Vasyl for turning our mother.

I had wrestled with this in my mind the whole day, and basically ever since I was told to have the "talk" with them.

Vasyl looked my way and I met his gaze. He was trying to nudge me into saying what I had to say, I could feel his subliminal nudge.

"It is time," Vasyl said, "to tell them our *other* secret."

A sickening thrill went through me then, and my stomach tilted.

"Oh, don't tell me," Randy said, smiling confidently and holding out a palm to us. "You're having a baby!" *Oh crap!*

My mouth fell open in disbelief and I made a half-gurgling chuckle. If only they knew! My life was so complicated even Dr. Phil would not be able to unravel it. *He would need to consult himself in this matter.*

"No," Vasyl said, his hand seeking mine. He looked into my eyes. "Not that we are not trying."

I made a gasp. *Yeah, like about thirty minutes before you guys showed up.*

"Oh! How wonderful. You two will make great parents," Constance said.

"But that's not what I'm trying to tell you," I said, my face warming.

"Oh, I can't wait until the family Christmas gathering at Aunt Shirley's this year," Constance went on without hearing me, eyes gleaming.

"I can just see cousin Doug's face when he meets Vasyl. He and his wife went to Paris in the spring, and are *still* bragging up a storm about it." Randy laughed. "Here we got ourselves a real-to-goodness Frenchman in our family now."

Constance rose. "Excuse me," she said.

Vasyl stood. I wished I'd had a camera when Randy awkwardly got half way out of his chair, mimicking Vasyl, dropping his napkin. He sat back down, leaned over and grabbed his napkin. Constance padded into the bathroom.

I let go a held breath. Crap. How was I going to bring up vampires after the subject of making babies, Frenchmen and Christmas parties was the primary subjects now?

I twisted the ends of my gloved fingers thinking hard on how to breach the subject when a scream came from the bathroom and Constance threw open the door and bolted from the room.

We all stood.

"Someone," she gasped. "I don't know how... He's-he's in t-the mirror!" She screeched, pointing toward the offending room.

"A man? In the mirror!" Randy repeated. "Just how much wine did you have, Con?"

"Oh, crap," I muttered, and Vasyl gave me a most disproving look. He knew it could only be one person who could appear in mirrors. And maybe he *felt* the Undead in the house. Because I sure felt the metaphysical imprint of Dante's aura.

Dante suddenly materialized in the wide opening of the threshold between the living and dining rooms, giving me a deep one-knee bow, his long black tresses falling down around him like a cape. Constance cried out and darted behind Randy. Vasyl swore in French, Randy swore like a sailor, and I swore under my breath.

"Many pardons, my Lady, but I held off as long as I could," Dante said, and looked up at me.

"What is it?" I asked.

"A demon is requesting audience. He says he knows you." *Aw crap.*

I looked over to my brother and his wife.

"Yeah, see, my life has gotten way different in the past months," I said to them as if that would explain everything. To Dante I said. "What do you mean he says he knows me?"

"His name is Jacob. He tells me that he met you while you were in Dark World."

The name was familiar, but I still didn't remember him.

"Why does he want to see me?"

Dante smiled lightly. "Apparently he misses you."

"*Sacrebleu*," Vasyl said.

"Get rid of him," I said.

"As you wish," Dante bowed his head, never rose, and disappeared.

Constance fainted. Randy caught her and somehow propped her into a chair and then glared at me.

Chapter 13

Truth or Consequences

"Sabrina? What the hell is going on here?" Randy demanded.

Twisting the fingers of my gloves, I said, "That's sort of the reason I asked you over."

The girl's tinkling laughter from the other room filtered to me, making me glance toward the French doors. Beyond, I saw someone making shadow puppets on the wall, or on the drapes. I was so grateful Dante waited until they were out of the room to do his sudden materialization.

Vasyl moved to close the space between us. He leaned slightly toward me and said, "I have him within my control, Sabrina." While this was good news, it only slightly reassured me because of the dark look Randy was still giving me. His wife, meanwhile, was still out, and slumped over the table, but comfortably seated in a chair. I worried about her hair having dipped into the gravy boat, however, and chewed on my lower lip thinking about how she fusses with that bountiful mane of hers.

"Okay," I began, "this is how it is. Vasyl is a vampire. Dante is too, but he's an Undead." Scrunching my nose, I added, "Well, he died and that's why, but it's really, really complicated and I can't go into that right now." I took a breath. Randy was still staring at me, but didn't interrupt. "I worked for vampires in Chicago. In fact my boss, as well as my husband, are both master vampires."

After twenty seconds Randy's lips stretch across his face and then split into a guffaw. A hand slapped against his thigh. "That's a good one, Brie! *Haw-haw-haw!*"

"I'm serious!" My worry slipped to annoyance as my fingers curled to make fists at my sides.

"What do you wish me to do?" Vasyl asked quietly.

I watched my brother wipe tears from his eyes, he was laughing so hard. Some were streaming down his cheeks.

My frown hardened. "Can you pull out your wings?" I wondered.

"Of course." He yanked off his shirt, revealing that milky-white skin, and a viral chest and abs. This got Randy's attention and he quit laughing.

"What are we doing here?" he asked, looking thoroughly confused and somewhat concerned.

Vasyl's wings grew out of his back. It was quite fascinating, and my eyes were riveted as well as Randy's. Gradually, he opened them, but not fully. They were too huge to open wide, but the leathery membrane and claws at the ends, and the two thumbs tipped with large, wicked claws at the bend were terrifying enough. A good thing Constance was still out. Or maybe Vasyl also maintained a strong thrall on her at the same time.

Vasyl lifted his head slightly, looking down his nose at Randy. It was that haughty I'm-more-powerful-than-you look I've seen him use on other men, and other vampires. It never failed to put them in their place. Randy was overwhelmed. He began to shake.

"Maybe that was a bit too much," I said low to Vasyl.

Vasyl's eyes darted off Randy, to me for only a second before returning it on Randy. "You need not fear me, as I do not drink human blood," Vasyl said. "But many of my kind do. Some do not have control over their needs and desires."

"Good... that's good," I quietly cheered him on. "Keep going."

My brother stared back at Vasyl, wordlessly taking in what was said to him. I presumed that Vasyl had put him under a slightly stronger thrall, now, so as to impart the message, make him aware of the dangers surrounding him and his family.

"O-kay," Randy said, continuing to stare.

"Tell him he has to stay indoors at night—all of them—and not answer the door or let anyone in," I said to Vasyl. "Rick put a really strong ward on their house, like he did mine."

Vasyl nodded.

"Neither you, nor your family must go out after sunset," Vasyl said. "Your family must stay inside your home. You will be safe if you stay inside and do not go out for any reason after sunset. Do not let anyone inside that you do not know well."

"Wear crucifixes," I suggested low.

"Wear crucifixes. Put one on each child, yourself and your wife. All of you must wear one," Vasyl commanded. I wondered how many times you heard a vampire telling a human to wear a crucifix, and stay indoors at night.

"Okay," Randy said in a calm voice. "I'll do that."

"Now. I will escort you home," Vasyl said.

"Good idea," I said, turning to him.

Constance made a rousing noise as she sat up. Looking very confused, she touched her drooping hair, discovering something wet (gravy), in it and made a face as she drew fingers over the length of a few strands and sniffed. Then she tentatively tasted it, her face making a grimace, then a confused squint at it.

"I will be with them until they get inside the house," Vasyl said, turning toward me and taking hold of my arms. He drew his hands down my arms until he held my hands. Drawing them up, he kissed the backs of them.

"Good," I said.

"You will be safe until I return," he said.

I nodded.

"Girls?" Randy called, moving out from around the table. "Come get your coats on."

"What?" Constance said. "We're leaving now?" She looked around the room. "I–Sabrina?" She got up unsteadily, and caught herself on the edge of the table. "Whoa,"

"Did you—?" I looked to Vasyl, made a significant look.

"I altered her memory, do not worry, *cherie*," he assured me.

"Good." I did not want Constance remembering seeing Dante popping up in the bathroom mirror while she was doing her business. It was bad enough she would have to wash gravy out of her hair.

In a few moments, Randy had coats on both girls, and himself. Constance was still looking slightly dazed, as if she wanted to ask questions, but couldn't bring herself to it. They all trouped out the door. Vasyl, still shirtless, and shoeless, led them out. No one asked about his state of dress—or undress—as they stepped out into a bitterly cold night.

I sighed with relief, and shut the door.

"I will clear the table, if you wish?" Cho offered.

I turned to address him, was about to say, "No you don't have to do that," when someone popped in again.

Dante was into a low bow once more. "My Lady. The demon, Jacob, is very persistent. I detect he is no threat to you. He only wishes to impart something. I feel it would be wise to entertain his wishes."

I flicked a gaze to Cho before I returned it to Dante. I sighed. "Oh, good grief! Fine. Have him come in."

Dante bowed once again. A few seconds later someone materialized beside him. He was handsome, and in some weird way I recognized him, but couldn't place where I'd seen him before. It was one of those odd moments of wondering where I'd seen this person before, but not able to bring that particular memory up. Then a scene of a bath—and not your normal sort of bath, but something larger-than-a-jacuzzi sort of bath—hit me. Then, as if my brain could not hold it back—it was like a locomotive chugging down the track—what we did while in that bath played out and my face reddened. *Holy shit... crap... hell... I did do it with a demon!*

"Sabrina," the demon said, with a bow, which dropped his longish dark hair down into his face and he had to flop it out of his eyes when he straightened. I felt an edgy sort of desire go through me. *Damn it all to hell and back.*

"My Lady, remember the ring controls him," Dante reminded. Then he added without speaking, but went directly to my mind, *He is an incubus, my Lady. Quickly!*

"Oh. Right." I held up my hand quickly. Then realized I had the glove covering it. I hurriedly pulled it off and held my hand up again. I trembled all over. He was on the gorgeous side. No wonder I had had such a good time with him in that huge bath on Dark World. Sheesh!

Jacob blinked at my hand, then at me. "Your powers I cannot ignore," he said, then gave another bow. "Give me an order so that I might please you in some way so as to show you a small token of my devotion to you, mistress."

"Right." I looked at Dante. Dante shrugged.

Jacob waited. I thought a moment. What could I have Jacob do, more to keep him occupied and not bothering me? Especially bothering me in the bedroom, because there was no room for an incubus there. I sure didn't need him complicating my life any more than it already was. Then, I had it. Thankful that Constance had brought it up at dinner time.

"Jacob, do you know how to get to the Black Veil?" I asked.

"I have heard of it."

"Good. My cousin, Lindee, is there. She works in a palace in Targosvite. The palace belongs to Drakulya. She works as kitchen help, there. Do you think you can find her and bring her back?"

"I will do my best to please you, mistress," he said and bowed again. Then, he vanished.

I slapped my hands together. "There. Another problem solved." I glanced at Cho who smiled as he picked up the dishes and took them into the kitchen. The sound of him loading up the dishwasher filtered to my ears while I slumped over a chair.

"Where is your husband, my Lady?" Dante asked.

"Vasyl left to escort my brother and his family back home."

He bowed. "I will hold vigil until his return," he said and vanished.

Cho sailed out of the kitchen and grabbed up empty and almost empty glasses from the table.

"Here, let me help you." Needing something to do, I moved and grabbed up silverware and a few stemmed glasses, and together we loaded the dishwasher.

"Did you tell them about the vampires?" Cho asked.

"I did. Well, not exactly me." I straightened from the dishwasher to look at him. "Vasyl did most of the talking. I'm glad he was there to, um, soften the blow, so to speak."

He nodded. "Of course. I saw *zhūn* with your *jiā rén*."

"My huh with my who-what?"

"Difficulty with your family, in the beginning."

"Oh."

"All of it worked out, for now. But I fear that things may happen that are out of your control," he warned.

"Story of my life." I turned on the dishwasher and looked at him. "Wait. Was that advice, or a warning?"

Eyelids dropped into a blink, then his erudite eyes lifted to engage my gaze. "You have *qián*—great creative power and skills. I have seen it in action, but I also know that you hold back. You seem unsure. Waters untested, you seem to dip your toes, instead of immerse yourself wholeheartedly into your job."

I gaped at him. I suppose he was right. "I didn't ask for this." My answer felt lame.

"No. And yet you are in the thick of it, as it were," he said. "You must accept who and what you are. Until you do, you will be ineffective against your enemies."

"How old are you, anyway? Like. Ninety-five?"

He smiled "No. I am twenty-five. You must agree that I am right."

I scrinched my lips slightly at his seriousness. I hated to admit he was right, but he was. Damn. Before I could say another thing, an odd tingling at the base of my spine caught me off guard. I stood there, eyes swimming around the room, not focusing on anything but rather waiting to understand what the sensation meant. It felt not unlike the seconds before when someone had shot at me.

"Something is happening," I said.

Cho grasped my upper arms. "Tell me what you feel?"

"I don't know. It feels wrong, somehow. Like right before I was shot. Something—"

The sudden noises made me jump. Outside, there was a loud racket. Cho's grip on my arms tightened slightly. I say slightly, because I knew he was a hell of a lot stronger than he looked. And because he was touching me a whirlwind of visions came off him and I really needed him to let go and step away. Finally, looking up he did. We both looked up.

"What *is* that?" he asked as something thumped against the house, and some sort of terrible slashing cut across the roof.

"It sure isn't wind," I said. "Sounds like vampires fighting." I recalled how Vasyl had fought off a master from South America who was after me a few months back. I sure hoped they wouldn't come through my picture window again. That put me back a good sum. I only just got the insurance check the other day.

The tingling went up a notch and displacement of air made me jump slightly. Dante appeared.

"Sabrina, both of you, get into a windowless room. Now!" He vanished.

"Windowless room! I don't have one of those." I paused. "I don't think."

Cho grabbed my hand. "I have an idea." He pulled me along. Unfortunately he had grabbed my ungloved hand. He pulled me into the dining room and then pulled open the door to the far right. It creaked a little bit. We plunged into the darkness, down the steps and onto the landing where the steps turned. I drew in musty basement smells. Cho shut the door. Thankfully he had released my hand. I was surprised I didn't go into full-blown synaptic over-load from contact with him. There were a lot of dark things I now knew about him.

"Oh, don't shut it!" But he did. And now we were in complete darkness.

"Why shouldn't I have shut it?"

"The door knob is so old that it won't turn from this side of the door," I explained.

Cho tried it. He must have pushed, and the door refused to open.

"It doesn't matter—"

BOOM!

I jumped from the noise, and bounced off of Cho—at least I hoped it was him. "What was that?"

He hushed me. I froze and became quiet. It had come from the outside door that led to the basement. Fortunately my father had put a very sturdy metal door for the outside entrance. It wasn't for safety so much as keeping raccoons from gaining entry. They were like small bears in the winter trying to get inside the house.

We remained silent for a few more moments. I allowed Cho to hold me because I was scared out of my mind. My heart was beating so hard I could hear it—that's how quiet it had become, momentarily.

This wasn't good. A pang slid through me. It seemed distant. It wasn't my pain, I realized, but Vasyl's. I tried to reach up and locate the light switch. I was nowhere near the light switch on the wall, which was four steps up. The back of my legs were against the steps and I turned, stepped up a few risers, my hands slipping and groping along the wall. I felt around, until finally, my fingers found the light switch and I flipped it on. Overhead a single bare light bulb, which had a colored glass lamp shade that mimicked real lead glass around it, came on. I blinked until my eyes weren't burning any more.

Cho gave me a questioning look.

"Sorry, but I don't like the dark. It freaks me out."

"We are fine, for now. The noises have diminished."

I paused to listen, and tried to *feel* our perimeters. "They've stopped fighting."

The door which we had come through suddenly opened. I screamed, jumped the two runners down onto the landing, almost falling. Cho caught me, then let me go. He twirled me around, getting in front of me in a lightning move, going into one of those Kung-Fu stances.

"It's me," the familiar voice said. "Sabrina? Are you okay?" It was Dante.

"Yes. I'm fine. Scared to death, but fine. What the hell was going on out there?"

"We were attacked. It began when Vasyl returned from your brother's. He called on his sentinels, but there were too many attacking us." Dante said this as we climbed out of the stairway, and he surged for the front door. I wondered who he was letting in as he opened the door.

Vasyl half-fell and half-staggered inside. Dante was there to catch him. Cho darted in front of me to grab Vasyl's other side. I was momentarily frozen with dread. Why would Vasyl need to be carried? Then I saw it, in the limited light, all the blood. The pain I'd felt *had* come from Vasyl's fight. I didn't want to look too closely, but his hair was matted in tacky blood, and the pants he had worn were shredded and stained with dark blood. They moved Vasyl inside, arms leaning heavily upon both men's shoulders, head drooping with his hair falling like a wild horse's mane.

I darted to the door and shut off the cold blast of air, and saw more than I really wanted to. The blood was everywhere. There was a trail of blood up to the door through the snow. At first I didn't know whether it was all his blood, or the incidental bathing he'd gotten while dispatching other vampires. Then I saw the chunk taken out of his shoulder. It was as though someone took a bite out of him like he was a cookie.

The sight made me go woozy and I grabbed for a chair. Missed the chair and fell to the floor. No one was looking. Good.

"Sabrina," Dante's voice brought me back. I was looking up from the couch. How had I had made it into the living room? *Must've fainted. I'm such a wus.* My brain tried to catch up with things. Then I remembered Vasyl's horrifying wound, and all the blood. Okay, yuck.

"Huh?" I managed not to up-chuck. I was stronger than that. I had to be.

"Your wards on the house—they're down," Dante said. They had maneuvered Vasyl into the bedroom and onto the bed. The only noise was from Vasyl. He made incoherent sounds (some in whispered French), and I wasn't sure if he was swearing or giving directions, or both.

While I got myself together, and comprehended what Dante had said, I wondered how my wards on the house had come down. Then, it dawned on me. When I let Ophelia and Declan in I had said something that would let them gain entry past the ward. Mrs. Bench had told me how to close it again. *Oh crap.* The moments after Vasyl had picked a nasty fight with me, I'd forgotten to close them again.

"Crap," I said and stepped to the doorway of the bedroom. I winced.

"He needs blood," Dante said. "He needs human."

I stepped into the room, as though it were my duty to give my blood to him. Hell, I'd just donated my plasma to Tremayne. Why not? Dante stepped in front of me, hands firmly on my shoulders. He looked into my eyes, his glowing with an eerie incandescence that gave me chills. The whites of his eyes looked dark. Crap. Dark red, like bloodshot.

"No. Not yours," he said. I shook. My knees weakened. I dipped. Dante's hands grabbed me underneath my armpits and held me up easily. If it were not for the fact he held me, and we were closer than we should have been, I would have been on the floor at that point. Again. I couldn't look into those terrifying eyes, so turned my head away. Frowning, I looked over where Cho stood next to the head of the bed. He bared an arm and made a fist, and the veins popped all along his arm like little snakes. *Crap-ola.*

"You cannot, Sabrina," Vasyl said as if in response to something I'd said.

"My blood is—like—magical," I said in protest, but it was a weak protest. I actually didn't think I'd be able to give blood the way I felt.

"No," Dante said and I looked into his eyes. The redness leaving the whites, the silver rimming the dilated pupils. I wondered if I had been imagining those terrible eyes. "You would be in jeopardy, should you give him blood." The warning was stern.

"Besides, Sabrina, you must give plasma tomorrow," Cho reminded. "It would compromise you significantly. They won't take your plasma if they find you've given a pint of blood." He had a point.

Cho placed his bulging forearm before Vasyl's face. I wondered if he would bite, as he had avoided drinking human blood for a long time. But he didn't hesitate. I glanced away, stunned by his huge fangs and the sight of him biting a human arm like a large dog chomping down on a bone.

"Come," Dante said, pressing me back out of the room. I was glad he pushed me away. I couldn't have moved away on my own.

Without warning I simply broke down and cried. Dante held me until my sobs were spent. He leaned, grabbed the box of tissues and I blew my nose into a wad.

"Vasyl lost several sentinels, he will have to call up more, once he is strong enough," Dante explained. "You must get the ward back up on the house. Even though these vampires could not gain entry, there are still those who you invited into your house who can come inside without further invitation."

Yep. Nicolas and Leif. Two vampires who would happily stop by on their murdering rampage and do God knew what to me.

I nodded. "I'll call him."

"Do it," he said firmly. "Now, I must go and feed, as my powers are quickly fading, my Lady." He bowed, and then vanished while in the bow.

My cell phone... where is it? I looked for my cell phone, trying to both remember where I had it, and ignoring some of the sounds from the bedroom. None of the sounds came from Cho. I was pretty certain.

Finally locating my cell phone from my purse, I went through my contacts—the reason I didn't use the house phone—and found Rick's number and hit send. He answered on the second ring.

"Girlfriend, what's up?" he asked. Music, and conversation in the background filtered through. The music was of the Celtic variety. He was at Tom's Hideaway

"Uh-m, hi, Rick. Hey, I'm sorry to bother you, but—"

"No bother. What's up, toots?"

"I somehow brought the ward down on my house, and I need it put back up," I explained.

"Wow, how did you do that?" he wondered.

I quickly explained about allowing the Nephilim—Bill's sister—in, and that I'd forgotten to put it back up. "I didn't know I could do that," I said.

"Actually, you do have that sort of power."

"Wow. Really?" I gasped. "How would I be able to do something like this?"

"It would take practice, on small stuff, and then you move up."

"Wow. Really?" I sounded like a broken recording.

"So, everything is cool, otherwise?"

"Well, not really. We were attacked by vampires tonight. We need to get the ward back up quick."

"Okay. Sure, toots, I'll get that back up for you. No problem."

"Thanks a lot," I said.

"Any time."

We hung up and I hoped that the ward was up soon. I paced around, looking out windows, worried about one of my past vampire visitors coming in unwelcomed.

Cho stepped out of the bedroom, pulling down the shirt sleeve. Our eyes met briefly, and I was first to look away.

"Don't worry about me," he said. "I do this more often than you think. I started out as a donor, in fact."

Nifty. I wasn't certain how to react to that, so I kept silent. Was he in it for the sexual gratification, or what? He certainly looked more perky than he had a right to be.

"He asked me to send you in to see him," Cho said. "I'll go clean up." I didn't know what he was going to clean and left it at that.

I nodded and strode toward the bedroom door. I hesitated and poked my head in.

"Knock, knock," I said working to place a smile on my face.

"Please, Sabrina. Come to me," Vasyl said, a hand out to me.

I bit on my lower lip, and stepped around the bed. Sitting on the edge of the bed, I look down at him and took his hand. I nearly let it go because tacky blood coated it. It was all over his arm, and in his hair. His one eye was swollen, but it healed before my eyes. Amazing. I tried to not look at his bloodied torso. I didn't want to wonder what else was done to him.

"You're a mess," I said, trying to hitch a grin on my face. I shoved a fist to my hip to sell it.

"Forgive me. I ruin your bed linens," he said, giving a sheepish look.

"That's okay. God, like you can help it," I said. That's when the chunk of flesh taken out of his shoulder grew back with an icky sound.

His eyes closed as the process took precedence over everything.

When his flesh mended he took a sudden intake of air, his back arched a little and then his eyes opened, and he released his breath and relaxed.

I sat down, grasped his hand again. "Are you—?"

"I am fine," he said. "Now." He took a few more breaths and went on. "The battle took a great deal from me." He frowned, looking up at me. "We were greatly out-numbered."

"Outnumbered?"

"Ilona and Nicolas both sent their sentinels. It overwhelmed mine. I do not understand how they came so close to the house."

"Dante said my ward fell. But don't worry, I called Rick. I'm sure he's put it back up again."

"I want you to forgive me for something else," he said and sat up, leaning back against two pillows propped up against the headboard.

"What?"

"Earlier. I was jealous."

"No-o-o," I gushed, smiling. "Of who?"

"When the Nephilim were here. Bill's sister?"

"You were jealous of Ophelia?"

"Not *of* her. Of the fact that—" He paused to consider how to word it. "The fact that the baby is yours and Bill's, and not mine." He screwed up his expression. "That didn't sound right. Did it?"

"I know what you meant," I said and quickly went into my apology. "I'm sorry. I-I—"

His hand came over my lips, shushing me. "I only wish to make a baby with you." He looked down at my midsection. "One *you* will carry."

Oh God. Here we go. But I was prepared. Sort of. "Not tonight," I said, a wry smile on my lips. "You've got a headache."

"No," he made a small chuckle, but a hitch made him cut it short. "But soon?" Hand around mine he kissed the back of it.

I looked away.

"You do not want to have a baby?" His words made me turn back to him.

"Not right now. There's so much going on… people shooting at me, trying to kill us."

"But you cannot prevent it, can you?" His question hung in the air.

"Actually," I began, "I can." I paused to look him in the eye. I had not wanted to have this conversation with him. Plus, I realized he was not up-to-date on modern medicine. He didn't know, nor did he want to know about technology. The way that Ophelia became a surrogate mother must have overwhelmed him. "I take a pill," I finally said. "It prevents me from becoming pregnant."

He stared at me, processing this new information. Then he sat up a little straighter, stared at me, lips pressed together. His action of getting out of the bed made me move away. "I am taking a shower. Then I will sleep elsewhere. Good night, *madam*." He strode through the room and went into the bathroom to take his shower.

My whole insides fell. I had made two mistakes today with him. Maybe I was the worst wife in the world. Maybe I shouldn't have married him.

Chapter 14

Cold

It had snowed overnight. The six additional inches on my Jeep was my biggest clue. I could make out the general boxy shape and the grill under the yard light of the Jeep. The circle of light cast illumination over the fantastic glistening snow scape below. The driveway was basically plugged up with four- to six-foot drifts, looking like waves in a frozen lake that you might see in northern Minnesota. I didn't think my Jeep would get through all that, I don't care what their commercials claimed.

I continued to look out the kitchen window into the darkness while the coffee brewed. I didn't know if Cho drank coffee. I wasn't sure if someone who fasted would drink coffee. I'd only seen him drink water. Coffee was made with water, so I made a whole pot, just in case. I'd had a short vision of someone actually wanting and drinking my coffee, but it wasn't Cho.

Mentally I was trying to locate my broom and snow shovel. Someone had been nice enough to shovel my steps and plow the drive each time it had snowed while I slept in. I hoped to discover who my mysterious snow-plowing, step-sweeping good samaritan was. No matter what, I needed to dig out my Jeep. An industrial-sized broom would be needed to push the snow off it today. That would be in my father's shop. Which was looking as far away as Siberia, right now.

Dressed in gray sweats and warm, thick socks, I stepped across the kitchen to the counter where my coffee filled the room with its rich aroma. I poured a generous amount of caramel latte creamer into my cup while I slipped back to that terrible moment with Vasyl last night, and the argument. Well, it wasn't an argument exactly. I had upset him and he'd left the room. After he showered

I'd heard him go upstairs. He most likely went to the "vampire room," as I like to call it. He had not used it since we had consummated our marriage. I guess this was the vampire's version of sleeping on the couch.

Replacing the pot of coffee back on the heating element, I realized that I had half coffee and half creamer in my cup. I took a sip. *Not half bad.* I paused, picked up my spoon for the sugar and put it down as I took another sip. Perfect. I replaced the spoon in the holder unused.

Settling into a kitchen chair, I plopped my feet up on another and cupped my hands around my cup to warm them. Only one night light glowed in an outlet lending light to my lonely vigil, as it was still dark out at six a.m. I don't know how long it had been since I'd gone to bed so early that I would get up *this* early. Not that I'd slept much.

A thump alerted me. I wasn't sure where it had come from. Upstairs? If it came from upstairs, it would be Cho, not Vasyl. My heart ached at the thought of my dilemma. I'd made things so bad between us I didn't know how I would make it up to him—or even if there was a way to make up to him. I was sure I would never be able to make amends. I had told him, basically, I wasn't going to carry his baby, meanwhile someone else was carrying mine from another man. Does that even make sense? *I am so screwed up.*

I sipped my coffee staring into space dwelling on my problem. After several sips I realized my cup was empty. I got up and refilled it, using plenty of creamer. Maybe it was a good thing I never got a taste for whiskey. But I decided what I did need was chocolate. Chocolate was a girl's best friend, not diamonds. You can't eat diamonds, and they really don't make me feel as good as chocolate does. I remembered I'd bought some decadent chocolate- caramel cookies the other day and went to the cupboard. I located the cookies and this reminded me I had planned on baking some for the holidays. But I'd have to give some away if I did, as I couldn't eat them all. I then thought of who I might share them with. Rick was addicted to my chocolate chip cookies, but he wasn't the only one who I needed to show my gratitude to. Hobart was one guy I needed to bake cookies for, and maybe cook a whole meal for. After all he was the one who provided me with all those deer roasts. And then I realized that Vasyl would probably have a problem with me inviting a single guy over for dinner. *Hrumph!*

The sound of a big engine revving in the drive pulled me out of my gloomy thoughts.

I peeked out the window and found myself staring at a white truck with a snowplow. It had carved a pretty neat swath into my drive. I was startled to see a man had hop out of the truck, and now trudge through the snow up to my porch. He was all covered up in a hat, coat and gloves. I had no idea who it was, and that made him someone off the grid, as I like to put it.

I was up and out of my chair, wondering who my mysterious snow-plowing guy was. I surged to the door as his knock sounded.

"Sabrina," came the gravely voice. I peeked through the window and brown eyes looked back at me as he raised a gloved hand in greeting.

Realization had me undoing my locks and pulling the door open for him.

"Hobart?" I said as a rush of cold air blasted me.

"It's colder than a witch's—" he broke off as he took a huge step inside. I closed the door quickly. Removing his gloves, he blew into his raw, red hands. "Well, it's really damned cold out," he amended.

I almost didn't recognize him. Aside from the fact that he'd cut off all his dreadlocks some weeks back, he'd grown a beard. Well, it wasn't actually a full beard, now that I took him in. I had to unravel what I was seeing. Some gray peppered his dark beard. His mustache was thick and heavy, and it grew down to the jaw, and joined to thick sideburns, leaving his chin almost bare. But he hadn't shaved that in a few days so it almost looked like a full beard. If it wasn't for his deep, gravely voice and gold-flecked brown eyes, I might have called in Cho to show him out.

"I saw the light," he said. "Hope you don't mind my barging in?"

"No. God. I haven't seen you in a while. You the one who's been plowing my drive and shoveling my steps?" I wasn't sure why he was so cold, and the snow on his shoes was melting onto my entryway rug. But that didn't matter too much right now.

"Guilty as charged. I just need to get warmed up, if that's alright?" he said.

"Sure, sure," I said, still stumped by his appearance. But I shouldn't have been. He had a soft place in his heart for me, plus I was an honorary member of his Were pack.

"You wouldn't happen to have some coffee on hand?"

"I sure do! I'll go get you some." His fingers looked stiff and red. I strode into the kitchen, knowing now who the stranger was in my short vision enjoying my coffee this morning. I grabbed a mug off the coffee cup tree, and poured. "You take it black, right?"

"Black is fine," he said.

I brought the mug of coffee to him. "Why are you so cold?" Large hands folded around the mug as I handed it to him.

"I came to plow your drive—" He paused to take a manly sip. It was hot, but he savored it as he made another groan of pleasure. "Oh-h-h, you make some great coffee, Alpha Girl." His voice had enough gravel in it to fill a dump truck.

"Thanks." I smiled at his pet name for me. "It's a breakfast blend." I noticed his shivering had stopped.

"My GMC, the damned heater didn't come on this morning. What a time for the thermostat to go out on it. At least, I think that's what needs fixin'."

"Wow. You need to get that fixed soon."

"No kiddin'. I'll give Dave a call, see if he can't fix it today or tomorrow."

"I thank you for plowing out my drive, anyway. But I can call someone to—"

He held up a hand. "Nope. My pleasure."

"But you'll freeze! It must be below zero out."

"Something like twelve, I heard on the way over."

"Well, if you need to warm up, come on in. I have to dig my Jeep out," I told him. "I have an appointment in town later."

"Leave it to me," he said. "Oh, is it okay if I..." he lifted the mug and pointed out the door with his other hand, indicating he wanted to take the cup with him.

"Oh, sure," I said, understanding coming to me. "Be my guest. I can give you a refill, whenever you want."

He turned, grabbed the door knob, and stopped. Half-turning he said, "You've got a good sound barn, by the way. Won't take but a few new boards here and there."

"My barn? What about my barn? You aren't sleeping in it or something?" I don't know why I said that, but it wouldn't surprise me, since he was supposed to be our outdoor guard.

"Mmm," he said while sipping the coffee. "No, no." He chuckled. Reddened, gnarled hands clutching the cup as though it were his life line. "I'm doing something for Vasyl."

"Vasyl?" If I sounded shocked, I was.

"I'm not to tell you about it." His eyes flashed and his voice went down into what for him was a whisper, but it sounded like sandpaper on a sidewalk. "It's a secret."

"A secret?" I echoed. Hobart had become Vasyl's scion, a few months back. Now they were plotting something with the barn. I gave him a startled look.

He was half way out the door with the cup of coffee once again when I stopped him with my question.

"Were you here last night?" I wondered.

"Last night? Nope. Why?"

"We were under attack."

"Really?" His eyes widened in surprised. "I had a meeting with the pack. Full moon is next week."

"Yish," I said. "Don't remind me." I would have to get the brew from Mrs. Bench that would keep me from turning. I was *not* going to go out in my altered state ever again.

"Anyway, Vasyl let me off for the night. Had his sentinels out here."

"Yeah. Well, thought I'd better tell you. Vasyl got pretty badly bitten and—"

"What? Really?"

"He's okay, now. Ilona and Nicolas sent their sentinels, and they overwhelmed Vasyl's."

Hobart dropped his gaze and ran a hand over his chin and scrubbed the Brillo pad there. "Well, I'll bring the guys out here tonight."

"But, werewolves can't go against vampires. Can they?"

"Don't you worry about it," he said. "I've got some friends." He turned again toward the door. "Thanks again. I'd better get back to your driveway."

"Right." I watched him slip out the door and shut it, but not before cold air hit me. "*Brrrr!* Crap it's cold out there." As I darted back into the warmth of my kitchen, I wondered why Vasyl would have Hobart work on the barn. I wanted in the worse way to go and wake him from his sleep and demand he tell me. But since he'd battled viciously with many vampires last night, and had been injured, I didn't dare do that. He deserved to be left alone.

Oh, and I'd have to apologize. *And* get pregnant from him.

I lifted the curtains to watch Hobart trudge through the deep snow toward his truck. He hopped in and settled the cup on his dash.

"Sabrina?"

I turned with a start, nearly dropping my own cup. "Ty!"

"Sorry," Cho said with a little shrug and look of innocence.

"Make some noise for crying out loud! I've only got so many lives here." We stared at one for a few eye blinks. When he said nothing, I said, "What?" My hands going out, one still holding the cup.

"You've got an appointment."

"I know," I said, "with BioPlasma. But that's not until nine o'clock." I strode back into the kitchen. "I've got coffee, if you want some."

"I'm good," he said.

"Right. Except you need to enter the room and make a throat clearing noise, or heavy stomping—something," I suggested, moving for the counter. I grabbed more creamer. I didn't quite make it to the counter. Everything went wavy and then all I saw was white.

"Sabrina?" Cho's voice was in my ear. "Are you alright?"

My ears were ringing when I came to.

"What? What happened? Oh." I was now prone, and couldn't discern where I was at first because it was dark.

"You had one of your visions?" Cho asked.

Okay, I'm on the couch. I reached for my woozy head.

"What?" I tried to pull in his form, but he was still a blurry smudge, so I stared at the ceiling for a while.

"You went into one of your visions," he said. "I caught you when you fainted and brought you in here so that you'll be comfortable." He wasn't as upset about what had happened as most would be. It was as though he saw it all the time.

"Good call," I said still staring up.

"Do you remember it?"

"What?"

"Your vision?"

I frowned trying to remember. "White. Lots of it."

"Snow?" he said.

"Probably. What else could it be?"

"Are you worried?" he wondered.

"About?"

"Snow."

"No. My Jeep can go through a lot of snow," I said, my voice confident. Someone knocked on the door.

"I'll get it." Cho rose and turned to get it. He was at the door before I could vocalize who it was.

"It's Hobart. He'll want to warm up and get a refill of coffee."

"I've got it. You just rest," Cho said.

I lie back thinking about my vision of snow. I guessed it was snow. What else could it be?

The door opened and in stepped the big werewolf, growling about the cold, and then he stopped short.

"Oh. Hello?" Hobart said. He hadn't met Cho yet.

"Hobart, Cho. Cho, Hobart," I introduced from my prone position.

"How do," Hobart said.

"I am fine. You are cold and would like a refill?" Cho said helpfully.

"I wouldn't mind, if it's no trouble," Hobart said, sounding apologetic.

"Not a problem. Coming right up." Cho ducked into the kitchen with the empty cup.

I sat up slowly—well, I got myself to my elbows, anyway.

"Is everything okay?" Hobart asked, peering in at me on the couch from where he stood inside the door.

"I had a vision," I said. "I'll be fine." I paused. "Actually, I'm hungry. Are you hungry?"

"Oh, I can always eat something, if you're offering?"

"Had one of your venison roasts last night," I said. "It was fantastic. Dante put it into the oven for me, and—"

"Dante?" he said. "I thought he was dead."

"Uh-um, he's Undead, actually." I slowly stood, wanting the dizziness to vanish, but it lingered and I stood half-bent over, holding onto to the couch arm.

"Sabrina," Cho was at my side. "Easy. Let me help you sit back down. No worries," he added as he helped me to sit down; my butt plopped back down and somehow I twisted and landed in the recliner. *Much better.* "I will make you breakfast."

"Great. Leftovers," I said, finding my heartbeat had elevated from my episode. "Heat it all up in the microwave."

He bowed and left me to go back into the kitchen. I still wasn't exactly comfortable with him being my waiter and whatever else he was to me. God, I'd have to talk to him. I hadn't had a chance. *Do I pay him?* Then my eyes fell on Hobart.

"How's the plowing?" I asked him.

"Done." He had unzipped his parka and stood waiting for his fingers to thaw. "I thank you for the coffee, but you don't have to feed me."

I held up my hand. "Nonsense," I said. "You do a lot around here. Plus it's cold as a witch's—whatever." I slid him a look.

"It sure is." He chuckled.

Chapter 15

White-Out

The roast and all the trimmings were just as good as they had been last night. Possibly better, since I didn't have a nervous stomach, this morning. Hobart and I greedily devoured the remains.

"You sure you don't want any of this?" I asked Cho.

"No. I'm fine." He stood at the counter making himself a cup of tea.

"Sorry I only had Lipton." I apologized.

"This is fine." He gave me a small smile. "I am almost done with my fast."

"That's good," I said and looked across the table to Hobart. He scooped the last of the roast that was left in the bowl, and plopped it onto his plate. In a matter of a few scoops, he shoveled it into his mouth. Chewed. Swallowed. Gone.

"Aw, this was great, Alpha Girl," Hobart groaned and sat back in the chair, hands resting on his belly.

"Don't thank me. I didn't lift a finger to make it or heat it up."

Hobart sat up and held my gaze. "Don't be so hard on yourself, woman," he said in a more stern way than I'd ever heard him speak to me. "You have to realize that you're the one everyone needs to do for."

I stared at him trying to understand and accept that. Was I that special?

"Mr. Hobart is right," Cho said. "You are like the flower, and all of us bees gather around to please you."

Hobart's gravely chuckle filled the room. "You do realize that could be taken in a different light."

"It was well intended," Cho defended. "As you have said; she is important."

"Mr. Cho has pretty much put it in a nutshell." Hobart stood. He wore a flannel shirt over a thermal long-sleeved shirt. I had always wondered if my dad were alive if he would like any of the men who have been inside this house in the past few months. He wouldn't have liked Hobart, at first. I wasn't so certain about him myself in the beginning, but he did tend to wear on you. I think Dad would have eventually liked the big Were.

"You are the sibyl," Cho went on. "You're important to us, we need to protect, and show you our respect."

I opened my mouth to say something, but I could think of nothing. I didn't want to be this important to anyone. Not to Hobart, not to Cho, and especially not to the world. I still wondered what part I played in saving the world. I mean, the *whole friggin' world?* Come on!

Hobart stood and said, "I thank you for your coffee, food and hospitality. Now I've gotta go see Dave about my thermostat."

And I had to give my plasma so that Tremayne didn't die a horrifying death. Maybe my life *was* important, in a small way. I only knew that if Tremayne died, Ilona and Nicolas would take over the North American Vampire Association. I couldn't let that happen. Not on my watch.

After I showered and dressed, I was ready to leave for my appointment. Boots, mittens, a thick sweater, a heavy coat and knit hats were the automatic choice for winter gear in the northern part of Illinois. Cho had only his leather jacket that seemed extremely thin and I couldn't see him walking around like he came from Florida and had nothing better to wear. I found my father's winter coat and we discovered that Cho wore the same shoe size. I had not been able to go through my dad's things to send them off to Good Will. If someone could wear them that needed them, why not let them have them?

We trudged out to my Jeep. Hobart had done a good job plowing and shoveling, and unearth my vehicle from the snow. He had earned his coffee and meal a few times over, I figured. Cho and I climbed into my Jeep and slammed the doors. Our breath clouded inside the vehicle, threatening to ice up the inside of the glass before I stuck the key into the ignition and turned it.

Come on, start, I almost prayed under my breath.

I was happy to hear the thing turn over slowly, at first, and catch. Tonight I would not leave it out in this cold. I would definitely get it put away in the garage.

I looked over at Cho. "Were you worried?"

"Not at all," he said.

"Right."

"It's so cold," he said.

"I know."

"Perhaps you should have started it and waited for the engine to heat up a while?" he suggested.

"But we'd be late if I did that," I pointed out.

"Perhaps you could have gotten ready sooner?"

I frowned. "Perhaps," I said, doing my best to not sound angry at his suggestions. "Well, we're going now, so put on your seatbelt." I clicked mine in, pulled the parking break and pushed in the clutch. Cho's seatbelt clicked and I put the Jeep into first, and we were on the move. The tires made that odd rubbing-crunching sound over snow covered ground.

Maneuvering out of the drive, I realized the only tracks on the road were those made by Hobart's truck. I followed them through the otherwise pristine snow, finding where he must have dropped his blade to cut through a wall of snow. I gripped the steering wheel tightly with my gloved hands, feeling the Jeep dig in as I kept it in Low-2.

At the crossroads, I noticed Hobart's tracks headed straight. I had to turn right. I had hoped Hobart had gone into town. No such luck. The township's plow had not been down these back roads, yet. Nor would it be, any time soon, if memory served.

I turned onto the crossroad, and drove on, noting that the wind was picking up. Snow drifted across the open fields, creating huge drifts. We both remained quiet as I drove and the Jeep lurched over a few moguls. These were nothing. I knew my Jeep could go through much deeper snow. I had ground clearance, I told myself confidently.

"You saw white," Cho said. "Perhaps it was a warning. Perhaps we should turn back?"

"Cho, this is fine. I've driven through worse conditions than this. Believe me."

We went a few miles, passing the last farm houses when the wind picked up like a demon was blowing it. The road became blotted out by a wall of snow. I could barely see the hood of my Jeep. Creeping forward, I was sure we were still on the road, but who knew? I remembered seeing people getting all the way out in a field on one extremely bad winter's night while my father drove us home. I was pretty small back then. But still, I held my breath, my hands ached because I held the wheel so tight.

Air from the vents didn't seem warm enough, and I turned up the heat. Good. At least we'd be warm.

Cho hissed something. It sounded like he said "*Xùn.*" Which I remembered meant "wind". No shit.

Then we hit something. Hard. Our shoulder straps held us, and I was a little amazed that the air bags hadn't inflated because we really hit something. Strange. The Jeep had come to a complete, dead stop. It took a few seconds to realize the engine had stopped completely—that's why it was so quiet.

"You okay, Ty?"

"Yes. What happened?"

"We hit something." I looked out through the windshield. White. My eyes tried to pull in all the information so that my brain could understand it, but it took me more time than it should have. Then I saw the front part of the Jeep had disappeared. *What the—? Oh...shit.* It was buried in snow. Thing was, I couldn't see where the snow bank ended beyond. Everything was absolutely white. Had I gone snow blind?

I reached for my sunglasses. Stupid of me not to put them on before this. When I did, the UV rays were blocked and I could see better. I didn't like what I saw.

"What happened?" Cho asked again.

"Snow bank. I'll back up." I tried the engine. It wouldn't turn over. In fact nothing happened. "Oh my God," I said it softly at first. I tried to start the Jeep once more. Again, nothing but a click. "OH MY GOD! Shit!"

"This isn't good," Cho said, and turned in his seat to look around.

Understatement of the year.

All I could see around us was *white, white, white.* No buildings, no trees, not even a stupid fence line to give me reference. I figured our visibility might be down to a quarter mile, maybe less. Now what?

"We can't be stuck!" I undid my seatbelt, threw open the door and tried to climb out. The door opened about six inches, enough for me to step onto the running board. When I did, my foot sunk into snow. It covered the running boards, that's how deep the snow was. I wrangled my body and stuck my head up over the door frame. Snow blasted me like sand and I weaseled my way back into the Jeep and closed the door, breathing hard. My face felt like a pop sickle.

"We're trapped," I said. "We'll freeze."

"You didn't bring your cell phone?" he asked.

My heart lunging with hope, I grabbed my purse. Already the temperature inside the Jeep was dropping. We would freeze if we stayed, and freeze if we tried to walk out of here. Walk? No way could we walk through this snow unless we had snow shoes and damn it all to hell, I'd left them in the barn.

Desperately, I rummaged through my purse. I was sure I'd brought the cell phone. *I know I put it in there. Please let me be right. Please let me have done something right today!*

My cold fingers found my wallet and threw it out onto Cho's lap. He grunted in a strangled way with a flinch. It *was* pretty heavy.

"Oh. Sorry," I said looking up with an apologetic wince. Grasping my brush and comb, I laid those out on my own lap, and once these larger items were out of the way, I plunged my hand deeper. Something was down there. *Please let it be my cell phone.*

I gasped when my gloved fingers fumbled with the flat object. I pulled it out. Yes! Cell phone.

I looked up at Cho. "Who do I call? A snowplow?" Yeah, right. Like that would work.

"Call your friend, Rick."

"Right!" I would have thought of that eventually. I was panicked and wasn't thinking straight. Maybe the cold had gotten to my brain and I couldn't think past my conditions. I scrolled through my contacts. "Got it!" I tried to press send, but it wouldn't go through. "It's not working."

"Here. Let me," he said. I handed the cell phone to him. He was the least panicky of the two of us. In fact if we were on fire, I'd hand him the fire extinguisher.

He pressed my phone and lifted it to his ear while the wind rocked the Jeep. *Wow.* The front of my Jeep now had an inch of snow over it. We'd be buried in a matter of a few minutes. I looked up. The skies above us were clear blue. The wind was picking up snow from the field and drifting over us as we sat there.

He handed my cell phone back to me. "It is ringing."

"Thanks."

"Girlfriend. What's up?" Rick's voice was in my ear.

"Help! I'm stuck in a snow bank! The Jeep is stuck. The engine quit," I explained, trying to give him all the information I could think of that was important. "We'll freeze!" I added. "Come bail us out. I have to be at BioPlasma, like, in ten minutes!"

"Sure, toots. Where are you?"

"Somewhere down on Ram Road. You know that road that leads to my road?"

"I think I can Google Earth you," Rick said. "Hang tight. I'll be there in a few seconds."

I closed the cell phone and looked across at Cho. "He'll be here in a few—"

"Hi, toots!" Rick's voice came from the back seat.

Startled, I turned around to find him sitting in the back seat like he'd been with us the whole time. He at least had a coat, hat and a scarf around his neck.

"Hi, Rick. Thanks. That was fast!"

"No problem. Holy crap it's cold! Can't you turn up the heat in this thing?"

"The engine stopped," I explained.

"Oh. Right. Well, I'm here," he said. "You need to get to the plasma place in town, right? Hold hands. They're on the same ley line I used." He smiled as he held his hands out and leaned forward. "I get to hold hands with you," he boasted to me. Then his eyes flicked right. "Oh. Ty. Didn't see you." He made a slightly strangled chuckle. "Here. Give me your hand, too." Both of us turned in our seats and reached back for Rick's hands. It felt like my brain was left behind for about ten seconds, and my body felt squeezed, and my ears needed to pop from air pressure.

The ground came back beneath my feet, glass doors and windows appeared out of the gloom in front of me. It was cold. We were outside and our breath puffed out in clouds. The sidewalk was shoveled, and although it was cold out, it wasn't quite as windy here, because we were in town.

"Thank you, Rick!" I gasped, slipping my hand from his. Ty had already let go and took a few steps forward, looking around.

"Just keep walking like we came from the parking, lot, kids," Rick said, and that's what we did. We strode through the doors into the lobby. The warmth of the place surrounded me. Its modern and hospital-like interior gave way to high ceilings, and sterile-looking white walls. I spotted all the stations where the plasma collection areas were beyond the nurse's desk. My Were senses were taking in a cocktail of scents from humans. Some of which hadn't bathed in a while, and some just plain smelled of stale cigarettes. We strode forward toward the reception desk, and a woman looked up smiling at us.

"May I help you?" she asked.

"Yes," I pulled off my hat and unbuttoned my coat. "My name is Sabrina Strong and I'm here to—well, give plasma…" I trailed off, not sure that it was right to say who it was for.

The woman looked over her ledger. "Ah, yes. We have you down." She handed me a clipboard with a bunch of papers on it, and a pen.

"Fill these out, please. When you're done we'll have you step back to the donation center."

We all trouped toward a warren of seats by the windows with a jungle of plants. My legs became weak as my adrenaline crashed, and I had to sit, amazed that I had held up so well under the current stress. I looked at the pile of papers I was given to fill out. *Gak.* There were fifty pages—well, maybe not fifty, but a small booklet. Mostly waivers and such. I had to fill out my name soc. number, address, next of kin, and lots of other things, and sometimes the same thing about twenty times, at least.

"Thanks, again, Rick," I said while I filled out the papers.

"No problem." Preoccupied with his iPhone—or whatever he called it—he walked around looking at it, his fingers texting so quickly he sounded like a small woodpecker on a tree limb.

Cho sat next to me, looking around, but being quiet.

"I am sorry," he said out of the blue.

I looked at him. "Why? What did you do?"

"I saw this, you saw this too."

"No." I wanted to brush his enthusiasm over taking the blame away. "Well. You might have, but all I saw was white. Remember?"

He smiled again. "The hexagram showed change, wind and shadows. The inner, or personal aspect related to the outer trigram; wind. It seems I missed something in the reading of it." He looked vexed at himself.

"Oh, don't worry about it, Ty." I wanted to assure him he couldn't have seen that coming. But *I* should have, since I was the clairvoyant here.

"Possibly. But the Trigram *Gèn*—mountain—was there also. Mountain. Snow drift?" He made a grimace. "Possibly." He said out-loud, as if conflicted about it. I didn't have anything to add, so I returned to filling out sheet after sheet after sheet.

"Sabrina, I've just sent a text to Tremayne's compound," Rick said. "Told them you made it here and are about to give your plasma. They are sending someone who will come and pick it up."

"Pick it up? Like UPS?" I said, distracted. I couldn't really grasp what he meant.

"Oh, much better, Brie," he said, then leaned toward me conspiratorially and said, "One of the elves will come and take it back through the magic network."

I looked up at him. "Oh. Right. Got you." I remembered that Morkel had mentioned this to me the other night.

"Todd?" a male nurse called out as he stood beyond the threshold of a doorway. I noticed there weren't that many people in here. I figured it was the bad weather. I watched the man shuffle forward. He followed the nurse back through the doorway.

"Are you guys going to be able to go in with me?" I asked, after I'd taken all the paper work to the desk, and returned.

Rick made a shrug. "Probably not," he said. "Some places don't allow anyone back there but the donor." He looked down at his cell phone, and then up, as though something caught his eye. "Kiel?" he said almost under his breath.

I looked across the room and saw a woman in a black slacks and red leather jacket enter the room and then immediately turn away and dart back through the doorway, her auburn hair flying.

"Kiel? Hey, Kiel!" Rick shouted. "Aw, crap." I watched his face as it went through a couple of quick emotions, the first one was surprise, the next one was something like suspicion, and the third looked like worry.

"What is it?" I asked. "Who was that woman?"

"That was Kiel," Rick said and blew out through his nose like a bull about to charge. He turned back to his iPhone and tapped some message on it rather vigorously. "This is fucked!"

"What? Why?" I said, exchanging glances with Cho.

"Kiel's a witch," he said while tapping some more on his iPhone. "She's also my ex, but that probably has nothing to do with it." He stopped and looked up. "At least I hope not." He resumed his tapping a little more vigorously with his thumbs. "Christ!"

"Should I go after her?" Cho offered.

Rick looked up briefly. "Knock yourself out."

Cho jumped up and sprinted through the room and disappeared through the doorway, almost barreling into someone else coming out, but he turned his thin body in order to miss her. The woman he narrowly missed shuffle through, looking back at where Cho had gone as if trying to understand what was going on. Shaking her head, she went up to the desk.

"Sabrina?" A female nurse stepped through the doorway. I recognized her from the other night from Tremayne's underground complex. She was the blonde elf nurse.

I stood and looked over to Rick. He was pulling on his ear. I figured it was like scratching his head, since he couldn't reach his head easily. I think it was his own nervous reaction to stress. "Is everything going to be okay, Rick?" I asked.

"I'll deal with this stuff. You go and get your plasma taken. I'll keep my eyes on things out here," Rick said, his eyes darting around.

I followed the nurse toward the doorway, worried about the significance of the woman, Kiel, being here while I'm supposed to give plasma. Was she here to screw things up? I paused to look around. It was open, no walls, only the machines to block my view. Where could the woman have gone?

I remembered the elf's name and greeted her. "You're Ariel, right?"

"Yes. Is everything okay?" she asked in a hushed voice while we walked through the donation area. She stood a little taller than myself and her hair was styled away from her face, but not so that the tips of her ears showed.

"I'm not sure," I said. We paused and she crinkled her brow.

"Why? What's wrong?"

"Well, did you see a woman with deep auburn hair, short, and styled kinda… I don't know—" I motioned with my hands around my head. "Sort sticking of out all over her head like she's put her finger in a light socket?"

"I guess I missed her." She chuckled. "Why?"

"Rick called her by the name of Kiel," I explained. "He said she's a witch."

Ariel paused, and I stopped again to look at her. This information made her uncomfortable, I could tell.

"We weren't prepared for a witch, I guess," Ariel said, looking around. "You say Rick knows her?"

I nodded. "She saw Rick and flew out of here." I didn't mean that literally, but now I wondered if she'd used the ley line connections to leave the premises.

"That's understandable," she said. Then she grasped my arm lightly. "I meant that in a good way." She laughed, and the freckles on her cheeks stood out with the way her cheeks rose.

I chuckled with her to show I understood. "He indicated they had some history."

"Oh?"

"And he wasn't sure if she was here to do something, or what."

"I see." She turned toward a machine like the last one I had been hooked up to. "Here you go," she directed me to one of the chairs. Not quite as comfortable as what I'd had last time. Darn.

"Let me get you all hooked up."

I nodded, glad that she had shown up. If I'd had a regular nurse touching me, that would have been bad. I got no read from Ariel because she was an elf. She put on the latex gloves and while I looked away, she stuck the needle into the crook of my arm. At least she was quick about it. It felt like a hard pinch and then that was it.

Ariel was bent at my side placing my arm on the platform, and then she dipped to the floor.

"Oh, is this yours?" She came up holding an earring. Antique-looking, it was dangle-y with what I guessed were amber beads. *Yep, amber and silver*, my Knowing supplied.

"No. It's very pretty. I—wait a moment," I said, thinking back to that woman Kiel. She had been wearing those types of earrings, come to think of it. "I think I know who it belongs to. May I have it?"

"Of course," she laid the earring into the palm of my other hand, which was still covered with a glove.

"And could you ask Rick to come back here?"

She made a quick glance toward the front. "Sure," she said low, and then left me.

I clenched my fist like I'd been told. I became chilled during the process and had the same metallic taste in my mouth as before. I had no blanket, so pulled my coat up to cover myself with my one free hand, the best I could. But it didn't help much. I kept shivering. I wondered if this second donation would help Tremayne get better all the way, or would they expect me back for more. I hoped not. This was not a fun way to spend a good part of an hour.

"Sabrina?" I looked up. Cho and Rick appeared around the machine. They looked like a two-faced totem pole looking in at me.

"Hey," I said. "Look." I held out the earring to Rick. "Look familiar?"

Cho eyed it and I lifted it up by the hook for him to look at.

"She was wearing earrings like that," Cho said.

"Yeah," Rick said, plucking the earring from my fingers. "Those are like what she'd wear." He looked up. "Where did you find it?"

"Actually Ariel found it on the floor, right here." I lifted my eyes to Cho. "What happened to you? Did you lose her?"

"I did," he said. "I tried to follow, but she vanished."

"She can travel the ley lines. There's a pretty good one here," Rick said, looking around.

"I must have been too nervous to notice," I said, shivering. "Now I'm just cold."

"The blood leaving you does that," Rick said. "You're lucky that Ariel came to do this. She's pretty good."

"Rick. You said we were screwed. Why? Because of Kiel being here?" I asked.

He hedged. "Maybe. Like I said. I don't know why she was here."

"Let's find out," I suggested.

Cho and Rick exchanged glances.

"How?" Rick asked.

"Here." I handed him the earring. He took it. I then held my hand toward Cho. "Take the glove off my hand." He did as I asked. "Now, Rick, place the earring in my hand. I may go into a swoon, but I'm almost lying flat, and have nothing better to do."

"We'll stand guard," Rick said and carefully settled the piece of jewelry in my hand. My skin tingled, and then heat radiated from the object. I pulled in a surprised breath. After a moment, the tingling dissipated.

"You okay, Brie?" Rick asked, his hand hovering over mine.

I swallowed, looking into his brown eyes. I waited. I felt an odd *something*, but nothing specific. "I'm getting nothing."

"It might be charmed," Rick said.

"Okay. Get rid of it." I paused. "Wait. Put it in my purse." I pointed to my purse on the floor.

Rick took the earring out of my hand and stuck it inside my purse.

We were quiet for a few heartbeats. Then I had to ask.

"Tell me what you know about this witch?"

"Kiel Saint Thomas is no saint by any means," Rick said. "I knew her about five years ago. We dated." His eyes slid back to Cho, then on me. "I thought things were going great. And then I realized she was using me to learn… things."

"Learn things?" I said. "Like what?"

"Well, ley line travel, for one."

"You knew she was a witch?"

"I knew it the moment we met."

"Where did you meet?" Cho asked.

"In a club on the north side."

"Really?" I said.

"And we sort of hit it off." He beamed and slid his eyes again to Cho and rolled them. "The sex was fabulous."

Cho and I wisely kept silent.

"She had me help her in certain spells," he said slowly, eyes cast down. "I didn't like what those spells were for."

"Why? What were they for?"

"She was trying to raise the dead."

"Oh, come on!" I said.

"No. I'm telling you the truth!" He put up three fingers like a boy scout. "It's been done by famous witches like John Dee, and others. Anyway, once she asked if I knew any vampires. You know, personally?"

"And you probably did," I supplied.

"I did. But I was getting some bad vibes off of her and where she wanted to go with her witchcraft. I thought it sounded more like black craft than white. She wanted to go after certain people who had wronged her, that sort of thing. Also, she wanted to raise a demon."

"Yes. Definitely black magic," I said.

"Of course, I hesitated in introducing her to any vampires. But it doesn't take much to find one, especially if you're a witch." He shrugged. "Anyway, I broke it off. I had to have another witch put a protection spell on me so that she couldn't hex me."

"Really?" I found it hard to believe he couldn't put up his own wall of protection.

"It's a bit complicated," he said, seeing my dismay.

"Kiel probably has found a couple of vampires by now," I stated the obvious.

"No doubt."

"Rick, I'm not sure what level Kiel is at, but if she's in with the wrong vampires..." I trailed off.

"You mean the likes of Ilona and Nicolas?" he suggested.

I slid him a look. "Yes. Them. She may be in cahoots with them to find me and do something to prevent me from giving blood, today."

"Most likely," Cho piped in. "Maybe she was here to take your donation and keep it from reaching Tremayne so that he would die?"

"Yep," Rick said. "That would be just her style, too."

"No doubt Cho is right." I sat for a moment thinking, shivering again. My coat had slipped off me some. Cho moved it up and arranged it around my shoulders. "Thanks." I held the coat in place with my free hand. "I'm wondering if I were to take the earring to another witch she might learn something from it?"

"I don't know," Rick said. "Worth a try, I guess."

I thought of Mrs. Bench. I owed her a visit. The last time, she had brought over rum cake and we talked about Bill's death and consoled one another. I thought about what I could bring to her. Cookies? I made a mental list of things in my refrigerator and cupboard. I knew she liked my peanut butter cookies.

Someone's cell phone rang.

Rick pulled his out and looked. "Not me."

"Oh. It's mine," I said looking down toward my purse on the floor. "I can't reach it."

"I'll get it." Cho dipped and reached into my bag. He rose from his stoop with the phone at his ear already. "Hello, Ms. Strong is not available right now, this is Ty. Can I take a message?"

Rick's brows rose as we exchanged impressed glances.

"Who?" Cho said. Then covering the phone with his hand he said to me, "It's Hobart."

"Oh!" I reached for the phone and Cho put it in my hand. "Hello?" I said.

"Sabrina? Are you alright? I found your Jeep—it was buried over on Ram Road!" Hobart had never sounded more frightened and relieved.

"Yes. I'm fine. I'm in town at BioPlasma, having my plasma taken from me."

"How did you get out? Hell, I've been worried sick!" Hobart must have been panicked, as he never used curse words in front of me.

"It's alright, Hobart. I'm okay. Rick came to our rescue. Ty and Rick are both here with me. I'll probably be another half hour here. Then I'll pop back home. Where are you at?"

"I'm actually at your place. I couldn't get back home. I couldn't go anywhere, in fact. It's this storm. It's picked up big time. They're closing roads everywhere. They say it's a Nor-eastern."

"Wow. I'm glad you made it back to my place. You're inside?"

"Yeah. Door wasn't locked. I hope you don't mind? I had nowhere else to go."

"No. Make yourself at home. I'll be back soon. Just, whatever you do, don't go upstairs. Vasyl is up there."

"Oh. Yeah. Got you. Not that he'd be up."

"Well, being a master, he could get up any time, since we've got a nasty storm."

"Right," Hobart's gravely voice rumbled in my ear.

"Okay, I'll be back in a while. Don't be startled if we suddenly appear, 'coz we're going by ley line."

"Ley line?" he asked.

"I'll explain later. But we'll be there in a little while." We said good bye and hung up.

Closing my cellphone, I looked up at the two guys next to me. "Hobart's at my house. He said they're closing roads—this storm became worse since we left. Said it's a Nor-easter, and he couldn't get home."

Rick consulted his iPhone. "Odd," he said.

"What?" I said.

"That the weather forecast for today was windy, but with sun. How did we go from that to a storm?" He met my eyes.

"Demons can control weather," I said, brows raised with the significance.

"So can witches. Strong ones," Rick said.

"*Gèn*. Mountain. It also means *northeast*," Cho said.

I had another chill. I'm not sure if it was from the plasma giving process, but I shivered.

Chapter 16

Over—night Guests

Giving plasma a second time had drained me both in spirit and energy. Ariel had taken my donation and she assured me she would take it to Tremayne herself. We parted company at that point, her going one way and us going another.

Cho held me up as we stepped outside (in order to not startle anyone by our vanishing act). The wind whipped at us as Rick and I joined hands, and Cho held on to me. Two seconds later, I was glad to be home where it was warm and I knew we were safe. My ears popped when we returned to my house.

"Holy Living Hell!" Hobart's grating baritone startled us as we popped into the dining room.

"Sorry," I said taking in the big Were standing in my living room, one hand over his heart looking as though he'd seen three ghosts and passed a kidney stone at the same time. "I tried to warn you about our appearing out of thin air when I called you," I reminded.

"I thought… I mean," he trailed off. "I didn't realize that's what you really meant."

"Sorry," I said again. I looked up at Cho who still held on to me like I was going to fall. "I'm good, now, Ty. You can let go of me."

"Of course," he said and his strong arms released me.

I pulled off my coat. Rick was ahead of us and darted into the bathroom. I was beginning to wonder if Rick had a bladder problem or he simply liked the fancy soap I used in my bathroom and the plush towels.

After shucking off my boots, I padded through the living room, and angled toward my bedroom. "Everything okay?" I asked over my shoulder.

"All is quiet," Hobart said. He was watching TV, what I gathered was an old black & white western. He turned it off.

I opened up my bedroom door and slid it closed and locked it for privacy. The wind battering the north side of the house took the place of the noise of the television. Windows, although new, rattled in their fixtures. In fact it was colder in this north room—the direction of the wind—and I wanted to get changed pronto and out of there.

I came out, and slid the pocket door shut. I now had three men in my house and had to mentally take stock of what food I had available while I changed back into my sweats. Bulky, warm, and comfortable they'd be appropriate for my motley male company. While I wasn't sure if Rick would stay overnight, I knew I now had to put Hobart up somewhere. I still had room, in fact if push came to shove, I had a fold-out bed in the couch in the den, and one small extra bed in my old bedroom upstairs, and there was also a cot. The cot was put away in the extra room where we stored things we didn't use often. Our camping equipment, extra chairs, some old suit cases and large bins with extra clothing for seasonal change, filled the unfinished room. My dad had not fixed it up since we had no need for another bedroom.

I emerged from my bedroom in my sweats, thinking that Vasyl was better off upstairs in his own cocoon of quiet and darkness. Although I knew he would not have been awoken by any of the activities down here, but then I wasn't certain what would wake Vasyl up during his sleep, which was usually very deep. But yesterday, he'd woke when Bill's sister came over (but then, he was downstairs where all the action was).

Rick was back out of the bathroom looking at his iPhone again.

"Alright!" he said. "Ariel texted me and said that she arrived at Tremayne's compound, and they're giving him the plasma as we speak." He looked up at me. "She says that she'll get back to us in twenty-four hours to let us know how it went."

"Good." I stepped into the kitchen to peek into the refrigerator and then my cupboards. I stopped my motions, overwhelmed by my emotions. *Please let him get better. Please?* I didn't know if God cared about vampires. I didn't know if asking God was right, in fact. I could not predict the outcome of this. I had to force myself to move on. I sucked it up and worried about feeding people in my house. Cho, of course, was still on his fast, which meant he was one less mouth to feed.

I did a mental walk-through of what I had on-hand. I had plenty of staples, like rice, pasta, noodles, and dried beans, and plenty of stewed tomatoes. I also had beef and chicken stock, knowing full well I would want those things once winter set in. Good that I had thought ahead and bought things I might need. There was never enough warning when a bad storm, like this one, would come in during the winter. I mentally patted myself on the back.

I moved to the freezer to check on my home-grown frozen vegetables. There were plenty more out in the larger freezer. Our garden, which my father and I had planted in the spring, had boasted a good yield. I'd harvested it all myself. I'd managed to freeze the beans, corn, plus there was a bushel of carrots, onions and potatoes each put away in the basement where it was cool and dark. I noticed one frozen pizza—which was not enough to share—deer sausage, and ice cream. The ice cream would not be desired tonight. I thought about making up a batch of hot cocoa to warm everyone up maybe later on. I really had not planned on having house guests, but it was good that I could make due with my larder, thanks to all the sweat and toil I went through to keep it all, including two dozen quarts of tomatoes, minus one I used the other night. I decided to make another pot of soup. All I needed was another deer roast. Hobart, the werewolf guy, would definitely want the meat.

"I need a volunteer to go out to the deep freezer in the shop and grab me a deer roast."

Hobart rose. "I'll go." Entering the dining room, he grabbed his boots where they sat on the big rug I'd put out for snow boots. They looked warm and impervious to snow.

"If he knows where it is, I can take him," Rick suggested and wiggled his eye brows.

"Oh, yeah," I said. "That would be better than making him trudge through the snow."

"Which is getting deeper by the moment," Rick reminded.

"Unless he isn't willing to be transported by magic," I amended, glancing at Hobart who gave us a confused look.

"What do you mean?" he asked, standing into his boots.

"I mean Rick can take you out directly to the shop and bring you back, you don't have to go through the snow," I explained.

"Naw," Hobart said, and bent back down to work on his boot lacings. "I'd rather do it the old fashioned way with my own two feet. I'm not too crazy about traveling in no magical way."

"Okay, suit yourself," Rick said and ambled into the living room, found the remote and deposited his rump in one of the two recliners. I knew he'd be disappointed because I didn't have HBO, or two hundred channels to surf through, as he liked to do. He would become bored as soon as he figured this out.

Hobart went out the door, and the bitter cold swept in momentarily.

Meanwhile, I pulled out a large cast iron pot. I realized only then that Cho was nowhere to be seen. I didn't see when he'd gone upstairs. Probably while I was changing.

After about six or eight minutes, Hobart came through the door again, stomping his feet loudly. I poked my head out to take him in. He was covered in snow. From head to foot. Mostly his legs were caked in the snow he had to trudge through.

"It's cold out there!" He stood holding my roast like a football, and it was nearly as large as one.

"You okay?" I asked because he didn't move, except for the shivering.

"As soon as my eyelids unfreeze from my eyeballs, and my joints thaw out, I'll be fine."

"I offered to get you in and out," Rick muttered from the living room.

"I'd take you up on it, if I had to do it all over again, friend," Hobart said.

I plucked the frozen roast from his hands. It felt as solid and as cold as a piece of ice chopped from an iceberg. I would have to thaw it out in the microwave. I had a quart of tomatoes out, but I was ahead of myself. The roast would need to be cooked and cut down to bite-sized pieces first. I had to plan out what to do when it came to cooking for a group of people. The last time, I had *planned* to make the soup, but had to go to Kansas and never ate any until this morning. Today, I realized I had all afternoon to cook the soup. Lunch was whatever they could find. Maybe I'd pop some popcorn, later.

Hobart pulled off his boots and coat, hung his coat up and joined Rick in the living room.

My house phone rang. I surged to grab it.

"Hello?"

"Brie?" It was my brother. Crap. I should have called him earlier.

"What's up? How are you guys? Everything okay?" I asked rapid fire.

"About as good as they can be under the snowstorm," he said. "But I called to ask you something."

"Shoot."

"What the hell happened last night?"

"What do you mean?" I asked with trepidation.

"I mean, I don't remember leaving your place, all I remember is getting home and wanting to place garlic all over the house and wear a crucifix, and make everyone else wear one. Constance thought I'd lost it. But I feel compelled to do these things. So, I'm just wondering—y'know—if you know what's going on."

My first impulse was to deny I knew anything. That was my normal response and I knew immediately that was the wrong way to go about this. My brother and his family were in danger. I hoped not in as much danger as me, but the likelihood of vampires messing with them was high.

"Yeah. About that. Are you sure you don't remember anything I, or Vasyl told you?" I prompted.

"Vasyl?" There was a pause and I could almost hear the wheels spinning. "Wait, I remember something." He chuckled. "Oh, wait. Yeah. There was something about vampires."

"Yes. We spoke to you about the real danger vampires pose—"

In my ear Randy burst with laughter. I pulled the ear piece away and looked at it as though I could see him laughing. I waited until he became breathless.

"Are you through?" I asked.

"Brie, if you're joking around—"

"I'm not," I said with a serious voice. "Randy, listen, you have to keep your family inside during the night and don't answer the door. Although Rick put a pretty good ward on your house, you never know what sort of tricks they may use." I heard dead sound. "Hello?"

"I didn't understand one word you said just now. And who's Rick?"

"Uh, right. Rick's a friend. Anyway, don't go outside at night and don't answer the door." As I said this I turned toward the double windows over the sink. They faced north. White blocked my view. Snow had wedged itself in between the screen and window making a white wall. It was as though we were buried. Maybe we were.

"Because?" Randy asked in my ear.

"Vampires—the bad ones—may try to attack you. They attacked my house soon after you left last night."

"Vampires," he said, deadpan.

"Yes. Vasyl had to fight them off, he was injured, but he's okay, now."

"Vasyl fought off the vampires?"

"Yes. He's a vampire master. Remember? We told you all this last night." Gads it was like talking to a three year old.

Another few seconds of no sound except his breathing. "Is Vasyl there right now?"

"He's sleeping."

"Sleeping?" Randy repeated. "Oh. Because he's a vampire, right? And I suppose he sleeps in a coffin?"

"No. He sleeps in a bed. Vampires don't have to sleep in coffins," I said. "But they do sleep during the day."

I heard him pull in a deep breath and blow out, sounding like an exasperated bull. "Brie, I don't know what's going on with you anymore, but when Vasyl does wake up, you have him call me. I need to speak to someone who isn't hallucinating." I wasn't going to let his snide remark get to me. I ignored it.

"I'll have him call you, later on, when he is up," I said. "Good bye." I hung up, my nerves all jangly as I did. If he didn't believe me, how much more would he believe Vasyl? Of course, Vasyl might have the power to control him over the phone. But I wasn't sure, since he hadn't bitten my brother.

"Everything okay?" I turned to the voice and found Rick standing in the threshold of the kitchen.

"It's fine. I had to set my brother straight on a few things."

"Right."

I stepped over to the other windows to find I could look out these, but all I could see were white drifts surrounding the house and between the buildings. Blowing snow didn't allow me to see past the barn.

"Rick?" I turned to find him rooting around in my refrigerator.

He popped his head back out and closed the door of the refrigerator, looking guilty. "What? I-I mean..."

"Are you hungry?" I was hungry too. I stepped over to the freezer and peeked inside. I couldn't think of anything else we had to appease the appetites as quickly as a pizza. I pulled it out. It was large sausage, mushroom, and five cheeses.

"I'll put this in the oven."

"Oh. Good." He looked a little relived. "I was considering going out for lunch."

"Are you kidding? Besides, there won't be anything open." I switched on the oven.

"Tom's place is *always* open," he said.

"I suppose it would be." I smiled thinking of the small bar called Tom's Hideaway, where leprechauns and supernaturals seemed to congregate.

The lights flickered. Both Rick and I looked up at the lights. I had a gas oven, so we were good with food. But if we had a power outage, my freezer and fridge wouldn't work, and the well couldn't work. Without water, we couldn't flush the toilet, and that would be bad with this many people in the house.

But the lights went back on, and stayed on.

"Good," I said, relief rushing through me. "I don't think we want to sit around in the dark."

Hobart stepped in. "You know you have a generator out in the shop."

I looked up. "Yeah, but I don't know how to hook it up. My father knew."

"I could do it. If we have a problem," he offered.

"I hope we don't have a problem," I said. "But thanks. It's reassuring to me you guys are around."

"Vasyl wouldn't know how to?" Hobart asked.

"Are you kidding?" I scoffed mildly as I set the oven temperature for 400°. "He hardly knows how to turn on a light, let alone do anything mechanical or electrical." The two men exchanged glances. "He's from the first century, don't forget."

"Yeah, but other vampires as old as he are up with the times," Rick argued. "Look at Tremayne. He's as modern as they come."

"Not Vasyl. He is not interested in technology at all. He doesn't approve of most of it. He doesn't even wear shoes for crying out loud! I had to ask him to shove his feet into some shoes last night for company, and he wouldn't do it."

"Wow."

"No way would I let you have a black-out, toots," Rick assured. "Leave it up to me."

"Thanks, Rick." I sighed and looked at the back of the pizza box for the instructions.

"So, we're having pizza for lunch?" Hobart asked, eyeing the box in my hand.

"Well, I know it's not much, but I don't have much in my freezer, other than frozen vegetables."

"Too bad we're stuck in a blizzard," Hobart said.

"Why?" Rick asked.

"I was thinking of what I had in my refrigerator," Hobart said, giving Rick a smile.

"What?"

"Ribs. A full rack."

"What?" Rick said. "Oh, I could go for some ribs."

The two men were considering the possibility with vacant, far-off stares.

"I could pop you over there," Rick suggested, wiggling his brows.

"You could? Really?" With hands on narrow hips Hobart glanced down at the leprechaun.

"Yep. Just direct me, and I'll get you over there."

"What kind of ribs are they?" I asked.

"St. Louis style. Got a whole slab. Won't take more than twenty or so minutes to heat up," Hobart said.

"Okay," I said. "Go and get them and grab whatever else you want for overnight. Like beer?"

"I'll do that." Hobart looked down at Rick. "You can really get me there?"

"Does the bear shit in the woods?" Rick said.

"Hell." Hobart paused. "Well, okay. Let me get my coat and boots—"

"Won't need them," Rick said, fingers splaying. "But you'll have to hold onto my hand."

Hobart looked at his hands situated at his shoulders.

"You don't want to get lost in the network. That would be really bad," Rick said.

"It's like a blink of an eye," I assured him.

"Alright," Hobart said. "I'm game."

The two meandered into the next room. The oven pinged to tell me it reached the desired temperature. While I slid the pizza into the oven, the two men vanished.

The lights flickered again, but came back on and stayed on.

Fearing that the lights might go out and never come back on, I decided to get my roast into the microwave before I couldn't use it. Of course, Rick would probably keep my electricity running, if it came down to that. It was good to have a leprechaun around in times like these. I remember once we went without electricity for two and a half days. That was ridiculous. Especially when we didn't have any water supply for either drinking, washing or flushing the toilet.

We only had the fireplace to keep warm in the one room. My father took us to the nearest motel.

The atmosphere bent. I could see a portion of my kitchen become wavy, like a portal was opening. This was really unusual. I gasped and shunted back and collided with the stove. I cried out as I jumped away when my skin came into contact with the hot stove. I grasped the fingers of my glove in my teeth and tugged it off. Something was coming in here and I hoped it was a demon. Or a vampire. *It couldn't be a vampire. Not yet. Oh, my God, I can't believe I wished that a demon was coming into my house!*

Two bodies plunked down in my kitchen. At first I didn't recognize them.

"Oh, shit!" The voice I recognized. Then the black hair and her familiar build as she turned around. She blinked at me.

"Lindee?" I gasped. Her eyes popped, gaping at me. She wore a floor-length black dress with a white apron and some sort of small bonnet on her head.

Ignoring the fact that there was someone else in the room, and that she had come through a ley line network that whisked her from one planet to this one, she crossed the room and embraced me tightly.

"Ohmygod! I can't believe I'm here!" Lindee looked around when we let each other go. She spied my microwave, saw it running with the light on. She rushed over and embraced it. "Oh! Modern technology! God! I miss it *sooooo* much!" She kissed the top of the microwave, and patted it affectionately. Quickly she let it go. I imagined it was somewhat warm to the touch.

My chuckle was interrupted by a pair of arms going around me and I was again embraced by someone.

I pushed at him. "Jacob, stop," I said, looking up into a pair of brilliant blue eyes that threatened to consume me if I continued staring. I averted my gaze.

"But I brought your cousin home. Do I not get a hug?" he asked dolefully.

"Well. Yes." And he hugged me again. "But that's all." I pressed my hand with the mystical ring into him, and that did the trick. He stepped back, releasing me, but looking as though I'd burned him.

"Sorry."

He turned to Lindee. "You see? I wasn't lying."

"No, you sure weren't. Thank you!" Lindee excitedly grabbed my hand. "Oh! I have to tell you everything!"

The stench of body odor and wood smoke invaded. I stood back, leaning my head away, putting a hand over my nose. "Oh, my God, Lindee. You need a shower. Bad!"

"Yeah." Letting go of my hand, she wrinkled her nose and lifting her armpits, sniffed. "They really need to figure out the hygiene thing, I mean there is *no* deodorant. Just perfume and soap. And all day long I'm working over a wood fire. It's hot and nasty."

"I thought you loved it," I said.

"I did. At first, because it was different. And it wasn't home. And it was sort of fun." She shrugged. "A challenge."

"Right."

"But, God, I miss this!" She put her hands out, palms up. "Electricity, and just *everything*."

"At the moment we have a blizzard and I don't know if the electricity will stay on."

She turned to the microwave. "What do you have in here, anyway?"

"Venison. It's thawing out. I'm making soup for tonight."

"Sounds great!"

"For lunch I've got a pizza in the oven and a couple of friends went out to grab a few other things. They should be back soon."

"Meanwhile, could I please take a shower?" Lindee said. "I don't want to meet your other friends smelly, and wearing this." She grasped her black maid's dress and drew it out at her sides.

"Agreed. Go to my bathroom, and I'll dig up something you should be able to wear." We both migrated out of the kitchen. Lindee blabbering all the way to the bathroom. Jacob in tow.

"I mean, ohmygod!" she gushed. "That place. The vampires!" her voice echoed in the bathroom. "Did you know that Dracula was there? Oh, yeah. You'd have seen him. But ohmygod!"

I continued on to my bedroom while Lindee had diarrhea of the mouth. I opened the bathroom door and went in, pushed Jacob out and held up my magic ring in warning. He looked slighted, but left the room. Lindee stood between the sink and tub/shower peeling off her skirt and top, her voice muffled for a moment, and she grunted with the action. She got down to her camisole and bloomers, still blabbering about Black Veil, Dracula and all his relations.

I'd been there and knew pretty much all of it, so everything she said wasn't news to me.

I moved for my bureau, knowing I had an older pair of sweats that she would easily fit into, since she was about my size—except in the bust area. I also had some "emergency" undies. I brought these items into the bathroom and settled them on the small chair.

"I mean Drachen was a dreamboat, and I let him take blood from me—"

"Lindee!" I gasped, looking at her.

"It was cool. I mean, really. It was *very* cool. But Jett's father, Dracula? Crap, he was scary as hell. I mean I was so afraid he'd want to do things to me."

"Was it getting that bad?" I asked, arms folded in front of me.

"I had the feeling, you know, at times when he'd call me in to bring him blood—you know that kind in a bottle—?"

"Yes." I certainly did know what kind she meant. The vampires of Black Veil ruled their world, and people did donate blood willingly, and some were paid well for it.

"Anyway, he'd give me these looks over the rim of the glass as he drank. He'd make me stay until he was satisfied by the quality of it. I just had these creepy feelings about him and what he was thinking. Y'know?"

"I sure do," I said. "But I was promised no vampire could touch you, because you were already house help. Plus, I did something for Drakulya." I'd saved his wife's life. He had considered me his warrior, in fact, and owed me.

"I know," she said. "You saved his wife, and got rid of all those creepy things—"

"Dreadfuls," I supplied.

"Yeah. But things were beginning to get a little, I don't know… strange." She stood completely nude before me and *I* was beginning to feel strange. I had to avert my eyes to give her privacy.

"Everything okay in there?" the male voice startled us making us scream.

I turned to find Jacob had stepped into my bedroom once again. He certainly had nerve.

"Get out of here!" I muscled him back out of the room and shut the door. "You aren't helping things, you know?" I scolded.

He made a puppy-dog face. He looked cute doing that, and made me feel horrible. *Damn it. I'm not going to let him get to me.*

"That's not going to fly," I said. He stood close to me, and moved closer.

"I have missed you," he said, his hands gliding over my arms. The fact that I could not remember him or what we did, was not helpful. But because he was an incubus, I was pretty sure we did have sex since I'd had little odd memories pop into my head. These little overtures made it obvious.

"Listen," I said, pointing a finger in his face. "I'm married to a vampire now. So don't even think about it."

"Vampire? Interesting." He squeezed his chin in thought. "Your cousin, however is unmarried?"

I gave him a glare. "You try it and I'll send you back to Dark World."

He crossed his arms in front of him. "I do not believe you can do that."

"Try me!" He didn't budge. "Move. Out! Out! Out!" I said, thrusting my right hand, mystical ring uncovered, in his face.

This time he could not help but do as I said. He scurried out of my room, a mixed look of outrage and surprise as he did. I felt awesome and powerful, and drew my head back and laughed. *God, that felt good.*

But now I had a demon in my house. Not *just* a demon, a frigging incubus. My vampire husband would probably have a real hissy fit. That made one leprechaun, a Were, a demon, a vampire, and if Dante showed up, God help us!

The shower going in the bath caught my attention. I thought about the things Lindee had told me that happened to her in Black Veil. I wondered if she was planning on going back. If she didn't, and stayed, would she go back to her looser days of drug and alcohol abuse? I wished there was some easy way to help Lindee stay here, and stay out of trouble.

My emotions dropping from a great high, I wandered back into the living room and shut my bedroom door. Voices from the kitchen told me Rick and Hobart were back.

"Well, I'll be a fairy on a pile of dog shit!" Rick said. "Jacob! How the hell are you?"

I groaned and surged for the kitchen where the men were getting acquainted—or re-acquainted. Rick was telling Hobart how he, Tremayne, and myself wound up in Dark World about a month back, and met Jacob.

"... And the women took us back to this room with the biggest bath you've ever seen and they—"

"Okay," I said, holding up my hands. "I don't mind you telling Hobart what you did in that place, but I don't want to hear it. Okay?"

"Oh. Sure, Sabrina. Didn't mean to." Rick became suddenly red in the face, and said on the sly, "I'll tell you later." Hobart nodded.

My eyes took in Hobart and then slid to Jacob. How the hell could I have forgotten him? He was too delicious. My only thought was that perhaps my synapses had been burned somehow, at some point after. Or, perhaps it was some after effect of being with an incubus. Could they erase your memories of having been bedded by them?

"Brought lunch!" Hobart said, holding up a couple of grocery bags. He knew how to change the subject quickly. He took out the package of ready-to-heat ribs.

"Fantastic! I'll get them into the oven. As you can see I have a couple of guests to add to the fun." I reached down to get a baking sheet for the ribs. "My cousin was brought back from Black Veil by Jacob, here. She'll be joining us shortly."

"Wow. More people," Rick said. "It's like a party."

Hobart had his nose to the air, his Were senses going. He already knew another woman was in the house, I could tell by the way his eyes dilated.

"She's had trouble, guys. She went to Black Veil, willing to give up everything—like drugs and alcohol in order to dry out. So, be mindful. Okay? She might have some issues… with things." I was trying to hint, but I wasn't being hint-y enough because I got blank stares.

"Never mind," I said and worked on opening the package of ribs. I pulled out aluminum foil and tore off a large sheet. Pizza smells filled the kitchen. Checking my timer, I read the directions for the ribs. It was a different temperature. I would wait until the pizza was done before putting in the ribs.

"Here's the deal. I will heat up everything and you guys eat whatever you want." I went to the cupboard and pulled out some plates. "The pizza will be out in a few minutes," I announced.

Ten minutes later Lindee's voice pierced the house with her exuberance. "I smell pizza!"

I turned to watch her flounce into the kitchen, hair still wet, her large boobies bouncing, making me blush for her, since she didn't have the sense to.

"After weeks of not shaving my legs and underarms, I'm finally smooth!" She drew a big-toothed comb through her thick hair. "I haven't had pizza in ages!"

"You actually made a rather good one, I recall, when I was there in Black Veil," I said with a smirk.

She looked at me squarely. "I did as best I could with the ingredients. You'd think these people would have heard of tomato sauce! Sheesh!" She banged the heel of her palm to her head, then shook it sadly, stepping away. She stopped and took in Hobart and Rick. "Oh, are these your friends you were telling me about?"

"Lindee, this is Hobart, and this is Rick. Rick is a leprechaun." I said.

"Oh, hi!" She strode forward and shook hands while I did the introductions. Then she stopped mid-way between Hobart and Rick. "Oh crap!" She looked at the hand that was attached to Rick's shoulder by about four inches of wrist. Her eyes went large. "I'm sorry. I feel so *stupid*." Her apologetic wince and a touch on his shoulder made Rick smile.

"No problem kid. It's a birth defect. I'm used to it."

"Yeah, you're used to it. It's taking me a few minutes to not stare." Lindee let out her trade-mark infectious laugh that got us all laughing. Lindee turned her attention to the ribs. "Ribs too? Wow!"

"Yep. I'll be putting them in when the pizza gets done." I arranged them on the sheet of aluminum foil and began to fold the ends.

"We brought the coleslaw and potato salad too," Hobart said, beaming. "I was planning on having that tonight."

"Well, you'll be sharing it with all of us," Lindee said.

"Don't mind sharing." Hobart gleamed at her.

Mine was not a small kitchen, but add several people to it, it became small quickly.

"Okay, everyone," I said. "I'll call you when things are done. Why don't you go into the other room and make yourselves scarce." The men filed out of the room. I heard two pull tabs being popped. Hobart and Rick both had beers. Figures that Hobart would bring back beer. A good thing he did, I was nearly out. "Hey!" I said, and they twisted their heads to look at me. "It's barely past noon and you're drinking already?" I was having fun with them.

"It's four o'clock somewhere, sweety pie," Rick said, and took a healthy sip.

"Besides, we're celebrating the first real blizzard in years!" Hobart said looking positively excited. I wasn't sure why he'd celebrate that. Unless he snowplowed for money.

I turned into a pair of arms and was embraced. The smell of ozone and brimstone filled me.

"I missed you," Jacob said softly over my head.

"Jacob, take yourself into the other room with the guys." I pulled away from him, then I surged for the refrigerator and pulled out a cold one. "Here." I handed it to him. He gave it a curious look.

"What do I do with it?"

I snapped the tab back. "Drink it." I placed it into his hands and pushed him out of the room.

"God, even I didn't drink until late afternoon," Lindee said. "So, give me the low down on this Jacob? He is hot! Didn't you say he was a demon of some sort?"

"Yeah." I studied her. No make-up and no nose- and eyebrow-rings, she almost looked like the girl I once knew. I'd missed her and couldn't help myself and pulled her into a fierce hug. "I worried about you. Not just when you were in that place." We let go and looked at one another. "But always," I finished.

She glance down. "Yeah. Thanks. I thought about you a lot, too." She glanced up. "They told me what you did. I mean *there*. I don't understand it, exactly."

"That's okay. I'll try and up-date you. Since you know about vampires—"

"Oh, boy do I know about vampires!" We chuckled.

I smiled patently. "I'm married to one."

She bent forward, eyes popping as she grabbed my arms. "Get OUT!"

"Vasyl. He's upstairs sleeping."

"Right. He'd be sleeping during the day," she said, nodding. She let go, remembering she shouldn't be touching me because I might go into a semiautomatic state and spout about things she's been up to. I can't edit what I see.

"And Hobart is a werewolf, by the way. He's a nice guy, but I'm telling you, he can seriously hurt people. Plus, he saved me from a burning building once."

"Really!" she gasped.

"Oh, hell," I said, realization washing over me. "I can't catch you up in just a few hours. It would take days."

"That's alright," she said with a wave. "We'll have time. I don't plan on going back there." Tucking the dark hair behind her ears, she bent to peek in at the pizza. "This looks done."

We took out the pizza and placed it on a cooling rack, then adjusting the temperature, and slid in the ribs.

Lindee leaned against the counter, an oven mitt on her hand. "I know I've been a pain in the ass to everyone," she said, hands moving. "I think the best thing that happened to me is going into that portal and winding up in that place, as strange as that sounds." She made an exasperated sound, and shook her hair back. "Figures *that* would only happen to me."

I settled on a chair and leaned my head on a hand, elbow on the table. "I didn't want to leave you there unless you were sure. You seemed so… happy."

"I was." She crossed her arms and looked down at her feet. Flipping her hair back, she looked at me. "I don't know what you told my parents, but…"

"Oh, I'll update you on that, but they think you've been in a rehab place to dry out. I think they'll be amazed at the change."

She laughed. "Yeah. I think it'll shock them." She ran her hands through her still-damp hair. The curls were springing back. She hated her hair. "No more hair-do." She tugged on a strand and let it spring back. I noticed the brown roots and wondered if she would still color it.

"You should call them, let them know that you're here. You can say that I picked you up from the airport and you're staying here because of the blizzard."

She let out a puff of air. "Not yet. I'm not ready to talk to them just yet."

"Okay. When you are, I'll tell you what I told them," I said.

"I'm not real concerned about what I'll tell them, as to what to tell Ron, my boyfriend."

"Don't worry about it. You'll come up with something."

"But I am. I mean… shit," she said dismally. "I was *gone!*"

"If you think he can handle the truth, I'll back you up," I suggested.

"Wow." She looked at me. "I don't know if Ron is ready for me telling him about vampires, let alone traveling to some other planet."

"No. I suppose not, unless we can include quantum travel," I said and that got a bark of laughter out of her.

"Quantum travel, that's a good one, Brie." She laughed and slapped her knee. "You know he's into quantum theories?"

"That's funny." I laughed with her.

"But really what I have to tell him is I might be in love with someone else."

It was my turn to show surprise. "Who?" I hoped it wasn't Jett, or, worse, Drachen.

"Joha," she said, smiling broadly. "He's so cute. And intelligent!"

I chuckled, picturing the straight-laced, studious young man who liked to wear a top hat inside the palace all the time. I didn't think that Joha seemed very interested in women. But perhaps my cousin had turned his head, somehow. "When did this all happen?" I wondered.

"Oh, pretty much after you left. I don't know how it got started, but we've begun seeing each other."

"Sneaking around?" I wondered, hardly able to believe that Joha's father would allow him to be seeing a commoner.

"No. We were actually going to balls. His mother is a doll! She's given me dresses and nice jewelry."

"Yes. Gwendolen is a wonderful human being."

"And I can't get over the story that you saved her life," she said. "I wonder if I wasn't meant to go there. It was almost like I had gone back to another time."

"That portal in that park was put there on purpose, and you were lured to it," I reminded. "I didn't want to tell you this before, but that was a trap for me."

"A trap? What do you mean?"

I wanted to let her know as much as I could in only a few words as possible. I began by telling her about how I came into the vampire world, then briefly told her about Ilona, and how she was behind much of what happened to her and to me, lately. I explained that at this moment the only master vampire who could stop this was deathly ill and I was trying to help him out.

"Ilona has been trying to kill me from the start," I said, "and she's not likely to quit. If she was bold enough to trap you, to get to me, she'll go after someone else in my family next," I said, and paused for a heartbeat. "I'm afraid they may go after my brother and his family."

"Randy? Really? Why? I mean I don't get what they have against you."

I realized I hadn't explained that part, yet. "I'm what they call the sibyl. I have weapons that can maim vampires and kill demons and a few other things and they don't like it. But mainly they want to take over all of the vampire association in the U.S., and I'm in their way."

"Wow. Really? What sort of weapons?"

I suddenly felt like she was about eight years old and I was telling tall tales to her. "Well, I've got this dagger made of pure silver. And with this ring—" I held up my right hand to show her the mystical ring "—I can control demons, and vampires can't thrall me."

"Cool."

"Jacob is an incubus, and according to everyone who knows—" I looked at the doorway to make sure no one was within earshot "—he and I have done it."

She covered her tittering laugh. "I thought so. He is so whacked about you."

"I can keep him under control if I use this ring on him."

"God, I'd love a demonstration."

"I won't use it unless I have to," I said. "For your information, this house is under a very good protection spell they call a ward. So, we're safe from vampires attacking." I only wish I hadn't messed with the ward yesterday. I didn't want to overwhelm Lindee with any more information about my crazy life. It was bad enough I had to tell her this much.

Lindee breathed in. "Yum, the ribs are heating up. I'm starved for some good ol' American fast food."

"But you're definitely not going back?" I asked, wanting to make sure.

She slid me a look, no longer confident. "Well, if I do, I'm going to buy a butt load of razors, deodorant, and maybe two cases of tomato sauce."

"Better buy a can opener, too."

Chapter 17

Chance

Rick threw the dice onto the playing board. "C'mon, doubles!" he cried. When the pair of dice stopped a collective groan ran through the rest of us. "Hot damn! I still got it! Woo-hoo!" He leaned and grabbed the small car off the playing surface of the *Monopoly* game board where I had set it up on the coffee table. The five of us had settled on the floor around it. We were still working on getting our choice of playing pieces. Everyone wanted the car or the top hat, so we had to throw for it. I was in last place. I'd thrown a six on the dice. I knew I'd wind up with either the cannon or the iron. I took the iron to make things go quicker. *What do I care if I have an iron or a frigging car... it's only a game.* Hobart had grudgingly taken the top hat, while Rick snagged the car because he had "snake-eyes".

A stitch in my left side made me put a hand to it. No one noticed, but the pain surprised me.

Rick moved the car around the board making car noises, and then a squealing breaks sound when he brought it to a stop on GO, where the rest of us—or our playing pieces sat.

Earlier, there was nothing on television, and the guys looked restless— Hobart paced and looked out windows, Rick was watching something on his iPhone, and Cho was being Mr. Unsociable, and had remained upstairs. And my demon kept following me around. Okay, so the guys weren't all restless. But, I needed something to occupy everyone. I considered watching a video, but wasn't in the mood to dig out the box of videos (I had no DVD player, but wanted one, and thought about buying one this Christmas for myself). I decided to bring out the board games. I gave everyone a vote. *Monopoly* won out. I hadn't played since I was maybe twelve or thirteen, with my brother who *always* won. And, naturally, he always chose the car, and I'd take the iron. I don't know why I always took the iron.

"Now we toss for who goes first, second, third and last," I said. The pain in my side persisted. I tried to ignore it, but it really concerned me. *Maybe it was the cold air in my lungs earlier?*

"I'm going to buy up all the good places first," Rick bragged. "I used to be pretty good at this game when I was in the orphanage. We had the oldest version—probably the very first one—with wooden houses and motels," he went on. "A few of the cards were gone, and we had to draw and cut out our money from notepaper, 'cause it always got lost. But, I always won."

I exchanged glances with Lindee. We used to play marathon games, when she came over to stay for the weekends when we were much younger. She gave me a wink. We'd had a pretty long talk after lunch. I could tell that although she was happy to be back home, she had missed it. I asked her about it.

Looking off in the distance as she'd said, "It was like I was living some other life. Or a life in the past. You know?" I nodded, feeling there was more she wanted to say. "For the first time, while I was there, I felt the most comfortable, the most wanted, or needed. It was like I fit in there—I don't know how to explain it." Her lips trembled as she spoke, and my insides twisted. "And for once I was doing something I've always wanted to do—cook." I gave her another hug at that point. Her need to fit in ran deep. She didn't seem to fit here, on Earth, and tried to look as weird as she could. Maybe it was her frustration with her mother—she had mother issues—and the fact she never did well in school. But also she ran with the wrong crowd. I had the feeling Lindee was still confused about who she was and who she wanted to be, and maybe where she should be; here, or on Black Veil.

I could also see the danger in her being left on a planet where vampires ruled. I couldn't talk her out of returning, but she couldn't get there without my help. But she was so fresh away from it. Maybe in a few days, she might have a change of heart. After all, she seemed to be happy returning to where we had electricity and microwaves and deodorant.

After we figured out who went first on the board game and who went next, we began playing. Jacob had wedged himself between Lindee and me at the coffee table. He had questioned everything, of course. I was the only one who hadn't lost my temper with him asking a million questions. I explained the game to him, and I coached him through each step. He had picked the boat for a playing piece, looking at questioningly it when I told him what it was.

While I was turned away, Rick had changed the color of the houses and motels.

Lindee said she wanted hers to be pink and orange. Hobart said the green houses were fine with him. Jacob said the green things looked nothing like houses and wanted a castle for his house and motel. I was considering giving the whole playing board the heave-ho. That's when something thumped above us. Everyone's eyes went to the ceiling.

"Must be Ty," I said. "Maybe he's practicing his Martial Arts."

"Who's Ty?" Lindee asked.

"Oh, yeah, I forgot," I said shaking my head, realizing she hadn't met him yet.

"He's Sabrina's protector," Rick said in a sly way. I had to wonder if he was jealous of Ty.

Lindee squinted at me. "I thought that was Hobart's job."

"Uh, it's complicated," I said.

"Yeah. Complicated," Hobart said and threw the dice. A seven came up. He moved his piece to CHANCE. "Oh," he said and picked up a card. "Hell."

"What?" I said.

"Go back three places." He moved his piece back, and of course had to shell out two hundred dollars. "I've never liked this game. It's too much like life. I always gets screwed."

"You don't have to play," I said. He met my eyes and smiled.

"My aim is to go bankrupt gracefully, and step out of the game early. That's the only part about it that isn't like life. I can quit, if I want." Hobart winked.

"That's right, you sure can," I said, chuckling. I figured he wasn't into playing a board game, and merely went along with the rest of us.

"Not me. I'm going to buy up all the expensive places, like Park Place and Boardwalk and make all of you losers pay through the nose just like a good republican would," Rick said.

"You sound so like Donald Trump," Lindee said.

He scoffed. "I'm a leprechaun. What do you expect?" He threw the dice and got another double—a pair of sixes.

"Ah. A leprechaun," Jacob said, eyeing Rick suspiciously "He has a certain advantage over the rest of us."

"Rick, you aren't cheating and using your magic on the dice, are you?" I asked in a warning tone.

He looked up at me, squinted and made a deep sigh. "Sorry. It sort of happens when I'm competing. It's my nature. I won't do it again, Sabrina." He looked around and apologized to everyone.

"That's good enough for me," I said.

After twenty minutes of playing, Rick had bought both Park Place and Board Walk plus a utility and a railroad. I'd never seen such a run of good luck as he had, and such bad luck for Hobart, who got another CHANCE card and wound up in jail. I didn't wind up on Rick's properties, but I did land on Luxury Tax. I had three properties plus B.&O. by the time I'd gone around the board once. I felt that was a comfortable spot to be for a first round of playing. Lindee had bought all the small-fry places claiming gleefully she was well on her way to becoming a slum lord. Jacob had bought nothing, but just kept throwing dice and making his rounds. He didn't want to buy any property, but just wanted to watch us.

The sound of feet descending the stairs made us all look to the door in the dining room that led upstairs. It opened and Cho emerged, his straight black hair lifting from the air current he created with the door.

"Is that your *other* protector?" Lindee whispered to me, unable to take her eyes off him. I didn't blame her.

I nodded and she made a growly sound in the back of her throat.

"Sabrina?" Cho called from the doorway, leaving the door open and it sort of irked me; he was letting the warm air up the stairwell. The wind outside chose that very moment to gust. It sounded like a train going past my house. Then the pain in my side flared up again. It doubled me up and I put my hand over it. Cho was on his knees, at my side instantly.

"Are you alright?" he asked.

"I don't know," I said.

Jacob put an arm around me, his concern genuine, but this was an excuse to touch me, I knew that.

"You okay, hon?" Lindee had gotten to her feet and now leaned over me with her hand on my shoulder, and worry lines rippled across her forehead.

The pain let up and I straightened. "I'll be fine," I assured, but I said it with a catch in my voice.

Cho took a step back and said, "Vasyl has awoken. He wishes to see you. Also he requests some bottled blood. Do you have any?"

"Yeah," I said, moving toward the kitchen. He headed me off.

"No. I will get the blood. You go up and see him. I will bring him the blood."

"Okay," I said, my heart racing, and stomach flipping. Reluctantly, I turned and opened the door. "Go on without me," I said to everyone still in the game." Closing the door, I climbed the stairs—I'm not ashamed to say—slowly. After last night's fiasco of his anger over my stupid mistakes, I didn't know what to expect.

Each upstairs room had a small electric heater for winter, they were only turned on when someone needed heat. Heart throbbing against my chest, I wondered how Vasyl was, and what he'd say to me after yesterday. I treaded quietly down the hallway to his door, knowing he'd hear me, even before I stepped on that annoying floorboard that popped every time.

I moved my hand to knock, and didn't quite get my knuckles to the wood when he said, "Enter."

I opened the door and peeked in at him. "Hi," I said, noticing he had a small lamp on, for my benefit.

"Sabrina, come in." He motioned for me with an outstretched hand.

I cautiously stepped forward. The room was chilly because he didn't have any heat on. Obviously, he didn't need it on.

"How are you?" I shut the door quietly, as though it was a sick room. A heavy coppery scent filled the room. That wasn't good. My stomach knotted with worry. He looked overly pale, and his lips had a blueish tint to them. That couldn't be healthy for a vampire, could it?

"I need blood, and can't hunt for it." I noted that he didn't answer my direct question. I got a read that he was still wounded. I didn't understand how that was possible.

"Cho is bringing up a bottle. "As I spoke, Cho's footsteps approached down the hall. Odd how he somehow avoided that creaking floorboard. His knock elicited Vasyl's bidding.

"Come in."

Cho entered and made a bow. "*Bonsoir, Vasyl. Ici, sest le sang.*"

He spoke French?

"*Laissez-les sur la table, s'il vous plaît.*

Vasyl must have asked that Cho place the bottle next to him on the table, because that's what he did. When he headed for the door again, Vasyl asked a question to him—in French. I wasn't sure what the question was but the word "loup", which means wolf, was the subject of the conversation.

"*Le loup-garou est au rez-de-chaussée,*" Cho said.

Vasyl nodded and made an imperialistic swish of the hand, and Cho withdrew, closing the door quietly.

I had caught the word *loup-garou* only when Cho replied. That meant werewolf. Yes, Jeanie had taught me a few choice words in French. Wish I knew more than a few. They had been talking about Hobart.

"You want me to open that for you?" I asked, nodding toward the bottle.

"It is open, and it is warmed up. Cho has done it for me."

"Oh." *Duh*. I felt incredibly useless.

"He tells me he has been with a vampire ruler before. I find him adequate as a servant."

"Nice," I said. I probably didn't need to tell him that Tremayne had asked him (or someone), to escort me to his secret below-ground condo. I *knew* that Cho and Vasyl had had a long conversation this afternoon. That's why Cho had not come downstairs before this. He had been with Vasyl a long while. Probably giving each other the history on their respective lives.

Vasyl patted the side of the twin bed as an invitation to me. "Come, sit with me." I did. He reached for the bottle with his left hand and grimaced.

"What's wrong?"

"I am injured on my left side," he said. "Would you—?" He grimaced. That was the same side my pain was on. What's wrong with him?

I got up and went around the bed and handed him the bottle.

"*Merci.*" He took a long pull, swallowing, and settled the bottle on his stomach. He was not wearing pants. This I could see as his white legs were sticking out from the white sheets. My eyes automatically saw blood stains. *Crap!*

"You're still bleeding?" I gasped, horrified. I looked down to find a blood-soaked cloth around his stomach.

"*Oui*," he sighed. "You can do nothing for me."

"But—" my side-stitch made me put a hand to it. "I'm feeling this?" My astonishment on my face. He watched my face squeeze from the pain.

"We have shared blood. You feel my pain, as I feel yours."

"But, it should have been healed."

"Sabrina, I ask that you send the leprechaun up, after you leave me. I believe he may know what weapon has done this to me."

I grimaced as a thought came to the forefront. "You think it was sliver?" *Oh, God no. Not him too!*

"I do not know. But it is a possibility."

We sat for a moment not speaking while he drank the blood down.

"Are you still mad at me?" I asked.

"*Mon amour*, I love you," he said. "Yesterday you angered me beyond measure. But I love you. I always will. Had I known what you'd planned to do for the Nephilistic one, I would have forbidden you. Now, it is too late. *Ce que sera.*"

I sank on the twin bed across from him, thinking about that for a moment. I was now bound to him, in marriage. Last night, I'd realized that being married to him I would have to work hard to not piss him off. I seem to be going at it all wrong, making the wrong choices.

He took a longer pull of blood, swallowed and looked at me. "I now make my request." He paused and went on. "No. It is not a request. It is more than that." He frowned and murmured to himself in French. I gathered he may have been trying to find the English equivalent.

"Ah. Yes." His right hand opened. "I *demand* that, however you have been avoiding getting pregnant with me, you stop doing it."

My eyes went wide, and my mouth opened with surprise. A grimace replaced my expression as the phantom stitch at my side flared up.

"I understand that modern women have a pill which they take in order to avoid getting pregnant." He engaged my gaze. "You have until tonight to relinquish the pills to me."

I must have looked stunned because he gave a small triumphant smile. He took another pull on the bottle of blood and nearly drained it. My face flushed. In fact, my sinuses warmed as my nostrils flared.

"Why?" I asked.

Vasyl's eyes flashed. "You are my wife, and that is my demand." I somehow kept from huffing, or snorting at his "demand."

"You demand that I get pregnant against my will?" I said, brows gathering in the middle.

"This is not about what you want. The prophesy must be met."

"It's only a prophesy. It doesn't mean we have to do this *now*. Besides, it's my body and if I choose at this moment to not get pregnant, it's up to me." I crossed my arms and glared at him. We both grimaced and put our hands to our sides with sudden pain. After ten seconds the pain let up. I was panting when it was over. Damn, that hurts!

"This isn't the fourteenth century," I went on. "I live in a free country where women vote and can chose to get pregnant or not."

He let out an exasperated sigh, eyelids half-closed. "Sabrina, this is not about you. It is what is important to the world of vampires. If you do not birth the savior—"

"Savior!" I blurted, slightly shocked by the sound of this.

"It is what some call it. Yes."

I shook my head. My brain felt like it was going to spin with everything going on. "Look. First, we'd better make sure you are healed," I said, nodding toward his injury. The idea that he thought that it was caused by silver had me frightened. After seeing what it had done to Tremayne I could barely manage to not burst into tears.

I stood. "I'll send Rick right up. He has people who can help." I stepped toward the door.

"There are people in the house I do not know," he said, stopping me.

Hand on the door knob, I turned. "Yes."

"Who are they?"

"My cousin, Lindee, and the demon, Jacob."

"That's right." He looked away, as if remembering. "He is the one who came to you, last night, and you sent him away on a mission."

"Mission accomplished."

"You will send him away, then please."

"Yes, master."

Vasyl frowned. "He is an incubus. I do not want an incubus anywhere near you." He tipped the bottle again, draining it.

My frown gave way to a tight smile. "Of course. God forbid I become pregnant from an incubus."

"Take this, *merci*." He held up the empty bottle. I turned back to him, and took it from his hand. I would need to recycle it, but I highly doubted the courier for the Tremayne Inc. Bottled Blood would be making his rounds tonight, unless he had a sled and six tiny reindeer.

"Send the leprechaun to me..." Upon seeing my look he added, "Please?"

"I will." I glanced at him, and my insides went cold with the memory of how I'd last seen Tremayne in that hospital bed, his skin flaking off, hands bandaged. The horrible stench of his rotting flesh coming back to me. God, I didn't want that for Vasyl. And I could tell he was still in a weakened state—because we were blood-bound, I could actually feel his weakness. It weighed me down, and my side twinged suddenly over the phantom wound. I paused, touching my left side. It was on his left side, under the ribs. Silver would prevent him from healing. Someone in that battle last night had used a blade made of silver to attack him. I guess I'm not the only one with a silver dagger.

"Do not forget, later, to bring me your anti-birth pills," he reminded me. I turned to see his stern look, stifling any further protest from me.

Anti-birth pills—humph! I left his room, breathing through my nose like a bull. My knees suddenly went out on me. I caught myself against the wall, trying hard to hold back not only the tears but the huge sob that was caught in my throat. Thoughts of Tremayne had me thinking of my latest donation of plasma, today. I wondered if he had gotten it. Was he going to live? Maybe I could find out from Rick, later. But this being done to Vasyl blew me away completely.

The rousing noises of the game reached me before I opened the door to enter the dining room. When I stepped through, five sets of eyes tracked me. I had spent five minutes in the upstairs bathroom getting myself put back together, blowing my nose and worked on not looking like I'd been crying. Which is impossible, I know. My emotions were off in all directions right now.

Hobart stood up from the table. Long strides took him to the kitchen, my guess was for another beer.

"Hey, Alpha Girl, how's the boss?" he asked in passing.

I followed him into the kitchen. "He's still weak," I said. "He's got a bad gash on his side that won't heal."

Opening the refrigerator, he grabbed a beer. I hoped his twenty-four pack would last him and the others. The snow storm hadn't relented as yet.

"Oh, yeah?" He looked at me. "What's wrong with him?" Before I could answer, a request from the other room reached us.

"Hey, Hobart, bring us another cold one!" Rick shouted from the living room.

"Got it covered," Hobart yelled, and ducked back into the refrigerator, and brought up two more beers from the fridge. I halted his motions with my hand on his shoulder. "Vasyl wants to see Rick, and the demon is going home."

Our eyes met. "Okay. This one's for your cousin." He held up the one can of beer in his other hand.

"I'll take it into her," I said taking it from his hand and feeling the cool can through the material of my gloves.

Shrugging, he swung around and I followed on his heels. Back in the living room I found that my playing piece, the lowly iron, had traveled all the way around the board and was presently parked on Park Avenue, which had three houses (gray with black roofs), and three hotels (tan with red roofs, and one seemed to have a swimming pool behind it) on it. Great. I set the can of beer down in front of Lindee.

She looked up and thanked me. "I moved your piece for you when your turn came."

"You're welcome for the beer, and thanks," I said. "Who do I owe and how much?" I asked the room at large.

"Five hundred bucks," Rick smiled, holding out his greedy paw. If he could put his two hands together he'd have been wringing them greedily.

"Okay," I said picking up my pile of money—which looked very thin. "By the way, Rick, Vasyl wishes to speak with you." Rick met my eyes as I counted out the play money and handed it to him across the table.

"Oh sure, girlfriend." Rick struggled to his feet, pushing off the coffee table with one hand.

"I also need to talk to you." I got up and walked him toward the steps.

"What is it?" he asked, voice low.

"He's got an injury that won't heal. We think it may be from silver."

"That's nasty. Where's he hurt?" He looked into my eyes and I had to look away with the pain of emotions stirring inside. "C'mon kid. It'll be alright," he assured, patting my arm.

I nodded and pointed to where I still had the phantom pain. "In the side. Here. He's still bleeding. Is there anyone you can call to ask about it?"

"Sure can." He was looking at his ever present iPhone with all the icons plastered across the screen. He tapped something with a thumb. A whole screen pulled up. It looked like his calling list. "I'll take care of it. You go on and enjoy the game." He turned to the living room. "Guys, I'm out. Divvy up the loot and take all my motels and houses off the board, put the properties back with the bank."

Hobart and Lindee hooted their excitement.

"He has quit?" Jacob asked. "Why?"

I turned to watch Rick climb the steps. "He's second door to the right," I called up.

"Got it... Hello, Andrew?" Rick's voice echoed, his feet thumping up the stairs. He was talking to Morkel on his phone, and I knew the elves would come and see if they could work their magic. Flicking on the hallway light, I closed the door.

I turned away. "Jacob?" I called. He looked up. I crooked my finger to him.

"What do you wish of me, my mistress?" he asked as he rose from the floor looking a little too eager. "I am having a very good time here."

Sadness over the fact I had to send him away drew over me. It wasn't fair, but it would be a constant battle to keep him away from either myself, or my cousin. "I know, and I'm glad you did. But you have to go back, now."

He gave me the sad puppy-dog look again.

"I'm sorry. And thank you for bringing Lindee back home. But I may need you to return her at some point. I'll call you then." I made sure my ring was visible so he could only obey me.

He bowed. "As you wish." Then he vanished. I had expected him to argue his case. But maybe he had other fish to fry.

With my life spinning out of control, it was actually good to have such *power* that I could command demons. I could see how it did have its advantages. My side squelched again, bringing back the worry about Vasyl. I wondered if Dante had seen what had happened last night. Maybe he could shed some light on who had the weapon.

"Where did you send Jacob?" Lindee asked, slipping up alongside me, beer in her hand.

"I sent him home. He's a demon," I added.

She laughed. "I thought there had to be something special about him." We stepped back into the living room. "He was flirting heavily with me while you were out of the room," she said low, snickering.

"That figures." Bad enough Hobart was sizing her up. As an eligible female in the room, she probably didn't mind the attention too much. But, eventually, she would have to fight them all off. Getting rid of a few wouldn't hurt.

She eased into the living room ahead of me. Cho was seated at the end of the coffee table, looking over the game, and apparently took someone's spot.

Crescendo

"So, is Hobart your first name, middle, or nickname?" Lindee asked Hobart as she plopped back down to the game on the coffee table.

"Ty is my first name." We all looked at him, then over at Cho, whose first name was also Ty. "Actually it's Tyrone. Yeah," he said catching Cho's expression. "Get over it. My mother liked the name. Okay?"

"Ty?" Lindee said with a giggle. "I like that."

"You can only call me Ty if you know what I wear under my jeans. Otherwise, it's Hobart," he said in that gravely note.

Lindee whistled and then chuckled darkly and met my gaze. Then she looked at Hobart.

I felt a blush coming on. I could certainly call him *Ty* from this requirement, since I had been bedded by him—well, in the werewolf sense. But no one need know that we had been intimate—in a wolfy way. Waking up with a stranger the next morning is not something I wanted to repeat. Ever.

Hobart's eyes flashed at me. He smiled. "The moon'll be full soon." The look in his eyes told me he wouldn't mind having another wolfy-one-nighter with me. I would have to reach Mrs. Bench soon for that elixir to keep me from turning.

"Ohmygod, you guys have 'done it'!" Lindee said and then laughed.

"Shhh!" I said, seeing Ty Cho's eyes take us all in, but averted his gaze almost shyly.

Hobart merely smiled knowingly, like the dog he was.

"Don't you dare tell anyone!" I warned her. "We were in our wolf skins at the time." Not that that would matter to her. I was right.

"OH!" She laughed harder and jiggled and then fell over, in full-blown laughter. Damn it. There was no taking it back now. It pissed me off that a portion of my personal life was now out in the open.

Angry, I rose. "I'm going to start the soup."

Lindee was still laughing, holding her stomach as I stood up. "I just got a visual of it! Ho-hahahah!" She rolled a few times on the floor.

"Lindee, stop." My hands went to my waist. "Quit laughing and come and help."

* * *

Hobart had gone upstairs as soon as it became dark. I thought of how many people might have been upstairs in that room with Vasyl. It must have gotten really crowded. My Knowing told me that other people were upstairs with him. People who had not been in the house with us before. Since I could get no real reads, I figured they were elves. Rick had been up there a long time. Cho, too, had joined all the men upstairs. I wasn't sure if I'd be serving dinner upstairs or down.

A few hours later, the game of Monopoly sat in the living room abandoned when I plugged in the Christmas tree. I stood looking at how the many lights cast a more cheery glow over the room. Meanwhile, the house had become quiet, aside from Lindee and me talking and laughing and reminisced while we put together the soup. I suggested she call her mother again.

She made a sound of protest.

"You should call your mother," I said, as I rose from the kitchen table. The rich aroma of our soup filled the warm kitchen. "She loves you, and really misses you."

Lindee finally agreed to call, albeit reluctantly. But I could tell she really felt she should.

"Use my phone in the living room, if you like." Despite the Christmas tree lights, it was now dark in the house. I clicked on a small light in the dining room for her.

Moving through the living room, I glanced at the abandoned game. I would have to pick it up. It took me back to when I was much younger. Memories were dashed when I noticed movement and shadow in the den. My heart lurched at the sight of someone standing in front of the fireplace, plus the French door was slightly ajar as though making it an invitation. Steadying myself, I knew it couldn't be anyone who shouldn't be here. There was another stairway that lead down the front of the house, through the hallway, which lead into the den. But I doubted anyone knew about it but me and Lindee as another door closed it off. The fireplace was burning brightly, casting jumping shadows against the amber backdrop in that room. I didn't know who had started the fire. Probably Hobart when I had been busy. It flared now, and the front of the person who stood there glowed. Their long, black hair and black suede coat made the identification easy. Dante. My heart did a tattoo in my chest. What was wrong with me? I should have been able to know that he was here with my abilities. Probably I was messed up because of too many sups in the house.

The French door slowly opened on its own, creaking slightly on the old hinges. A bit of the vampire magic was available to him, apparently.

Stepping through, I peered in at Dante. "Hi," I said. "Is this a party, or a funeral?"

"Neither," he said in his usual stoic way.

I stepped all the way in, watching him warming his hands, like he did the last time.

"I can't feel the warmth. I can't feel cold, either." He looked up at me. "I can feel nothing." His voice low, vibrating through me like a bow on a cello string. "Except for the emptiness inside where my heart once beat."

My own heart squeezed with sorrow at his words. What could I say? "I'm sorry," came to mind, but that seemed inadequate. "Is there anything I can do?" I said instead, and it came out so lame I wanted to duck back out of the room and re-enter. Or not enter at all. My fingers twined and twisted, thumbs thrust toward him. "I-I don't know what to say to you." I kept at least three feet away from him, knowing if I got any closer I wouldn't be able to resist him. His control was amazing, as I felt the pheromones rolling off him as strong as any master vampire I had ever known. The smell of pine and woodsmoke becoming like an intoxicating perfume. His own scent was just as enticing. My ring, of course, could hold back his thrall, should he lose control, but still, I felt desire trickle through me. *Damn, I shouldn't feel this way for him. Not now.*

"There is nothing to say. Even if I were to hold you, I cannot have you. If it were not that I was already dead, it would kill me waiting until I could."

"You mean, when I die?" I said unable to stop myself. *Shit.*

Gray eyes glittered silver sparks as he looked at me, as though the very thought of having me all to himself excited him. He didn't need to confirm it. If I died, I knew that I would be with him. I wouldn't be alone. At least that part of dying would be good. Maybe.

"Aren't you afraid of Vasyl? What he might do?"

"No. I am not afraid of him." He smirked. "Thank you for reminding me. He can do nothing to me." Because he was already dead. A regular vampire, even a master, had nothing over an Undead. "It's you I worry about."

"Because?"

"You are not happy." *Well, yeah. Duh.*

My glance fell to the flames. "He wants me to have his child. He became upset that I gave some eggs for Bill's child."

"It's because of The Prophesy." It wasn't a question. He knew about the prophesy, of course. Seems that all vampires knew about this damned prophesy. But, I had told Dante about it the day after I'd been told of it.

"Two masters who are opposites—we know who they are—will seek the sibyl," he said. "She who holds the ring—that's you—while two powers struggle to take over the new continent." He was paraphrasing, but he got the gist of it. "The last sibyl—that's you—holds the key... blah, blah, the descendant of the *Watchers* holds the *seed*. In the abduction there shall be salvation and redemption... yada, yada, and a new race shall be born." He looked directly at me while he recited this. I stared at him for a few heartbeats. The fire snapping wasn't the only sound. From the other room, Lindee's voice became loud and she laughed while speaking to her mother. I had to say something to break the near silence between myself and Dante.

"Yeah, well, Bjorn had his chance with me, so I guess it's only fair Vasyl gets in his licks, too." I shrugged.

Dante gave up a dry chuckle.

"Gosh. I didn't know I'd made a joke," I said, frowning.

"You weren't listening, were you?"

I threw him an irritated look. "Yes I was."

"Then you don't know who the Watchers are, or *were*, do you?"

I didn't say anything at first. This was like being caught day dreaming in a classroom while the teacher was at the blackboard. I gave an exasperated sigh. "What?"

"Watchers. They are the ancient ones. The nephilim are closely related. A *descendant*."

I frowned harder. "What are you trying to say? Or not say?"

"Bill's seed. Your's and Bill's child."

"What?" I said, hands out, unable to comprehend this riddle.

"Will be the king—the Dhampire," he said.

I frowned, my eyes searching the darkness for clues that weren't there. Then it slowly dawned on me what he meant. "You mean..."

"Yes," he said. "No matter what happens, the king of vampires has already been conceived." He chuckled, seeing my expression and turned toward the flames, putting his hands toward them. Though he was an Undead, I could nearly feel his own deviant glee over this development.

"Oh. My. God." My heart skipped a beat, and my skin suddenly chilled with the adrenaline rush of realization.

"Say nothing to anyone about it," he said, his hand up in a warning.

"No. Of course not." My heartbeat deepened at the very idea of such a huge secret. "Are you sure?"

Hand out, palm down, he wiggled it. "Pretty sure. It makes sense."

"It does," I agreed. *This lets me off the hook.*

"You will have visitors," he announced abruptly, after a moment of silence between us.

"Today?"

"Tomorrow."

"Who?"

"They are a group who you have never met. They are called the Priory of Sion."

"The Priory of Sion?" I tumbled the words around in my memory banks. "Are you sure?"

He nodded.

I remembered how I had been introduced to Jamie North through Chris Duran, the werewolf I met in Colorado Springs. But they were a different group of wizards and sorcerers. They were called Sons of Solomon. I couldn't get a read from Jamie when I'd met him. Rick had assured me he wasn't a demon, but something else. I'd learned later he was a sorcerer. The Sons of Solomon had wanted to enlist me as their priestess—which I found really difficult to accept—and attend some of their rituals, one of which was coming up. I really didn't have time for that.

"I have told you everything I know." Dante smirked. "And now I must leave you." Black hair and fringe flying, he half turned, then misted out of existence. The flames in the fireplace jumped explosively out of the grate as the air where he once stood was displaced. The scent of pine needles gone, only the wood smoke from my fire remained.

I stood there staring at the spot where Dante had stood. On top of everything else going on in my house, I'd have visitors from some mysterious group. Dismissing that for now, I mentally ran through the more important information Dante had given me. I tried to absorb it. If it was true, about mine and Bill's child, it meant I need not have anyone's child—if I didn't want to, that is. Our baby was growing inside Ophelia's womb. This information had to be protected. I would say nothing to anyone. Those who knew would, hopefully say nothing to anyone else.

My resolve to remain steadfast in my head-strong decision to not honor Vasyl's request intensified with this new information. I really did not want to have a baby. Not now when things were getting too crazy. Knowing what I had to do, I moved for my bedroom, opened a drawer, found my pills. I thought about hiding them, but that meant I would have to remember to continue taking them. But, also I would have to give Vasyl something in order to placate him. I looked at the pill pack trying to think of a way to make it look as though I were giving the pills to him, but really wasn't. It had to look convincing. After a few moments I had a stroke of genius and wondered if Lindee could help me in my deception. *Of course she would!*

It had become quiet again, and I found Lindee quietly stirring the soup in the kitchen, wiping away tears.

"Everything okay?" I asked, hand on her shoulder, looking at her face.

She nodded, pulled in snot and then turned to me and threw her arms around me. Crap. I wish she wouldn't do that. Her emotions filled me full-blown. Grimacing, I drew away from her and stepped back from her reach. "You've forgotten. No touching," I reminded.

"Sorry," she said, knowing why I pulled away. Her hands went to her face again. "I told her about Joha."

"Hopefully you didn't tell her he's from another world?" I said, and almost checked my own sanity after saying it.

"No," she chuckled her answer.

"I'm glad you and your mom had a talk, Lin." I moved to find the tissues on top of the refrigerator. I pulled the box down and presented it to her. She snapped up several tissues and blew snot, cursing softly at herself.

"Soup's done, by the way," she said followed by a hiccup. She giggled around the tissues at her nose and then blew once more. "God, I'm pathetic!" She threw the tissues into the wastebasket, and while I went to the cupboards for bowls, she washed her hands.

"No, you're not," I said, noting I had a set of six soup bowls. I did a mental count of who might be eating and carried five bowls into the dining room. I never did break the table back down to its shorter length from my dinner with my brother and his wife and kids from last night. In fact it still had the same table cloth on it. After tonight I'd have to break it down and wash the linen by hand.

After Lindee dried her hands, she brought in napkins and spoons.

"Wish I had homemade bread," I said.

"Oh, hell," Lindee said. "I wish I'd known. It was bread-baking day at the Drakulya's today. I could have brought a loaf."

"Oh snap!" We laughed.

Lindee and I transferred the soup into my mother's soup tureen, then lugged it out to the table steamy and hot.

I leaned on the table watching Lindee move a few pieces of flatware to within a millimeter of straight lines. She must have taken lessons at Drakulya's house from the maids. "Lindee, after dinner, will you help me with something?" I asked.

"Sure. What is it?" she ladled the soup while I held a bowl up.

"It's kind of devious, and difficult to explain. I'll tell you about it later." My glance went toward the door to the stairs. I didn't totally trust that vampires couldn't hear everything you said, even on a different floor.

"Sure! You know how I love devious," she smirked.

"That I do."

Once we had the soup served up, I opened the upstairs door, and yelled, "Come and get it! Soup's on!" Then I shut the door, cutting off the cool air rushing down, and the warm going up. The chill from the stairs caused me to shiver.

I wasn't sure if Cho would eat, I took the chance that he might be ready to break his fast with a little soup.

The clatter of heavy feet announced their eagerness to eat. The men all filed down into the dining room. I was happy to see Cho, who sat among us, looking hungry.

"How's Vasyl?" I asked.

"The elves are working on him," Hobart said.

"They think it might have been elf-made silver that they used," Rick said, actually placing his iPhone down for once, but eyeing it every three seconds.

"Really?" I dipped my spoon into the broth, noting it was rich and the steam opened my sinuses. "Is that common?"

"Sure as hell isn't," Rick said sounding angry. "Anyway, they cauterized the wound on his ribs. He isn't bleeding any more. There didn't seem to be any internal damage."

"That's good. Right?"

"Best we can hope for," Rick said.

"It means that if a vampire wielded it, then it may have been on the tip of a spear," Hobart said.

I nodded, tentatively nibbling on small chunks of hot potato and carrots on my spoon.

"Since it didn't hit any organ, he'll be fine, Sabrina. It'll just take a while," Rick assured, seeing my worried face. I did not want to see Vasyl begin to die a slow death like I had seen happen to Tremayne.

"Thank God. What's going to happen now? Is there anything we can do?" I meant that as *me*, but it went out as all inclusive.

"He can't be moved," Rick said. "He's still healing. They can't do anything about his wings."

"Wings? What's wrong with his wings?"

"They were shredded with the same weapon."

"He's had something like nine pints of blood," Hobart said. "Plus about one of mine."

"*Nine*?" I said. Totally grossed out, I met Lindee's gaze. We both put down our spoons.

"He's not going to wind up like Bjorn, is he?" I asked.

"Oh, no," Rick said. "He was beginning to heal up when we came down."

"Speaking of which, how is Bjorn doing?" I asked, thinking this was a good time as any.

"He's much improved." Rick took a spoonful of soup. "OH! Girlfriends, you make the best soup!"

"Thank you," Lindee and I both said and smiled at one another.

My relief for both Vasyl and Tremayne poured through me. Two things which only moments before had been on my mind all day. Now I didn't have to worry about these issues anymore. I had other things to tend to. One was high up on my to-do list.

Chapter 18

Deception

Lindee made the slit in the plastic at the base of the blister pack of my birth control with the exact knife I found in my father's junk drawer. She had a very steady hand. A good thing since I didn't trust myself to do this.

"Aspirin," she said as she settled one birth control pill down next to several others on a blank piece of typing paper. I used cellophane tape to hold each contraception in place. I'd already wrote the days down on the paper, that way I wouldn't get confused when I went to take them each day.

I shook out another low-dose aspirin and set it down in the space next to where she worked on my dresser. I could think of no safer place to do this than in my bedroom, with doors locked so no one could barge in. We kept our voices at a whisper.

"I hope this works," I said.

"It did for that spoiled brat who roomed with me," Lindee said low. "She wore my cloths, ate my food and even stole my boyfriend."

"Wow."

"I went and found her pills and did this to them." She turned the pack over to the silver blister side. "See? You can't tell I did anything to it. It's a small slit. Pop the pill out. Pop another in its place, and you can't tell the difference."

"Did she get pregnant?"

Lindee nodded, smiling broad. "Omygod, she was royally pissed, but her mother was even *more* pissed. If you thought *my* parents were over-bore with their religion, you should have heard all the tear-filled phone conversations between Katie and her mother."

Lorelei Bell

I was appalled that Lindee had gone to such extremes to get back at her roomie, but I could see how someone like Katie would piss you off. Especially if she stole a boyfriend. But, this was different. I was to present this pill pack to Vasyl tonight. I knew this was being deceitful, but I was not going to get pregnant now. My gut was telling me this was a bad time to be in a delicate way. I hoped that no one would figure out what I was doing. I was pretty sure I was right about it. Besides, the Dhampire had been conceived, and that seemed to be all that mattered, no matter how it happened.

In another fifteen minutes Lindee had replaced each of my birth control pills with a baby aspirin. If you didn't look close—as they were a generic brand—you couldn't tell the difference and she had somehow made only one slit just large enough to shove the birth control pill out, and the small aspirin in through the plastic that held it in place on the pack. Then the sleeve went over it, more or less hiding the fact it had been tampered with.

"There. Done." She quickly slid the pack of phony birth control pills into its sleeve and handed it to me.

"Thanks, Lin. I don't think I would have thought of baby aspirins." We both giggled.

"Hey, glad to help out." She settled her hands on her hips and looked around. "Where are you going to hide those?" Her head inclined toward my sheet of paper with the real pills secured on the page with tape, with the dates and days over and under each pill.

"I don't know. I hadn't thought that part out."

"You don't want someone coming across those by chance."

I sat on my bed thinking.

"Wait. You don't have anything in the medium canister in the kitchen," she suggested.

"That might work. But I'll have to do it when no one is looking."

"I'll do it."

A knock on my door made us both jump slightly.

"Who's there?" I said.

"Me. Ty."

I gave Lindee a wide-eyed look of panic. It was Cho. I really didn't know who's side he was on and didn't want to find out now.

"What's up?" I asked calmly.

"Vasyl would like to see you, and requests that you bring the pills with you."

"Right. I'll be out in a minute." Now I knew he was actually on Vasyl's side since he knew about my pills.

Lindee put a finger to her lips to keep me from saying anything further. Then she mimed with the piece of paper with my birth control pills taped down that she was going to do exactly as we had discussed. I nodded, and she stood next to the bathroom door, ready to go through to the bathroom and wait until everyone was busy.

I pulled on my heavy winter slippers. I had dressed in jeans, and pulled a sweater over my camisole after my shower. I wore the sweater because I would have to go up to Vasyl's room where he convalesced. It was cold up there and the thick sweater would keep me warm.

Earlier, Rick had gone home—wherever that was. Hobart was watching a football game on TV, and Cho was being the go-between between myself and Vasyl. They didn't want him venturing down the stairs yet. There may have been other things he wasn't supposed to do, which had been alluded to during the dinner conversation by a few snickers from the men that I would have to rate as fifth-grade-ish. Men.

Lindee scooted into the bathroom and shut the door quietly. I was sure glad I had her around tonight. I slid open the pocket door to find Cho standing waiting for me. I had the pill dispenser in my hand. I hoped that the cuts on the packet Lindee made would not be too evident to the keen eye of a vampire. I also hoped that he would trust me enough not to have to look at it—at least too closely. But we were presuming that he would at least look at it.

"You are to go up to him now," Cho said, and smiled.

"Okay," I said, and went on up the stairs. I rapped on Vasyl's bedroom door.

"Come in, Sabrina," Vasyl said.

I opened the door. Warm air pour out. I had expected it to be freezing in here by now. Cho must have turned the space heater on for my benefit. I would have looked over at the dial on the heater, but my eyes were kind of busy. Vasyl lay in the bed partially covered by the dark blue sheets, and that apparently was all. His naked torso and bare, lean legs shown stark white against the dark contrast of the sheets. Cho must have changed the sheets because they had been white, before. Vasyl held a bottle of Organic Red in his hand, resting in his lap in a suggestive way. I wondered if he was naked underneath the sheets. *Oh!* My abilities told me he was indeed nude. *Okay.*

"*Bonsoir, madam.* Good evening," Vasyl said, his eyes half-lidded. I swallowed, but my throat was dry.

"Hi," I said, fanning myself. "Wow. It's warm in here. I think I'm overdressed."

"I happen to agree." His dark violet eyes flicked over my form. The sheets were rumpled in the right places. Making me even warmer.

The lock on the door slid in place and I looked back, initially startled, but realized Vasyl's vampire powers were alive and well.

I held out the pill pack in my hand. "I brought it."

"*Bon, d'accord,*" he said, dark eyes flicking toward it, then back up to my face. "Throw it into the trash." Something had changed. I wasn't sure what. I didn't hesitate and stepped around the bed and threw it into the wastebasket on the other side.

"Sit beside me," he said, patting the narrow bed.

I sat on the edge. There really wasn't much room for me.

A knock on the door made me turn.

The lock on the door disengaged. "Enter," Vasyl said.

Cho stepped in with a round tray in his hands like a manservant. Two tall-stemmed glasses balanced upon it. One had a deep red liquid in it—blood. The other looked more like white zinfandel.

Without a word, Cho drew the tray before us. Vasyl placed the empty bottle on the tray and lifted the glass of blood from it. I mimicked Vasyl and took the fluted glass with wine in it.

Cho turned away, the tray with the empty bottle on it in his capable hands, and slipped out the door as silent as though he were a ghost. The door's lock clicked into place again.

I looked back at the door. "I take it we won't be disturbed?"

"No one will venture upstairs at all. I have made certain of it. But I like locks on the door."

I did too. I smiled back at him.

"To the future," Vasyl said, lifting his glass toward mine. I tipped mine so that it would clink against his. We both took a sip. All was forgiven, and we were back on level ground.

I repositioned myself on the bed and tugged at the neck of my sweater. Relationships were difficult to maintain. A lot of give and take. And some deception required at times.

"You are hot? I suggest you take that off," he said with a gleam in his eyes, crooked smile and arched brow.

I handed him my glass. He held it while I pulled the sweater off and tossed it on the other bed. Now my shoulders were bare, save for two spaghetti strings that held up a maroon cami. He handed my glass back to me.

"How's your owie," I asked, a half-smile on my lips.

"Owie?" His confusion obvious with his rumpled brow.

"Your wound?" I said.

"Oh. That." We both looked downward at his left side. "It is now healed."

I leaned over to check. His skin was marble white and the only mar was a red slash across his ribs where I gathered the injury was. "Fantastic." Astonished, I sat back up and sipped my drink. His hand took my drink away from me and placed it along with his on the side table.

"I wasn't finished," I complained.

"We have all night."

"You promise?"

"I do."

"But I thought you had to take it easy," I said moving in toward him, my hands glided up his arm and chest. His own cool hands touching my warm flesh nearly sizzled like water in a hot frying pan. I leaned, pressing my chest against his. His lips easily found mine. My face warmed. The warmth spread down my neck to my chest to my inner thighs and there was a happy dance down below.

He broke the kiss. "I am. You are going to do all the work," he said huskily with a devilish grin.

I smiled, biting my lower lip with the thought. "Nice." Sliding my hand down his abdomen, it slipped beneath the sheets and found that his own happy dance had already begun. His hardness filled my hand and I squeezed a little.

"*Mon Cherie*, take your things off. I have been waiting for you for too long."

Chapter 19

Priory of Sion

Panting, I opened my eyes and found that the bed had moved at least a foot away from the wall due to all my rocking motions. The amazing part was the bed wasn't on casters, and it rested on carpet.

I was balanced precariously on top of Vasyl, drenched in sweat, in the last throws of ecstasy. The mattress below us had moved as well. It was now pitched at a forty-five degree angle, more or less, and my balance became jeopardized by weakened leg muscles from all my activities for the past two hours. My knees had about four inches of room on either side of Vasyl's hips and that was it. The mattress buckled below my right knee, I pitched over, and tumbled to the floor.

"Ow." My hair, moist from sweating from both having sex with a vampire and the too-warm room, fell down in my face.

Vasyl's laughter rang in my ears.

"Right. You try balancing on a two foot-wide mattress, buddy!" I said heatedly.

He laughed harder, holding his hand to his stomach as though it hurt from laughing too hard. Then, pointing at me, he said something in French that sounded like an insult, yet sexy as hell.

I mopped matted hair out of my face and scowled. He probably said I looked like a baboon. I found myself wanting to laugh, now looking at how we'd wrecked the bedroom, and the way I must look. He, on the other hand, looked entirely too comfortable with himself, like a nude study by Michelangelo. In contrast, my skin was coated in sweat and I needed a shower. I felt like I'd been mud wrestling. This had been the third or fourth time the mattress had wiggled askew from our love making. We had both fallen on the floor together before this. But this time Vasyl had somehow managed to remain poised on the top corner of the stupid little bed.

I threw a pillow at him and he easily swatted it away, still remaining balanced on the edge of the bed. *Bastard.* I tried to move my feet. Couldn't. The sheets were twisted around one of my legs. *Son of a bitch!* I couldn't locate the bedspread. It was moot at this point. I worked to untie myself from the sheet, which was somehow anchored somewhere beneath the mattress. Vasyl reached down and pulled the sheet and freed me easily, his laughter finally dying.

"I am sorry, but you looked so silly," he said.

"Eff you," I spat.

He chuckled sinisterly. "I think you already did. Would you like to eff me more?" he asked with a sly smile and his voice going coy.

"No. I'm taking a shower." I struggled to my feet and looked around. I realized I had no clothes up here except the ones I'd had on. I was *not* going to put a sweater and jeans back on over my sweat-soaked skin.

"How are you getting into the shower?" He gathered up the sheet, and held it out to me. "Would you like to don my sheets, madam?"

"No." *I could just jump the line in the house, couldn't I? How hard could it be?* I reached out and felt the vibration of the ley line. If I could make myself jump millions of space miles from Black Veil back to my own bedroom, I shouldn't have any trouble moving about ten or so feet below where I stood via the magic of ley line jumping. I screwed up my face in thought and closed my eyes. I thought about where I wanted to be and suddenly that floaty feeling came over me, and I basically dissolved. A few seconds later, my feet were again on solid ground. I cracked opened one eye. Then the other. Darkness pressed in on me. Panic threated.

Sounds of the TV—football announcers—told me I had made a perfect landing inside my bedroom. Yep. There were the red glowing numbers on my clock. *9:46pm.* Good thing I had closed my door before I'd left the room earlier. I realized I hadn't locked it and now I padded to the door and felt for the lock and slid it in place. Sneaking around in my own house was ridiculous, but necessary when I had two other men and one woman in the house. I didn't want someone to walk in on me.

Grabbing my robe, I donned it and edged the door to the bathroom open. No one was inside, I knew this from my own abilities. I quickly turned on the light, locked the outer door and prepared to take a nice hot shower. Then, I'd take a long nap.

*　*　*

Activity and noise woke me. I was in my own bed alone. I squinted at my alarm clock. *10:35 am.* My memory came back with a resounding throb. *Oh, yeah. I remember.* I flopped onto my back thinking about the things Vasyl and I had done last night. I hoped he was able to put the bed back together. If not, there was the other twin bed he could sleep in. I stared up at the ceiling smiling. I had no idea I could move a bed a *whole* foot while having sex. That was a new one. The mattress too, but it was a small bed, so it hardly counted. I would want to recreate the same thing down in this bed, the next chance I had. *Maybe tonight?*

Voices filtered through my closed oak door. Hobart and Lindee's voices. I couldn't quite hear what they were talking about, but I was still sleepy. I rolled over trying to ignore that my stomach began turning inside out. Did I have anything to eat in the house?

Knock... knock.

Why is it when you want to sleep in someone comes and knocks on your bedroom door?

"What?" I said to the knock. I hardly had to use my abilities to know it was Lindee.

"Hobart and Cho went and dug out your Jeep."

"Oh!" I said, my eyes popping wide. I couldn't believe I'd forgotten about that. I pictured my Jeep being buried in a snow drift down a country road. And then pictured Hobart digging it out. Poor guy.

"I'm going to the store," Lindee said. "You're out of everything, girl. I need some money, though."

"Okay. Wait a second." I threw the covers off and swung my legs out of bed. I was in my warm pj's. I slid my toes into my warm fussy slippers and padded to the door. Mentally I tried to figure out if I had enough cash, or should I let her use my debit card. I pushed the door back a foot revealing Lindee's smiling face.

"Morning, sunshine!" Lindee said. "You had quite a night."

I chuckled, feeling a flush coming on. "Did we make too much noise?"

"Like two elephants going at it."

"Crap," I muttered. "Sorry."

"No problem. Sounds like you were having a good time," she said.

"I moved the bed. You know—during?"

A bark of laughter filled the house, and she put her hands over her mouth. "That is *so* cool!"

I couldn't help but smile. "Where's Hobart?"

"He's taking me to town. You have money?"

"Tell him to wait. I'll get dressed and I'll come with."

It was easier to get dressed and go along. Thing was, Hobart had a truck with only a front seat. With three of us in there, there would be no room for groceries. I decided I'd take my Jeep, instead. It needed to run after being stuck in snow up to its eyeballs, anyway.

I dressed quickly and came out to find Lindee and Hobart waiting for me. I didn't know where Cho was. Probably sleeping, like I had been.

"I think we'll take my Jeep," I announced.

"Oh, well, you guys go ahead," Hobart said. "I've gotta head home. Make sure every thing's okay there."

"Oh. Sure," I said. He did have his own house and probably wanted to have his own space. I couldn't blame him. "Thanks for digging out my Jeep."

"No problem. You put up with me, and fed me," he said.

"Hey, it was fun." I shrugged. "Besides you brought some of your own food."

"I did, didn't I? Well, call if you need anything." Hobart turned and headed out the door. "Bye. Oh, and take the main roads, yours is still plugged up."

"Okay, thanks. Bye," I called back. I looked at Lindee. "You need a coat if you're going with me. And some boots."

"Oh," she looked down at herself. "Yeah." I'd given her a pair of jeans to wear yesterday. She still wore the old sweatshirt I'd given her. Crap, she was now a homeless woman.

I dug out my older coat and gave it to her to wear. I had more than enough pairs of shoes, but her feet were larger than mine. We went with a pair of snow boots that belonged to my dad. She didn't mind. I guess she was happy to get out of the house. As was I. 'Cabin fever', they call it. One day stuck indoors because of a storm was plenty of reason to want to get out and do something else.

I grabbed my checkbook, and the cell phone and dumped them into my purse. As Hobart had indicated the main roads were plowed and passable. Winter in northern Illinois brought out the best and worst in weather. You put up with heat and humidity in the summer, and snow and sub-zero temperatures with wind chills across open fields and parking lots in winter.

The main roads had been plowed and the blacktops salted. We got to town without a problem and I pulled into Moonlight's Market where it looked like nearly everyone had the same idea to stock up, or re-stock. I had to figure out how much food I'd need. Lindee threw two loaves of bread into the cart.

"Wow, why so much bread?" I said gaping at the large loafs of plain white bread. I liked wheat. I grabbed a loaf that I liked and put it into the cart.

"I might make stuffing," she said.

"Seriously? Stuffing? Do you mean like in a turkey?" I gaped at her.

"I don't know. Maybe." She plodded down the aisle in my dad's huge boots. She looked like a refugee from North Dakota on a mission to stock up for the next blizzard for her farm house. She swung around the end of the aisle. Pushing the cart along, I found her standing before a display of canned cranberries. She plucked a can off the shelf and began reading the contents.

"I actually know how to make this from scratch." She looked up at me. "It's much healthier. Doesn't have corn sweeteners in it. I make it with sugar. In a few minutes it's done."

"Really. You're going to bake a turkey?" My mouth watered. I know Thanksgiving had barely been two weeks ago, but I didn't get to enjoy it much, what with the demon who posed as my Grandma Rose and had attempted to kill me over the Thanksgiving table. I would have to tell Lindee about that one. It was one crazy night. Remembering that made the trip with Tremayne surface and I had to squash it.

"How was Thanksgiving?" she asked.

"Wild. I've got to tell you all about it. But not here. It involves Rick, Tremayne and a demon." I faltered as the store and Lindee hazed out and a vision took its place. Lots of faces I didn't recognize, and some I did. All of this blipped through my head like a movie reel gone crazy.

"What about Thanksgiving?" Lindee asked. That was the last thing I heard. When my vision cleared, and the store aisle surrounded me, I found myself looking up into a handsome Indian face.

"Dante?" I said, my head still woozy, and my eyes trying to focus.

"Where'd you come from?" Lindee said, her voice piercing while staring at Dante.

"I am always with her. I am never far away," Dante said. To me he said, "Are you alright?" He was holding me while I steadied myself, getting my feet beneath me.

I nodded, grasping something solid. Dante's shoulders. "Yes. I think so."

"That's so cool," Lindee said, taking us in.

"Wow," I said, hand to my forehead.

"It's a good thing you caught her," Lindee said and chuckled. "I wouldn't have been able to do that. She'd have been on the floor. They'd be calling for the ambulance and stuff before I could figure out what happened." She looked at me. "You okay?" I nodded. "You sure?" She kept asking and I kept nodding.

"I'm alright." I was still in Dante's arms when I noticed people were staring at us. Dante all in black, and Lindee in the oddly matched clothes, and me—well, I may have been the only normal-looking one for a change, but I had done something weird. Plus he was holding me. I stepped back from him.

"I'll stay," Dante said, and moved to put an arm about my shoulders, then he slipped a kiss on the top of my head, like he was my boyfriend.

"Aw, you two look like such a cute couple," Lindee said. Then she covered her mouth, over a gasp. "I mean… oh, shit. I forgot you're married to—"

"Shhh!" I said, eyes glancing around. Near the end of the aisle a lady in a mock fur coat slid me a disdainful look. Probably because the Indian had his arm around me. She probably saw him kissing my head and thought this was disgraceful. I didn't need to read minds to get this from her. It was all on her face.

I turned the cart away and wheeled it to the end of the aisle, then I pushed it toward the frozen section, Dante at my side and Lindee shuffling along in the too-big boots.

"Lindee, this is Dante. Dante, Lindee, my cousin."

"Hi," Dante said, nodding her way. "She's the one you were looking for in Black Veil?" he asked.

"Yep," I said.

"I don't think we've met," Lindee said, squinting at him. "Is he one of those special guys who appear and disappear?"

"Yes," I said low, looking around. We were by ourselves. The closest person was some guy with a beer gut choosing his beer in the liquor aisle, totally engrossed in whatever beer he wanted. He grabbed a 30 pack of Miller. "Dante is an Undead," I whispered the word "Undead".

"Oh, how awful." Lindee simpered, looking up at him with empathy.

"You know what an Undead is?" I asked.

Hand up she said, "No. Wait. Don't tell me. I think I can guess."

"I am actually a returned spirit," Dante supplied.

"He died," I explained. "He and I were in love when he was alive. Now we're dealing with the fact that he's dead and I'm alive. The whole we-can't-be-together-any-more thing."

"How tragically romantic! But he looks solid." She touched his arm. "He *is* solid. He's not a ghost?"

"Shhhh!" I said in warning. The same woman in the coat emerged from the chips aisle nearby. Spotting us, she leveled us a scornful look, turned and fled in the other direction. "He's not a ghost," I went on. "He's *Un*-dead. He's a vampire, in other words."

"Wow. Another vampire?" She shook her head. "Girl. You and your vampires…"

"I'll explain it to you later. Right now we need to get what we came here for."

Dante had turned away from us and opened up a glass door of the frozen section. In a minute he returned with several things in his hands. Frozen bags of vegetables, and two cartons of my favorite ice cream. God, I loved him. I missed him cooking for me, I missed him being with me. If only he hadn't made the transition from a mouse to human so quickly, he wouldn't have died.

Lindee's eyes went round. "Oh! I didn't think of ice cream. Was there any Chunky Monkey, or, you know, the Moose Tracks one?" Without waiting for an answer she zoomed across the way and searched the shelves of ice creams. The frozen section was large with an open freezer in the center. I thought a frozen pizza for tonight would give Lindee a break from cooking dinner. I thought two pizzas would work for the three of us. I wondered if Cho liked pepperoni. I know Lindee did. My choice was always sausage and mushrooms.

"Your vision, can you remember?" Dante asked, as he added the third ice cream container to my cart. I'd have to put some of this outside in the larger freezer, there'd be no room for it all in the fridge.

I looked up at Dante. "I saw some things. I don't know what it all means yet."

"Let me help you put it all together," Dante said, pushing the strands of hair out of my face that tend to flutter around my eyes and mouth. He stood close and it was so natural for me to put my hands on his shoulders while his went to my waist. His lips touched mine giving me little shivers along my spine, and a throb below. *Nice.* I searched his eyes. Yes. He was a vampire, and as such he could help me remember my visions. And give me a thrill with his touch as an extra bonus.

"What did you see?" he asked, his tone serious.

"See?" I said, my eyes fluttering slightly. He made a click of his tongue as if exasperated with me.

"Think. Quiet your mind and let me have the vision," he said. We stood there like that for—I don't know—maybe two minutes while I did as he said. Then the vision cleared, and separated. I saw Ilona… and Nicolas. And many more people. Some men I'd never seen before. My Knowing came back strong. Dante's auto-suggestion had worked.

"I'm going to get a call soon," I said. "From someone I know…" I trailed off. I squeezed my eyes, thinking. The name wouldn't come to me right away. Finally it did. "Chris Duran. The Were I met at Lonny's, in Colorado Springs."

"Yes. I remember." His hands gently cradled my head. His nose touched mine and then our foreheads came together. "What else? What do you remember?" This wasn't him being romantic, but he was using his abilities to help me remember my visions and bring forth the Knowing. At times I have trouble doing this by myself. It sometimes took hours before I could put them together, too. Vampires acted like a bridge between my conscious and sub-conscious with merely a touch of minds.

"I know I was somewhere else in one of the visions. I had this sense of being far away from here on a clear night. I don't know where. An open place. It's really cold. Lots of snow, with… Oh! Women dressed in black." My eyes popped open. "I think I was tricked."

"By who?"

"Witches!" Something about this one vision terrified me.

"Look at this, you guys!" Lindee said, interrupting us. "They've got a sale! Two for six dollars, so I got two more!" I looked over. She was holding up another two cartons of the ice cream. Her face registered that she realized something was wrong. "I'll put them back—"

"No," I said. Dante and I pulled away from one another. "Go ahead and put them in the cart."

"One is pumpkin pie spice," she said hopefully. "That's alright isn't it?"

"I have to go," Dante said, looking around.

"Crap." I no more than got that word out when he made his turn and vanished.

"It wasn't something I said, was it?" Lindee said, worry lines deepening on her forehead, looking at the empty space where Dante had been a second ago.

The woman in the fake fur who had been more or less spying on us, had seen Dante vanish. Her eyes bulged and she yanked her cart around, careened into a little old lady's cart, corrected her course, and darted down the aisle. I was certain she must now think she'd seen a ghost. I saw her abandon her cart and race out of the store through the automatic doors. Poor lady. She'd forgotten her purse.

I sighed.

"I'm sorry. Did I ruin a good thing?" Lindee gave me a pout.

"No," I said on my sigh. I grabbed our cart. "Go ahead and get those if you want." I pointed to the ice cream she held in each hand. "If you promise to make homemade cranberries. And that pumpkin pie. And the turkey?"

"Okay. Done!" She put them into the cart. "You sure?"

"Yes. And now we'd better get actual food here," I suggested and rolled toward the meat department. I'd never need to buy ice cream again. Until summer.

Twenty minutes later we had our purchases. It was a good thing we didn't have another body with us. The bags took up all of the back compartment in my Jeep. We did wind up getting a twenty-two pound turkey, and whole, uncooked cranberries plus a pound of sugar, and the makings for a pumpkin pie. I had my heart set on the cranberries and turkey and all the trimmings. Naturally I had to get whipped cream to go with the pie.

After loading up the back of the Jeep, we climbed into the front. The notes of a familiar song played from inside my purse. It was my cell phone. It was the call I was anticipating. I turned the key in the ignition and started the Jeep and turned on the heat before I dug for my phone because it was dang cold. I knew who it was before I touched the phone.

"Hi, Chris."

"Hello, Sabrina. How are you?" Chris said. He sounded happy.

"I'm good. How are you?" I adjusted the heat and let the Jeep run while I spoke to him since I had a stick-shift.

"Can't complain. I finished a down-hill snowboard race and got second place," Chris said in his husky voice. I liked his voice over the phone.

"Wow. That's great! You'll be heading for the Olympics soon." He laughed. "You want to tell me someone is coming over to my house," I prompted.

There was a pause. "Yes. I—" He chuckled. "I guess you would know things like that. Wouldn't you?"

"Yep. Who are they and what do they want?" As I said this I had the Priory of Sion in my head. Dante had told me about them yesterday.

"We've got ice cream and cold stuff in the back," Lindee reminded.

"Here." I pulled the phone away from my ear and put it on speaker, then handed it to her. "Hold that so I can hear him and talk while I drive."

Lindee held the phone up close. I put the Jeep into first gear.

"You there?" Chris asked.

"I can hear you," I said. "I'm on my way home and I've got a stick shift."

"Oh. Got it. Well, we've been contacted by members of the Priory of Sion who wish audience with you."

"Okay," I said. "How do you know them? Or is it the other way around?"

"Facebook," he said, and there was a shrug in his voice.

"I see. So they aren't affiliated with you guys at all?"

"No. It's entirely up to you whether or not you want to see them," he said. "You have a ward on your house, and need to take it down so that they can come to your house and speak with you."

"Okay." I drove to the stop sign. I had to wait for traffic to clear. When it did, I sped across the intersection, went through the gears, and we were on our way home.

"What do they want with me?" I asked. Chris's coven members, Sons of Solomon, had helped save me from a cave-in while I was in Colorado Springs trying to out-run trouble. I was still beholding to them, and was leaning toward letting this other group come to see me.

"We aren't sure," he said. "I'm just a go-between. They asked me to contact you so that they could come and see you. They're in your area, waiting for my call back. I'm sort of setting up an appointment, so to speak."

"I see. Well, thank you for that."

"So, uh, how are things?" he wondered.

"Not great." The miles out of town were blanketed in snow. I had to dig out my sunglasses to cut the glare. "Remember what happened at Lonny's?"

"How can I forget?"

"Well, turns out Tremayne needed my plasma," I said, and went into how he had looked when I last saw him a few days ago. "He's recovering nicely now, after two donations of my plasma." After my news, Chris told me he was no longer working for Lonny, but went back to work for a restaurant in town.

"Smart move," I said.

"The vampires were a little too crazy for me to stay involved, and he let me go if I wanted."

"Lonny let you go?"

"I asked him to let me go, and he understood, and cut me loose. I'm no longer under his thrall. He hasn't summoned me, at least." But I got the hint that if Lonny wanted to he could, since Chris bore his bite.

We talked until I was almost home. Lindee's arm was tiring and so I had to let Chris go with a promise of calling him around Christmas-time to catch up.

"What about the Priory? What do I tell them?"

"Ah, tell them to come out this afternoon around one," I said. "I'll have the ward down then." We hung up.

"You know, Brie, I used to feel sorry for you because you had no boyfriends," Lindee said, looking at me with admiration.

"Yeah?"

"Yeah. But I'm no longer feeling sorry for you. I'm in awe of you."

I chuckled. "A lot of these guys aren't my boyfriends. A bunch of them are looking to use me in some way. But, Chris is just a friend."

"Friends can become lovers."

"So I've found out."

"Tell me more about that Indian guy. Dante? He's gorgeous. Why didn't you marry him?"

"He never asked. He never told me he loved me, even. That was his fault, not mine," I said. "Because of it, and a few other things, when he died, he couldn't move on. He came back because he wanted to." Plus he was a shaman in life, but I couldn't explain that to her.

Fifteen minutes later, after we got groceries put away, I called Rick. Some of the ice cream had to be put out in my larger freezer in my dad's shop. Since Lindee insisted on getting two cartons—six in all—I made her trek out into the snow and cold and store at least four of them. She didn't argue, since she still had the boots on.

Rick wasn't busy when I called. I'm not sure if he ever was busy, but I didn't want to be a pest. When I told him who was coming to my house he paused.

"They sound familiar," he said. "I'll pop out there in a wink."

I didn't realize he meant this literally. I was standing holding the phone and he twinkled into existence right before me, making me jerk with surprise.

"Jesus, I thought you were kidding!" I said.

"No I wasn't, and don't take the lord's name in vain," he said, shaking a finger at me.

"Oh. Sorry," I said, and hung up my phone.

"So, Priory of Sion is coming out and you need me to take down the wards," Rick guessed.

I nodded. "You remember what happened when *I* did it," I said.

"You forgot to put it up, yeah," he said, shoving his iPhone into a pocket. "You know any of these guys?"

"The Priory of Sion? No," I said. "It wouldn't be a bad idea for you to stick around. I mean, if you can, of course." I didn't want to be presumptuous.

"That would have been my suggestion," he said. "Wait. Weren't those guys we met in Colorado Priory of Sion?"

"Ham and the others? No. They were the Sons of Solomon."

"Oh. Gotcha." He pulled out his iPhone again. "I'll take down the wards. They've got an hour to get here before I put them back up. I'll monitor things from my iPhone for security reasons." He stepped into the living room, gazing at his phone.

"Wow. You can do that?" I followed him.

He turned his iPhone around to me. "See that?" He pointed to the screen. It looked like a bird's eye view of my house from above. "This is your house. I've got it all set up in Google Earth so I can watch everything that comes within a hundred yards of your house."

"Wow," I said, looking at the picture of my house and snowy grounds, and the green outline around its perimeter. "That's so cool!"

"When I bring it down, the green is replaced by red. I decided to do this because of that problem we had the other day." He plopped into one of the recliners, feet going up because they couldn't reach the floor. With a snap, he made the foot rest pop out. *What would it be like to be him?*

"I think that was yesterday," I said.

"Really? Wow. That seems so long ago, now." He squinted at his screen. "I had fun, though." He looked over at the Monopoly game still out.

"I'm glad." I looked at the game and bent to pick it all up.

"You ever get snowed in again, give me a call."

"Oh, Rick. You are always welcome here," I said, picking up all the piles of play money and began to put each bill in the right holder. The houses and motels were back to being green and red respectively. That was good. "In fact, Lindee is going to bake a turkey. Not today, maybe tomorrow. But she's doing cranberries from scratch and I know she's gonna bake a pie and there'll be stuffing. I didn't get to enjoy Thanksgiving."

"Right. That was crazy at your brother's place that night."

"No kidding."

The door opened and Lindee plodded in, snow falling off the over-large boots onto the rug.

"I'm gonna change," she announced. Then she saw Rick. "Oh. Hi!"

"Hi, girlfriend," Rick said. "Is it true you're gonna bake a turkey with all the trimmings?" His voice went high in hopeful mode.

"I intend to. But not tonight." She sat on the chair near the door and pulled off the boots. She slid her feet into the slippers nearby. "Pizza tonight."

"I've got people coming over, but they shouldn't be staying long," I told her.

"Just keep them out of the kitchen. Once I get started on the pie I don't want to be interrupted." She stood now in her stocking feet.

"Pie?" Rick watched her walk across the room and disappear into the bathroom. "I think I'm in love," he murmured. Then he looked up at me. "After you, of course, sweetheart."

I chuckled at him while folding up the game board. For Rick to fall in love at a moment's notice a woman only needed to cook for him to win his heart. He loved my chocolate chip cookies.

The door opened to the stairway. Cho emerged.

"Good. You are home," Cho said.

"Yes. And we're going to have visitors," I said. "Priory of Sion. They want an audience with me." I said it jokingly, but he didn't laugh.

"I know. I read the yarrow sticks. You must be seated regally when they come," Cho said, looking around the room. "But not here. Perhaps in the other room? The one with the fireplace." He moved toward the living room, going directly toward the French doors that closed off the den.

"I will set things up," Cho said, entering the room.

"You'd better get something nicer on," Rick suggested. "Whoever these people are, you don't want them saying something snarky on Facebook about you, or how you looked."

I looked at myself wearing the worn-out jeans. "Eww, you're right. Wouldn't want that." I headed to my bedroom. I closed and locked the door. I looked over my choices, I didn't want to put on a dress. But I wanted to look more professional. Fifteen minutes later, I emerged wearing a pant suit. One of the ones I'd bought for my job with Tremayne Towers. It was gray with a lavender top beneath the suit coat. I felt silly dressing up in my own home, but hey, guests were coming.

To my surprise Hobart now stood in my living room.

"Hobart, you're back?"

"Hi," he said. "Got a call from Rick to be here as part of your entourage." He said the word *entourage* stressing its significance, with bushy eye brows lifting. I tried to not giggle.

"Cool." It would seem I had more people in my "entourage" than I'd at first thought.

"What do I do?" he asked.

"I don't know. Just be you, and be ready to back me up, if the need arises."

"Who's coming?"

"A group of people called 'The Priory of Sion'. I don't know why they're coming to see me, but I have to look presentable." I made a motion at my apparel. "Good?"

"Yes. You look *very* presentable," he said and smiled. "I think the suit jacket makes you look professional. In a good way, of course."

"Too business-y?" I unbuttoned and flipped the coat open.

"No. Leave it on. I think it looks fine."

"Okay."

"Ready?" Cho said from the den.

"They're already here?" My chest burned with panic, and my stomach twisted in knots.

"Yes," Cho said moving passed me. "They just drove up."

"Come in here," Hobart said, hand extended for me to go ahead of him into the den. I entered to find that Cho had started a nice fire, plus some candles were going. I looked appreciatively around and nodded at the effect.

Cho answered the door while I settled in a chair that Cho had chosen and placed before the fireplace. He had moved the couch further back, and brought a reading chair from the other room.

The door was opened and Cho greeted our guests. I felt silly sitting in a distant room waiting for Cho to lead them into the den like I was some sort of royalty. I tossed a look up at Hobart who stood at my right.

"Nervous?" I asked.

"Not at all. You?"

"Like a cat in a room full of Dobermans," I said. He chuckled.

He wore a Green Bay Packer's sweatshirt. I had no idea he was a Packer's fan. Then I suddenly knew he was originally from Beloit, Wisconsin. My Knowing was working well today.

I turned back to look out through the doors—both of them opened wide. Five men, all of various sizes and ages, stepped inside my door. Cho took their overcoats, their voices filtering to me. I *knew* who among them was the leader. I knew several things about him all at once, such as his age—34—and that he was married, had two children and his name was Alan Tish. A few other names floated to me. In the next two seconds, I *knew* they would not tell me their real names. I smiled, my Knowing was working fine and dandy. A few were from Chicago, and others from various suburbs. None were from my neck of the woods, thankfully.

Alan Tish strode directly behind Cho, and led the others. He wore a dark blue suit and striped power tie over a white shirt. *Ah, a lawyer...* He was definitely the leader. His dark brown hair was cut business-short. The others wore suits, but one wore a red sweater over a shirt and tie.

Cho stepped into the room, but drew aside to present the assemblage of men.

"Sabrina, may I present the members of The Priory of Sion," Cho said, making a little bow to me.

The leader cleared his throat. "Sabrina Strong, on behalf of all of our members, thank you for allowing us audience with you, today."

I nodded, not trusting I wouldn't say something lame, so I said nothing.

"May I present a few of our top members? This is Rene, Vaughn, Dajae (he pronounced it *Day*), Rodolfo, and I'm Voltaire." He held out his hand to each member and then pressed his hand to his chest as he made a little bow. I had to keep my chuckle inside. *Voltaire indeed!*

My jaw clenched before I answered him. "Those aren't your real names," I said, one brow raised and a little challenge to my voice. I wanted to see how they'd react to this.

The shoulders of two of them fell. One gasped—either Vaughn or Rene—and all but Voltaire exchanged looks of astonishment. Alan—aka Voltaire—merely smiled. In fact he almost looked delighted with my abilities.

"How did she—" one of them sputtered.

Voltaire held up a hand to quiet them. His smile broadened.

"She's the real deal; the sibyl, after all," Voltaire said, turning slightly to them and back to me. "Of course she would know these things." He made a slight bow to me. "Our real names are not important."

Rick made a scathing noise from a chair in the corner and tried to hide it with a fake cough, but continued to study his iPhone.

"Your name is Alan Tisch," I said. If I wanted to I could name all of them right then and there, but I'd already astonished them to this degree, any further and I'd only be showing off.

Alan/Voltaire bowed a little deeper. "You are, of course, correct. Nevertheless, I go by my alter name when in the service of The Priory." He looked at his companions. "If I may continue with our business, then?"

"Go on," I said, feeling no small amount of dread filtering through me. I already knew what he was going to say to me. And to quote Lindee, *Omygod*.

"We are here to invite you to our meeting on the twenty-first. We ask that you be our priestess during the proceedings."

I glanced back at Rick in the corner where his own gaze was exclusively on his damned iPhone. "What exactly does a priestess do at one of your meetings?" I was starting to get an image, but something was blocking me. Or someone. I glanced at the others. Vaughn was a little harder to read, than the others, but I could crack through if I really wanted to. I could also touch him and know everything.

"First of all, we have a gift for you." Voltaire turned and the one who wore the sweater and went by the name of Rodolfo, handed him a white jewelry box. He opened it and lifted something shiny and interesting looking on a silver chain. I wasn't about to touch it. Before I could say anything he said, "May I?" Meaning he wished to put it around my neck.

A growl sounded behind me. Hobart, protective as always, surged around in front of me to block him. I looked up at him silently questioning why.

"That's silver," Hobart said in his low, gravely voice. "She can't touch silver."

"Oh." Voltaire blinked and looked back at his companions. "Why is that?"

"That's really none of your concern," I said before Hobart got into the real reason. I didn't want other people to know that I changed into a wolf-lady at the full moon. If they couldn't tell me their full and real names, then eff them. I didn't have to tell them anything about myself. They were all strangers, and as far as I was concerned, they could remain such once this meeting came to an end.

The piece of jewelry dangled from his fingers. It was a five-petaled flower, in the center, from what I gathered from my Knowing, was a diamond. Nice, but not my style.

"Oh. Too bad. Silver is the metal that a priestess wears at a gathering," Voltaire said.

"Aw, snap," I said. My sarcastic remark made both Rick and Hobart chuckle softly. None of the Priory men were chuckling. I felt their tension rise a degree. The one named Vaughn squinted at me. There was anger building up in him. Most likely he was insulted. *Oh! He picked it out for me.* I didn't need to be an empath to feel that these men had become offended. *Oh well.*

Voltaire gave the jewelry box back to Rodolfo.

A vision of a piece of jewelry popped into my head. An earring. Familiar. *Why is this in my head, all of a sudden?*

Clearing of a throat brought me back. My eyes re-focused on Voltaire's face. "Is everything alright?" he asked.

"She was having a vision," Cho said. I glanced over at Cho. His dark eyes were staring at me intently and unblinking.

"Really?" Voltaire looked impressed and glanced back at his group.

"Sabrina can have a vision at any moment. Sometimes they are small visions. Other times, they are grand," Cho said. I smiled at him. He made a bow.

"Wonderful, wonderful," Voltaire said, looking as though the very thought of it made him excited beyond words. "Perhaps if I explain the nature of our group—"

"Cult, you mean," Rick said from his corner, still punching away on his iPhone. I suddenly realized he may be looking these guys up on the Internet, or texting someone who knew about them.

Voltaire slid him a look, then he made a nervous clearing of his throat and went on in what may have been his lawyer voice. "The Priory of Sion is devoted primarily to the celebration of the female. We believe the sacred female should be honored, and have an honored place in our society." Voltaire held out his hands with his explanation. A large ring on his left hand shimmered. His wedding ring. It threw little sparkles from the lights in the room.

"That's nice," I said to his explanation.

"We recognize the power of the female and her ability to produce life. Without her," he looked around the room, "none of us would be here."

"Exactly," I said. "You all had mothers."

"That's right," Rick said. "Even I had a mother, and she brought life to me, and then left me on the steps of a local church, and I was raised by nuns. So much for motherhood."

"Oh, Rick. You are loved," I said. He snapped his eyes up at me.

"I love you, too, girlfriend," Rick said, smiling. His gaze dipped back to his phone.

My face flushed. I hadn't meant for these sentiments to be said in front of a crowd. My eyes teared up, in fact. I knew about Rick's terrible past, his mother was a drug user and had dumped him. Plain and simple. Fortunately, the sisters of the convent had raised him, not knowing that he was a leprechaun. I wondered how Sister Fred, the nun who had been closest to him, had dealt with his magical abilities, and not revealed them to anyone else. That had to have been trying.

"Down through thousands of years, the predominantly male church has made the woman look as though she is the enemy, is unclean, and unworthy," Voltaire went on.

"Sometimes I feel unclean," I said under my breath. Hobart chuckled over my right shoulder.

"But you are worthy, Sabrina. More worthy than you could possibly know. Being that you are the sibyl, especially, puts you above all the rest. That is why we wish to bring you to the pinnacle of our society. Our priestess. Our *goddess*."

"Okay. Wait a minute. I thought I'd heard of The Priory of Sion," Rick blurted from his spot in the corner. He was looking at his phone, as though reading directly from it as he said, "The original Priory of Sion group dissolved back in the sixties. The head guy was a fake and phony, or at least whatever bullshit history he made up about himself and that group isn't real."

"We admit that this is true," Voltaire said working to keep his face neutral. "However, we are *not* that group. We have begun our own group, separate from the original one. We, of course, agree with their beliefs of the sacred female. We need our goddess. We need Sabrina."

"Right. Right." Rick turned to me. "What he really means is he wants you to be at their ritual so that one of them can have carnal knowledge with you and gain… what do they call it?" He looked at his cell phone again. "Oh, yeah, spiritual orgasm."

"Wha-at?" my voice went up an octave. Now the scenes that had played out in my head a few minutes ago made sense. They had been disgusting and obscene, and, although I couldn't see the faces, I knew that a man and woman were coupling inside a circle of on-lookers.

"Yeah. In other words, you'll be on your back most of the time, while one of their chosen ones has sex with you." Rick eyed Voltaire. "Him, probably." He chuckled, shook his head and looked back down at his iPhone. "You can fool some of the people some of the time, but you can't fool a leprechaun."

"Or a sibyl," Cho put in.

"Right on," Hobart chimed in, smiling. Then his eyes flashed at the group and his smile disappeared, and he re-crossed his arms more firmly. "Shall I show these bums out?"

I held up my hand. "Thank you, Hobart, Rick." I glared at Voltaire and the rest of the group. "Is this what you need me for? Sex?"

Voltaire put out his hands in a placating way. "We only wish to acknowledge the sacredness of the female. We are incomplete without her."

"You sure are, buddy," Rick said, a smirk on his face. "What he's trying to say, is, they want to experience God through sex. They call it *Hieros Gamos*." He was still reading this off his iPhone.

"This isn't *just* sex," Voltaire said, his voice becoming harsh with anger now. "It has nothing to do with something unseemly, or erotic. It is a way to achieve *gnosis*—the knowledge of the divine. It is the oldest way to achieve the ultimate spiritual moment. It's been done down through the ages, since time began for humans. We are able to glimpse God through the act of sex during that one moment of total incapacity at orgasm."

"That's a nice way of puttin' it," Hobart rumbled behind me. Then chuckled like he just got the joke.

I sputtered with a chuckle myself. *That's exactly what I was doing last night. I glimpsed God several times.* My laughter became uncontrollable and I snorted, then fell over sideways against the arm of the chair as I continued to laugh and snort with the hilarity of it all.

"Sabrina?" I didn't know who said my name. Tears in my eyes, I levered myself up on an elbow and wiped away the tears. I gained control from laughing long enough to say, "I decline your offer." Holding back the words I really wanted to say, I turned to Hobart. "Cho, Hobart, show these men out of my house. And Rick as soon as they are gone, put up the ward."

"Right, girlfriend," Rick said and jumped down off the chair and stood. "It might go up a little prematurely." He made a devilish sound as he chugged out of the room.

Cho and Hobart moved around the couch toward the men. They effectively put themselves between myself and them.

"But you have to listen to—"

"Go. Or you'll wish you had done so ten seconds sooner," I said, watching Hobart's lips curl back from his teeth and he growled more menacing than before. All the men turned and scooted through the French doors.

"I knew we should have brought one of the women," one of them groused as they left the room.

I moved out of the room and stood near Rick, listening to the men donning their coats silently. The door opened and finally closed. They were gone.

Rick chuckled. "You are getting popular with the boys."

"Too popular," I said, a smile still on my lips.

"What was so funny, anyway?" Rick asked.

I batted the air. "Never mind. Private joke. But I wish you'd found out about these guys sooner. I wouldn't have had to let them into my house."

"Sorry, but it took me a moment to realize I'd heard about them somewhere. I decided to take a chance to see if they were out there in the cosmos." He held up his iPhone. I now was happy he had the thing.

"I'm glad you did," I said. "And, I meant every word I said."

He looked up. His face red along the hairline. "So did I, kid. So did I."

Chapter 20

Good Witch

The aromas from the kitchen were mouthwatering. Lindee's pies were out of the oven cooling. She'd baked two! I could hardly wait to have a wedge topped with a glob of whipped cream on it. But pizza was in the oven for tonight's meal. I invited Hobart and Rick over for the turkey dinner tomorrow, before they both left for the day. Hobart said he had a meeting tonight with his pack. And Rick had things to do. It sounded like he had tickets to a basketball game from the way he and Hobart were talking sports before they went their separate ways. I decided it would be our Thanksgiving together, Hobart, Rick, Lindee, Cho and me. Cho said he was glad he was done with his fast. He loved turkey. In fact, he had missed out on Thanksgiving all together. He didn't go into details.

The last thing that Hobart said to me was, "Full moon is in three nights." He gave me a significant look over his shoulder. That had me thinking I had to go see Mrs. Bench. "We always meet right beforehand to make plans where to meet," he added as an aside.

I didn't know what he'd meant by the plan part. I didn't want to be part of the pack's werewolf games. I wasn't going to lope around on all fours and get it on with something furry through the three nights of the full moon. No Effing. Way. Been there, done it, hated it.

As soon as I shut the door to Hobart (Rick merely vanished in his usual way), I went to the phone. Pizza aromas made me glance inside the oven. "Almost done?" I asked.

"Yep," Lindee said. Oven gloves on both her hands, she bent and peered into the lit oven. "I'll be taking them out in about three minutes."

"Good. I'm going to make a quick call to my neighbor." I lifted the phone's handset and ran my finger over the little list of names and numbers on the side. It had a tape recorder for messages, and the list was on that portion of the phone. I found Mrs. Bench's number and dialed. She answered on the third ring. I was afraid she wouldn't answer. I didn't know why I thought that.

"Hello?" the familiar, somewhat craggy voice answered.

"Mrs. Bench?"

"Yes. This is she."

"Sabrina, here. Hi, how are you?" I said, finding myself at a loss as to how to ask for a favor. But she was a sweet old lady who just happened to be a witch.

"I'm fine, Sabrina. What do you need?" she asked, shocking me. Well, she was pretty good at precognition too.

"I—uh—the full moon is coming and I need some potion so I don't turn. You think you can help me out?"

"Oh, yes. Of course! As a matter of fact I was doing up some potions tonight. Come over later on, why don't you?"

"Oh, great," I said. "After dinner? Say around seven?"

"That would be fine, Sabrina," she said.

I hung up, turned and found Lindee looking at me, a wry smile on her lips. "That was a very strange conversation."

That's right, she didn't know I turned into a were-creature.

"You need some potion because of the full moon for some reason?" Lindee said. "Sounds like werewolf potion to me. Girl, we need to talk!" She chuckled.

"Yes. You caught me. I was bitten about two months ago by a werewolf. I now turn into Were-girl."

"Wild!" She looked impressed. "So, you change every full moon?"

"Yes."

"Super! You sure know how to have a good time, these days."

"Not gonna happen," I said. "Mrs. Bench can make a potion for me that keeps me from turning."

"Oh, really?" She then made a devilish chuckle. "Not ready to party with the big bads?"

"You met Hobart, right?" I said.

"Yeah."

"Hobart is a 'big bad'. I wound up with him one full moon night. That's how I got to know him."

She guffawed. When she was done laughing and straightened up, she said, "I wondered about that. You two seemed on familiar terms. I just thought you'd dated."

"No. Hobart and I are just friends."

"Just friends huh?"

"Yes!" It wasn't like I'd made a conscious decision as a human to jump in the sack with Hobart.

"I don't see anything wrong with him." her inflection made it sounding as though she would choose him. That *so* figured. "Why wouldn't you?"

"Because she is married," Vasyl's voice startled me. It was as if he'd popped into the room. Maybe he had. I made a half-turn, and his arm draped over my shoulders. I smiled up at him. We kissed. "Oh, yeah. Lucky, lucky me." I put my hand to his bare chest. "You feeling better, hon?" *Hon?* I'd never called anyone that in my life. *My God, now I'm beginning to sound married.*

"Better, *oui*," he said and our lips met again. "Thanks to everyone." He kissed my nose. "Especially you. Last night."

I smiled, trying to hide my discomfort at the subject. The heat rose in my face and I pressed it against his cool shoulder. He had a shirt on, but it was left unbuttoned. I didn't like that he was showing his hunky white chest and six pack off to my cousin. I buttoned him up, at least four buttons. He didn't mind this little treatment. I think he actually enjoyed my attentions.

"I need to go over to my neighbor's after I eat," I said.

"I heard, and approve," he said, kissing the top of my head, then crossed the room and opened the refrigerator. The bottle of liquid refreshment clanked against another as he took one out. I was so glad that Rick was able to bring me several bottles of Organic Red II, which was mostly horse blood, and the rest animal. In other words, it had no human blood in it. I didn't think my delivery man would be coming tonight either.

He turned with the bottle in his hand, twisting the top off.

"Let me get that warmed up for you." I took it from him. Lindee watched me put it into the microwave.

"Ohhh, you warm it up for him. Good idea," Lindee said, slightly mystified by these proceedings. "Pizza is ready. How many pieces you want?" She held the spatula and the pizza wheel over one of the pizzas on the counter.

"None," Vasyl said.

I shot him a frown. He smiled lopsidedly at me. He was in a good mood. "Two for now," I said.

"You want the loaded one, or the other with barbecued chicken and spinach?"

"One of each," I said. The microwave beeped. I grabbed the bottle, which felt hot, and set it on the counter. "I think I over heated it."

"In a glass, then?" he suggested.

Lindee was closest to the glasses, and chose a wine glass. I took it and poured, watching the thick red liquid slide into the glass. I used to get grossed out by this, but I'd become used to it.

I handed Vasyl the glass. "Here you go. Enjoy."

"I shall," he said, raised the glass in salute and sauntered out of the room. From the next room where he spoke with Cho.

Lindee sighed. Both hands covered in the oven mitts were fanning her face. I chuckled, but she shucked the mittens off, took up another wine glass, went to the refrigerator and clinked around and emerged with a bottle of the white Zin.

I grabbed my plate of pizza. "Cho, come and get some pizza or I'll eat it all!"

"In a little bit," he called back.

"Okay. I need this bad," Lindee said, and poured the wine into her glass. She drank about half the glass before she set it down and wiped her mouth on the back of her sleeve.

"You okay?"

"I haven't had sex in months. I'm horny as hell," she said.

"Oh... I see." I settled into a chair at the kitchen table, absorbing what she'd just said. No wonder she'd been flirting with all the men. Lindee grabbed a large wedge of pizza and took a huge bite and came over to the table with her plate. "You mean you haven't had any guy since you disappeared into the Black Veil?"

"Yes."

"You mean to say that you haven't done it with Joha?"

She ate and chewed and drank before she answered. "No. Joha is a perfect gentleman. That gets *so* boring." She looked annoyed by that fact, and snarfed down the pizza wedge as though she were starving. "I'm so horny, and here you've got all these guys hanging around you. I just want *all* of them." She made a snarly-look and then chuckled. Then she drank down the rest of her wine. At this rate she would tie on a good buzz in no time and be offering herself up to any man in my house. Not a good idea. One vampire and Cho, who I wasn't real sure where his gentlemanly virtues would lie—or even his sexual preferences—as far as available and willing women went.

I put my gloved hand on her arm. "Slow down," I said. "Take it slow and breath. If you really love Joha, you'll be strong."

She gasped. "I'm trying."

"Good."

* * *

"Come in, dearie," Mrs. Bench greeted me at her door.

"Hi." I stepped in out of the cold. The heat hit me first, and it was welcomed after my cold walk from my place across the road to Mrs. Bench's house. It smelled like an herb/candle shop and bakery all in one. The door from the porch opened up directly into her kitchen. In the middle of the kitchen, her old Formica table was covered in open books, notebooks, and lots of herbs, dried roots, flowers, and bark nested in their own parchment wrappings. Pots boiled on the stove. Fragrant steam rose and fogged up her windows. Sticky notes pasted on the overhead exhaust fan and cupboards revealed ingredients and instructions in too wild a scrawl for me to interpret.

When I tell people Mrs. Bench is a witch, I can imagine that there are those who would think she'd be dressed in a black shawl, some sort of long dress and a pointed hat. And have an old crone's face. This was not Mrs. Bench. She wore her usual matching sweats—tonight they were deep rose colored—and white canvas sneakers. Her white hair styled in soft curls fell below her ears, just touching the collar of her white shirt underneath. She looked like any elderly lady you would meet anywhere. Rectangular glasses were perched on her nose. She gave a book on the table a quick glance, turned and poured something from one of those pieces of parchments into the boiling water. She seemed energetic, spry and nimble.

"I'll be with you in a jiffy. I need to keep at what I'm doing, or I'll forget where I'm at." She made a cute chuckle. "Make yourself comfortable." She gestured to a chair. I took it.

Mrs. Bench's age was indiscernible to me. At times she looked ancient, and moved as though her bones were brittle as dry spaghetti. But tonight she moved around her kitchen as though she had a fire under her ass and she was forty, not seventy-something, which is where I pegged her age at, because she'd always looked the same age since I was a child.

"Have a cookie," she said, stirring a pot.

I looked around. "Uh, I don't see any," I said, feeling embarrassed.

"Oh, under the star anise."

I still didn't know where she meant, but lifted books and parchment carefully, and finally unearthed a plate of cookies from beneath some dried things that did look like stars, and smelled like licorice. Mrs. Bench bakes great cookies. Better than mine. These were the kind with the Hershey's Kiss in the center.

"Oh, these are good," I said, biting into one. *Heaven!*

"Have another one. I've got plenty more."

I did. Only one more, because I was full from dinner.

"You need to be careful," Mrs. Bench said.

I halted the last cookie to my lips, thinking she meant the cookie.

"I've consulted my crystal ball. You need to be careful of a woman you've just met."

I thought on this. It couldn't be my cousin, since I knew her all my life.

"I don't think I've met anyone recently. Unless you mean Ilona," I said.

"No. You already know about her. This woman you've just met," she said and turned off one of the burners.

I thought for a moment. I could think of no one. I hadn't been out of the house—wait a minute. I *had* been out of the house. Twice. Once at the grocery store, and also when I went to give my plasma.

"Oh," I said. "Oh! I think I know who."

Mrs. Bench turned around to look at me over the rims of her glasses, which were steamed up. "Who?"

"She's a witch." I tried to remember her name. Rick knew her, and said she was a witch.

"Yes. She's dangerous. Don't talk to her." Using a small funnel, she ladled some liquid into a small vial.

"I don't know how I'd come across her again. In fact, we didn't actually meet. I only saw her from a distance. Someone I was with knew her. Then she simply disappeared." Seems I was forgetting something about that day. So much had happened in the past twenty-four hours. A good thing my head's attached. The earring came to mind, but I didn't know how that would count. Plus, I'd left it at home. It was too cold and windy to trudge back to get it now.

"Here you go, dearie," She held up three vials of brownish potion in a white dish cloth. "They're hot, so be careful." She moved to set them on the counter. "We'll let them cool for a while." She sat across from me. "Remember that you have to take one vial after the sun sets and before the moon rises. You may want to check the time of moon rise on those days."

"Okay." I looked at the vials.

"I'll have another batch for you next month, and the month after that. I made plenty." She pointed to her pot on the stove. "I think there should be enough in there for three more months." She smiled sheepishly at me. "I don't have enough small vials to give them to you right now. When I do I'll call and have them waiting for you."

"Okay. Do I owe you anything?"

"No. No. I don't take money for my potions," she said, waving a hand at me, and taking a cookie off the plate and bit.

I nodded with a smile. We enjoyed eating cookies for a moment. "It wouldn't be right. I'm helping you, and anyone else who needs help," she said through a mouth full of cookie and stood and brushed the cookie crumbs off herself. Grabbing potholders, she moved the pot from the stove onto a heat pad on the counter. "I understand that I'm to be a great grandmother." She smiled over her shoulder at me.

"Oh? That's wonderful."

She made a cute gesture with her hand to her mouth as if covering her titter. "You know what I mean," she prompted.

I didn't have a clue.

"Ophelia was over the other day? Carrying *another* woman's child?"

Like an idiot, it dawned on me slowly. "OH!" *Duh.* "Yeah."

"That was very, very sweet of you to do what you did. Bill's last request, and you honored it. Blessings to you, dear!"

I blinked at her trying to decide if she realized the impact of what I'd done. Maybe she did. I hadn't realized it until Dante had told me. But as I stood there in the witch's kitchen, it hadn't really hit me, until now this impacted her as well. *My child is inside another woman's womb, and it will grow up to be something the world has never seen before.*

"No one else knows," I said. "I mean Ophelia and her family know, of course, because it is Bill's child," I explained hastily. "But I didn't tell anyone in my family. And the less people who know, the better."

Crescendo

"Absolutely!"

"Mrs. Bench, I did the right thing. Didn't I?"

"Emma. Call me Emma."

"Emma," I said. "I feel like I've cheated on Vasyl."

"Oh, no, my dear," she said. "You're second guessing yourself. You didn't do any hanky-panky. So, no, you didn't cheat on anyone."

"Yeah. I know."

"The vampires will have an ultimate leader. A king. That baby is yours and Bill's, sure, but the prophesy has come true!" Her hand was lifted, palm-out, like someone making a pledge.

"That might be why some people want me dead," I said, moving a finger to one of the vials. It was still really hot.

"You have your protectors. And you married your vampire," she said. "You need to allow them to help you."

"I'm trying. It's hard to get used to."

Her bony hand clutched my shoulder. "You will. And you will find more people will come and help you, once they know who you are."

"What about Ophelia? Who protects her?"

"Her people." Mrs. Bench stared at me.

"Then… you know they're—who—er—what they are? Bill and—oh, my God!" My hand went to my mouth with realization as Mrs. Bench nodded, a kindly old-lady smile on her lips.

"Of course, I know. I'm their grandmother." She made a little cock of the head. "I'm only part Nephilistic. My mother's side."

"That's why you can do witchcraft?"

"Yes. It came from them."

"That explains it all," I said.

"Those might be cool enough, now," she said, nodding toward the vials. I took this as a subtle hint our business was finished here and I should leave her so that she could continue her work.

I touched them. They were hot-warm, and I picked them up and slid them, clinking lightly, into my coat pocket. I edged toward the door. "Thanks, Mrs. Bench, for—"

She took my face into her warm hands and I was looking into her bright blue eyes, surprised at first I wasn't getting a read, but I knew why.

"No, my child. It's Emma, or you may call me grandmother if you wish, from now on."

"Right, Emma," I said. I wasn't really related to her, as I had not married Bill. We hadn't even done it, and I wasn't the one pregnant—that's how crazy this all was. So I couldn't call her 'grandmother', it didn't feel right; and yet, looking into her kindly eyes, I felt that we were more related than I was to my own grandmothers.

"Once more," she said, "tell me how Bill died. I need to make absolutely sure he will not come back as a vampire."

"Oh," I said and swallowed. She looked straight into my eyes. To show her I wasn't lying, I looked straight back. "The rock that fell on him, cut him in half. He barely had much time to tell me the things he did."

"And then he died?"

"Yes."

"And his body turned to ashes?"

"Yes."

"Good. It was terrible how he died. But the fact he turned to ashes is a good omen, I think." She didn't show any sorrow, just smiled at me, then she hugged me hard. Harder than I gave her credit as far as strength. I hugged back.

I left her warm, cozy, aromatic kitchen, trying not to shed tears as I did. The cold made me tremble as I stepped out onto her porch. I didn't really shiver so much from the cold, as from what she'd told me earlier—her warning. Walking toward my house, across the quiet snowy road, I kept looking back at the house. The golden lights glowing through the windows making the snow around the house glisten. I stood still for a few heartbeats, listening to the quiet. That's what my father said snow did; it absorbed all sound, so that on a windless night you could hear a pin drop.

I looked up into the black sky. Pin-pricks of starlight shimmered above. I had that illusion of smallness then. Yet, I was the center of attention. Attentions I didn't want—from the Priory of Scion, to the vampires, and anyone else who wanted a piece of me.

And Bill! If he hadn't been dying, and asked me to grant his dying wish, I would not have done what I'd done. It was as simple as that. Fate, or whatever you call it, had caused me to make a decision that I wasn't all that sure was the correct one for *everyone*. Myself, included.

The horn of a train two miles away, brought me out of my thoughts. I could usually hear a train's horn on a quiet night. It sounded closer, and mournful to my ears.

I turned back toward my house, wiping tears from my face.

Chapter 21

Bad Witch

"Well, I'm going to bed," Lindee announced, opening the door to the den.

I looked up at the clock on the wall. It was only a few minutes before nine. She was in the pajamas I had given her to wear.

"Really? So early?" I asked, not that it bothered me.

She wrinkled her nose. "Yeah, I think I've still got the ley-line-lag." We both chuckled.

"Well, good night. And thanks for cooking," I said.

"I didn't do any real cooking," she said.

"Yes you did. You baked those awesome pies and you'll be working like crazy tomorrow."

"I don't mind. Keeps me busy. Mom wouldn't let me do things my way in the kitchen. I love your kitchen. It's so large compared to my mom's."

"Well, I'm glad you're here," I said and gave her a big hug. She hugged back. It was the night for hugs.

"Aw, now, don't start that." She pulled away and wiped a tear. I could see she was embarrassed. I don't know why. We were cousins, but I guess we were never that close, in high school and beyond.

"Sorry, but I want you to know you've been missed," I said.

"Stop it. 'Night." She twirled away, and shut the French doors quietly. A small light within revealed her movements through the sheers. Earlier, she had pulled out the bed inside the couch and got it made before I had come home. Cho was upstairs.

The light clicked off and I turned to the bedroom where Vasyl was settled on the edge of the bed. I went to him. He put his arms around me, and kissed me. "You are going to bed now?"

"I'm exhausted," I said. "I hope you don't mind."

"Not at all. I will watch over you while you sleep."

"My protector." I patted his chest and kissed him. He rose, looking down at me.

"When will you take the potion against your turning?" he asked.

"Not until the first night of the full moon. Which reminds me, I have to ask Hobart what night is the first night. I think he said it was coming up, but I can't remember when." I thought I should call him, but remembered he had a meeting tonight.

"*Bonsoir, mon amour*," he said and gave me another quick kiss. Then he vanished. I knew he went outside to watch over the house, as always. I felt safe knowing he was back, strong enough to watch over me.

I walked through the house, turning off lights, and then closed my bedroom door, locking it. Anyone wanted me could knock. I went to my drawer and unearthed my birth control pills (I'd moved them back into my room earlier, fearing I wouldn't remember them), still feeling guilty about taking them behind Vasyl's back. But also feeling as though this one decision was the only smart one I'd made in a while. I undressed and shimmied into my nightgown. I padded into the bathroom and took my pill. I went through my night regiment and returned to my room, looking forward to a good night's sleep.

My house phone rang when I slipped under the covers. I let go a sound of aggravation and flopped the covers off me. "This had better be important." In fact, I would turn off the ringer so any other calls would go to my messages. I padded out into the living room to answer the ringing phone. I thought it might be a salesman. Or, maybe Mrs. Bench. And since I couldn't get a read from whomever it was, I thought it might be Mrs. Bench calling me for some reason. That both intrigued and frightened me. Something about the phone call wasn't good. But I had to answer to find out why.

"Hello?"

"Is this Sabrina Strong?"

"Yes," I said. "Who is this?" It was then that I got a flash of the woman in the plasma place running away, red hair flying.

"You don't know me," she said. "My name is Kiel—"

"Kiel St. Thomas," I said. It wasn't a question. "You're a witch."

Pause. She may have been thinking about how I knew, and then it clicked.

"Yes. Rick told you who I was, didn't he?"

"Yes." *That you're evil.*

"I'm sorry to bother you, but I just wanted to ask if you'd found my earring. I was there that day, giving plasma, in the same chair you were in. I didn't want to run into Rick. You know, we sort of had a bad parting and I didn't want to—um—have an ugly scene?"

"Right," I said, rolling my eyes. "What does it look like?" I didn't want to admit I had the earring, and at the same time if it was hers, she needed to identify it.

"The earring? Well it has beads made of amber. They're one of a kind. I had them made by a lady in a Wicca shop. They're very expensive and I'd like it back, if you have it?"

"I do have that earring," I said. "You want me to mail it, or—"

"That would be nice. But could you make sure that you still have it? You might have lost it."

I was feeling chilly standing talking to this woman. "Sure." Fortunately I had the cordless phone and had returned to my bedroom. I stepped over to the jewelry box where I'd stashed it. I had wanted to show Mrs. Bench, and forgot it when I'd gone over.

I opened the box. The earring lay on top of the junk I store to one side. "Yep. Still got it."

"I know this sounds really weird and all, but could you make sure that the beads are all there, there should be thirteen."

"Thirteen?" I repeated. Why did that not surprise me? But why did she need me to count the beads? "Why? I mean that's a really strange request."

"I contacted the woman who made them and told her that I'd lost it, and asked if she could make me a new one. But if you have it—"

"I do."

"How many beads are on it? I just want to make sure they're all on there."

"Okay," I said, and picked up the damned earring.

"You have it in your hand?"

I frowned at the phone. "Yes."

"Good."

Over the phone I heard someone chanting in the background and then Kiel's voice chimed in. *What the hell?* Before it dawned on me that something magical was happening, before I could comprehend that I was in danger, my body dissolved in a flash. Alone and small as particles in an atom, I could see nothing. I could hear nothing. This lasted for about ten seconds, making my inner self panic. And then suddenly sound came back like a crash. As did my awareness while a zing of fear lit through me. In an instant, I was on solid ground—which was super cold—and no sooner than I could blink two people had me by the arms and hauled me backward, dragging me through the snow, my gaze going up into the night's black sky, my bare heels slicing through snow. My scream became lost in a cloud of vapor when my body was thrust against something solid.

"Let me go!" I cried, my whole body going ridged, fighting against the two women who were tying me up against a cold pillar, my feet chilling quickly in the icy snow. I didn't know where I was, but, obviously, I was outside.

Once my eyes quit darting around fearfully, I took in my captors. I counted thirteen, including the ones that had tied me up, who were now returning to the outer circle of women who had gathered around me. With everything going on I tried, but couldn't find the ley line to get the hell out of here.

"Quickly! We must work quickly!" A woman with a lot of tattooing around her eyes said. Her robe blowing wildly in the wind. They all wore black robes, and cowls over their heads, so I couldn't identify any of them—but really I didn't need to see their faces. I knew who they were instantly. One was definitely Kiel St. Thomas.

They began chanting. The chant was in Latin—or that's what it sounded like—and I had no idea what they were doing to me, but I felt an odd pull of energy right away.

"Stop it! Let me go!" I screamed at them. Terror stabbed my inner being. Whatever they were doing, it was working. I felt suddenly weak, and the chill of the wintery air penetrated me to the marrow. I shivered so hard I thought my limbs would break off. Witchcraft wasn't something I practiced, but I knew enough about it to know they were conducting black magic. The very air electrified with it. They were draining me through their magic. Draining my chi or aura—something basic that would take away my essence. My whole body tingled at first, and then a burning sensation grew as the ugly curse slid across the cold night.

My head snapped up as this wild magic coursed through me, flooding my mind with numbing cold and I screamed. I might have been screaming a name, but I could barely make my lips move around the vowels—my lips were frozen.

After several minutes of their chanting, I couldn't hold my head up. My chin sagged to my chest, and my body listed to one side. The weight of my body pulled on my arms, and the ligaments became strained. I was in pain, but I could only suffer through it, because I simply couldn't move. After another minute, I couldn't hold my eye lids open. The witch's voices became distant. A floaty feeling came over me, possibly my aura had lifted from me, I wasn't sure. Not right away.

Then, tingling with lightness, I floated above them. I now looked down on the whole scene. The circle of women with a bonfire nearby and candles stationed at all four corners of a five-pointed star drawn in the snow. My body was in the center, my head bent down. My arms bound in a way that looked extremely uncomfortable. This was weird to see myself while outside of my body. Why, or how I had separated from my body, I wasn't sure. Had I suddenly found a way to separate my astral body from my physical one? Or, was I dead?

While pondering this situation, I saw something white, cloud-like, appear next to my body and then it moved around it, close, and yet not touching it. It circled my body, and each time it circled it went faster than before, until it was a blur, like a propeller that went around at full bore. The very air seemed as though charged with energy, and the witches were aware of it. They stopped chanting and looked on as though taken by surprise.

At the same time, I noticed thin gold and red lines led away from my body into the hands of these witches. But, as the odd wisp, or cloud, gained momentum, the little lines stopped leaking from me. It was as though this thing, this entity, had somehow stopped the leakage. I noticed this began to frustrate the witches. Their concentration broken, they stopped chanting completely and looked around at each other.

Kiel, the leader with all the tattooing, dropped her hands and shouted to the others, "Stop! Something is wrong. Something is blocking us!"

The others dropped their hands. A few of them staggered and one fell to her knees in the snow, as though the ritual had also drained them. Or, possibly it was like pulling on a rope in a game of tug-o-war, and my end let loose.

That was when I noticed those odd gold-and-red lines were now pulled from those who had staggered. These energy lines—what I perceived them as—surged back into my own body.

That's when a tug came on my aura. I was being pulled back into my body, but I resisted. I felt wonderful. Nothing hurt, and everything below me too interesting to watch. The strange cloud stopped whirling around me, and became stationary. Then, it formed into something solid and black. It took about five seconds before I made it out to be Dante. He stood there all in black, his long black hair flapping in the wind.

"Witches!" Dante said, his voice strong, deep and dangerous. "You dabble in things you have no business meddling with. This is the sibyl, and her mate is not pleased. More importantly, I am very, *very* angry."

"Who the hell are you?" Kiel snarled. "Whoever you are, you get a dose of my powers!" She thrust her hands forward. Two large bolts of light jettisoned from her hands toward Dante. He held up his hands and absorbed the power. His laugh sounded belittling.

"Thank you! I have not fed so well in a while," Dante said, his deep voice resonating somehow more forcefully than before, and I barely recognized it.

Kiel, who looked as though she couldn't believe he didn't die on the spot, shot more power bolts at him. He absorbed them again. I guessed Kiel wasn't too bright a witch. Dante could not be killed, and any energy thrown at him was a repast for him.

"Nice. That was better than the last one," Dante said, giving her a cocky smile.

Kiel stopped and bent at the waist, panting, red hair flopping down in her face. She'd poured everything into that last one, I could tell. She stared at him through the snarly hair, looking as though she couldn't believe she'd butted heads with someone stronger than herself. She tossed her auburn hair back. "What are you? A demon?"

"Oh, no. Much better," Dante said, his voice sliding with belittling contempt.

Looking frustrated, Kiel shouted to the others, "Don't just stand there! Get him!"

Three women near her wound up and threw flaming bolts at Dante, the air hissing from the energy. It hit him in a shower, lighting up the whole area like an explosion of firecrackers. Individually they weren't as strong as Kiel, but together they seemed as strong.

Instead of absorbing the energy, Dante threw it all back at them in one big, evil red bolt. It hit them like a bowling ball hits the pins, and all three women were knocked off their feet, arms flailing, and fell on their backs in the snow. They didn't move. If I were in my body and conscious, I would have laughed. I *was* laughing, but it sounded, and felt odd.

Kiel's head swiveled left and right, hair flying like a red cape, as she took in what he had done to the three witches. She gave Dante a look that really scared me.

"I'm tired of playing nice," Dante snarled. "You've taken something that doesn't belong to you. And that doesn't rest well with the rogue."

"Rogue? What are you talking about?"

Before she got the words out of her mouth another form misted into reality beside Dante, and turned quickly into a tall man with large tattered black wings. It made him look quite evil. Formidable. Vasyl was royally pissed. Steam jettisoned out of each nostril, as he leveled an evil glare her way.

"You dare to touch that which is mine, witch?" Vasyl's roar made the rest of the witches jump up from the ground, and scatter into the night.

"Wait! Come back!" Kiel shouted, but all of her cohorts fled into the darkness. Now she was alone. The distant, but distinctive sounds of car doors slamming and engines turning over reached my ears.

"I believe she would help you heal all the way, if you were to take her blood," Dante suggested with a smile.

"It has been decades since I've taken witch's blood. Thank you for suggesting it," Vasyl said and moved forward.

The last thing I saw was Vasyl stepping toward Kiel. Things went black momentarily. All sound was sucked into a vacuum and swirled around, the sound bent and distorted. My astral body could no longer resist the call to join my physical body.

When I opened my eyes again, my arms were no longer pinned back, but the muscles in my shoulders, arms and back were sore. Disoriented, I thought I had been on a merry-go-round, up-side-down. After my head quit swimming, and the feeling came back to my hands—it felt like little razors slitting my flesh. The opposite was true with my feet. I had no feeling in them at all.

"Ow. I feel like shit," I muttered, opening my eyes. Dante peered down at me. He held my body in his arms. Things were not right. "Where am I? Where's Vasyl?" I tried to look around, but it was black.

"I'm taking you back now," he said, a smile on his lips.

"You mean I'm not dead?" I said, immediately feeling stupid for saying it.

"No. Not yet." Dante smiled, and let out a small snicker, as though he found my words—or me—funny.

"Darn."

He turned around. My body shifted from his arms to someone else's. Now I was looking up into Vasyl's face.

I weakly drew my hands around his neck. "I want to go home. I'm cold."

"That's exactly where I'm taking you," he said.

The trip was instantaneous. The last thing I was conscious of was the cold night air around me. Then, the warmth of my house both surrounded and soothed me. But I still shivered violently in Vasyl's arms.

"Cho! Lindee!" Dante's voice made my ears ring.

"What is it?" Lindee's distinctive voice sounded sleepy, when she entered the room. I caught a glimpse of her disheveled hair and shocked look on her face. "What's wrong? What happened?"

"She was abducted by witches," Dante said.

"What? Witches?" She laughed. Her laughter died. Must have been the nasty look Vasyl had given her. "There wasn't anyone here," she said, voice nervous. "I was right next to her, in there." She pointed.

"Never mind. She needs to be warmed up." Dante pulled back the covers on the bed. I was lowered into the bed. My shivering continued. It was like the bed itself had absorbed all my cold, and became an ice block.

Lindee felt my face. "Oh, my God, she's freezing!"

"I can't feel my feet!" I said through chattering teeth.

Lindee looked down at my feet. Her eyes went large. "She might have frostbite. We need a basin of cool water."

"I can do that," Cho said, standing at the threshold of my bedroom, wearing sweats and no shirt. He rushed away.

"Lindee, do you know where more blankets are?" The question came from someone. I didn't know who. There was so much commotion, it was as though I was in a hospital.

"I have plenty on my bed," she said.

"Then get them and put them on this bed," Vasyl said.

"No. I will get more blankets," Dante said. "You help Cho with the water. Make sure it isn't hot, or even warm, just cool."

My head thrashed from side to side while my body quaked.

"I have no warmth to give her," Vasyl said.

"Nor do I," Dante said.

"We need a human," Vasyl said.

Dante nodded. He vanished from the room. It might have been two minutes or two seconds, I had no conception of time, I was so cold I couldn't comprehend much. Then someone slid in beside me. Warm arms went around me. Lindee. Her warm little body spooned me.

"Oh, my God, she's like an iceberg!" Lindee said and tried to hug warmth into me.

"We need another," Vasyl said.

"Me?" Cho suggested.

"It will have to be you. There are no other humans. Place the basin on the floor there."

Another warm body slid in on my other side. Cho's long, sinewy body was warm, his arms muscular and strong. The fact he wore no shirt barely phased me. He coiled his arms around Lindee's and they tried to hold me down. I was like a bucking horse that wouldn't let them ride. After a minute, my teeth quit chattering. The shivers came and went.

"Is there some brandy in the house?" the question came from Dante. He shook out the blankets he'd found and covered us.

"We need to get her feet into the water," Lindee said from behind me.

"There's brandy up in my room," Cho said. "It's not mine, by the way. I hate brandy."

"I'll get it," Dante said.

"It's in a bottom drawer by the bed," Cho called out.

"Let's get her feet into that water," Lindee said. She drew away from me. With many hands helping, I was propped up on the side of the bed. My legs were drawn out of the covers, and my feet brought down into water that felt like fire.

I screeched and pulled my feet out. It was like someone had set them on fire.

"Oh, that hurt?" Lindee said. "It's because your feet are so cold. You have to leave them in there, hon."

"No! It hurts too much," I said, refusing to put my feet back in, water dripping from my feet into the basin.

"Guys she won't put her feet in the water," Lindee said.

Vasyl leaned to me. "Sabrina." His hands took my face in them, and he stared into my eyes. "Sabrina, look at me. Listen to me. You must put your feet back into the water. It will—" he looked at Lindee. "What will it do?"

"It will bring the warmth back to her feet," Lindee said, patting my thighs, trying to press them down. "My brother had the same thing happen to him when he was a kid. We did the same thing, and he was okay afterwards. He didn't lose any toes."

"Sabrina, put your feet back into the water," Vasyl said, violet eyes staring into mine. "It will feel only warm to you." His command hitting me just right. *Yeah, I should do this...*

I paused, my anguish softened slightly. I let my feet down into the water. No burning. Weird that I couldn't feel much, but I knew in the back of my mind that Vasyl had been able to thrall me. He could sometimes override my ring's ability to block any vampire's thrall because we had shared blood a few times.

"Hey, wait. She's got an electric blanket in here," Lindee said, standing in front of my blanket hutch. "Here, help me put it on the bed."

Vasyl moved away from me. "Should we not put it over her, now?"

"Good idea," Lindee said. "Here. Plug it in over there." She pointed to an outlet.

The two worked on getting the electric blanket plugged in and arranged around my shoulders and over my legs.

"Be careful not to get it in the water," Lindee said. "We don't want to electrocute her."

"Here's the brandy," Cho announced, returning to the bedroom. Dante had the brandy bottle in his hands.

"Get a small glass and put some in it," Lindee said. Cho turned out of the room, heading for the kitchen. She leaned to me, placing a hand to my back. "Is that beginning to warm up?"

I still shivered, but not as violently as before. I nodded. The blanked was beginning to warm up.

"Maybe I should get a bath started. She needs to have her core temperature go up," Lindee said, and then left my side.

"Here's the brandy," Cho said, presenting a tumbler glass with about an inch of dark brandy in it. Blackberry. I had no idea my father had blackberry brandy stashed in his room. I had never seen it when I had cleaned the room weeks ago. Then, again, I really didn't want to know. It might have been his only vice, drinking alone, in his room at night.

I took the glass from his hand. I wasn't a fan of hard liquor. This tasted sweet, and went down my throat warm. It hit my stomach like a torch.

"Take only sips," Vasyl coached while knelt beside me, looking up at me with those incredible violet eyes. I was moved by everyone's caring and quick actions.

"Thank you," I said to him and looked up at Cho. "Thanks. Both of you." I looked at Dante. "I'm so glad you were there to rescue me."

He bent in a bow. "I am always with you, Sabrina."

"We are here for you, Sabrina," Cho said.

I took another sip. Lindee started a bath, from the sound of the rushing water. I would have a warm bath. It sounded soothing.

"Tell me how did the witch get you?"

I shivered more at the thought of how it was done. Through trembling lips, I said, "The day I went to give my plasma at that place, I found an earring." Actually I didn't find it, Ariel had found it. But for some reason I kept it. "Tonight, after you left, and just as I was getting into bed, my house phone rang. It was the woman who Rick recognized while we were there. Her name is Kiel St. Thomas. He told me she's a witch. I didn't think I'd ever come across her again. I'd meant to take the earring to Mrs. Bench and see if she could get something from it."

"Like what?" Vasyl asked.

"I don't know. I couldn't read anything from it at all, come to think of it." I frowned down at the brandy in my hands, noticing they weren't trembling anymore.

Vasyl looked briefly up at Cho, then back at me. "Obviously the earring was embedded with a spell, but it would have needed to be invoked. How was that done?"

"They invoked it while I was on the phone. She had me go and dig it out. Gave me a lame excuse about making sure it had the same number of amber beads on it, or something. Anyway, it worked to get me wherever they were." I sipped on the brandy. "I think they were draining me of my powers."

"It's very possible," Cho said. "Witches who are power-hungry will always try and find ways to gain more magic. Sometimes they find special people from which to drain in order to gain power."

Vasyl stood. "He is right. They were draining you of your powers." I looked up at him. "Dante came to your rescue in time to stop them from taking all of it."

"It's true. I felt—feel—drained," I said and shivered a little. My shivers now came in spurts. The blanket felt wonderful but I was still cold. "I still feel like I'm drained. Exhausted." I sneezed twice. "Maybe even sick." My mouth trembled as I spoke.

Dante's dark shadowy figure appeared in the doorway. My bedroom door had been pulled all the way open.

"I took the power they harvested from you into myself. I will be able to return it to you..." his voice trailed off, and his gray eyes lifted from me to engage Vasyl's.

Vasyl had already turned to him. "Then do so." His hand was outstretched to me.

"Sabrina is not a witch. She is a magical creature who absorbs power through touch."

"So, touch her," Vasyl said, gesturing to me. "Make her better."

Dante blinked and dipped his head down holding it that way for several seconds as though he were contemplating something. He drew his head up and looked at Vasyl. "Forgive me, Vasyl, but it is not that simple. She must take it from me and I must give it to her in a very intimate way." He paused again. Vasyl looked clueless. "Through coupling with her."

"*Sacreblu!*" Vasyl said, and a string of French spewed from him, hands whipping the air around him, his words bombarding my ears.

"Hey, no one speaks French, in here. Translate, please," Lindee said.

"I speak it," Cho said. Lindee gave him a look.

"You're kidding." She looked incredulous.

"No I speak French, Italian, Spanish and Mandarin."

"Whatever." Lindee stomped away.

Vasyl complied. "You are not making this up just so that you can have her in your bed, are you?"

"I assure you, I am not." Dante crossed his arms and returned the glare Vasyl gave him. "Of all the people who would know, since you are from the first century, you should know the sibyl gains new powers from her lovers. She's born with some, but some she must gain by her consorts."

"It is the way of the sibyl," Cho agreed, with a nod of his head and a slight smile, looking at each of us in turn. "I might add it is not unheard of the sibyl attaining power through sex from a powerful sorcerer. The attraction is the power exchange that the two might share. A certain ability, or affinity, can be given in exchange for the other's. Its only price might be that they share their greatest powers. Obviously a sibyl would not want to, or be able to share her power with a known enemy."

Dante looked validated.

"However," Cho went on, a finger came up to drive home his point, "in Sabrina's weakened state the more powerful sorcerer must understand how much power she can hold. It is not unusual for certain powers to overwhelm the receiver. There is also a great danger to her that afterwards she might become insane, or possibly die from too much power."

"It is too dangerous," Vasyl argued vehemently.

"I know Sabrina well, I was her lover in my human life. I can gauge how much power to give her."

Lindee appeared through the threshold of the living room, gaping at the scene between the two vampires. "The bath is ready. Oh, wow."

Vasyl's head swung to her. "What?" he growled at her. I wanted to chastise him, but I didn't have the strength to bark at him.

"Uh, the bath's ready?" She shrank back into the darker room and waited.

"Let me take her to the bath." Vasyl turned back to me. Cho took the glass of brandy from my hands. Vasyl pulled the blanket off and lifted me, my feet still wet, and carried me into the bathroom. "We will discuss this further, shaman," he said over his shoulder.

"I sensed something happening. I... hey—" the new voice belonged to Rick who was standing in the living room.

Vasyl looked over his shoulder.

"What's wrong?" I asked, looking around Vasyl's head to find Rick. My breath caught seeing Rick in a surprising disarray. He wore gray sweats and his hair was messed up as though he had been in bed. He wore bedroom slippers, and no socks. I'd never seen Rick in this state, even when we had shared a motel suit while traveling with Tremayne. Something was up.

"Wait," I said. Vasyl stood with me in his arms ready to transport me into my bath.

"Uh, did I come at a bad time?" Rick asked, looking uncomfortably at me in Vasyl's arms. I was still in my nightgown, my feet dripping wet, plus I was shivering, and sneezed a few times.

Rick's eyes roved to the next room and saw the other three standing around. "Crap! Whatever the hell you guys do at night is none of my business, but—"

"Sabrina was abducted by witches, she needs to get warm, as she was outside wearing nothing but her nightgown," Dante explained at length. "Why do you need to speak with her?"

"The ward went down around her brother's place. I have no idea why," Rick said, holding up his iPhone. I remembered his saying that he'd had an alarm rigged up on his wards through his iPhone.

"What?" I said, casting a worried look up at Vasyl. "Are they alright?"

"I will go and check," Dante volunteered.

"I can go with you," Rick offered.

"No. I can do it without being seen," Dante said. He turned to us and said, "There may have been a dual purpose that the witches chose that moment to snatch you. I'll be back shortly."

Chapter 22

Power

Submerged in the bath water, I was alone, at last. After five minutes in the warm water, I quit shivering, *finally*. Vasyl had put me into the tub of water, and although it felt warm, I was told the water was lukewarm. Gradually Lindee drained the cooler water, and added hotter water as I became used to it.

Lindee's babbling on and on had worn on me, tiring me further.

"I could have been a nurse, you know? I don't get squeamish over puke, or blood, and shit like that," she said while seated on the toilet lid. "You know they had me chopping heads off of chickens at the palace? I'm their main chicken-head-hacker." She threw her head back with a burst of laughter. "And it doesn't bother me." She shrugged, and turned off the hot water.

"Get out so I can warm up," I said in a calm way, so as not to ruffle her feathers. She had been very helpful, but really, I'd had enough of her constant babbling, and her wild laughter for one day. I realized why I did not spend much time with her. She drained me on a day when I felt normal. Right now, she made me woozy.

"Oh, sure. I'll get you something warm to wear."

"My sweats," I said. "Put them on the bed. And shut the bathroom door, please?" The door leading from my bedroom to the bath was open, creating a chilly draft.

"Done! Enjoy your bath." Lindee was up and out of the room, closing the door quickly.

Silence.

Vasyl, meanwhile was in a meeting with Rick and Cho. I was unable to get a read as to where they were exactly. Normally, I couldn't read any one of them, because one was a vampire, and one was magical. And for whatever the reason, I never could read Cho very easily. Either he blocked me, or there was another reason, but I should at least get an idea of where they were in the house. That meant that my powers were completely drained. If my clairvoyant powers were gone, it meant the witches had drained me completely. I suppose Vasyl was explaining to Rick what had happened, and why I was taking a bath at such an odd hour. I could hear the exchange of three male voices in the other room. Vasyl's deep and resonating; Cho's softer yet deep voice; and Rick's higher, almost plaintive tenor. Then Lindee added something about warming me up with brandy... "Her feet might have gotten frost bite if I hadn't of acted quickly!" I caught her words easily through the door.

"*Oui*. Rick knows this," Vasyl said, cauterizing more of her input.

I wiggled my toes. First the tingling and burning had begun in my toes. They were still white, now. The feeling had come back after being in the warm bath water after about ten minutes. That was a relief. I didn't want to lose my toes. I mean I really liked painting them in the summer. They looked blah right now. Maybe I could have Lindee paint them the plumb color I liked.

With the door closed to the others, I lay back against a rolled up towel Lindee had placed there for me, letting my inner babble drown out the outside babbling going on. Steam curled up around me with the shower curtain drawn to hold in the warm air. I reached for the glass of brandy placed on the ledge and lifted it to my lips but stopped. I could drink no more of it. My stomach would heave if I did. I forgot I didn't like brandy. Too bad she didn't give me some wine, instead.

I eased a sigh through my lips. What a night!

The two developments—Rick's ward going down, and Dante announcing he could give my powers back to me only if we had sex—were swimming around in my head. Was Dante that desperate to have sex with me he'd make something up like that? I knew Dante could find someone to have sex with, without trying to trick either me, or Vasyl into something like that. But Cho had argued that what he'd said was true. But I simply couldn't see Vasyl saying "Sure, go ahead and boink my wife."

It didn't matter. Until I heard that my brother and family were safe, I had no desire to do the nasty with Dante, no matter how desirable he was.

I decided, since my hair was already wet, I'd wash it. I used the mint-raspberry shampoo, and delighted in the scent as I sudsed up good and then leaned back to dunk my head into the water. I used the conditioner and rinsed a little more thoroughly with my large cup. Then I leaned back to relax. Exhaustion still ruled my body, and I felt in no hurry to get out of the tub.

Silence invaded. I didn't hear any noises or voices from the other room. I nearly fell asleep when the sound of something moving caused me to jerk with a start.

"Oh!"

"I'm sorry. I didn't mean to startle you," Dante said, sitting on the toilet lid, the shower curtain drawn back. Sans shirt and pants but wearing—uh—okay, it looked like Indian underwear. My brother called them "blanket butts", and I really took exception to that. Lean hips and legs uncovered, he wore the traditional loin cloth made of soft doe skin, intricately decorated in quill work. It was almost as handsome as the man who wore it.

"Your brother and family are fine," he said, brushing a length of black hair out of his eyes.

I leaned back with a long drawn out sigh. "Thank God."

"I sensed activity, earlier, however," he said, his voice grave. "But perhaps when Rick realized the ward had gone down, and he'd put it back up quickly enough before whoever would have come and tried to hurt them."

I lifted my hand out of the water and patted his brown one on the side of the tub. His hands were strong, and very knowledgeable about what I liked in bed. *Oh, God what am I doing thinking about that for?* He could easily read my mind, being that he was telepathic.

"There is the matter of getting your powers back," he said, grasping my wet hand before I could pull it away. Holding it by the fingers, he lifted it toward his mouth, turning it so that my wrist was exposed to his lips. I thought he would kiss it. Instead, he opened his generous mouth and opened. White teeth clamped down, not hard, but enough for me to feel it. He didn't have fangs, like living vampires did. He didn't need them. A sudden surge of pleasure simmered through me. His mouth released my wrist and a tongue flicked across the pulse. A shiver of desire coursed through my body. *Shit!* He invoked the bite!

"You-you're despicable!" I groused.

He only chuckled at me.

"Not fair!" I complained.

"I know. But I've always wanted to do that. See what it does to you."

"Satisfied?" My brow went up.

"Probably not as satisfying for me as it was for you," he said.

I crossed my arms and shifted my head showing my disdain, but since I was naked in a bathtub I wasn't able to sell it.

"Did you talk to Vasyl? About—the problem?" I asked.

"I did."

"And he said yes?"

"Reluctantly. I had to persuade him."

"How?"

"I told him you might die."

"Would I? Die, I mean?"

His shoulder hiked up. "You might. Remember how I became sick after I shift changed too quickly?"

I glanced away. I swallowed thinking about how lost I had been, how his dying had left a hole in my heart. Those feelings flipped through me and I had to put a hand over my lips to stifle the despondent sound that caught in my throat.

"Hey," he said in a gentle tone. "I'm here."

I squeezed my eyes, ridding the tears that had collected in them. Yes. Here, but not alive-here.

"I know." I pushed my emotions away best I could and looked up at him. This wasn't something I'd wanted to talk to him about. "So, you told Vasyl I might die and he said yes?"

"Not right away," he said, a smile lifting his lips. "I told him if you died, you would be *all* mine. That's when he decided it would be wise."

I chuckled. I couldn't help myself.

"I need to give you back some of this power that's raging through me that I pulled from those witches. You need your powers back in order to fight the vampires, and others."

I became nervous thinking about it, about fighting the vampires, if and when it came down to it. I wasn't feeling myself, and had to get back my powers. I couldn't describe it as weakness, but it was almost as though someone had taken a piece of me, and I damn well wanted it back!

He gazed away from me. "There is no privacy here, in this house," he said—meaning for us to get naked and make noises, because we would. "May I suggest *my* place?"

"You have a place?" I said, finding this rather unbelievable.

"Of course I do. When I wish to be alone."

"Right. I suppose, since you have this place we could go there." I had no idea where his "place" might be.

"And since you're…" his gray eyes crawled over my nakedness in and out of the water. "Properly unclothed."

I twisted my lips in thought. "I might be missed. By the others."

"Not necessarily. Time does not exist where I will take you." He still held my hand in his. Things around me shifted. The bathtub, walls, the toilet—the whole room—winked out. Then we moved, not so much physically, as, well, from one place to another in an instant. I blinked, and things swished passed my eyes, making me dizzy; everything around me moved too swift for my human eyes to pick up. I closed them, waiting what seemed like five minutes, but I didn't know when we stopped, until the sensations stopped. I opened my eyes again.

We were somewhere warm, or maybe hot would be the best term for it. Rocky outcroppings, and beyond was dessert. Distant mountains cutting it off with hoodoos and colorful cliffs along the basin. We were high above the surrounding landscape. The distant hills were banded with pinks, ocher and tan.

"It's beautiful. Where are we?"

A small chuckle escaped him. "It is called Dante's View. And no, I didn't name it. We're in Death Valley."

"For real?" I then looked down at myself. Whoops. Naked. Shyly, I attempted to cover myself.

He chuckled again. "No need. This is the most desolate place on earth that I could find, and yet be able to stay near you."

"Near me?"

"In my world, nearby means you are only a second away," he explained. "Come." He took my hand and I padded carefully among the rocks. The rocks were warm beneath my bare feet, and I moved quickly. I was now warmer than I'd been even laying in that bathtub. My hair still wet, it dripped on absorbent rock and sand, and I left wet foot prints in my wake, but my skin and hair gradually dried. The air was like a greedy sponge pulling any moisture it found and absorbed it. On top of that, it was night and a bright, not quite full moon was shining above us, so that made the whole experience feel weird. We descended natural stone steps along the rocky cliff. At one point the distance between stones was too large. He turned, grasped me by the waist and brought me down beside him. His lips were on mine before I could take a breath. Those hands of his ran down and then up my sides. Palms cupping my breasts. "It's been a long time," he said against my lips.

"Mmmm," I said, finding the taste of him intoxicating. It had, indeed, been a long time since we'd touched, let alone kissed. I'd missed it.

His hands slid around me, and suddenly I was in his arms. Desire flamed through me as he carried me into a dark hole. I realized it was a cave—or cave-like. It had all an Indian could want: a cot, hand woven blankets, and a hand woven rug on the floor and a pit fire place in the center. Above it a hole for the smoke to escape. Sage and pine scents filled me. The fire was out in his fire pit.

"It's a little chilly," I mumbled as he set me down on the cot. When the cot didn't give I realized it wasn't a cot, but a carved ledge into the rock wall. Not what I'd call comfortable. Definitely not a Sleep-Number bed, and certainly Spartan in comparison to a hard motel bed.

Dante no sooner heard my complaint of being cold and he looked toward the center of the room. There came a whoosh of sound and light. Flames now licked the darkness from the fire pit, and smoke curled up through the hole in the roof. My werewolf sight had helped me see before the amber flames lit up the room, but now upon further inspection of the walls, I understood this wasn't a cave at all, but a hogan. The outer wall was made of brick-like rocks fitted together. The back side was made of the rest of the naturally curving cliff wall.

"I like your place," I said from the hard bed. My skin brushed against softness. I sat on a blanket made of fur. Very soft. Possibly rabbit, as it was sewn together: black, white and brown. I couldn't help but smooth my hand over it.

"It makes my heart glad to know you like my place." He looked around himself. "It brings me serenity when I am alone." He looked down at the fire. His words made my heart actually squeeze with emotions I could barely keep from surfacing. My eyes watered thinking how things might have been different, if he had simply admitted to being in love with me, instead of running away and ignoring it. But then again, upon review of all the things that had happened to me to this point. Dante, as an Undead, was the only one who could have saved me tonight, before the witches had killed me.

Before I could say anything, he turned to another section of the hogan, another ledge held several things that caught my curious eyes. One was a large skull of a bison, the rest was not discernible to me. Feeling odd laying there, I sat up and placed my feet on the floor. My toes came in contact with something thick and lush. I looked down to find a bison skin covering the floor.

"Before we begin," he said, choosing something from the ledge that looked like a bit of wood, "I need to purify us and this work place." He turned to look at me. "What we are about to do is magic. It is not about sex."

"Oh, okay," I said. *Could have fooled me.* The fire warmed the air, but I still felt a chill. I couldn't stop the sneeze when it came.

"You are cold still?" He turned and with one hand grabbed a folded Indian blanket. He shook it out and handed it to me. "Put this around yourself."

Well, yeah, as I'm nude, came my thoughts.

"Thanks." It was hand-loomed in warm colors of the southwest. I should have gotten a read of the woman's fingers who lovingly and with long hours sat at her loom to make this blanket, but I didn't. The usual Aztec designs with Kokopelli playing his flute along the edges made me smile. I loved Kokopelli, who brought joy and happiness to the land with his flute playing. Ancient legend said he was a god. I remembered also he brought fertility to, not only the land, but also to human women. *Okay, therein lies the hint.*

Okay, maybe Dante only had this one blanket, but *Eeek!* Glad I'd taken my birth control earlier. Wait, Dante couldn't impregnate me. Duh. My brain was spinning, and my stomach was in knots. You'd think this were our first time, and I'd just met him in a bar or something the way I was feeling.

"As I said, this will be a difficult undertaking, Sabrina," Dante said in a serious voice, interrupting my inner turmoil. Turning to me, he had something in his hand. I realized it wasn't a piece of wood, but a smudge stick, which is a combination of dried herbs, like sage, tied together with twine. He would light it and get it to smoke, then wave the smoke over us. It was usually used when running water wasn't available—which wasn't available around here.

"I have only done this once before." Dante leaned to the fire with the smudge stick.

"Really? When?"

"Ten years ago. She was Cherokee," he said, bringing up the flaming smudge stick, moving it around so as to have it catch the whole end. Then, he blew out the flame and let it smoke. Sage and pine smoke curled thickly from it.

"What happened?" I wondered.

"Stand," he said. I stood, my toes digging into the thick hide.

"Were you successful?" I asked.

"No. This is what I want to stress to you, Sabrina. The amount of power I will give to you has to be given a little at a time. It will become a need, a craving for you to draw it into yourself like someone dying of thirst needs water. I must caution you, do *not* take more power from me than I give you. I control how much I give you."

"Got it," I said, nodding.

"You say that now, you must hold firmly to that. Because if you do not, you'll turn out like my friend did."

"What happened to her?"

"She died. Painfully."

"Oh. I'm sorry." I dropped my eyes from his gaze then. This was serious stuff. I'd never dabbled in any sort of magic, until tonight.

"It was my fault as much as hers," he went on. "We didn't know any better. I have never gotten over it. I caused her death."

"How sad," I said, not knowing how to be sympathetic enough.

"Nevertheless. We must be careful."

"I'll try and be careful," I said.

"Don't just try, you *must* keep your head. It will become unbearable for you and you'll want more of the power. Too much at a time will kill you. Your aura had been ripped from you during those creatures' dark ritual. My siphoning out what little bit of your powers and bits of you that I could was only just enough to get your aura to return to your body." I had not heard this explanation before and stood stunned. I'd nearly forgotten what their ritual had done to me. My aura *had* floated above my unconscious body for a while. That wasn't a dream after all. "Right now you can't take in too much at once. We need to go slowly."

"I understand," I said. My stomach had begun to butterfly more with his words. This sounded too weird.

"Communication, too, is important. You let me know if it becomes unbearable. If you feel a burning sensation that becomes intolerable."

"I will." I nodded. Was this like learning to drive a car, I wondered? I'd failed that test twice!

"Now, take a breath, close your eyes and think of something positive, something wonderful. A sunrise, perhaps, or a rainbow. I will perform a cleansing of our bodies and this place from negative thoughts and vibrations."

I closed my eyes. "Okay, I've got something," I said. I had once seen something that I didn't know what it was at first, during a sunset. I'd learned later it is called a sun pillar. The sun had set below some purple clouds, and this one shaft of red beamed straight up from the horizon. My heart had fluttered and my eyes had teared up. It had been one of those things in nature that dazzles and makes you feel so very special when you see it because you might be the only one, or one out of a few people who see it, and never see it again. I held this feeling inside me, as it was still fresh.

Dante's wonderful voice chanted as he faced each of the four directions. Then he drew the smoke up my front, and then down my back, all the way to the ground. The Lakota language is so beautiful. It melded well to my vision of the sunset in my mind.

He continued the same for himself, drawing the smoke over his body in the same way, while chanting rhythmically. His voice went up and down in a deep sing-songy way.

Then he put out the smudge stick. I didn't know he was finished until he said, "Now sit down. You can keep the blanket around you for now." He pointed to the ground, where the bison hide covered the ground.

I sat cross-legged. He sat down behind me, and arranged his legs around my hips. His face leaned near mine. His breath, when he spoke, fluttered my hair. "You should feel anything from light electrical current along your skin, to a pull on your chi. It's like a game of tug of war and it goes like this: I give you power, then you return it. We repeat it all over again. We'll go back and forth with our exchange." He paused and said, "Think of it like a teeter-tauter." I nodded. "Then, when I think you can handle more, I'll return a little more power. Each time we exchange power it will reform, become something larger. Are you ready?"

My mind balked. Was I ready? This sounded dangerous. "I-I think so." I didn't know what would actually happen, but I was about to find out.

He removed the blanket from my shoulders, it slid down over my arms. The fire in front of me, which was three feet away, kept my naked flesh warm. Dante pushed the length of my hair around to my front and his breath feathered over my shoulders. I wasn't certain what to expect, until his lips lightly grazed my flesh. The sudden jolt, made me jump and cry out.

"Sorry. That was too much, then," he said, paused a few seconds as if to get more control over himself. Once again he lightly kissed along my shoulder. This time it was something like static shock, only different, as it went right through me.

"That was better?"

I nodded.

"Good, I'll continue."

His lips trailed along my shoulders, across my back, up my neck and down to the other shoulder. With every kiss he delivered little shocks went through me, and it took a little bit to get used to.

"Hold on to it," Dante said, lips against my skin. "Don't let it go. Not yet." He continued kissing me, going back over my shoulders, neck and back, a little faster this time. There came what felt like a buildup of power—I couldn't come up with the word for it, but I had the sensation of feeling "full". My brain, my senses, my chi, all of it, full. I hunched against his touches now.

"No more! No more!" I gasped.

He stopped. I fell back against him and looked up into his face.

"Return it, Sabrina. Let it go. Release it back to me." He leaned down and pressed his lips against mine. It wasn't a kiss in the traditional sense, but more like our lips merely meeting. I felt something like pent up energy, and when I kissed him I somehow released it back to him I *felt* something leave me. Invigorating, but at the same time, it gave me a slightly washed-out feeling. I needed some of that back.

He now kissed me, taking my face into his hands and I wound up with my back on the ground, the soft bison rug against my skin. The tingling began anew. I took as much as I could, feeling like a spring inside me was being wound, tighter and tighter until I couldn't hold it any longer and I released it. *Hey, this isn't so hard.*

Dante moaned into my mouth. "That was a good one," he said.

I panted, looked up at him and licked my lips with anticipation. "Yeah," I said. "Give me more next time."

His body was stretched out alongside mine, and he now drew over me. He was naked. *Wow, when did that happen?* I hadn't expected that, but he was literally quicker than the eye. His body held above me, he kissed along my collar bone, lighting my senses, making me feel like a firecracker that had been lit and ready to blow. I drew the power into me, seeking more.

"Easy, easy," he said, slowing his kisses. "Equalize, now."

I did. I held what he'd given me, and really didn't want to let the power go back into him, but I couldn't hold it much longer and released it. He grunted as though I'd released too fast. Maybe I had. I looked up at his face, his eyes were pinched.

"I'm sorry," I exhaled abruptly.

"Don't be. That felt *really* good," he gasped. His eyes flicked opened and he looked fine. "Ready?"

My skin prickled in anticipation. I nodded.

"Relax. Just relax. Let this happen."

I nodded again, reaching up to wind my arms around his neck. I smiled and tried to spread my legs for him, but his own were around mine and kept them in place. And he pulled my hands back down to my sides.

"No. Not yet. We won't become one for a while, not until you can take more."

He delivered light kisses around and on my mouth, sending tingles of desire through me. My brain lit up with bright lights when he delivered power into me then. *That was a little different. More powerful!* I could taste him inside my head, and in my soul. He was delicious in some other worldly way I couldn't describe. I could barely comprehend this, but it felt fantastic! Tears filled my eyes. I wanted him to touch me with his hands, body and the rest of himself badly.

My hands came up, but he quickly pressed them down to either side of my head. I turned my head to both sides, then looked up at him, trying to ascertain how he wasn't touching me anywhere but with his lips, only when he pushed my hands down. I looked to find he was actually hovering above me, like he was a helium balloon—which looked really weird. But he was an Undead. Plus his supernatural powers were jacked up. I could feel that.

Trapped this way, beneath him, I felt a stab of desire rush through me like no other time with a guy, even those times with him, as a man.

He nuzzled one breast, lapped at it, making the nipple erect. I gasped.

"You're able to hold more, I can feel it," he said, and slanted his lips across mine. His tongue slipped into my mouth and I gently clamped down on it with my teeth.

A spine tingling rush tumbled through me. My brain lit up again. I saw Dante there in my mind, but other people as well. Lots of other people, all of it way too rushed for me to comprehend. I realized whatever he was doing to me, these sensations were happening within, not without.

I kicked my legs impatiently. I could stand it no longer.

"I want you inside me. Now!" I said.

His slight chuckle broke as he said, "Whatever my high priestess wants." His body gently lowered to mine, and without warning, he plunged into me.

My breathless cry filled the hogan. His lips covered mine again. Bright red light splashed against my brain and the rush was like an ocean wave crashing over rocks—he was the ocean and I was sand and rock.

"Oh! God!" I cried. I looked up at him. "That was excellent!"

"I thought you would enjoy that," he said. "But don't be stingy. Give it back to me, and I will give you something even better."

"Promises," I muttered while he withdrew from me. He had released my hands and so I plunged my fingers into his hair, slanted my lips and pulled his toward mine and shoved power back into him. I heard him moan. *Damn, I'm good!*

That's when he plunged into me and it was mind numbing. Glorious. I cried out with a sudden orgasm, then panted, feeling spent. I thought I would pass out as little stars danced around my eyes.

"Oh, shit, oh shit..." I muttered breathless.

"Too much?" he asked.

"No. Just right," I said, and grabbed his face and kissed him hard, bit his lip, and poured what he'd given to me back. He groaned. Then things went into higher gear as we tumbled around grinding our hips and rolling like two animals on the ground.

At some point I had something like my twentieth orgasm and I could hold no more power. He slipped away from me. I lie on the ground, panting, sweat drenched, but I felt more like myself again, but, I definitely felt *very* powerful. I looked up at him as he crouched near the fire.

"I must take you back, now," he said.

"Wow, no snuggling afterwards?" I leaned up on an elbow.

He chuckled lightly, but didn't look at me. "You do not belong to me. I must take you back." His seriousness was a downer. I touched his shoulder. He turned to look back at me.

"You, Dante Badheart, belong to me," I said. "If I'm a sibyl, then I can have a consort as well as a husband." It had been something in the back of my mind as of late. I realized I was not like any other woman in the world. I was the sibyl. I knew things now that I didn't know before, probably through our power exchange. No other man or vampire had a right to tell me how I would live from here on out.

He blinked and smiled. His hand slid over my fingers.

"You've ruined me, you know?" I said. "For other men. I won't be as satisfied."

"No," he said. "You have it wrong. You have ruined me. I will not be able to have sex with normal women any longer. It will not satisfy me. I'll hunger for you, our exchange of power. But that is the only way we can now be together. Thus, we will not be able to have casual sex anymore."

I bit my lower lip, startled by this bit of news. "Really?" I gasped, but the smile on my lips said I was pleased. *I* had ruined a guy? How wild!

"You now hold much more power than you had before. I've given it freely, all that I could, I gave to you."

I could think of nothing else to say but, "Thank you, I think."

He chuckled, squeezing my shoulder. "It will help you fight against demons, vampires, and even witches, now."

"Cool," I said, leaning up on both elbows. "I'd like to be able to kick a little witch butt every once in a while."

He smiled back at me. "You sound more yourself, as though you feel much better, now."

"I do." I sat up.

He moved and pulled up the blanket I had been wrapped in, and draped it around me. "I will take you back, now." His arms drew around me as he slid up behind me again.

I didn't quite get the word "Okay" out when my pulse jumped, my ears popped a little, and all sight of the hogan disappeared. Darkness swirled around me and then I came to a stop. As I lay curled up in my bed and it only took me a second to find the red numbers on my clock at my bedside. A little after midnight? I thought he'd said we wouldn't be gone long, but I had no idea how long this whole ordeal had lasted from when I was abducted to now.

The house was still. No lights on. I wasn't sure what everyone may have thought about my disappearing act. Maybe they figured I'd left with Dante from my bathroom.

Sleepily, I rolled over and I was out.

Chapter 23

The Bait

I heard voices. They seemed to be in my head, but when I woke fully, I ascertained that they definitely came from outside my room.

"I don't know, she's been asleep all day. I didn't want to disturb her," Lindee was saying on the other side of my bedroom door, which put her in the living room. "Dante said to let her sleep as long as she needs. I was in there a few hours ago to make sure that, you know, she was... alive."

"She is alive," Cho said, confidently.

"How do *you* know?" Lindee challenged.

"The master would have been down here grieving over her."

"The *master*," Lindee repeated the word in a snide way. "Like he's-he's your master?"

"He has had my blood. He commands me now, and so, yes, he is my master." I imagined Cho making a head bow at this point to my cousin. In other words, he was now a scion to Vasyl until he released him of the bond.

Lindee let loose one of her terrible laughs that held a note of humiliation in it. "He had your blood?"

"Yes."

"Wow."

"I'm awake," I said, finding that my throat was dry and my voice came out like a frog's croak. I cleared my voice. My throat felt sore. Well, it isn't a wonder, I'd almost lost my toes in that freezing cold. I could use something warm, like coffee, if only to wake up and ease the pain in my throat.

The two had become quiet near my door.

"Sabrina?" Lindee said in a near whisper.

"I'm awake," I repeated, struggling to move my body into a sitting up position. I noticed the same blanket which had been around me in Dante's hogan was slightly crumpled on the top of my bed. I was under my own covers and pulled them up to my neck because I was certain I was naked.

The door rolled back nosily and the two of them stood there peering in at me. It was as though I'd been entombed and was now coming back from the dead, instead of sleeping in my bedroom. *What a terrible thought!*

I hesitated in pulling my covers off, not certain if I was dressed or not. I definitely was sweaty. I recalled only having been swept away by Dante in my birthday suit. But somewhere along the way, I'd been clothed in my nightgown. *When had that happened?*

"My nightgown is on me?" I said, looking up at her.

"Yeah, sweetie, I washed it for you," Lindee said. Then she crinkled her nose. "It had mud on the hem. I really had to scrub it. I thought it wouldn't come out."

"Oh, God. You didn't have to do that, Lindee."

"I didn't mind," she said with a shrug. She glanced up at Cho. "Not like I don't do a hell of a lot more at the palace." Hand on her hip, she let go a sharp laugh and threw back her head, her wiry hair falling out of her face.

"Well, thank you, however you did it." I wanted to know if she dressed me, but I couldn't ask with Cho standing there. "Please go tell Vasyl that I'm awake. What time is it anyway?"

"What time?" Lindee and Cho exchanged glances.

"Yeah. Is it night or day?" I looked at my clock. It read 5:15. It was dark in the room. I couldn't decide if it was morning or night, since the sun sets at four thirty P.M.

"Dang girl, you've been sleeping and out of it for two days, now," Lindee said.

"Two days!" I looked at them flabbergasted. "How—I mean, what's—" I couldn't form my question. Actually, I had too many to ask.

"I will go and tell the master she is awake. He will be happy," Cho said, and left us.

"God! No wonder I'm famished," I let myself plop back onto my pillows.

"Stay right there," Lindee said, hands out to me, as if she could keep me down with the gesture. "I've got some soup. I'll heat it up quick in the microwave and bring it to you. You must be weak as a kitten." She flounced away. Soup actually sounded pretty good.

Lying back, I stared up at my mauve ceiling. Frowning, I tried to remember something from my dreams. Nothing came. Then the recollection of what Dante and I had shared before I was returned came back in full, vivid memory. *Oh, my God...* The sex had been incredible! He'd ruined me completely for anyone else. Including all vampires, and yes, *even* Vasyl, who was excellent in bed. Dante had to be aware of this fact, and I wouldn't doubt that it pleased him to no end, since he competed with him on that level.

I also remembered that I'd told Dante he was my consort. I'd made a decision, at that point, that Vasyl didn't own me. Not my mind, or my body, and especially my spirit. My heart was another matter entirely. It was confused. I loved Vasyl, but I also loved Dante. My attraction to Dante wasn't just sexual. There was a longing to be with him more than the mere few moments that I got to see him each day, and sometimes not even that much. I would have to rectify this somehow.

Or, could I?

Lindee's noises in the kitchen came loud to my ears—a drawer slammed, silverware clanked, and the refrigerator opened and closed a few times—interrupting my thoughts. I could see her moving around in the room, working on fixing me dinner. The soup was beef with lots of vegetables in it. Good. I wasn't in the mood for more deer meet...

Wait. Oh, my God! What? I sat up.

I'd just seen Lindee doing this in my head, clear as though I had a camera poised in the corner of the kitchen, and I watched it up on my own private screen inside my head. I had never seen such clear pictures of what people were doing out of my own sight, in my life. I might have had flashes, or *knew* what they were doing. But never have I had running pictures of someone while they were going about their business in real time. *Wow!*

I'd have to be careful where, and who I aimed my mind camera at. *I wonder who all it would work with.* I thought about Cho, and concentrated. I saw him clearly in the dark hallway, upstairs. He knocked on Vasyl's door. Vasyl told him to come in and he did. I not only listened in on their conversation, but could see them as though I were standing right there with them. I couldn't manage to see two places at the same time, however, but this was cool. This was magnificent! I could see and hear Cho speaking to Vasyl just as if I were right there with them.

"Your wife is awake," Cho said to Vasyl.

"Thank you," Vasyl said, smiling.

"Her cousin is feeding her as we speak," Cho said. That's when I realized they spoke in French. I understood it all and I don't speak a bit of French.

"Then, I will allow her to eat, and gain her strength back before I go to her side."

Lindee sailed into my room, busting the little vision I was enjoying. I jerked slightly. It was like I had been in two places at the same time.

"Here you go, sweetie," she said, holding a little tray with legs. I didn't know we still had such a thing. It had little folding legs that was made to place in bed for a person to eat off of. I think my father may have bought it to treat my mother to breakfast in bed on Mother's Day, once.

"Where did you find this?" I asked.

"In a far upper cupboard when I was cleaning."

"Cleaning?"

"Yes. I got bored and began cleaning the house."

I didn't think anyone could be *that* bored to climb a ladder—because you'd need one—and go clean out *those* cupboards way above the others. They held a lot of Christmas trays and decorations, and kitchen junk that we never used any more. She was definitely OCD.

I picked up my spoon, and dipped it into the steamy broth, going for the carrots and chunks of meat. "Looks real good," I said, lifting the spoon to my mouth. Then I had a huge stabbing pain in my head. "OW!" The spoon fell, clanking to the bowl, splashing me—and whatever else.

"Oh! What's wrong? Soup too hot?" Lindee said.

"No." I was holding the top of my head. How would soup being too hot hurt the top of my head, unless I dumped it there? "My head suddenly began hurting."

"Still?"

"Uh, no. But—" Again there came a stabbing pain. "Ow!"

"Oh, jeeze! You're having an aneurysm! I'll call a doctor." She ran out of the room.

"I'm not having an aneurysm!" I cried. "I'll be fine. Don't call a doctor."

"But..." her voice faded. "Oh, you have a couple of messages in here."

"You mean on my house phone?"

"Yes."

"See what they are, save them if they sound important." The pain throbbed in my head. "Dante? Are you there?" I called out quietly, knowing he'd be close by in the astral plane. I now saw him in his little hogan seated before the fire, eyes closed. *Crap! I've got some sort of new vision going on here!*

The displacement of air heralded Dante's appearance at the foot of my bed. He bowed, fist to chest, his long black hair draping over him like a cape. The soft scent of pine and woodsmoke filled my room. "My lady. How can I be of service?"

"My head hurts. Real bad." I still held my hand on top of my head.

He stepped over to the side of my bed. His large hand came to rest on my head. "Here?"

"Yes."

"Did you just wake up?" he asked.

"Yes."

"What did you do when you woke up? Anything unusual?"

"No, I—wait. I had visions. Only they weren't normal visions. I mean, I could actually see what everyone in the house was doing as they did them." I looked up at him. "I saw you sitting in your hogan, eyes closed."

He hummed at that and stepped back giving me a critical look. "A new magical power."

"New? Yeah. I guess. But why is my head hurting?"

"The new powers may put a strain on you because you are not used to them. How long did you use it?"

"I dunno. Maybe about five minutes?"

"On who?"

"Well, besides you, and Lindee, I looked in on Cho and Vasyl, upstairs."

"Three separate places and groups of people?"

"Yeah." I gave him a pity look.

"Possibly it was too much, too soon. I would not use it often. At least not yet." He shifted away from me, looking at the doorway. Lindee stepped in. Dante's presence surprised her and she made an intake of air.

"Oh, shit. I mean, hi," she said, smiling to cover her embarrassment.

Dante nodded. "Thank you for watching over Sabrina. She should continue to rest for the night." He nodded to the soup. "And she needs her nourishment." He turned to me. "I'll be close by, should you need me further." And he vanished.

"Crap, girl. He is *soooo* hot," she said, fanning herself with her hand. I wasn't about to tell her that Dante had probably heard her say it, but more importantly, he probably picked it out of her brain. Of course, the way she ogled him would tell any living man what she thought, too. I forced myself to ignore it, but her sexual needs were getting almost creepy.

"I'm feeling better," I said, picking up the napkin to daub up the soup that had splashed all over the tray.

"Oh, here." She handed me a couple of paper towels and we both worked on soaking up the soup I'd splattered.

"What were the messages?"

"Uh, one was from a Mr. J. Curtis Ewald *the Third*," she emphasized the last, then giggled. I chuckled.

"Sounds like a lawyer. What did he want?"

She gasped, eyes wide. "How did you guess? Oh, wait, don't answer. I'm stupid." She chuckled. "I wrote down his number." She handed me a sticky note with the man's name and number on it. "He *is* a lawyer—um, he said he was the D.A.—and spoke about some case against Mark and Marry Woodbine and that it would be going to court in January. What's that all about?"

"Oh, crap. I forgot all about that." I put down my spoon. "That's a hell of a long story. The short version: Mrs. Woodbine and Mark tried to kill me." There was a sharp intake of air and her eyes went huge. "You remember Jeanie?"

"Isn't she your bff?"

"Jeanie is now a vampire."

"Really? How cool."

"Not," I said. "She was dying. I had to make a quick decision. I didn't want her to die, and I had the vampires turn her. So, because of that, she couldn't be seen by any of her human family or friends—well, except for me. Anyway, her mother, Mrs. Woodbine, was trying to find her. Believing I knew where Jeanie was, she kidnapped me in order to force me *with torture* in order to tell her where she was." I could not go into the whole horrifying ordeal. I still had nightmares about it. Now, it was coming to trial. I really didn't want to do this, did I?

"Wow. Nasty bitch," she said, and bit on her lower lip. "I wouldn't figure her to be so whacked."

"Well, it turns out they're both insane murderers. They killed a local pregnant woman, cut the baby out of her womb and buried it simply because she had been having an affair with someone."

Lindee gasped, holding her hand in front of her mouth. "You're shitting me! God! How horrible!"

"Anyway, I helped solve the crime, but the two tried to kill *me*. They burned down houses, too. So, there's arson to add to murder, and attempted murder and kidnapping charges, just to name a few."

"Oh, my *God*! I just realized we don't talk anymore," she said, plopping on the end of the bed, looking at me and patting my blanket-covered leg. "You really need to tell me what's been up with you, girl!" She grabbed my foot and wiggled it.

"I know. What was the other message?" I managed to spoon soup into my mouth. "This is very good, by the way," I said after swallowing.

"Thanks. Your brother," she said, frowning at her note. "He said something about having a getaway. Something about having a free two-night stay in Chicago?" She handed me the note.

"When?" I asked.

"Well, he said Friday through Saturday. He and family should be there now, since this is Friday night."

I took the note and squinted at it. "Crap, it's too dark in here." I couldn't reach my light, and I was hemmed in by the tray with a bowl of soup that I hadn't finished.

"Here." She came over and flicked on my night-stand light. "He's staying at a place called Tremayne Towers. I've never heard of it but—"

"Tremayne Towers!" I choked.

"Wow!" She bent to me and patted my back. "What's wrong with Tremayne Towers?"

"Everything! Dante!" I cried out between coughs.

Dante appeared at the foot of my bed again. "Did you hear? My brother's gone to them. He's been tricked! Damn it all to hell!"

"Where?"

"Tremayne Towers," I said.

"Calm down," Dante said, palms out. "I will go and see where they are. Meanwhile, if he is there, can you call him?"

I looked at the note. "What's the room number? Did he give you one?"

"He had a phone number, but it was garbled at the end," Lindee said. "So, what's wrong with Tremayne Towers?"

"It's a haven for the bad vampires. It was once run, and as far as I know, is still owned by my boss, Mr. Tremayne. But now the bad vampires have taken it over, especially after his status was lowered to rogue, and he was on his deathbed. Now Ilona and Nicolas have taken over all of the North American Vampire Association, and have brought back hunting humans—making it legal for them to hunt humans, and they don't get into trouble for it from the ones who rule."

"Most of that I didn't understand. Who rules them?"

"Demons, and a few others that are not very nice. Believe me." I let out a frustrated sigh. "Randy was given those free nights in order to lure me to them! Shit!"

"Oh," Lindee said. "This doesn't sound good. Why do they want you to go there? Wouldn't they have invited you?"

"No. They want me dead," I said.

"Jeeze!" she gasped, eyes wide with fear. "Why?"

"Because I'm the sibyl, I have the power to overthrow them. Especially now, as I've got special powers. They won't like that. But, then again, they won't know about them." I squinted in thought, wondering if Kiel and her witches had been hired by Ilona to drag me out into that field and drain powers from me. I wouldn't doubt it, given that she had tried to kill me multiple times already. And Nicolas, too. *She must be holding his dick in a vice.*

"This is really bad. How are you going to get your brother—"

The house phone rang. We both froze and looked at one another. I felt a stab of ice run through me. I *knew* it was Ilona. How I knew I chalked up to my new powers, since I never got a reading from vampires at all.

"Should I answer that?"

"NO!" I said. Then, "Wait. Maybe you should before it goes to messages. Grab the cordless in there." I meant the one in the living room.

Lindee charged out of the room for the cordless. She picked up.

"Hello?" She paused and then held her hand over the mouth piece. "It's for you. A woman."

"I know who it is. Ilona." My scalp actually crawled like a tarantula was marching up the back of my skull to the top about to dig it's fangs into me. *Crap!*

"What do you want me to do?" Lindee said in a frantic whisper, holding her hand over the mouthpiece. Long pause while I thought. I really didn't want to talk to her, but if she was calling me, I knew my brother and his family were in trouble. "She's waiting. She wants to talk to you."

"Yeah. I know." I held my hand out. She brought the phone to me. My stomach roiled. I put the phone to my ear.

"What do you want?" I wanted to add *hag*. But didn't dare. Not yet, anyway.

"By now you may already know that your brother, his sweet little daughters, and lovely wife are here in the towers," Ilona said in a falsely sweet voice. She then switched to a haughty, slightly nasally way. "If you wish to save their lives, I suggest you get your ass out here as quickly as you can."

"Listen to me... hag," I said, my mouth turning down into a cringe. "If you touch a hair on their heads, I'll kill you with my bare hands."

She gave a cackling high laugh. "You and what army?" she said in an almost sweet voice. "Get over here. You have one hour from now. Oh, and if you *dare* bring anyone—especially a vampire—with you, I'll kill your family members one by one," she paused for effect, "in front of you." She hung up on me.

Chapter 24

Ultimatum

"Bitch," I said into the receiver, but Ilona was gone. I held out the phone to Lindee, noticing my hand shook. She took it from me before I dropped it. "Can you get this out of my way?" I motioned to the tray. I didn't trust myself to move it. I'd have soup all over me and the bed, the way I was shaking.

"Oh, sure. Just a moment." She hung up the phone, and came and took away the tray. "You didn't eat much," she observed.

"The way I'm feeling I can't eat. I'm too upset." I swung my legs out of bed with the intention of standing. Wrong move. The whole room and my bed swam and I pitched over to my side. This wasn't good. How was I going to fight Ilona if I couldn't stand up at all?

Dante appeared in the room. I only knew this because I smelled sage, smoke and pine needles. I looked, or rather, I steadied my eyes and moved my head to find him near the doorway.

"Your brother is fine," he said. "I observed them in their room. They are about to go to dinner."

"They don't know they're in danger," I said. "Good. I just had a call from that hag, Ilona. She told me I've got an hour to get there—"

"What is going on?" Vasyl asked. I looked up. Vasyl and Cho step into the doorway.

Tears welled up in my eyes as I took them all in. "Ilona has tricked my brother and family into going to Tremayne Towers. She's given me one hour to go to her, or she kills them."

"I have checked on them," Dante said. "At the moment, they have not been harmed, or know that they are pawns in capturing Sabrina."

Vasyl swore heatedly. "I shall go—"

"No! You can't. I was warned that if I bring any of you, she'll kill them all, one by one in front of me," I said. My hand trembled as I wiped my eyes.

"She will want your blood," Dante warned. His eyes flashed at me. "They will know how to subdue you."

"I have to find a way to bring someone with me," I said.

"Or, send someone afterwards," Dante suggested, brows going up.

"Dante, I want you to be with my brother and his kids," I said, my lips trembling. I could barely speak, and then I found resolve deep down and wiped away the tears. "If someone comes for them, you'll be able to stop them."

"But what of you?" Vasyl said, his voice rough. "We need to send someone, but who?"

"I will go, my Lord," Cho said with a bow.

"You are strong, but, not against vampires," I said. "They'd kill you easily."

"Not unless I take the magic serum," he said and smiled, then gave Vasyl a knowing look.

"What serum?" I asked, confused.

"It is a mixture of vampire blood and various other hard-to-get ingredients," he smiled more deeply. "It is an old Chinese elixir. I've always a supply on hand, just in case." He turned to Vasyl. "I would need only a very small amount of your blood. Three drops, at the most."

"I will supply it. What happens when you take it?" Vasyl asked.

"I become as strong and as fast as a vampire, and it lasts for at least forty-five to fifty minutes, depending upon the strength of the vampire I take the blood from. It may last an hour from someone like you, my Lord." He bowed.

"Well, don't take it until we are ready to leave," I said. I pressed my fingers to my forehead. The ache was back, but it had moved to my forehead. *Wonderful.* "How fast can you get my brother and his family back here?" I asked Dante.

"I can only take one person at a time through the lines," Dante said. "I don't dare take more. I never know when my powers will weaken."

"That will leave the others vulnerable while you're gone," I said. "I don't like that. I wonder where Rick is." Pressing my fingers to my temples, I decided to use my new powers, and searched for him. *Rick?* I called out mentally.

What is it toots? Hey! I can hear you in my head! How are you doing that?

It's my new powers.

Cool!

Where are you? I need your help. I moved to sit up, gradually. Lindee helped me. She tried to speak to me, but I held up my hand to quiet her.

I'm with Tremayne. Rick answered in my head.

Where? I could hardly contain my excitement and anxiety.

Kansas, in the middle of friggin' nowhere, sweetie.

Why? What's going on? I was beginning to get a visual on him. He was standing in a hallway that had odd concave sides. I knew where he was. He was in that old military silo, where I had been a few days ago.

Tremayne's gonna come to Chicago to kick Ilona's ass out of his towers. He chuckled.

So, you're there to bring him back here?

Yep. Why? What's happening your way?

My brother has been tricked into going to Tremayne's towers, and Ilona has threatened me with their lives if I don't show up.

Oh crap, girlfriend! He shifted his weight and leaned against a console. Then his eyes slowly widened. *Look, we'll be there within the hour. Mr. T. is giving some last minute instructions to his minions.* Rick chuckled.

I need to be there within the hour, too, I said in my head, and pressed on despite the pain in my temples. *But also, if I show up with anyone, my brother and his wife and kids will be killed.*

That bitch! What are you going to do if you can't bring anyone with you?

Don't think that bitch can outsmart me, I said. *Cho is coming, and so is Dante. Dante has been able to find my brother and family, because he can stay invisible. He can take them one at a time out of there. Once they're out, I won't have to worry about their safety.*

What about yours, toots?

I paused. *I'm gonna make it up as I go along. I may need you once you get there.*

Okay. I'm gonna go with Tremayne. A few of his minions are meeting us in front of the building. We're gonna storm the north tower, like friggin' X-Men for real.

Good luck, I said ready to disconnect from him because the pain became too much for me to bare.

You too, kid. I'll find you. Don't worry.

I cut off my connection and grasped my pounding head with both hands, and fell back on the bed squeezing my eyes, as if doing so would somehow make the pain go away. It didn't.

"What was it she just did? I'm lost here," Lindee said, looking worried.

"She was communicating with Rick," Dante said.

"Really? I didn't hear anything," she said, looking amazed.

"Telepathically," Dante explained.

"What is Rick doing?" Vasyl asked.

I opened my eyes again and gasped, "He's in Kansas with Tremayne. He's going to bring him to his towers in Chicago." I frowned wondering why Rick had to help him.

"He is better from the plasma you gave?" Vasyl asked. That reminded him, he might still be a bit peaky.

"He's up to speed," I said. "Rick says Tremayne's going to storm the north tower."

"Alone?"

"No. His minions will meet him at the front somewhere," I said. "My brother will be in the south tower—the human side." I tried to sit up, but the pain threw me back. I slid my eyes to Dante. "You'll have to take Cho. I can't show up there with anyone." I slid my eyes to Cho. "They have cameras everywhere."

Cho nodded his understanding.

"Bring him in through the underground garage. They've got fewer cameras there." I paused. Dante would know this, in fact, because he'd worked there before me. "They may not notice or care who he is, if he takes the elevator up," I added.

"My thought's exactly," Dante said.

"How will we find you?" Cho asked.

"Dante always knows where I am, and can read my mind. I only have to communicate with him what floor I'm on, and what's going on around me. I can't take the risk that you show up too early."

"You need to take more nourishment," Dante observed. "And stop using your new powers. It taxes your strength."

"No need to tell me. I've got a king-sized headache," I said, holding my head with my hands.

"I'll get more soup," Lindee said and dashed away with the tray.

Eying Dante, Vasyl made a jerk of his head and Dante stepped out of the room. They spoke low, but I could hear them.

"Why is she so weakened?" Vasyl asked. "What you did weakened her!" His tone was accusing.

"No. She is using a new power that she gained through me. I gave it to her of my own free will." There was a pause and he added in a voice that was clearly vexed. "It must have been a power that one of the witches held. It may explain why they knew what Sabrina was doing and where she was at any given moment."

Vasyl made a puff of exasperation. "Explain."

"She is able to see—and with certain people, like Rick—communicate telepathically with them."

"Why does it hurt her so?"

"Because it stresses the synapses in the brain, especially when one is not used to using it."

"I will go, too," Vasyl said.

"But you can't show up with Sabrina," Dante warned.

"I know. I'll be there, nevertheless. I must be there to ensure that she will not be harmed."

"I think that is why all of us are going to be there," Dante said dryly. "One thing to note: They brought werewolves, as back-up."

"With, or without the serum, werewolves are no threat," Cho said, joining the conversation.

"They are armed," Dante said in a warning tone.

"Guns have been known to fly out of hands when I am around. I am like the wind." Although I was unable to view him from where I sat, I knew he smiled. "If you would, master, allow me to take three drops of your blood?" Cho said.

Shifting of feet, their steps lead away from the living room. Closing my eyes, I allowed myself to rest, at least physically. Mentally, I was a mess. How was I going to take on Ilona and a pack of nasty, dangerous werewolves by myself? I wondered what sort of a greeting they'd prepared for me. I also wondered if they knew I would use the ley lines to get there. That was the only way I would be able to get inside without them knowing I was there—until they were alerted by the many security cameras, of course.

"Here you go," Lindee sang as she swung into the room with another bowl of soup.

"I think I'd like to sit at the table, actually."

Dante stepped in. His strong hands helped me sit up and then slung an arm around me and helped me stand. His warm breath against my ear he said, "You must not forget. Nicolas has had your blood."

I drew in a breath and gave him a startled look. "He'll know when I'm there."

He nodded solemnly. I had forgotten about that.

He moved me out of the bedroom.

"What did you do to me?" I said, moving my legs slowly as he helped me. "Why did you give me these powers? I can't handle them."

He chuckled lightly. "I knew that you could hold more power, and so gave you more. That is all I did. You pulled some extra powers from me. The telepathy and ability to communicate with others was one. But the long-distance, or remote viewing, is new. That's not something I had."

Right. "I heard you tell Vasyl," I said as we stepped through the living room. "I can't do this, Dante. I can't," I said on verge of tears. I leaned heavily against him.

"You will be able to do this, my Lady. I assure you," he said. "You can do much more than you are willing to admit." I plopped into a kitchen chair. "Eat something. Get your strength up."

Vasyl and Cho stood over the sink, their bodies close together. I could smell the blood. Vampire blood was fragrantly sweet smelling. I suppose there was a reason for this. I felt a slight twinge inside. It lit up my brain a little bit. Cho turned away with a small vial in his hands filled with the dark vampire blood. He smiled as he stepped out of the room, holding the vial of Vasyl's blood. He went upstairs. If I wanted to, I could simply "watch" him—Dante called it "remote viewing". That's exactly what it was, but I didn't dare. It would give me a hellacious headache, although it only lasted a minute or two.

Vasyl drew down his shirt sleeve and looked at me hunkered over the bowl of soup. I wanted to lift the spoon, but couldn't. I absolutely didn't have the strength at this point.

"She will not be able to face off with another vampire like this," Vasyl complained, his hand thrust out at me.

"What do you suggest?" Dante challenged.

"There is only one way to bring her strength back." He rolled up his sleeve again and with an elongated fingernail, which turned into an incredibly sharp talon, he made a slit in his white flesh. A line of red appeared. Lindee's eyes went large as pigeon eggs while she watched him draw up beside me. He lowered his forearm to my mouth.

"You will drink my blood," Vasyl said. "It will bring back your strength."

I sighed, looking up at him, trying to not look at the blood leaking down his arm. It normally grossed me out, and yet I felt compelled to drink it. I actually *wanted* it.

"Drink!" he commanded. I leaned and put my lips to his forearm. Vampire blood is oddly sweet, tasting nothing like blood at all. I'd heard it could become addictive. But I wasn't addicted to it. Or, at least not prior to this moment, I wasn't.

I licked the flowing blood, and was surprised at my own body's reaction. I became aroused. This had never happened before either. I moaned and clutched his arm with both hands and my lips latched onto the flowing blood like a voracious eel.

Dante grabbed my shoulders and Vasyl jerked away. Vasyl looked at me slightly startled, and drew his other hand over the cut, which I was sure was healing quickly. His eyes flicked up to Dante.

"It may be a manifestation of her new powers," Dante explained. "I would not offer her blood again."

"No shit, Sherlock," Lindee said, hands on hips. "You eat the soup, hon." She pointed at the bowl with a large wooden spoon. "You two, get out of here!" She held up the spoon threateningly toward both men, the look on her face menacing.

The two vampires vacated the room. I had to admire her tenacity.

I looked despondently down at my bowl of soup. I wanted Vasyl's blood instead. But I did feel better. In fact, a surge of energy ran through me at that precise moment. Oh, *hell* yes! I felt pretty damned good, all of a sudden and straightened up in the chair. I ate the soup, now hungry for it.

"Your hair is so long," Lindee said and she lifted it from my back. It startled me at first, but then I melted into the attention she paid me. A little chill coursed through me as she pulled my hair back and ran her hands over the ponytail. "Oh, you know? I could braid your hair like that girl in *Hunger Games*. Then, it'll be out of the way when you fight."

I wasn't probably going to be doing too much fighting, but I didn't want to stop her from her attention to my hair. "My brush is in the bathroom, first drawer on right," I said. "Must be a mess." Touching my hair—yep, snarly—I already knew what I would wear. Black yoga pants, a crew neck black knit top with long sleeves. And my boots. The very ones I'd kicked the Were in the jelly beans with. I might have to do that again, and now relished the thought.

Nerves and apprehension made me shiver while Lindee brushed out my hair. The men stayed out of the room, and Lindee babbled on and on about tomorrow's meal, and what sort of stuffing she'd make. I was sitting, swallowing my soup, wondering if any of us would be in attendance.

Chapter 25

Sacrifice

There were no long-winded goodbyes or anyone kissing me like they'd never see me again. Lindee acted like I was going to do nothing more dangerous than go to a sports meet as Dante, Vasyl, Cho and I stood in my living room about to depart—me via ley lines, Dante in his usual mysterious way, and Vasyl as vampires usually travel. Dante would take Cho.

"Go kick ass," Lindee said, both thumbs up to us.

Earlier, while she was braiding my hair, I told Lindee that Dante—or someone—may bring my brother and his family members back here for safe keeping, and to expect their sudden appearance. I had to calm myself in this last moment, before leaving. I was about to save my brother and his family from the merciless Ilona and Nicolas. Hopefully we were in time.

Dante left before me, taking Cho with him. Vasyl had a running—or a flying—start. I knew that I could get inside the Towers and I had to make sure I put myself in the south tower, not the north. It sounded as though all hell would be heading that way. Thankfully, it wasn't happening in the tower where my brother and family were.

When I misted into existence, I found myself in the lobby of the south tower of Tremayne Towers. As always, after traveling the ley lines, I had to get my bearings. I faced the doors and took in the lavish furnishings and décor. Hunter-green carpets, with peach and cream accents, and matching drapes. The brown leather couches huddled around a hooded fireplace. Although it was a gas-fed fire, it would be warm. I longed to sit down and stare into the licking flames and try to pretend I didn't have a care in the world. Truth was, my problems weighed me down.

I turned away from the lure of butter-soft leather and a warm hearth, and headed for the desk. A small group of people were checking in, a family and two individuals. The whole idea of the human side of Tremayne Towers was merely a money-making enterprise for Tremayne. The north tower was where the vampires lived and worked. The south tower was accessible from the north through a sliding door which needed a code card, much like the one used for certain elevators in the north tower. A few months ago, Tremayne was the only vampire who had a code card that accessed the south towers. I was told that silver was used on surfaces where a vampire might have to touch—such as the elevator buttons, a strip of silver on the hand railing of the sweeping steps, and other places. This also meant that werewolves had a little trouble accessing those same spots. I got around it because I wore gloves, which meant that anyone else who knew about these little headaches could wear gloves too. When I started working for him, Tremayne had given me a suite in this tower to use as my "home away from home". If I'd wanted to, I could have gone there, but I hadn't exactly had that many good experiences there. Besides, I wanted to find my brother.

I waited in line, watching nervously for trouble. I was hopeful they wouldn't expect me to pop in using ley lines. I suspected they really didn't think I would have the balls to do this. I smiled, thinking I had this one big jump on them. It urged me on, but I knew that it wouldn't last long. They'd find me soon enough once they caught my image on camera, or, maybe Nicolas would have already felt my presence the way a vampire could tell his human donors are within striking distance.

Finally, my turn came, and I stepped up to the clerk at the check-in desk.

"May I help you?" the manager asked.

"Yes. I believe you have a Randy Strong staying here—him and his family? I'd like to know their room number, please."

The young man didn't hesitate and looked on his monitor. "Are you a friend or a guest here?"

Oh crap. I didn't think about changing my name or anything. Giving my name would be the biggest tip-off. But then again, I was certain it would not take them long to know I was here. I needed to buy more time. "I'm a friend of the family. He called and said if I was in town to come by and say hi." I was going with the hope that finding me might take my enemies a while.

"I'll call them, and let them know you're coming. Can I have a name?"

"Elvira Bench," I barely got it out with a straight face. It was a joke we'd had as kids. My brother had had a crush on Elvira—the late night hostess of horror flicks—he'd gone to see her movie and he was smitten with her for a while. Anyway, I had teased him endlessly at the time about it. I'd once told him that Mrs. Bench's daughter looked like Elvira—which was bogus, of course—and he believed me for the longest time—he was fourteen. I remember finding him using binoculars out the window to watch for her whenever Mrs. Bench had visitors. If the clerk told Randy that Elvira Bench was on her way up, he'd know it was me—at least, I hoped so. I had called him before I left, telling him to stay put in his room and don't answer the door to anyone but an Indian and a Chinese guy, or me. He thought I was joking around. It was the best I could do without alarming him. See the reason why my brother doesn't always believe everything I say?

But, I knew that this guy wasn't going to call my brother. I didn't have to get it from his brain—but I did tap into my new telepathic abilities and saw that he was going to alert whoever on the other end of that phone call that someone was coming up to see Mr. Randy Strong.

The desk clerk didn't bat an eye and said, "He's on the twenty-fifth floor, Ms. Bench. Room 1703."

"Thanks," I said, turned and headed for the bank of three elevators. I got on with a few other people and pressed for the seventeenth floor. Tremayne Towers had ninety-seven floors. The top ones were luxury penthouses and Tremayne's was on the top floor on the vampire side.

The elevator stopped several times on the way up, letting people off. At one point a tall man in a suit got on. Like all people who get into the elevator, he didn't look at me, but turned and faced out. There was something familiar about him. Not only that, the scent of pine and sage was strong. Eventually, everyone got off, and we were alone.

"What floor is your brother on?" Dante's voice came out of the stranger in front of me. My adrenaline shot up with excitement.

"Dante? Is that you?" I didn't move away from my place in the corner.

"I've chosen a disguise," he said. "Since they have cameras everywhere, but can't monitor sound in the elevator, I knew I'd be able to find you when you arrived."

"They have cameras in the elevators?" I asked, working to keep my face neutral.

"Yes. Look above my head to the left."

I looked and saw the small camera lens.

"What floor is your brother on?" Dante asked.

"Seventeenth."

"I'll ride with you. I expect an ambush." *Me too.*

"I'm on pins and needles as it is," I said, wishing this day would go away. "If I'm stopped, you can't help me."

"We're picking up Cho." His head turned slightly toward me, but turned back when the elevator stopped and the doors opened. Cho stepped on, smiled and turned away from me. Okay, that was smart that they didn't get on together. This was like a James Bond movie.

"You guys need to get to his room. I don't dare go," I said. "It's room 1703. When you get there, tell my brother that you're there to take him to a safe place. Do you have any plan as to how you'll get them all out together?"

"Like I said, I can only take them one at a time. If we try and leave in a car, we'll be followed," Dante said. "I'll have to take them one at a time through the ley lines."

"Then, do it however," I said, fidgeting with the vials of holy water in my pocket. If I had to use them, I would. I couldn't bring the dagger for a lot of reasons. Mostly because it had a mind of its own and would go after any vampire within striking range. But I had nothing to thwart werewolves. I would have brought my Uzi—if I had one, that is.

Dante pressed a button. Level 16 lit up on the panel. The doors opened. We were now on the floor below my brother's.

"What's going on?" I asked.

"We get out here and go up the stairs," Dante said. Cho and I followed him out. The hallway was clear.

"Can you use your remote vision and see into his room?" Dante asked, pausing to glance back at me.

"Uh, maybe. If I think about my brother hard enough." We all stood in a small cluster.

"Over here." Dante moved us toward the stairwell. I was aware of the fact that cameras were trained on us in the hallway. There was one in the inset before the stairwell as well, but at least no one would be able to look out their peep holes to watch us.

I concentrated on my brother. It took a moment, but I finally saw him watching TV. I saw the girls, but no Constance. I wasn't sure where she would be, unless she was in the bathroom or the bedroom.

"Everything looks normal," I said, but frowned. A slight twinge in my head made me stop looking in on them. I grunted and leaned back against the wall.

"You okay?" Dante's hands went to my shoulders. I opened my eyes. Dante was his normal-looking self. That was better. I couldn't get used to him looking like a stranger.

"Yeah." I nodded. "What if I pop into his room?"

"You could, but that might have a lot of shock value. Are you sure you want to do that?"

My eyes flicked up to the camera. Something else was happening and a twinge of Knowing came. *Tremayne.* I squeezed my eyes shut to concentrate. Second sight gave me a visual of several vampires that I recognized rushing in through the doors of the north towers—meaning this was about to happen soon. Rick was among them, almost unseen, but that might have been by design, since he was wiggling his fingers, which meant he was using magic. Tremayne was in the front of the pack. I felt a thrill go through me. It was like watching a movie where the good guys come charging in to save the day. *Alri-i-ight!*

"Tremayne is here!" I said, excitement gave me chills down my arms. "Look, we don't have a lot of time. Tremayne's group should keep them busy for a while. But I don't know how long."

"You're right," Dante agreed. "Can we hitch a ride?"

"Why not?" I reached out and grasped his hand and reached to take Cho's. "Ready?"

"Ready," they both said.

I tapped the line easily, and we blipped out of the hallway and inside room 1703. I felt our bodies twang the atmosphere around us. My brother jumped a mile out of the chair and cried out. I'd never seen the man get off the couch so fast in my entire life.

"Shit!" Randy said, eyes bugged out, taking us in, hand to his heart.

"Sorry, Randy," I said, calming hands out to him.

"You trying to give me a big heart attack or something? How did you get in here?"

He had no way of knowing I had unusual powers. And to explain it all would take a lot longer than I had minutes to spare.

"Never mind," I said. "You remember Dante?"

"Of course. Hi," Randy said, still breathing hard and holding his chest.

"And Cho," I added, motioning to him. My brother nodded and said hello to him.

"So, what's happening? What's going on? You made no sense over the phone," Randy said, hands to his hips. Anger now creased the middle of his forehead.

"I know I didn't. But you need to know we're all in danger and I have to get you out of here. Fast!" I barely got the words out when two little girls ran into the room, singing my name.

"Aunt Sabrina!" Little arms wrapped around my legs and two angel-faces looked up at me. Jena had her Barbie doll clutched in her hands, the one I gave her last year for Christmas. It reminded me that I had to get my presents over to them. Barbie had a new car, and gobs more clothes. First, I had to get them out of here so we could all enjoy Christmas.

I bent and hugged them. My heart beat wildly. We could actually get them out of here and no one would get hurt. "You ready to go for a magical ride?" I asked them both.

"Yes!" they both chimed and began to jump in place.

"Where's Constance?" I asked my brother.

"Not here."

"Where is she?" I straightened and stared at him. Crap. How did he let his wife leave the room, when I told him I'd be there in ten minutes?

The sudden crash made us all jump; both girls screamed; Cho and Dante both whirled around, legs braced in a fighting stance. Beyond them, three large goons stood glaring at us, guns in hand, the door hanging open from the hall. I remembered them from Tremayne's bunker. My earlier thoughts of an Uzi now came back to me because one of the men *did* have an Uzi, and another had a huge Magnum .357. After that I didn't have time to take in their arsenal. This was bad, and it really pissed me off that I hadn't been better prepared for this.

Both Tera and Jena ran screaming, and disappeared into the bedrooms through the hallway. That ended my thoughts of getting them quickly out of here. *This sucks!*

Cho and Dante both moved with speeds my human eyes could not keep up with. Two guns went flying. I ducked, not sure if these guns might misfire when they landed. My brother said, "Now wait just a cotton pickin' moment here!"

But I wasn't paying any attention. Cho went into kung fu moves like a Bruce Lee movie, and moving slightly faster than a human should be able to. The sounds of kicks, fists smashing into faces, and resulting groans and cries filled the room. Cho's hands and feet—what I could see—turned the big thugs into human mush, basically. I hadn't seen anything so terrible since I'd watched a *Rocky* movie with my brother—number four with the Russian, I think.

When someone misted into existence right next to me, I jerked to look down a dark gun barrel. Cho's stance stiffened. Dante, standing beside him and the pile of Weres, stopped his motions, too. In the next second, Dante disappeared and reappeared behind my brother. I *knew* what he was going to do next—I could read it in his head because we were so telepathically tied. He put his hands on Randy's shoulders and suddenly both men vanished. His quick thinking may have only saved my brother, and may have put the rest of us at risk. I still didn't know where Constance was.

"I believe you need to think it over." Nicolas' smooth voice made Cho halt in whatever action he was thinking about taking. The barrel of his .35 S&W coldly kissed my left cheek. I moved only my eyes to the far left to take in my nemesis, Nicolas. How had we come to this? He had made a play on me in the very beginning. I thought we'd become romantically involved—until Tremayne saw me, and had nixed all that. Now, it was like he hated me. But I reminded myself Nicolas was a vampire, and, like nearly all vampires, humans meant little to him. Other than blood that we donated, of course. And now he was willing to spill mine for Ilona.

Two more Weres stepped into the room from the hallway while the others remained out cold. They had black velvet bags in their hands. Something shiny circled the ends of these bags. I wondered what the heck the bags were for. Our heads? No they were too small, I could see that now.

"Be so kind as to put these on, my dear," Nicolas said, stepping a couple feet away, and motioning to the two men. I noticed one was the silver-eyed Were from Tremayne's bunker. They both came up to me, and slipped the two velvet bags over my hands. They tied the strings. I noticed that they wore blue polyurethane gloves on their hands. This tipped me off. The silvery twine wasn't twine but actually made of silver. Nicolas would know that I couldn't to undo the ties. And by covering my hands, I could no longer command the vampires, or anyone else, because the mystic ring was now covered. Leave it to him to think of this, since he knew I'd been bitten by a Were.

"A very awkward moment," Nicolas said, a sneer on his lips. "You were told not to bring anyone with you, and yet I see you have." He darted a glance toward Cho, and made a wag of his gun, gesturing for him to move away from me. He now stood against the wall. "Now—" I thought that he would fire his pistol, but someone new appeared in the room sidling up next to Nicolas.

"Now I'll have to eat someone." The new voice brought my eyes up to meet the icy ones of Ilona. I couldn't hate anyone more. My adrenaline shot up at the sight of her as she twitched into the room. Wearing a shiny blue dress, which looked like she'd gone all the way to New York to buy it. Her swept-up silver-white hair, and small silver gun seemed to go with the ensemble.

"Nicky, darling, there's some sort of disturbance in the north towers," she said. "Why don't you go and fix that." *Nicky? Gak.*

Without a word, he stalked out of the room. But, I caught the look of indignation rising to his features. Once he was gone, Ilona glanced around the room.

"Where are your family members?" Ilona asked, slitting her eyes at me.

I pressed my lips together and didn't look into her eyes. I knew the rules well. She had never had my blood, so she couldn't command me. Besides, in vampire years, she was but a teenager, and couldn't really make anyone do squat, unless there was eye contact, or some physical touching going on.

"Hmm, I see. It comes down to my searching your brain for them? That's fine," she said.

Crap. I'd forgotten about her ability to mind-search. The invasion is utterly uncomfortable, and I remembered it from a month ago by her. She may have covered my mystic ring, but she was *not* the boss of me. When the first touches of her in my mind came, I resisted with all my might. It was my will against hers. I squeezed my eyes and bore down on concentrating to block her.

"Get OUT of my head, you power-hungry BITCH!" I spat. Ilona jerked slightly. I don't know if my spit actually reached her from across the room, but she was surprised, nevertheless. She was no longer in my head any more. I basically kicked her out of my sandbox.

"That can't be," she said in a quiet, but startled tone. "They took your powers from you. You are powerless. You can't have any left!" If I'd had any doubts that Ilona had put the witches up to their ceremony to drain my powers, I had none now.

"You mean Kiel Saint Thomas and her hags from hell?" I said. "Sorry, but I got my powers back." *And then some, bitch.*

"Well, it hardly matters." Ilona turned to her two Werewolf henchmen, made a nod, and the two stalked passed me into the rest of the suite to search it. When I heard my two little nieces screaming, my heart fell. This was not right. She had been after me for months, having people shoot at me, tried to trap me on another world and have my blood drained. But this took it to a whole other level, and I was not going to take this lying down. I'd find a way to beat her. I had to.

When the two werewolves brought my screaming nieces back into the room, I wished I didn't have my ring covered, I'd throw the bitch out the window and then I'd kick these guy's jelly beans with my big boots.

"You've been a thorn in my side for far too long," Ilona said, glancing at me, a terrible look on her face that said she had me now.

"Aw, what's the matter? I'm in the way of your world domination plot?" I snorted, surprised at my ability to sound so calm and sarcastic under such circumstances.

She made a one-shoulder shrug. "Just my corner of it." She smiled cockily.

"Queen of the Vampires has a certain ring to it," I said. "Watch out that the King of Vampires won't come and kick your ass."

She threw back her head and laughed, and then became serious. "Time to get rid of you once and for all, so that the king won't be born." *Ah, so she knew about the prophesy, too.*

"Aren't you afraid of reprisal? Or that someone might kick your ass out of here?" I asked.

Jena wriggled and screamed anew in the hands of the silver-eyed Were. Tera screamed and squirmed too, and kicked at the other one. Both held the two girls at a safe arms' length away, but Tera's legs were longer, and she connected a kick, and finally connected with the Were's face. The sound of a shoe connecting to a jaw had a nice satisfying sound to it—*good job, Tera!* He dropped Tera with a muffled curse. She ran out the door and the big bad Were shook the stars out of his head.

"Oh, for the love of demons!" Ilona angrily turned to the two Weres. The injured Were bounded toward the door to chase, but stopped to the command, "Let her go."

Ilona then turned to the one holding Jena. "Stop it!" Jena went slack in the hands of her captor. Well, I guess Ilona could easily subdue little children. It didn't surprise me, but defeat washed through me. I struggled to undo the bag on my right hand, I'd send Ilona into next Thursday. But the Weres had tied knots in the silver twine.

She turned back to me. "Who's going to kick my ass?" She smirked. "You?"

"Not unless you take the bags off my hands. But that would even things up," I said. "But actually, I was thinking about Bjorn. He'd like to get his revenge on you for killing both his wife and his brother." I was stalling for time. It didn't hurt to put a little fear in her.

"Hah! My sources last told me, Bjorn was good as dead. You don't come back from silver poisoning." She paused and then added. "Oh, and thank you for that, by the way." *Snarky-snark-snark*, I thought. So, she'd heard that I'd had something to do with that. Obviously, Nicolas would have kept her informed, since he'd been there at the bunker in Kansas. But he must have told her about our attempt at giving him my plasma. I didn't know who was working with who. If Kiel St. Thomas had been hired to take my plasma so that Tremayne wouldn't get it, then, after that failed she was assigned to weaken or maybe kill me. Ilona believed Kiel had managed to maim my powers as a sibyl.

"Now, back to where we were," Ilona said in an oily voice, stepping over to the Were holding Jena. "I think I warned you what would happen if you brought your pals in to help you." She handed the gun to the injured Were, and easily took Jena from Silver-eyes.

I hadn't forgotten about Cho, who had slid a little further into the room while they were all preoccupied. He now stood by the couch, and about four feet from me. I slid my eyes to him. He gave me quick little sideways glances. Yeah. I knew what he was thinking. *Sweet, if it works, Cho. Go for it.* I hoped his little nod meant that my telepathic message was received.

Silver-eyes kept his gun on both of us. As long as a deadly gun was on him he could do nothing, at least not from several feet away.

"Oh, how delightful!" Ilona said, looking at little blond Jena who could only stare at her, as she was under Ilona's heavy thrall. She looked at me then. "You know that children's blood is sweet? They're so innocent that it's rather intoxicating to drink their blood. Almost as delicious as yours will be, my dear Sabrina."

My heart clenched. I couldn't let this happen. "Don't you dare!" I said, wanting to end her life then and there with my own two hands. If only I had brought the dagger with me. If only my hands were uncovered, I'd be able to do something! Even if I called the dagger it wouldn't get here in time.

She spared me a shrewd look of triumph. "Oh, but I do. Dare." She held Jena's slack body up above her head. "You can't stop me, so don't even think about it." Her eyes flicked down and up my form. "Without the dagger and your marvelous little ring, you have no powers to stop me." She moved little Jena slowly toward her as she opened her mouth and the fangs slid out.

"I wonder what sort of little vampire she might make" Ilona said in a caressing tone as though she were a loving grandmother instead of a horrible creature. "Wouldn't she be a little darling? I've always wanted a little doll to play with. I think that's what I'll do. Make her my adoptive daughter." She laughed evilly.

"NO!"

Chapter 26

Mayhem

"No!" I cried again, wanting to make the Were who held the gun on me disappear. But I couldn't do that sort of magic. "You need to stop NOW!" I wasn't sure what I was thinking right then, but I felt a burn in my chest that spread outward. The need to make her stop overwhelmed me. I closed my eyes and envisioned her turning into something solid, I don't know why. Ice came to mind first, but I rejected it quickly. No. Stone was better. More permanent. I saw Ilona as a granite statue in my mind's eye, and pushed the thought from the cosmos into reality. Beads of sweat formed on my brow and upper lip as I strained to visualize this as reality.

I heard someone take a breath and someone else gasped. I opened my eyes. Cho had shifted closer to me, but he was watching Ilona across the room, like everyone else.

Ilona had frozen in the position she had been in, holding Jena a little higher than her head. She had completely froze. Her hair took on an odd uniform gray. Then the skin on her arms changed from flesh to stone, then it spread quickly down the length of her dress. Her legs were next and lastly her shoes. A crackling sound accompanied these changes as she went through this metamorphosis. In the matter of a minute she had turned to solid stone.

Jena woke from the thrall, and made little fitful sounds, wriggling to get free from the stone hands of Ilona the statue. I moved to grab her, but stopped, my eyes meeting those of Silver-eyes.

The other Were's jaw fell. He looked over at Silver-eyes. Neither one put down his gun, not certain what to do now.

"What the hell happened?" the Were asked, shaking his head. "Is she… dead?"

"Stone," I said. "She's turned to stone."

"Oh, hell," Silver-eyes said, eyes meeting mine. His shoulders sagged slightly. He did a feint as if to move away from the other Were. Then his big fist swung around and rammed into the other Were's face. He crashed to the floor. Gun tumbling out of his hand. The Were was out cold along with the other ones.

Silver-eyes plucked little Jena out of Ilona's stone hands, and set her down on the floor. Crying, Jena ran to me, and wrapped her arms around me as I knelt down. My gaze never left Silver-eyes. Why the change of teams? Was this a trick?

Cho surged, and stopped in front of the Were. Sliver-eyes held up his hands the gun dangling from one finger stuck in the trigger hole, showing us he wouldn't attack or do anything. Cho relieved him of his gun.

"Why?" I asked.

"I'm actually a mole," he said. "Name's Dan. Dan Huston."

Cho looked back at me. I nodded at Cho. We were safe. For now.

"Dante?" I called.

Displacing air, Dante misted in front of us. He stood sideways, looking a warning at the Were. Dan held up his hands a little higher. He wasn't going to attack.

"I need you to take Jena to her dad," I said to Dante.

"Where's the other girl? Tera?"

"She ran. I'll have to find her."

Cho stepped over to me and untied the silver bands around my wrists and I shook off the velvet bags. I kicked them under the couch, hoping no one would come looking for them. I could now keep the vampire's thrall from affecting me, and I could do a lot of damage, if I had to. It was good to know I didn't need the ring for the only way to take care of a threat from a vampire. Or anyone for that matter.

"I can help," Dan said and touched his nose. "I've got her scent."

"Okay," I said. I bent down to Jena. "Hey, Jena, everything's going to be okay. You want to go see your daddy?"

Fists to her wet eyes she nodded.

"Okay, go with Dante—"

"No! I want to go with you!" Her arms wound around my neck like little snakes. *Oh hell.* I looked up at Dante.

"Children are intuitive. She senses that I am not as I once was," Dante said.

"Do you know if Rick is here?" I asked.

"Yes. They've made it inside the north tower and are fighting those who stand up to them," Dante said. If I had wanted to I could have done a remote vision thing, but I really didn't want to see the brutality of an all-out war between vampires. And on top of it have a killer headache.

"Rick? Are you busy? Can you come to me, please?" I said, slightly louder than a normal indoor voice.

Rick's appearance surprised the Were, eyes going wide.

"Wow," Rick said. His hat was on backwards, his face sweaty. "That's one hell of a battle!" His voice squeaked with excitement. "Quist came along and began cutting vampire heads off with his laser thing. It was a slaughter!" He paused to take us in. When he saw we had a child with us he made a nervous laugh. "Oops," he said and pulled off his hat and clutched it. "Oh, hey, girlfriend. What's up? What'd I miss?" He looked around. Then his eyes settled on Ilona's statue and did a double take. "Holy crap! You do this?" He pointed at Ilona, but looked at me.

"Yep," I said, smiling weakly.

"Wow. That's sweet! We'll have to nick-name you Gorgon." *Huh?*

Ignoring what he'd said, I went on. "Rick, I need you to pop Jena out to my house. Could you do that real quick-like?"

"Sure. Sure."

"She's really frightened right now, so can you do a little thing?" I said, squinching up my nose at him, hoping he knew what I meant. Leprechaun magic affected children. They had all been fascinated with him at the Thanksgiving table, and I knew Jena would remember him.

"No problem. Kids love me!" He walked over to us. "Hey, sunshine. Jena. Hey."

Jena looked up at him, sniffling. He wasn't much taller than her, but he bent from the waist, down to her level.

"You remember Rick, Jena? At Thanksgiving? Remember?" I prompted. She nodded, a fist to her eye.

"You want to go on a magic carpet ride? Here, take my hand." Rick put his hand out to her. She took it. "That's it." His hand was not much larger than hers, and she wasn't weirded out by the fact he had no arms. That had to be his leprechaun magic helping in that way.

"Really?" she said, brightening, forgetting all about the horror of a few minutes ago.

"Yep," Rick said.

"Where is it?" Jena looked around.

"What?"

"The magic carpet," Jana said, looking confused. One tear had snailed down her cheek.

Rick chuckled and looked at me. "Kids. Adorable, right? Okay." He snapped his fingers and a Persian carpet, about three feet wide and five feet long, appeared and hovered two inches above the floor. "Come on, kid. There's our ride." The two of them hopped on. "Catch you guys later," Rick said. Both of them waved and vanished into thin air.

"Oh, hell," Silver-eyes said on a gasp. "I'm never going to touch another drink as long as I live."

"Yes, you will," I said, straightening. "I have to find Tera and my sister-in-law."

"I'll go and try and find Constance," Dante said. "Where did your brother say she was?"

I thought for a moment. My remote vision showed Constance having her nails done. "She went to the salon."

"It's the spa and salon. I know where that is," Dante said. "It's in the north tower."

"Oh, crap." I turned to Cho. "You go and help him."

Cho didn't argue. I had a Were and a gun, now. Both Cho and Dante ran out of the room. I stepped over toward Silver-eyes. His eyes were almost glowing. When I closed in I caught a whiff of *his* scent. Nice and warm, like a sunny day in a wheat field.

"Okay, you said you can find my niece?" I said.

"Right." He ducked his head out through the door, gun in hand. Thick fingers motioned me to enter the hall behind him. I stepped over the mound of three Weres that Cho had taken out, and the one Silver-eyes had sucker-punched.

Out in the hall we moved in the opposite direction Cho and Dante had taken. They were heading to the elevator. I followed the Were.

Silver-eyes stopped and sniffed the air. He turned in a complete circle and stopped to look down at me. He bent his head toward me. "Oh, that's you," he said sounding slightly amazed. "I thought I caught your sent at the bunker."

I lifted an eyebrow. "I thought you said you'd be able to find my niece."

"Give me a moment. Your scent is intoxicating."

"So I've been told." I looked up at him. His *eyes* were intoxicating. My face warmed and I had to avert my gaze. *What the hell's wrong with me?*

"I understand that you were bitten by a werewolf?" he said.

"You understand correctly." I had no reason to lie. Besides, I wasn't embarrassed by it, it was simply an annoying facet of my crazy life. He probably smelled my scent through my other scents—*oh brother.*

"I didn't understand why we had to put the bags over your hands. Now it makes sense."

"I does?" I had to question it.

"You couldn't loosen the bags because the ties were silver." Then he squinted. "Then again, why cover your hands? You magical or something?"

"Or something," I said.

Nodding, Silver-eyes casually braced a hand against the wall, like we were making small talk, instead of watching for danger.

I held up my right hand. "This ring can control vampires."

His eyes crossed to look at it. "Nice old piece of jewelry." He nodded.

"Vampires and demons hate it. It's very effective in controlling them."

"You going with anyone? I mean, like, the master or something?" He was on a different page for sure.

I brought up my left hand, pulled off the glove on my left hand and showed him the diamond ring on my ring finger. "Married," I said. "Thank you for the complements. Now, my niece is still missing?"

His eyes had focused on my wedding ring, then slipped onto my face again. "What a shame."

I twisted my lips in annoyance. "Do you smell my niece, or don't you?"

"Not at all. Your scent is so overwhelming I can't smell anything else in this hallway."

I rolled my eyes. I was about to use my remote viewing, when someone shouted my name.

"Aunt Brie! Aunt Brie!" a small voice shouted from down the hallway. I turned and saw Tera dashing from the elevator, her long brown hair flying behind her. She must have been riding the elevator all this time, staying safe. Smart girl.

I ran and met her halfway. Going to my knees, I embraced her.

"That was smart of you, Tera," I said.

"Where's the bad lady?"

"I've taken care of her. She won't hurt anyone again."

"What about Jena?"

"I've sent her to my house. She went on a magic carpet," I said.

"Really?" her eyes lit up.

A rapid *thug, thug, thug* turned me.

Looking stunned, Silver-eyes jerked and half-turned. Then his legs gave out and he fell to the floor. Three dark dots on his back made my stomach lurch with dread. He'd been shot.

A shadow emerged from a doorway. Nicolas stood holding his gun ten feet away, now aimed at me.

"Tera, hold on!" I said, grabbing her under the arms. I made a quick decision, and we misted out of that hallway and the next second we were in my own suite one floor up. It was dark, the scents familiar. I set Tera down and managed to find the wall switch. One lamp lit up a cozy living room in peach, brown and cream.

"Oh wow! That was fun, Aunt Brie," Tera said. "Can we do that again?"

I smiled down at her, patting her on the shoulder. "Maybe later." She looked excited. Somehow the shots fired hadn't bothered her, or the Were being shot and kissing the floor also hadn't registered in her young mind. Maybe I'd taken her away before she'd turned around. I wasn't sure.

"Listen, Tera, hon, I need you to go and hide."

I led her through my apartment.

"Who's place is this?" Tera asked. I glanced down at her. Freckles lightly dotted rosy cheeks and dark hair was pulled into a pony tail. She was not really my brother's kid, he had adopted her after marrying Constance. Constance had been married to a soldier who was killed in Iraq about the time when she was born, so she never knew her real father. But, it wasn't blood line that entered the picture in moments like these. I hugged her. She was my niece and I loved her.

"It's my apartment," I said in a quiet tone.

"You have a really cool apartment, Auntie Brie."

"Thank you."

"Can I stay with you?"

"Sure." I licked my lips thinking of where to hide her. Not many choices.

Lightning flashed a few times, and thunder rumbled. I was glad that Tera wasn't the one who was frightened of lightning and thunder.

"This is the bathroom," I said, flicking on the light. The visions I'd had earlier—days ago—I now realized what they meant. Nicolas was going to be here soon. I had to hide Tera. At least have her in another room. "Hide in here. Lock the door and hide behind the shower curtain. Don't make any sounds. Pretend you're playing hide and seek from your sister. Alright?" Nicolas was after me, not her, and I would have to keep him busy until someone came. Or, if worse came to worse, I had to clobber him in a Buffy-the-Vampire way.

"Are the bad men coming?" she asked in a plaintive voice.

"Maybe," I said. I didn't want to lie to her. "Just go in there and hide like I told you."

"Okay, Auntie Brie," she stepped into the tiled bathroom, her shoes clicking along the tile. I shut the door and waited for her to lock the door. "Did you lock the door?"

"Yes."

"Okay, go and hide," I said. "Don't come out until I say you can. Okay?"

"Okay," her little voice echoed.

I turned. Lightning flashed again. I didn't take Tera back to my house because I feared if I had, Nicolas could follow me there on my ectoplasmic trail, and then everyone would be in danger. Because he had been inside my house before, he could come without my invitation. I wasn't sure if he had been inside my apartment. That one night he'd taken my memory from me, he might have gotten me to invite him in. I didn't know for sure. That's why I was being cautious.

My skin tingled, and my spine stiffened when the room filled with that exquisite spicy scent I remembered from when I first met him. Nicolas' dark form appeared there in my suite, next to an armchair. So, he *had* tricked me that night and had been able to enter my room. He had erased my memory of it, totally. For all I knew he might have taken my blood again without my knowing—*or done other things?* In the beginning he'd been able to draw me in, use his thrall like a band of steel that tightened around me. I wasn't sure that I could override his thrall completely with my mystic ring, because, like Vasyl and Tremayne, he'd also had my blood.

I back-peddled.

"No. Do not run," Nicolas said, that rich voice of his sending skitters through me.

"Don't run?" I said, voice shaky, already backing away… one step and then two. "Right."

"I was your first. I imprinted on you," he said, stepping closer in an easy, casual way, one finger sliding across the back of a chair as he went.

I jumped at the sudden cannon shot of thunder. I thought he'd shot me. Angrily, I concentrated on his gun. I began concentrating on it becoming hot. It took only a few seconds and he dropped it with a startled sound. He looked down at it on the thick carpet, his expression briefly going from confused to blank. He looked up at me with sudden understanding. "Some new tricks to your repertoire, I see," he said, stepping over the gun, dismissing it. "I don't need a gun, anyway." He kept moving forward, and I backed up more. There was no place for me to go as I backed into my bedroom. If I vanished, he would follow me, and wasn't going to leave my niece there alone. Besides, I pretty much knew he wanted me there. I had an edgy Knowing that everything was going to end here and now. I licked my lips trying to think of something to stall him.

"What did you do to Ilona? I no longer feel her presence," he said, looking slightly annoyed by this.

"I turned her into stone," I said, and hitched up one shoulder.

"Stone—?" he faltered, trying to take this in. His chuckle belittling. "You?"

"I don't know how you managed to fall for someone like that to begin with," I said, ignoring his inability to realize I had become powerful enough to turn someone to stone. Wherever *that* had come from, I sure as hell didn't know. At any rate, I wouldn't hesitate to use the mystic ring's powers on him.

"Ilona was upper society. Something you wouldn't know about." He sneered at me. "She had an iron will, I'll admit, but I had great admiration for her. I agreed with her ideas."

"And don't forget she was power hungry," I added. "She had her husband killed, and Bjorn's wife killed." I ticked off a couple of fingers. "She also took my best friend, Jeanie, who's now a vampire because of her." Tears leaked down my cheeks with the thought of all I'd gone through, because of her.

He chuckled. "Ilona didn't change her. You gave the word to change her," he said, indignant.

"True, but she was near death. You know this. You were there." My legs backed into my bed. Lightning flashed through the windows behind me, lighting up the dark bedroom and bringing eerie shadow and light to his features while he stood in the doorway. I tried feverishly to come up with an easy way to stop him. The mystic ring was uncovered, but something held me back from using it on him. Maybe he'd imprinted me in a way that kept me from turning *him* to stone. Shakily, I held my hand up, palm out to him. The ring's powers were automatic when I pressed it into service. One of those no-brainer powers I had. Too bad the dagger was *alllll* the way back home.

Nicolas stopped in his tracks, thick black brows slanting in. I still had power over him—*nah-nah-na-nah-nah*.

"True. I was. It was an unfortunate set of circumstances, I'll admit," he said. "But your friend was… expendable."

"Expendable," I echoed, and wiped my nose with the back of my other hand. "So, you fell for her. Ilona," I said turning the conversation back to Ilona. "Like a school boy." I remembered the visions I'd had of her and him together. I didn't see anything intimate—thank God—but I saw them alone in an apartment. His. They were working up a plot to take over Tremayne's camarilla back when I had first started with Tremayne Towers. Hell, it all probably began well before that. It would take one wicked bitch to have her own husband killed.

I tilted my head with new sight—picking up something from Nicolas himself, with a few deductions I put it all together. "She talked you into using Toby, your scion, who was already addicted to vampire blood, and had him drink the blood of his victims—all vampires—three nights in a row in order to turn himself. Then, she ordered him to hunt me, Dante, and Tremayne—and anyone else—down." Toby had shot Dante with a shotgun, but he had lived. Then, he came after me. Tremayne had come just in time to stop him from hurting me further, or draining me, because that was what he had intended. Tremayne had saved my butt more than once. These memories reminded me just how many times he'd been there for me, and why I had to save his life with my plasma. "Must have been something there for you to work against your own master." I was stalling, trying to find things to say to keep him busy, his mind off of what he was there for. Maybe I could talk him out of whatever it was he wanted to do to me. Survival tactics for a woman. However, I had a few other tactics and surprises in my bag.

"We shared blood and were sexual partners." He shrugged. "Is that what you want me to say?"

"TMI!" He looked a question at me. "Too Much Information," I said.

He cocked an eyebrow. "In any case, I'm no longer under her influence." Because she was now a piece of granite statuary.

"Oh, goody for our team." I shook a fist in the air. I edged around my bed when he stepped into the room. I had short little visions—stuff from his head—what he wanted to do to me. Things he had always wanted to do, but couldn't because of Tremayne's control over him. *Yikes.* There was bondage involved. And biting. Lots of it.

Lightning flickered brightly and the resounding explosion of thunder made me jump away from the window. When I did, Nicolas moved closer in his vampire-floaty way. Now, he was within striking range. I held up my right hand again, like a shield. He grabbed it, startling me and we looked each other in the eyes.

"I bit you," he said, dark eyes flicking over my face.

"I know. That very first night," I said, nodding. "You weren't really trying to take any werewolf venom from me. That was a story you and Steve drummed up to pacify me."

"Yes. But it worked. If Bjorn hadn't called me that night when I was in your bedroom, I would have had you. You'd be mine now."

I swallowed dryly. "So, you hate me now?"

"No. I do not hate you, Sabrina," Nicolas said. "But as some wise man once said, you can never go backward in time and undo what you have done." He reached under my chin, lifting it, as if to kiss me, his lips were inches from mine. His words came out in a tender stream as though he were talking intimately to me. "Tremayne always takes whatever woman he wants, adds them to his harem and the rest of us are left with his seconds."

"Boo-hoo," I said dryly. "And, by the way, I'm not one of his harem." I studied him. So, it was true, he had been hoping for a human-vampire relationship with me. "Did you even ask?"

"No. What was the point?" he said. "He was smitten with you." He paused and then said, "I now realize it was your blood I was attracted to." He shook his head. "No, Sabrina. Only a master can have you. You are the sibyl, after all."

I wondered why he was not overwhelmed by the scent of my blood. Maybe not all vampires were. He was one of only a few, I was certain. But it attracted him all the same.

"So, no hard feelings?" I said, hoping the sarcasm came through.

"That would be the rub." A small smile lifted one side of his lips. "I can't have you by the normal means, at any rate. I'm certain by now that you're pregnant by the *rogue*." He made the word sound dirty. "You are the prized cow, the one that we all wanted and only one can have, and now a *rogue* has you." He made a dry laugh. "What a pity Bjorn didn't take you that first night. All this might have been avoided."

"No. Don't put this on mine, or Bjorn's head," I said. "And Vasyl is more than just a rogue." Besides he was already in bed with Ilona—figuratively and physically—by the time he'd met me.

"That isn't the point!" His hands grasped my shoulders and shook me. Lightning lit up his face which contorted into hard lines. His black eyes like cold marbles, reflecting the lightning, and red flashed there. Just a flash, that was all. A chill skimmed up my back again and I shivered involuntarily.

"I'm not pregnant." At least I was pretty sure I wasn't. (In the back of my mind I remembered that for two days I'd been unconscious and had not taken the birth control, and I needed to remember to take both days and keep from having sex.) (What a time to think about that!)

"But you will be. You will have the Dhampir child, eventually."

I bit my lip before I blabbed that the Dhampir was already in the oven. "And that's bad because?"

"The last time a Dhampir existed it nearly obliterated us as a race. I don't want that to happen again."

"Sounds like you lived during that time," I said, trying to hold off the inevitable. His pheromones were working on holding me captive. I tried not to breathe in, but it had nothing to do with breathing. Silly me.

"I'd heard stories. He held reign for eight hundred years. Then, during the plague, he decided to let humans know we existed," he said. "People believed that everyone who had died from the plague were coming back as vampires—which was ridiculous! That was when they began violating their coffins and plunging stakes into corpses. That was in a time when our kind had not moved out of coffins, into regular homes with beds in rooms with darkened windows, or cellars, or attics."

I didn't mind the little history lesson, but I couldn't keep him talking forever. Also, I knew something he didn't. Even if I didn't live through this night, the Dhampir would be born—if no one learned Bill's sister carried our child. I didn't dare tell him, even if it would save my life, I wasn't going to risk another's—the child and the woman who carried it. I was going to have to use my powers on him if he didn't back off. At the moment, it didn't look likely he was going to.

"We no longer have plagues," I said. "Well, not like that one. And people aren't going to begin killing your kind because of superstitions. But they might, if you keep on killing *them*." I pressed my finger into his chest. "Bjorn lives," I said, looking up into his eyes. "So, back off and go ask him for forgiveness and mercy."

"I know Bjorn lives. I saw him. Fighting and killing other vampires." He chuckled huskily, then pulled in a shaky breath. "So much useless carnage." So. He had seen what had happened in North Tower, but had returned to find me. "No, Sabrina. He has no other recourse now but to kill me for my insubordination." Then he added. "If he catches me."

Lightning exploded, blinding me. I was thrown onto the bed, Nicolas on top of me. For two seconds I was startled by his sudden attack and tried to move my right hand into place, but he held my hands down. I screamed and I looked up to find his fangs long and sharp as pitchforks.

"I might as well get something out of it before I die," Nicolas said past the fangs. "A sibyl's blood is too exquisite to pass over, Sabrina. I'm very sorry." He didn't sound all that sorry.

"No!" I wasn't about to let him kill me. He moved one hand down at my neck, pulled at my turtle neck, ripping it with his claws. Hand freed, I shoved it into his chest. "Get OFF!" The power from the mystic ring lifted his body off me, and he now floated above me about three feet. I pushed and he dropped to the floor. He didn't tumble as I'd expected, but jumped back up, coming at me again. I put my hand up again to push him away, he stumbled back. At the same moment something large shot into the bedroom, Uber-vampire fast, and knocked the already backpedaling Nicolas into the window. Another crash—the glass of the window—and I sat up to watch the torn black wings of a master slashing air as the two of them tumbled out through the window. A huge bolt of lightning flashed, searing my retinas, and I covered my eyes with my arm.

Chapter 27

Thunder

Rain slashed through the window, drenching me one second, in the next, strong hands pulled me into muscular arms, carrying me out of the semi-dark room into a lit one, where it was warm and dry.

Sputtering, I opened my eyes and looked up into Tremayne's bloodied, young—well, younger than a thousand years—handsome face. The blood, I realized wasn't his and it was mostly dried.

"Are you okay?" his deep voice rumbled against my ear and the rest of my body, which was against his chest. He moved through my apartment, shifted and lowered himself, and me, onto one of the couches in my living room.

"Tremayne! Oh my god!" I said, tears brimming on my eyelids, chest squeezed with emotions. I roped my arms around his thick neck. I couldn't help myself. The last time I had seen him, he was on Death's threshold. Now I needed the comfort he offered me, and I buried my face against his chest with tears leaking from my eyes. The overwhelming reek of blood filled my nose. I looked up at him again, remembering... things. He needed a shave, the bristles of his beard rasped against my palms when I placed them on either side of his face. "You're alright!" I choked. His hair—all of it had grown back, long and buttery-yellow—was tousled. But other than that, not a mark on him. He looked like the old Tremayne I knew. He had yet to use the F-bomb, but that might happen in the next few seconds to let me know it was the real Tremayne. His expression went from relieved to slightly annoyed.

"Of course I'm fucking alright," he said, dark brows dipping. *It was him.* "Thanks to your plasma."

"Good." I slapped him, hard as I could, and jumped out of his lap.

The look of surprise was almost as satisfying as if I'd actually hurt him.

Hand to his slapped face, he asked with proper indignation, "What the hell was that for?"

"For what you did to me at Lonny's place." Hands on my hips, I glared at him. I'd never had the chance to be angry at him, what with his being poisoned by my dagger and all.

"Well, I guess I deserved that."

"Yes. You did."

"You have to understand it was all because of the prophesy."

"I'm sick of the prophesy!" I bellowed.

"To tell the truth, so am I. But I had to do something." His hands went out. "They expect it." He then pointed at me. "You'd better be pregnant by the rogue or get knocked up soon. I can't hold off the demons forever."

I shook my head, wrapped my arms around my stomach. So much was expected of me it was maddening.

"Where is he?" Tremayne asked.

I looked around my suite. We were alone. "Who?"

"The rogue, Vasyl," Tremayne said, the look of annoyance on his face. "He got here ahead of me."

"Wait." I moved into the hall and glanced through the doorway of my bedroom. Where was Vasyl? Where was Nicolas? The drapes fluttered in the wind, the glass broken, rain coming in. Lightning simmered again, followed two seconds later by a rumble. The storm, which had settled over Tremayne Towers, now had eased up from moments ago.

Frowning, I tried to get a remote-vision of Vasyl, and where he was. But the pain was excruciating, so I let up. "I had Nicolas backed off. I used my powers to push Nicolas off myself," I worked on the events as I remembered them. "There was a crash."

"They went out the window," Tremayne said in a steady voice.

I worked to remember exactly what I saw. Two bodies did crash out of my bedroom window. "Where is he? Vasyl should be back by now." I wanted to go and look. Tremayne's hand on my shoulder halted me.

"It's best if you don't," Tremayne said. He drew me back into the living room. I remained standing, while he sat back down, arms resting on the back of the couch. "He'll be back." His words should have reassured me, but they didn't. After a moments pause he said, "We took the towers back. I never saw Ilona."

He sat forward, arms on his thighs. "You don't happen to know where she is, do you?"

Smiling, I said, "Yup. We had a bitch confrontation, and then I turned her into stone."

Brows up, he gave me the look of surprise. I raised my hands and wiggled the fingers. "I won!" I sang.

A bark of laughter filled the room as he threw back his head. Laughter dying, he looked at me. "Sweet! What about your brother? His family? I heard they were here?"

"Oh! Right." Everything had happened so fast. "Well, my brother and one of his daughters are safely tucked away in my house. Which reminds me, I've got Tera locked in my bathroom. Excuse me." I strode to the bathroom door.

"Tera? Honey, can you hear me?" I waited. I called her name a few more times.

"Auntie Sabrina?" the little voice answered from inside.

"You can unlock the door, now. Everything is okay. The bad man is gone."

The door's lock disengaged, and the doorknob twisted. The door opened a few inches and Tera's sweet little face appeared, her eyes taking me in and going everywhere to make sure it was okay. Then, she stepped out and put her arms around my neck. I lifted her into my arms. She was heavy, but not too much I couldn't carry her over to the chair.

"Who is the big man?" she asked, pointing at Tremayne.

"He's my boss," I said. "He's a good guy."

"Cute kid," Tremayne said, taking her in as I held her close.

Cho stepped through the busted-down door, turning Tremayne around. His hair was slightly ruffed up, he had a scratch on the back of his hand and one on his cheek, and his shirt was ripped, but other than that he looked fine.

"Cho, did you find my sister-in-law?" I said.

"Yes. Dante is with her now," he said. "She fell asleep after a massage." He chuckled.

"She had no idea what was going on?" I asked, astonished, but thinking maybe that was the best thing for her.

"None whatsoever. We haven't told her much, only that she will be joining her husband and children soon."

"Well, that's a relief." I looked to Tremayne. "Can we get out of here?"

Tremayne hauled himself off my couch and stood. I'd forgotten how tall he was and had to crane my neck back to look up at his face. His head nearly brushed the ceiling. "I don't see why not."

"It would be wise," Cho said. "Paramedics and police are on their way up."

"Why?" I asked.

"The two bodies that fell out of a window, came from this floor. It's on the news right now." He looked down the hall into the bedroom and from where he stood, he undoubtedly saw the window was broken. "They are going to be here in a matter of moments. I saw them gathering at the elevators in the lobby before I came up."

"We'd better move out, then," Tremayne said, and we all hurried out of my suite. He directed us to an alcove where the stairs were, and we ducked through the door as the elevator bell chimed. I knew it was the police, and fire department. We didn't need questions battering us. I still wondered where Vasyl was. He'd be able to find me, though, no matter where I was.

We went down one flight, and Tremayne stopped on the landing for the next floor below—where I had come from—and we filed out into the hallway. I expected to see Silver-eyes, who Nicolas had shot point blank, crumpled on the floor and bleeding, or possibly dead.

"Where's the werewolf?" I asked, looking around near the spot where he'd gone down. There were spots of dark blood on the carpet. "Nicolas shot him! He should be right here!" I pointed to the blood stains.

"Who?" Tremayne said.

"His name is Dan Huston."

"Never heard of him," Tremayne said, shrugging and looking around. "But if he's a werewolf, regular bullets can't kill him. He probably got up and waked away."

"This is interesting." Cho stood in the open door of Randy's room, looking in.

We all migrated to the spot. Ilona's statue hadn't gone anywhere. My foot came down on something odd. I looked down. A Barbie doll. I picked it up and brushed her off.

"Jena's," Tera said. I handed it to her.

"She'll be missing it," I said. Tera agreed.

"Nice work," Tremayne said eyeing what had become of Ilona. "I think an ice sculpture would have been more fitting, though."

"Funny. I thought of ice at first, but wanted something more permanent." I stood there staring at the woman's face, remembering how she had held little Jena. "Now I wish I had. She'd be melting in a big puddle right now." My gut was telling me the head had to come off. I don't know why I still felt a threat from her, even as I looked at her stony features and soulless eyes, but anything was possible in this world. "We need to take the head off. Bury it somewhere."

"I'll have someone come up here with a cement saw that'll cut through stone," Tremayne said with a nod.

"Step back," Cho said. He had a deadly look in his eyes.

"Wind?" I said.

"More like tornado," he said, smiling at me. I nodded and we all stepped back out into the hallway. Cho backed up against the opposite wall, then his body whirled into motion, and disappeared into the room. A crash made me and Tera jump back and hunch together with arms around one another.

"Nicely done! I believe that will keep the ice queen from returning," Tremayne said, leaning in to examine the damage. I went to the doorway and found that Ilona's stone body lay in pieces. Arms and legs, and other large and small bits of her, including her head, were scattered everywhere. Where bits of stone had hit the wall there were gouges and scrapes, and one of her arms now stuck through the bathroom door like it had been a missile.

"Sorry about the mess," Cho said, and bowed to Tremayne.

"That's the sort of mess I don't mind," Tremayne said. We filed out and he closed the door, even though is sagged to one side on one hinge. He hung a DO NOT DISTURB sign on the doorknob, making me chuckle.

"You're still doped up?" I asked Cho, jokingly. He nodded as we advanced to the elevators. Tremayne pressed the button. The doors opened. We hopped on.

"Yes. Vasyl's blood is *very* powerful," Cho said, turning around to face the doors of the elevator.

"Sounds like I missed something," Tremayne said, pressing LOBBY.

"It's a very ancient Chinese serum, which uses three drops of vampire blood. Humans who drink it become ten times stronger. I took it before we left for here," Cho explained.

Tremayne looked at him. "Oh, I remember you. You're Ty Cho, right? From New York? You're in Capella's camarilla?"

"Correction. Was." Cho bowed. "But now I'm with Sabrina."

"That's right. I'd forgotten," Tremayne said, looking embarrassed. "I asked Capella to bring a human protector for you, before you came to see me." His eyes flashed between me and Cho. "I didn't think he'd let you go."

"I asked for the assignment. I've waited my whole life for the sibyl."

"Really?"

"Well… almost. It has been predicted to happen during my life-time," Cho said, smiling. "The I-Ching showed me she was born, and in this area."

Another person who had waited for me to be born, or tried to find me. My knees dipped from the momentum when we arrived at the lobby.

We stepped out and had to walk between four policemen, and two firefighters in full regalia. Once we stepped free of them, we found ourselves entangled in a much larger crowd of people who were gathered around a large TV screen mounted on the wall. News was on, and the reporter's voice did a speak-over while an overhead shot of the towers was being shown obviously being taken from a helicopter.

"So far no one knows the identity of the two individuals who were either were shoved or fell from the 18th floor, and were struck by lightning. Police, the fire department and paramedics are on the scene…" the reporter said. *"Oddly, no bodies have been found, but dozens of holiday shoppers, and people driving along the Magnificent Mile saw the explosion. Some claim they saw a fireball that lit up the whole sky and dropped several feet and died out before ever landing on the street below. As I said, no bodies were found anywhere. Not even their clothes. This is Melinda Coffer, back to you, Brandon, in the studio."*

I stared at the anchor woman, her lips moving but I couldn't follow a word of it. My brain wouldn't let go of the reporter's words saying that the two who went out the window—my bedroom window—were struck by lightning. *No bodies found.* I looked toward the glass doors. Police held back a crowd of reporters and on-lookers from outside. Anyone who was not inside the hotel already were not going to get in.

Vasyl must be out there. He must be. He'll be here soon, my voice of reason assured me.

I waited, heart throbbing in my chest. Why didn't he just pop in? He could simply appear right beside me, no one would know. *Maybe he doesn't want anyone to see him.*

Someone said my name, but I couldn't turn away, for some reason. Someone's arm went around my shoulders, moving me away.

"Sabrina. Rick is here," Dante's voice was in my ear. "He'll take you back along with your sister-in-law and her daughter. He needs to disappear in a private place, though. Over here."

"Okay," I said quietly. When I didn't move, he led me away. My feet moved automatically, not really watching where we went. Faces blurred passed me. I kept looking for Vasyl, but I didn't see him. We went into a darkened room where tables and chairs, and counter tops and a coffee dispensers were set up. *The breakfast nook*, my Knowing supplied.

"Is everyone here?" Rick's voice floated to me from somewhere.

"No. Vasyl's not here," I said.

"Sabrina." Tremayne took my shoulders, turned me to face him. A wedge of light from the partially open doorway lit up his face. "I'll go and look for him. Okay?" He bent his knees in order to get low enough to look directly into my eyes. "Don't worry. He's out there. I'll find him."

"Promise?"

"Promise. I'll bring him to your place. Okay?"

I nodded. A depression fell over me like a dark, heavy blanket as Tremayne misted out of sight. I felt something slip down my cheek, dripped off my chin, and another wet thing ran down my neck. I wiped it away.

"Brie? You want to go by yourself?" Rick asked.

I shook my head. The way I was feeling I couldn't walk, let alone use a ley line to get back home.

"Take my hand, then. We need to make an unbroken link," Rick said.

"I'll meet you there," Dante's voice was in my ear.

A small hand slipped into mine. I looked down at Tera.

"What are we doing?" Constance's voice plundered the silence.

"We're going to Sabrina's house," Rick explained.

"Now?" Her question echoed oddly in my ears as the dark room hazed out of sight. My body became a swirl of ectoplasmic vapor, and before I knew it, I became a whole person again, standing in my living room. Three pairs of eyes looked at us from across the way.

"Wow!" Constance blurted, clearly having had a good time. "That was fabulous!"

Snap. "You remember nothing," Rick said to her. *Snap.* "You remember nothing." He went around the room, snapping his fingers in front of my brother, his wife and both kids, making sure they didn't remember how they'd gotten here—and hopefully any nasty stuff they saw, because they saw plenty.

"Thank you Rick," I said.

"Well, what the heck?" Randy said.

"Uh, soup's on!" Lindee announced. "Come on. I've got the dining room table all set. Been expecting you guys."

"I'm not hungry," I said and turned to my room. I slid the door shut and locked it.

I sat on the bed in the dark. Dante misted next to me. He made the light come on with magic because he was nowhere near my little bedside lamp.

I looked back at him. "What sort of powers did you give me, anyway?" I asked, my voice flat.

"Whatever I've gleaned from the witches. Why?"

"I turned Ilona into stone just by thinking about it."

He didn't respond like Rick or Tremayne had. He paused, and stepped closer. "Be careful with your new powers, my Lady. They can be… dangerous."

"No shit," I mumbled. "Did you find him? Vasyl?"

"No," Dante said. "But I didn't look. Tremayne is looking for him."

Exhaustion and despair made me drop to my bed, then I flopped over onto my side. I couldn't help the tears. My face was wet, and my nose was running. Annoyed, I mopped my face on a pillow.

"Sabrina, don't worry." His hand smoothed over my head fondly. "Take a nap," he suggested. He pulled off my boots and in a moment had me arranged on the bed. He unfolded an extra blanket, the Kokopelli one, and drew it over me. "You'll feel better."

I curled into a fetal position. Sleep should have been the last thing on my mind, but it overwhelmed me.

And I dreamt.

Chapter 28

Reprieve

I woke thinking it was yesterday. Then, when I knew it wasn't yesterday, I wished I could go back in time and maybe things would have turned out different.

Darkness in my room lulled me into believing it was okay to roll over and stay in bed. But then I realized I still had my clothes on. My clock told me it was only 10:05, and the PM light was on. Voices in the next room affirmed my Knowing that people were still in the house.

Randy, his wife, and their two little girls were gone, however. I was able to read that easily enough. So, who was still here? I listened to the voices. Was the TV on? After a moment, I identified Cho's and Lindee's voices. Tremayne's deep voice rumbled something inaudible.

My memory, unfortunately, came back. Tremayne had gone to look for Vasyl, who had gone out the window with Nicolas. The memory of the terrible lightning storm returned along with everything else. I tried to use my Knowing, or any other sense to see if Vasyl was in the house. I couldn't sense him. But I couldn't sense Tremayne, either. *I must be exhausted.*

My throat tightened with the memory of Vasyl charging and tackling Nicolas, then, both arrowed out that window, and the bright lightning punishing my eyes in the aftermath. He had thought he needed to stop Nicolas from attacking me when I had already done so with my powers. How could he have been so foolish? The newswoman's words "no bodies were found," looped through my head then, until I thought I'd go mad. I put my hands over my ears for a moment, as though these words were actually being said outside my head.

No bodies were found. The lightning had hit them and they both went up in flames. End of story. Call it a wrap.

Why again? Why do I keep on having to go through this?

"How long has she been asleep?" Tremayne asked.

"About an hour."

"I'll wake her," Dante said.

The noise of someone trying to open the door made me jump a little. *Crap.*

"Sabrina? Wake up," Dante said.

I wanted to curl up into a tight ball, hide under the bed and never come out. They could bring food through the bathroom and leave it there. I'd be *just* fine.

"Saaa-breeee-na?" now Rick sang my name, as if that would get me out. "We have some good news for you," he sang again.

I rolled back over, flopping the blanket off myself and it wound up on the floor. I swung my legs over the side, tripped on the blanket when I tried to move and smacked myself into the wall. I kicked the blanket. *Stupid blanket. I hate it. I hate everything and everyone.*

Blindly I found the latch and flicked it, unlocking the door. I pushed the envelope door open and glared out into the living room. Rick, in the forefront, and looking as though he'd seen a three-headed jackal, stepped back. Tremayne and Dante towered close behind him, but didn't move. Lindee was off to one side, and Cho stood next to her. Both held smiles on their faces.

"Where's my brother? He go home?" I asked.

"Yes. We thought it was best to get them home. I took them back myself," Rick said, a hesitant smile curving his lips.

"I'm sure they were happy to be back," I said sleepily.

"Sabrina?" Tremayne said.

"What?" I snapped, and looked up. "Oh, I know. You couldn't find Vasyl. That's okay. I know you tried." I grabbed the handle of my door and tried to close it. Tremayne's hand stopped me. I glared up at him. He'd done a vampire move to get across the room to where I was. Damn vampires.

"I brought you a present," he said, and flicked two fingers at me with the universal "come here" signal. *I didn't need this now.*

With a gasp of resignation, I strode out into the living room. "What?"

Tremayne and Rick parted. The Christmas tree was lit. Lots of presents under it—I couldn't help but notice there were several new ones in silver and gold wrapping and bows.

"Okay, more presents. Big deal," I said.

"You're looking in the wrong place," Rick said. "Look. Over there." He pointed toward the couch. Someone was curled up there, back to us. I couldn't make out who it was. The afghan covered him to the mid-back. I took in the creamy-white shoulder, and there were raw wounds, with some blackening around the edges. As I watched, the flesh healed ever so slowly over the dark, burnt areas. I could make out short black hair, in a wild mess.

Then it hit me. I didn't want to believe. It couldn't be him. It couldn't. My life didn't allow for miracles. People I loved and cared for *died*. Always.

Not Tremayne. He didn't die, my little voice said. *And your brother, his wife and nieces all survived.*

I rushed to the man on the couch. Knelt down beside him, not sure if I could touch him. I looked back to Tremayne. "You found him?"

"He was clinging to a building when I found him," Tremayne said. "He wasn't struck directly by the lightning, but a side-flash caught his wings on fire. They're gone—permanently."

I covered the noise coming out of me—a yelp of tearful joy—with both hands over my mouth. Tears dripped down my face anew.

Vasyl's head moved, and then he turned over slowly to face me, rearranging himself on the couch. All of his hair had been singed too, some of it really short and the smell was horrible. His face was dirty, sooty. He looked like a kid who'd been playing in the mud and got mauled by a bear.

"Oh, my God," my voice wobbled. "You're a mess!" I picked at his singed hair. All of those beautiful waves, gone.

He smiled, put his arms loosely around me. "But I am your mess," he said.

"You need to shower," I said, reaching and snatching up some of his remaining curls.

"Only if you wash me." He smiled weakly.

"I'd love to."

* * *

Earlier that day in a cave in Colorado Springs, Colorado

The annoying *beep… beep… beep* accompanied the low sound of the Bobcat motor.

"We'll get this part cleared, and place some support beams over there…" the man with a yellow hardhat said to another man wearing a white hardhat. Niel Bronson, the engineer, who owned and operated the Helix Pipe and Mining Company, held a rolled up set of plans which showed the cave's many chambers and tunnels. Bronson looked toward the largest rock that stood in their path to open up the cave completely. The only light came from their machinery, some mine lamps, and their hardhats. Thick electrical cords snaked out through the cave's passages. He estimated they were about a mile from the entrance in distance through the cave. It was hell trying to find a small enough skid steer to get through the narrowest part, but they found one.

"We get that thing down to size, then we'll gain some ground!" he shouted to the other man, Daren Voss, and pointed to the boulder.

Voss nodded. "Was anyone hurt during the cave-in?"

"No. A couple of people did get caught on this side. But how in the hell they got out, I have no idea. Some of the rubble was pushed aside when the first responders came in from Colorado Springs Fire Department."

"Amazing." The men both stood looking over the cave's walls watching two men using pneumatic chisels on the largest boulder that had fallen.

"They want to re-open this up to visitors again by next spring," Voss shouted over the drills and air compressors.

"I don't think it will be safe. The rock isn't stable above. They'll have to keep it closed off. That's my final word on it. Can't have regular people in here."

"That's what I told them," Voss said, shaking his head.

A sudden cry sent a shock wave through the other workers. Machinery stopped, a drill held by one worker suddenly dropped it heavily to the stone floor.

Startled, the two foremen rushed over to the man. The other driller, being closest, came to the man's aide first. The foremen and other workers gathered around the injured man, Sweed Jorgensen. Blood ran freely from Sweed's arm, gleaming and oozing thickly on the ground in the pool of light from their hardhats. He held his hand over the gash but it leaked through his fingers. Blood dripped from the wound onto the floor into the dust below next to the stone.

"What happened?" Bronson asked, his voice clear and echoed slightly.

"Velázquez! Hey!" He whistled sharply. "Get the first aid kit!" Voss shouted to the man, Velázquez, who had been working the Bobcat, had paused in his work, but hadn't come over. "Quick!" Velázquez jumped off the Bobcat and rushed to get the large medical kit they always carried.

"I don't know. I hit something, and the fucking drill bit split in half!" the worker complained, grimacing in pain and swearing. "It slipped and tore me up real good."

"In the arm? Only the arm?" Bronson asked. The last thing he needed was another injury. He could lose his license if there was another lawsuit from an injured worker. There goes college tuitions, and he had a second mortgage on the house.

Voss looked worriedly on. Was the drill bit inferior? Or was it the rock, or Sweed's inattention that had caused the accident.

Blood pooled in the dust below. The dust was gray to dark charcoal, unlike the limestone dust from the rocks around them. It was fine ash, like the ashes from a fireplace, as though something had been burnt. Something large.

The first aid box was brought over. They cleaned the wound, and wound gauze around the man's arm. They put a tourniquet on him to stem the bleeding, and had him lie down. Voss rolled up his own jacket for his head. Another man put his own coat over him—it was damned cold down here.

No one noticed that the pool of blood on the floor near the boulder now smoked, bubbled and hissed. The men were all clustered in a circle around the injured man, talking about what had happened, their concern for their work mate's wellbeing high on their minds.

The smoke rose, and the blood, which had touched the ashes, bubbled. In less than a minute the ashes solidified into membranes and ligaments. In two minutes guts, bone, and eventually flesh grew over it all; fingers grew from the bloody-ash mixture, then a hand... then an arm, another hand and arm, a head formed, connected to a neck and chest, legs grew from the lower abdomen, and lastly the feet formed. The broken bits of boulder lying over the being shifted slightly. It covered half of the creature which had formed beneath it.

With a huge roar, the creature's—a creature, because it had leathery wings like a bat—hands braced against the larger piece of rock and pushed it off himself. It rolled with a grinding sound.

The workers turned to the noises. They couldn't believe what they saw—a man was pinned underneath the huge boulder they were trying to break apart with large pneumatic chisels.

"Oh, my God..."

"What the hell?"

The stunned men could barely comprehend what their eyes were seeing. There hadn't been anyone underneath the rock—not five minutes ago.

One man surged forward, thinking to help the poor guy. The others followed.

"How the hell did this happen?" Bronson roared when the men put their hands to the rock and tried to push. "Where the hell did he come from?"

"Bring the Bob Cat!" yelled Voss.

"I don't know!" one of them said through a grunt. "Who could survive after all this time?"

"Must have snuck in—"

"We can't budge this thing! Bring that Bobcat!" even as Bronson said this Velázquez had started it back up.

"Where the hell did you come from, mister?" Bronson bent to the man underneath the rock, going down on one knee. The light of his hard hat hitting the man squarely in the face and he screamed horribly, shutting his eyes and throwing an arm over them.

"Sorry," Bronson said, dousing his light.

The man on the ground motioned for him to come closer. Bronson went to his knees again, frantic to try and help. A hand clutched his arm. Then, with lightning speed it was drawn to the man's mouth, and he bit him with razor sharp fangs.

Bronson screamed. The other men jumped up, watching the man beneath the bolder biting him. Blood oozed down his arm and the guy was slurping it up like maple syrup.

"Holy Christ!" Voss said. He waived off Velázquez on the Bobcat.

"What the fuck?" Ben Mosley, the only black man on the crew swore.

Both men grabbed Bronson and tried to pull, but couldn't budge him away. Bronson kept screaming, "Let go of me! Let GO! Jesus LET ME GO!"

The creature finally let go of Bronson who staggered into Voss' arms. With inhuman strength, the thing pushed the rock off himself, releasing his body.

Jaws dropped as the men all stepped further away. Bronson had a chunk of flesh taken out of his arm, and was crying incoherently. He now needed the paramedics, too. One of the men's bowls let loose in his pants, and then turned and vomited. Velazquez grabbed the man by the collar and pulled him along, trying to keep him out of harm's way.

Nervously, they all rushed out of the hole, to the furthest end of the next room. Voss looked back, waiting to see if the thing that had bitten his boss was coming to get the rest of them. Where had the mysterious man gone? He was no longer where they'd left him next to the Bobcat.

The men shuffled around nervously. Voss had to make a tourniquet from Velázquez' bandanna. Velazquez had been talking Spanish excitedly the whole while. Voss, who only spoke a little Spanish only picked out a few words. One was "Devil", the rest was more or less a version of prayers to the Mother Marry.

"Can you walk?" Voss asked Bronson. Bronson nodded. They moved a little further, and then he fell unconscious. Voss and Mosley dipped to pick him up, wanting to move him and everyone toward the exit of the cavern. Or as far away from that maniac as they could until the paramedics arrived.

"Bossman, what the hell? I don't know how any man could just appear out from under a rock, but that was no man!" the worker yelled, pointing a shaky hand in the general direction.

Voss was not quite sure what they'd actually seen, or what had actually bitten Bronson's arm. That was when all the lights went out. They were in total darkness. Even their hard hat lamps had gone out.

There was about twenty seconds of absolute silence. Then Vazquez's scream rent the cavern. The sound of something inhuman growled, and it was coming toward them.

Chapter 29

Awakened

Wind Cave, Colorado Springs, Colorado

He stretched. He felt wonderful. Alive. Strong. Empowered.

And hungry.

At his back the twinge and electric feeling of his wings unfurling ushered an icy rush through his nude body. He had to enjoy this wonderful experience, momentarily absorbed by how strong and invincible he felt. Looking over his shoulders, expecting to find his wonderful white-feathered wings, he saw something dark, and utterly diabolical. Where there should have been white feathers, ugly brownish membrane stretched between each long finger of his new wings. The bend of his wings ended in a huge thumb-like appendage tipped by a terribly hooked talon on each one. He moved it, to make sure it was his. It was. He took his hands and felt along the stretchy skin, examined the tips of each long finger of the wing. Certainly, he would be able to fly very well with these.

His astonishment with such metamorphosis challenged his memory. *What happened to me?*

And then he remembered being in the cave-in. With her. *I died! But how am I here? Alive?*

Or was he?

Bill Gannon put a hand to his heart. Waited. He waited some more. Finally a *thump-thump* sounded under his hand. Strong, yet not the steady drumming of a healthy heart in a human body.

Dread filled him at first, but a cool calculating mind took over. *Vampire?* His need to understand quickly replaced by a cold intense need to feed… and to mate.

With her.

Looking down from where he stood on top of crumbled rock of the cave, he finally noticed the five men in hardhats looking up at him. Two of them now turned to scramble out through a small hole in the jumble of rock. Then the rest followed, carrying one of them.

Bill Gannon laughed.

As if they could out run him.

###

Dear reader,

We hope you enjoyed reading *Crescendo*. Please take a moment to leave a review, even if it's a short one. Your opinion is important to us.

Discover more books by Lorelei Bell at https://www.nextchapter.pub/authors/lorelei-bell.

Want to know when one of our books is free or discounted for Kindle? Join the newsletter at http://eepurl.com/bqqB3H.

Best regards,
Lorelei Bell and the Next Chapter Team

The story continues in:
Requiem by Lorelei Bell

To read the first chapter for free, head to:
https://www.nextchapter.pub/books/requiem-urban-fantasy

About the Author

Lorelei's interest in vampires came in her teens watching the original Dark Shadows on TV, and old horror movie classics of "Dracula" on TV late at night. As a result, she was considered odd because of her interests in the macabre, horror/vampire movies—way before it was 'cool'.

When not at her day job, Lorelei works on her novels, inventing new characters and places/parallel worlds where her main character, Sabrina Strong, has a few adventures, lovers, solves a mystery or two, and comes within a hair's breadth of being killed—all in a day's work by a sibyl like Sabrina. Her writing has been compared to Anne Rice's more gritty novels, but with a humorous twist in the tradition of Charlaine Harris.

Sabrina Strong Series:
Book 1 - Ascension
Book 2 - Trill
Book 3 - Nocturne
Book 4 - Caprice

Other books
Spell of the Black Unicorn
"*I wanted to create a heroine who has to learn who and what she was from the beginning and throughout the series, rather than plopping my readers in the middle of things and doing a lot of back story.*

My vampires all have their own personalities; you will not find a cardboard baddie among them. They each have their own needs, wants, and desires, and do fall in love—in other words are capable of human emotions.

I hope you enjoyed this book!
Thank you!"
Lorelei Bell

Lorelei can be found on Facebook and at her blog:
http://loreleismuse-lorelei.blogspot.com/

Lightning Source UK Ltd.
Milton Keynes UK
UKHW012334030221
378341UK00009B/469/J

9 781034 374633